VAMPIRES
THE GREATEST STORIES
EDITED BY MARTIN H. GREENBERG

MJF BOOKS

NEW YORK

Published by MJF Books
Fine Communications
Two Lincoln Square
60 West 66th Street
New York, NY 10023

Library of Congress Catalog Card Number 97-70824
ISBN 1-56731-167-9
Vampires: The Greatest Stories
Copyright © 1997 by Tekno-Books

Manufactured in the United States of America on acid-free paper

MJF Books and the MJF colophon are trademarks of Fine Creative Media, Inc.

10 9 8 7 6 5 4 3 2 1

Contents

Introduction

by Martin H. Greenberg

O f all the supernatural creatures that inhabit the pages of horror fiction, the vampire is perhaps the most fearsome simply because of what he is. The classic werewolf can be excused because he goes into a feral state, the animal transformation separating him from the rationality of the human mind. Werewolves know what they do. Ghosts can also be allowed a certain measure of latitude for existence, as they primarily appear in our world for revenge, or, if serving a good purpose, as a warning to the living. They come back for a reason and whether it be for good or evil, that is for the reader to decide.

But vampires know what they are and what they must do to survive—drink blood. They are true parasites, existing only to feed off of the living. In fiction, they live among us, quietly invisible, taking what they need so as not to draw attention to themselves, for that would surely lead to destruction. Until recently, they were only portrayed as figures of evil—tragic, but evil nonetheless.

However, authors such as Anne Rice have attempted to put a more noble spin on the ancient legend, transforming the inhuman creature known and feared in Bram Stoker's *Dracula* into a tortured soul who is a victim of circumstance. To be sure, the vampiric figure is attractive in its power, the way it commands man and animal alike, its mysterious eroticism a powerful lure for women (and usually their death as well). The draw of immortality is strong as well.

Of course, most power has a price, and vampirism is no different. Al-

ways forced to keep under cover of night, repulsed by the smell of garlic and the sight of the cross, unable to cross running water. And yet, despite its horrors, there is perhaps a small part, buried deep inside each
one of us, that wonders what it would be like . . .

The authors in this book have each given their versions of what this
most ancient, most evil of the creatures of the night could be. From an
insidious evil hidden behind the most innocuous of fronts, to a child
whose love can stop even the most hideous monster, the vampire in all
its forms can be found in the following pages. Turn the page and join
them . . . if you dare.

The Bat Is My Brother

by Robert Bloch

I

It began in twilight—a twilight I could not see.

My eyes opened on darkness, and for a moment I wondered if I were still asleep and dreaming. Then I slid my hands down and felt the cheap lining of the casket, and I knew that this nightmare was real.

I wanted to scream, but who can hear screams through six feet of earth above a grave?

Better to save my breath and try to save my sanity. I fell back, and the darkness rose all around me. The darkness, the cold, clammy darkness of death.

I could not remember how I had come here, or what hideous error had brought about my premature interment. All I knew was that I lived—but unless I managed to escape, I would soon be in a condition horribly appropriate to my surroundings.

Then began that which I dare not remember in detail. The splintering of wood, the burrowing struggle through loosely-packed grave earth; the gasping hysteria accompanying my clawing, suffocated progress to the sane surface of the world above.

It is enough that I finally emerged. I can only thank poverty for my deliverance—the poverty which had placed me in a flimsy, unsealed coffin and a pauper's shallow grave.

Clotted with sticky clay, drenched with cold perspiration, racked by utter revulsion, I crawled forth from betwixt the gaping jaws of death.

Dusk crept between the tombstones, and somewhere to my left the moon leered down to watch the shadowy legions that conquered in the name of Night.

The moon saw me, and a wind whispered furtively to brooding trees, and the trees bent low to mumble a message to all those sleeping below their shade.

I grew restless beneath the moon's glaring eye, and I wanted to leave this spot before the trees had told my secret to the nameless, numberless dead.

Despite my desire, several minutes passed before I summoned strength to stand erect, without trembling.

Then I breathed deeply of fog and faint putridity; breathed, and turned away along the path.

It was at that moment the figure appeared.

It glided like a shadow from the deeper shadows haunting the trees, and as the moonlight fell upon a human face I felt my heart surge in exultation.

I raced towards the waiting figure, words choking in my throat as they fought for prior utterance.

"You'll help me, won't you?" I babbled. "You can see . . . they buried me down there . . . I was trapped . . . alive in the grave . . . out now . . . you'll understand . . . I can't remember how it began, but . . . you'll help me?"

A head moved in silent assent.

I halted, regaining composure, striving for coherency.

"This is awkward," I said, more quietly. "I've really no right to ask you for assistance. I don't even know who you are."

The voice from the shadows was only a whisper, but each word thundered in my brain.

"I am a vampire," said the stranger.

Madness. I turned to flee, but the voice pursued me.

"Yes, I am a vampire," he said. "And . . . *so are you!*"

II

I must have fainted, then. I must have fainted, and he must have carried me out of the cemetery, for when I opened my eyes once more I lay on a sofa in his house.

The panelled walls loomed high, and shadows crawled across the ceiling beyond the candlelight. I sat up, blinked, and stared at the stranger who bent over me.

I could see him now, and I wondered. He was of medium height, grey-haired, clean-shaven, and clad discreetly in a dark business suit. At first glance he appeared normal enough.

As his face glided towards me, I stared closer, trying to pierce the veil of his seeming sanity, striving to see the madness beneath the prosaic exterior of dress and flesh.

I stared and saw that which was worse than any madness.

At close glance his countenance was cruelly illumined by the light. I saw the waxen pallor of his skin, and what was worse than that, the peculiar corrugation. For his entire face and throat was covered by a web of tiny wrinkles, and when he smiled it was with a mummy's grin.

Yes, his face was white and wrinkled; white, wrinkled, and long dead. Only his lips and eyes were alive, and they were red . . . *too* red. A face as white as corpse-flesh, holding lips and eyes as red as blood.

He smelled *musty*.

All these impressions came to me before he spoke. His voice was like the rustle of the wind through a mortuary wreath.

"You are awake? It is well."

"Where am I? And who are you?" I asked the questions but dreaded an answer. The answer came.

"You are in my house. You will be safe here, I think. As for me, I am your guardian."

"Guardian?"

He smiled. I saw his teeth. Such teeth I had never seen, save in the maw of a carnivorous beast. And yet—wasn't *that* the answer?

"You are bewildered, my friend. Understandably so. And that is why you need a guardian. Until you learn the ways of your new life, I shall protect you." He nodded. "Yes, Graham Keene, I shall protect you."

"Graham Keene."

It was my name. I knew it *now*. But how did *he* know it?

"In the name of mercy," I groaned, "tell me what has happened to me!"

He patted my shoulder. Even through the cloth I could feel the icy weight of his pallid fingers. They crawled across my neck like worms, like wriggling white worms—

"You must be calm," he told me. "This is a great shock, I know. Your confusion is understandable. If you will just relax a bit and listen, I think I can explain everything."

I listened.

"To begin with, you must accept certain obvious facts. The first being—that you are a vampire."

"But—"

He pursed his lips, his *too* red lips, and nodded.

"There is no doubt about it, unfortunately. Can you tell me how you happened to be emerging from a grave?"

"No. I don't remember. I must have suffered a cataleptic seizure. The shock gave me partial amnesia. But it will come back to me. I'm all right, I must be."

The words rang hollowly even as they gushed from my throat.

"Perhaps. But I think not." He sighed and pointed.

"I can prove your condition to you easily enough. Would you be so good as to tell me what you see behind you, Graham Keene?"

"Behind me?"

"Yes, on the wall."

I stared.

"I don't see anything."

"Exactly."

"But—"

"*Where is your shadow?*"

I looked again. There was no shadow, no silhouette. For a moment my sanity wavered. Then I stared at him. "You have no shadow either," I exclaimed, triumphantly. "What does that prove?"

"That I am a vampire," he said, easily. "And so are you."

"Nonsense. It's just a trick of the light," I scoffed.

"Still sceptical? Then explain this optical illusion." A bony hand proffered a shining object.

I took it, held it. It was a simple pocket mirror.

"Look."

I looked.

The mirror dropped from my fingers and splintered on the floor.

"There's no reflection!" I murmured.

"Vampires have no reflections." His voice was soft. He might have been reasoning with a child.

"If you still doubt," he persisted, "I advise you to feel your pulse. Try to detect a heartbeat."

Have you ever listened for the faint voice of hope to sound within you . . . knowing that it alone can save you? Have you ever listened and heard nothing? Nothing but the silence of *death*?

I knew it then, past all doubt. I was of the Undead . . . the Undead who cast no shadows, whose images do not reflect in mirrors, whose hearts are forever stilled, but whose bodies live on—live, and walk abroad, and take nourishment.

Nourishment!

I thought of my companion's red lips and his pointed teeth. I thought of the light blazing in his eyes. A light of hunger. Hunger for what?

How soon must I share that hunger?

He must have sensed the question, for he began to speak once more.

"You are satisfied that I speak the truth, I see. That is well. You must accept your condition and then prepare to make the necessary adjustments. For there is much you have to learn in order to face the centuries to come.

"To begin with, I will tell you that many of the common superstitions about—people like us—are false."

He might have been discussing the weather, for all the emotion his face betrayed. But I could not restrain a shudder of revulsion at his words.

"They say we cannot abide garlic. That is a lie. They say we cannot cross running water. Another lie. They say that we must lie by day in the earth of our own graves. That's picturesque nonsense.

"These things, and these alone, are true. Remember them, for they are important to your future. We must sleep by day and rise only at sunset.

At dawn an overpowering lethargy bedrugs our senses, and we fall into a coma until dusk. We need not sleep in coffins—that is sheer melodrama, I assure you!—but it is best to sleep in darkness, and away from any chance of discovery by men.

"I do not know why this is so, any more than I can account for other phenomena relative to the disease. For vampirism is a disease, you know."

He smiled when he said it. I didn't smile. I groaned.

"Yes, it is a disease. Contagious, of course, and transmissible in the classic manner, through a bite. Like rabies. What reanimates the body after death no one can say. And why it is necessary to take certain forms of nourishment to sustain existence, I do not know. The daylight coma is a more easily classified medical phenomenon. Perhaps an allergy to the direct actinic rays of the sun.

"I am interested in these matters, and I have studied them.

"In the centuries to come I shall endeavour to do some intensive research on the problem. It will prove valuable in perpetuating my existence, and yours."

The voice was harsher now. The slim fingers clawed the air in excitement.

"Think of that, for a moment, Graham Keene," he whispered. "Forget your morbid superstitious dread of this condition and look at the reality.

"Picture yourself as you were before you awoke at sunset. Suppose you had remained there, inside that coffin, nevermore to awaken! Dead—dead for all eternity!"

He shook his head. "You can thank your condition for an escape. It gives you a new life, not just for a few paltry years, but for centuries. Perhaps—forever!

"Yes, think and give thanks! You need never die, now. Weapons cannot harm you, nor disease, nor the workings of age. You are immortal— and I shall show you how to live like a god!"

He sobered. "But that can wait. First we must attend to our needs. I want you to listen carefully now. Put aside your silly prejudices and hear me out. I will tell you that which needs to be told regarding our nourishment.

"It isn't easy, you know.

"There aren't any schools you can attend to learn what to do. There are no correspondence courses or books of helpful information. You must learn everything through your own efforts. Everything.

"Even so simple and vital a matter as biting the neck—using the incisors properly—is entirely a matter of personal judgment.

"Take that little detail, just as an example. You must choose the classic trinity to begin with—the time, the place, and the girl.

"When you are ready, you must pretend that you are about to kiss her. Both hands go under her ears. That is important, to hold her neck steady, and at the proper angle.

"You must keep smiling all the while, without allowing a betrayal of intent to creep into your features or your eyes. Then you bend your head. You kiss her throat. If she relaxes, you turn your mouth to the base of her neck, open it swiftly and place the incisors in position.

"Simultaneously—it *must* be simultaneously—you bring your left hand up to cover her mouth. The right hand must find, seize, and pinion her hands behind her back. No need to hold her throat now. The teeth are doing that. Then, and only then, will instinct come to your aid. It must come then, because once you begin, all else is swept away in the red, swirling blur of fulfilment."

I cannot describe his intonation as he spoke, or the unconscious pantomime which accompanied the incredible instructions. But it is simple to name the look that came into his eyes.

Hunger.

"Come, Graham Keene," he whispered. "We must go now."

"Go? Where?"

"To dine," he told me. "To dine!"

He led me from the house, and down a garden pathway through a hedge.

The moon was high, and as we walked along a windswept bluff, flying figures spun a moving web across the moon's bright face.

My companion shrugged.

"Bats," he said. And smiled.

"They say that we—have the power of changing shape. That we become bats, or wolves. Alas, it's only another superstition. Would that it were true? For then our life would be easy. As it is, the search for sustenance in mortal form is hard. But you will soon understand."

I drew back. His hand rested on my shoulder in cold command.

"Where are you taking me?" I asked.

"To food."

Irresolution left me. I emerged from nightmare, shook myself into sanity.

"No—I won't!" I murmured. "I can't—"

"You must," he told me. "Do you want to go back to the grave?"

"I'd rather," I whispered. "Yes, I'd rather die."

His teeth gleamed in the moonlight.

"That's the pity of it," he said. "You can't die. You'll weaken without sustenance, yes. And you will appear to be dead. Then, whoever finds you will put you in the grave.

"But you'll be alive down there. How would you like to lie there undying in the darkness . . . writhing as you decay . . . suffering the torments of red hunger as you suffer the pangs of dissolution?

"How long do you think that goes on? How long before the brain itself is rotted away? How long must one endure the charneal consciousness of the devouring worm? Does the very dust still billow in agony?"

His voice held horror.

"That is the fate you escaped. But it is still the fate that awaits you unless you dine with me.

"Besides, it isn't something to avoid, believe me. And I am sure, my friend, that you already feel the pangs of—appetite."

I could not, dared not answer.

For it was true. Even as he spoke, I felt hunger. A hunger greater than any I had ever known. Call it a craving, call it a desire—call it lust. I felt it, gnawing deep within me. Repugnance was nibbled away by the terrible teeth of growing need.

"Follow me," he said, and I followed. Followed along the bluff and down a lonely country road.

We halted abruptly on the highway. A blazing neon sign winked incongruously ahead.

I read the absurd legend.

"DANNY'S DRIVE-IN."

Even as I watched, the sign blinked out.

"Right," whispered my guardian. "It's closing time. They will be leaving now."

"Who?"

"Mr. Danny and his waitress. She serves customers in their cars. They always leave together, I know. They are locking up for the night now. Come along and do as you are told."

I followed him down the road. His feet crunched gravel as he stalked towards the now darkened drive-in stand. My stride quickened in excitement. I moved forward as though pushed by a gigantic hand. The hand of hunger—

He reached the side door of the shack. His fingers rasped the screen.

An irritable voice sounded.

"What do you want? We're closing."

"Can't you serve any more customers?"

"Nah. Too late. Go away."

"But we're very hungry."

I almost grinned. Yes, we were *very* hungry.

"Beat it!" Danny was in no mood for hospitality.

"Can't we get anything?"

Danny was silent for a moment. He was evidently debating the point. Then he called to someone inside the stand.

"Marie! Couple customers outside. Think we can fix 'em up in a hurry?"

"Oh, I guess so." The girl's voice was soft, complaisant. Would she be soft and complaisant, too?

"Open up. You guys mind eating outside?"

"Not at all."

"Open the door, Marie."

Marie's high heels clattered across the wooden floor. She opened the screen door, blinked out into the darkness.

My companion stepped inside the doorway. Abruptly, he pushed the girl forward.

"Now!" he rasped.

I lunged at her in darkness. I didn't remember his instructions about smiling at her, or placing my hands beneath her ears. All I knew was that her throat was white, and smooth, except where a tiny vein throbbed in her neck.

I wanted to touch her neck there with my fingers—with my mouth—with my teeth.

So I dragged her into the darkness, and my hands were over her mouth, and I could hear her heels scraping through the gravel as I pulled her along. From inside the shack I heard a single long moan, and then nothing.

Nothing . . . except the rushing white blur of her neck, as my face swooped towards the throbbing vein . . .

IV

It was cold in the cellar—cold, and dark. I stirred uneasily on my couch and my eyes blinked open on blackness. I strained to see, raising myself to a sitting position as the chill slowly faded from my bones.

I felt sluggish, heavy with reptilian contentment. I yawned, trying to grasp a thread of memory from the red haze cloaking my thoughts.

Where was I? How had I come here? What had I been doing?

I yawned. One hand went to my mouth. My lips were caked with a dry, flaking substance.

I felt it—and then remembrance flooded me.

Last night, at the drive-in, I had feasted. And then—

"No!" I gasped.

"You have slept? Good."

My host stood before me. I arose hastily and confronted him.

"Tell me it isn't true," I pleaded. "Tell me I was dreaming."

"You were," he answered. "When I came out of the shack you lay under the trees, unconscious. I carried you home before dawn and placed you here to rest. You have been dreaming from sunrise to sunset, Graham Keene."

"But last night—?"

"Was real."

"You mean I took that girl and—?"

"Exactly." He nodded. "But come, we must go upstairs and talk. There are certain questions I must ask."

We climbed the stairs slowly and emerged on ground level. Now I could observe my surrounding with a more objective eye. This house was large, and old. Although completely furnished, it looked somehow untenanted. It was as though nobody had lived there for a long time.

Then I remembered who my host was, and what he was. I smiled grimly. It was true. Nobody was *living* in this house now.

Dust lay thickly everywhere, and the spiders had spun patterns of decay in the corners. Shades were drawn against the darkness, but still it crept in through the cracked walls. For darkness and decay belonged here.

We entered the study where I had awakened last night, and as I was seated, my guardian cocked his head towards me in an attitude of inquiry.

"Let us speak frankly," he began. "I want you to answer an important question."

"Yes?"

"What did you do with her?"

"Her?"

"That girl—last night. What did you do with her body?"

I put my hands to my temples. "It was all a blur. I can't seem to remember."

His head darted towards me, eyes blazing. "I'll tell you what you did with her," he rasped. "You threw her body down the well. I saw it floating there."

"Yes," I groaned. "I remember now."

"You fool—why did you do that?"

"I wanted to hide it . . . I thought they'd never know—"

"You *thought!*" Scorn weighted his voice. "You didn't think for an instant. Don't you see, now she will never rise?"

"Rise?"

"Yes, as you rose. Rise to become one of us."

"But I don't understand."

"That is painfully evident." He paced the floor, then wheeled towards me.

"I see that I shall have to explain certain things to you. Perhaps you are not to blame, because you don't realize the situation. Come with me."

He beckoned. I followed. We walked down the hall, entered a large, shelf-lined room. It was obviously a library. He lit a lamp, halted.

"Take a look around," he invited. "See what you make of it, my friend."

I scanned the titles on the shelves—titles stamped in gold on thick, handsome bindings; titles worn to illegibility on ancient, raddled leather. The latest in scientific and medical treatises stood on these shelves, flanked by age-encrusted incunabula.

Modern volumes dealt with psychopathology. The ancient lore was frankly concerned with black magic.

"Here is the collection," he whispered. "Here is gathered together all that is known, all that has ever been written about—us."

"A library on vampirism?"

"Yes. It took me decades to assemble it completely."

"But why?"

"Because knowledge is power. And it is power I seek."

Suddenly a resurgent sanity impelled me. I shook off the nightmare enveloping me and sought an objective viewpoint. A question crept into my mind, and I did not try to hold it back.

"Just who are you, anyway?" I demanded. "What is your name?"

My host smiled.

"I have no name," he answered.

"No name?"

"Unfortunate, is it not? When I was buried, there were no loving friends, apparently, to erect a tombstone. And when I arose from the grave, I had no mentor to guide me back to a memory of the past. Those were barbaric times in the East Prussia of 1777."

"You died in 1777?" I muttered.

"To the best of my knowledge," he retorted, bowing slightly in mock deprecation. "And so it is that my real name is unknown. Apparently I perished far from my native heath, for diligent research on my part has failed to uncover my paternity, or any contemporaries who recognized me at the time of my—er—resurrection.

"And so it is that I have no name; or rather, I have many pseudonyms. During the past sixteen decades I have travelled far, and have been all things to all men. I shall not endeavour to recite my history.

"It is enough to say that slowly, gradually, I have grown wise in the ways of the world. And I have evolved a plan. To this end I have amassed wealth, and brought together a library as a basis for my operations.

"Those operations I propose will interest you. And they will explain my anger when I think of you throwing the girl's body into the well."

He sat down. I followed suit. I felt anticipation crawling along my spine. He was about to read something—something I wanted to hear; yet dreaded. The revelation came, slyly, slowly.

"Have you ever wondered," he began, "why there are not more vampires in the world?"

"What do you mean?"

"Consider. It is said, and it is true, that every victim of a vampire becomes a vampire in turn. The new vampire finds other victims. Isn't it reasonable to suppose, therefore, that in a short time—through sheer mathematical progression—the virus of vampirism would run epidemic throughout the world? In other words, have you ever wondered why the world is not filled with vampires by this time?"

"Well, yes—I never thought of it that way. What is the reason?" I asked.

He glared and raised a white finger. It stabbed forward at my chest—a rapier of accusation.

"Because of fools like you. Fools who cast their victims into wells; fools whose victims are buried in sealed coffins, who hide the bodies or dismember them so no one would suspect their work.

"As a result, few new recruits join the ranks. And the old ones—myself included—are constantly subject to the ravages of the centuries. We eventually disintegrate, you know. To my knowledge, there are only a few hundred vampires today. And yet, if new victims all were given the opportunity to rise—we would have a vampire army within a year. Within three years there would be millions of vampires! Within ten years we could rule earth!

"Can't you see that? If there was no cremation, no careless disposal of bodies, no bungling, we could end our hunted existence as creatures of the night—brothers of the bat! No longer would we be a legendary, cowering minority, living each a law unto himself!

"All that is needed is a plan. And I—I have evolved that plan!"

His voice rose. So did the hairs upon my neck. I was beginning to comprehend, now—

"Suppose we started with the humble instruments of destiny," he suggested. "Those forlorn, unnoticed, ignorant little old men—night watchmen of graveyards and cemeteries."

A smile creased his corpse-like countenance. "Suppose we eliminated them? Took over their jobs? Put vampires in their places—men who would go to the fresh graves and dig up the bodies of each victim they had bitten while those bodies were still warm and pulsing and undecayed?

"We could save the lives of most of the recruits we make. Reasonable, is it not?"

To me it was madness, but I nodded.

"Suppose that we made victims of those attendants? Then carried them off, nursed them back to reanimation, and allowed them to resume their posts as our allies? They work only at night—no one would know.

"Just a little suggestion, but so obvious! And it would mean so much!"

His smile broadened.

"All that it takes is organization on our part. I know many of my brethren. It is my desire soon to call them together and present this plan. Never before have we worked co-operatively, but when I show them the possibilities, they cannot fail to respond.

"Can you imagine it? An earth which we could control and terrorize— a world in which human beings become our property, our cattle?

"It is so simple, really. Sweep aside your foolish concepts of *Dracula* and the other superstitious confectionery that masquerades in the public mind as an authentic picture. I admit that we are—unearthly. But there is no reason for us to be stupid, impractical figures of fantasy. There is more for us than crawling around in black cloaks and recoiling at the sight of crucifixes!

"After all, we are a life-form, a race of our own. Biology has not yet recognized us, but we exist. Our morphology and metabolism has not been evaluated or charted; our actions and reactions never studied. But we exist. And we are superior to ordinary mortals. Let us assert this superiority! Plain human cunning, coupled with our super-normal powers, can create for us a mastery over all living things. For we are greater than Life—we are Life-in-Death!"

I half-rose. He waved me back, breathlessly.

"Suppose we band together and make plans? Suppose we go about, first of all, selecting our victims on the basis of value to our ranks? Instead of regarding them as sources of easy nourishment, let's think in terms of an army seeking recruits. Let us select keen brains, youthfully strong bodies. Let us prey upon the best earth has to offer. Then we shall wax strong and no man shall stay our hand—or teeth!"

He crouched like a black spider, spinning his web of words to enmesh my sanity. His eyes glittered. It was absurd somehow to see this creature of superstitious terror calmly creating a super-dictatorship of the dead.

And yet, I was one of them. It was real. The nameless one would do it, too.

"Have you ever stopped to wonder why I tell you this? Have you ever stopped to wonder why you are my confidant in this venture?" he purred.

I shook my head.

"It is because you are young. I am old. For years I have laboured only to this end. Now that my plans are perfected, I need assistance. Youth, a modern viewpoint. I know of you, Graham Keene. I watched you before . . . you became one of us. You were selected for this purpose."

"Selected?" Suddenly it hit home. I fought down a stranglehold gasp as I asked the question. "Then you know who—did this to me? *You know who bit me?*"

Rotting fangs gaped in a smile. He nodded slowly.

"Of course," he whispered. "Why—*I* did!"

V

He was probably prepared for anything except the calmness with which I accepted this revelation.

Certainly he was pleased. And the rest of that night, and all the next night, were spent in going over the plans, in detail. I learned that he had not yet communicated with others—in regard to his ideas.

A meeting would be arranged soon. Then we would begin the campaign. As he said, the times were ripe. War, a world in unrest—we would be able to move unchallenged and find unusual opportunities.

I agreed. I was even able to add certain suggestions as to detail. He was pleased with my co-operation.

Then, in the third night, came hunger.

He offered to serve as my guide, but I brushed him aside.

"Let me try my own wings," I smiled. "After all, I must learn sooner or later. And I promise you, I shall be very careful. This time I will see to it that the body remains intact. Then I shall discover the place of burial and we can perform an experiment. I will select a likely recruit, we shall go forth to open the grave, and thus will we test our plan in miniature."

He fairly beamed at that. And I went forth that night, alone.

I returned only as dawn welled out of the eastern sky—returned to slumber through the day.

That night we spoke, and I confided my success to his eager ears.

"Sidney J. Garrat is the name," I said. "A college professor, about 45. I found him wandering along a path near the campus. The trees form a dark, deserted avenue. He offered no resistance. I left him there. I don't think they'll bother with an autopsy—for the marks on his throat are invisible and he is known to have a weak heart.

"He lived alone without relatives. He had no money. That means a wooden coffin and quick burial at Everest tomorrow. Tomorrow night we can go there."

My companion nodded.

"You have done well," he said.

We spent the remainder of the night in perfecting our plans. We would go to Everest, locate the night watchman and put him out of the way, then seek the new grave of Professor Garrat.

And so it was that we re-entered the cemetery on the following evening.

Once again a midnight moon glared from the Cyclopean socket of the sky. Once more the wind whispered to us on our way, and the trees bowed in black obeisance along the path.

We crept up to the shanty of the graveyard watchman and peered through the window at his stooping figure.

"I'll knock," I suggested. "Then when he comes to the door—"

My companion shook his grey head. "No teeth," he whispered. "The man is old, useless to us. I shall resort to more mundane weapons."

I shrugged. Then I knocked. The old man opened the door, blinked out at me with rheumy eyes.

"What is it?" he wheezed, querulously. "Ain't nobuddy suppose' tuh be in uh cemetery this time uh night—"

Lean fingers closed around his windpipe. My companion dragged him forth towards nearby shrubbery. His free arm rose and fell, and a silver arc stabbed down. He had used a knife.

Then we made haste along the path, before the scent of blood could divert us from our mission—and far ahead, on the hillside dedicated to the last slumbers of Poverty, I saw the raw, gaping edges of a new-made grave.

He ran back to the hut, then, and procured the spades we had neglected in our haste. The moon was our lantern and the grisly work began amidst a whistling wind.

No one saw us, no one heard us, for only empty eyes and shattered ears lay far beneath the earth.

We toiled, and then we stooped and tugged. The grave was deep, very deep. At the bottom the coffin lay, and we dragged forth the pine box.

"Terrible job," confided my companion. "Not a professionally dug grave at all, in my opinion. Wasn't filled in right. And this coffin is pine, but very thick. He'd never claw his own way out. Couldn't break through the boards. And the earth was packed too tightly. Why would they waste so much time on a pauper's grave?"

"Doesn't matter," I whispered. "Let's open it up. If he's revived, we must hurry."

We'd brought a hammer from the caretaker's shanty, too, and he went down into the pit itself to pry the nails free. I heard the board covering move, and peered down over the edge of the grave.

He bent forward, stooping to peer into the coffin, his face a mask of livid death in the moonlight. I heard him hiss.

"Why—the coffin is empty!" he gasped.

"Not for long!"

I drew the wrench from my pocket, raised it, brought it down with every ounce of strength I possessed until it shattered through his skull.

And then I leaped down into the pit and pressed the writhing, mewing shape down into the coffin, slammed the lid on, and drove the heavy nails into place. I could hear his whimperings rise to muffled screams, but the screams grew faint as I began to heap the clods of earth upon the coffin-lid.

I worked and panted there until no sound came from the coffin below. I packed the earth down hard—harder than I had last night when I dug the grave in the first place.

And then, at last, the task was over.

He lay there, the nameless one, the deathless one; lay six feet underground in a stout wooden coffin.

He could not claw his way free, I knew. And even if he did, I'd pressed him into his wooden prison face down. He'd claw his way to hell, not to earth.

But he was past escape. Let him lie there, as he had described it to me—not dead, not alive. Let him be conscious as he decayed, and as the wood decayed and the worms crawled in to feast. Let him suffer until the maggots at last reached his corrupt brain and ate away his evil consciousness.

I could have driven a stake through his heart. But his ghastly desire deserved defeat in this harsher fate.

Thus it was ended, and I could return now before discovery and the coming of dawn—return to his great house which was the only home I knew on the face of the earth.

Return I did, and for the past hours I have been writing this that all might know the truth.

I am not skilled with words, and what I read here smacks of mawkish melodrama. For the world is superstitious and yet cynical—and this account will be deemed the ravings of a fool or madman; worse still, as a practical joke.

So I must implore you; if you seek to test the truth of what I've set down, go to Everest tomorrow and search out the newly-dug grave on the hillside. Talk to the police when they find the dead watchman, make them go to the well near Danny's roadside stand.

Then, if you must, dig up the grave and find that which must still writhe and crawl within. When you see it, you'll believe—and in justice, you will not relieve the torment of that monstrous being by driving a stake through his heart.

For that stake represents release and peace.

I wish you'd come here, after that—and bring a stake for me . . .

In Darkness, Angels

by Eric Lustbader

f I had known then what I know now.

How those words echo on and on inside my mind, like a rubber ball bouncing down an endless staircase. As if they had a life of their own. Which, I suppose, they do now.

I cannot sleep but is it any wonder? Outside, blue white lightning forks like a giant's jagged claw and the thunder is so loud at times that I feel I must be trapped inside an immense bell, reverberations like memory unspooling in a reckless helix, making a mess at my feet.

If I had known then what I know now. And yet. . . .

And yet I return again and again to that windswept evening when the ferry deposited me at the east end of the island. It had once been, so I had been told by the rather garrulous captain, a swansneck peninsula. But over time, the water had gradually eaten away at the rocky soil until at last the land had succumbed to the ocean's cool tidal embrace, severing itself from the mainland a mile away.

Of course the captain had an entirely different version of what had transpired. "It's them folks up there," he had said, jerking his sharp unshaven chin toward the castle high atop the island's central mount. "Didn't want no more interference from the other folks hereabouts." He gave a short barking laugh and spat over the boat's side. "Just as well, I say," he observed as he squinted heavily into the last of the sun's watery light. "Them rocks were awfully sharp." He shook his head as if weighed down by the memory. "Kids were always darin one another t'do their balancin act goin across, down that long spit o land." He turned the wheel hard over and spuming water rushed up the bow of the ferry. "Many's the night we'd come out with the searchlights, tryin to rescue some fool boy'd gone over."

For just a moment he swung us away from the island looming up on our starboard side, getting the most out of the crosswinds. "Never found em, though. Not a one." He spat again. "You go over the side around here, you're never seen again."

"The undertow," I offered.

He whipped his ruddy windburned face around, impaling me with one pale gray eye. "Undertow, you say?" His laugh was harsh now and un-pleasant. "You gotta lot t'learn up there at Fuego del Aire, boyo. Oh, yes indeed!"

He left me on the quayside with no one around to mark my arrival. As the wide-beamed ferry tacked away, pushed by the strong sunset wind, I thought I saw the captain raise an arm in my direction.

I turned away from the sea. Great stands of pine, bristly and dark in the failing light, matched upward in majestic array toward the castle high above me. Their tops whipsawed, sending off an odd melancholy drone.

I felt utterly, irretrievably alone and for the first time since I had sent the letter I began to feel the queasy fluttering of reservations. An odd kind of inner darkness had settled about my shoulders like a vulture de-scending upon the flesh of the dead.

I took a deep breath and shook my head to clear it. The captain's sto-ries were only words strung one after the other—all the legends just words and nothing more. Now I would see for myself. After all, that was what I wanted.

The last of the sunset torched the upper spires so that for a moment they looked like bloody spears. Imagination, that's all it was. A writer's imagination. I clutched at my battered weekender and continued on-ward, puffing, for the way was steep. But I had arrived at just the right time of the day when the scorching sun was gone from the sky and night's deep chill had not yet settled over the land.

The air was rich with the scents of the sea, an agglomeration so fe-cund it took my breath away. Far off over the water, great gulls twisted and turned in lazy circles, skimming over the shining face of the ocean only to whirl high aloft, disappearing for long moments into the fleecy pink and yellow clouds.

From the outside, the castle seemed stupendous. It was immense, thrusting upward into the sky as if it were about to take off in flight. It was constructed—obviously many years ago—from massive blocks of granite laced with iridescent chips of mica that shone like diamonds, rubies and sapphires in the evening's light.

A fairy tale castle it surely looked with its shooting turrets and sharply angled spires, horned and horrific. However, on closer inspection, I saw that it had been put together with nothing more fantastic than mortar.

Below me, a mist was beginning to form, swiftly climbing the route I had taken moments before as if following me. Already the sight of the quay had been snuffed out and the cries of the gulls, filtered through the stuff, were eerie and vaguely disquieting.

I climbed the basalt steps to the front door of the castle. The span was fully large enough to drive a semi through. It was composed of a black substance that seemed to be neither stone nor metal. Cautiously, I ran my hand over its textured surface. It was petrified wood. In its center was a circular scrollwork knocker of black iron and this I used.

There was surprisingly little noise but almost immediately the door swung inward. At first I could see nothing. The creeping mist had curled itself around the twilight, plunging me into a dank and uncomfortable night.

"Yes?" It was a melodious voice, light and airy. A woman's voice.

I told her my name.

"I am so sorry," she said. "We tend to lose track of time at Fuego del Aire. I am Marissa. Of course you were expected. My brother will be extremely angry that you were not met at the quay."

"It's all right," I said. "I thoroughly enjoyed the walk."

"Won't you come in."

I picked up my suitcase and crossed the threshold, felt her slim hand slip into mine. The hallway was as dark as the night outside. I did not hear the door swing shut but when I looked back the sky and the rolling mist were gone.

I heard the rustling of her just in front of me and I could smell a scent like a hillside of flowers at dusk. Her skin was as soft as velvet but the flesh beneath was firm and supple and I found myself suddenly curious to find out what she looked like. Did she resemble the image in my thoughts? A thin, pale waif-like creature, faint blue traceries of veins visible beneath her thin delicate skin, her long hair as black as a raven's wings.

After what seemed an interminable time, we emerged into a dimly lighted chamber from which all other rooms on this floor seemed to branch. Directly ahead of us, an enormous staircase wound upward. It was certainly wide enough for twenty people to ascend abreast.

Torches flickered and the smoky, perfumed air was thick with the scent of burning tallow and whale oil. Uncomfortable looking furniture lined the walls: bare, wooden stiff-backed benches and chairs one might find in a Methodist church. Huge, heavy banners hung limply but they were so high above my head and the light so poor I could not make out their designs.

Marissa turned to face me and I saw that she was not at all as I had imagined her.

True, she was beautiful enough. But her cheeks were ruddy, her eyes cornflower blue and her hair was the color of sun-dazzled honey, falling in thick, gentle waves from a thin tortoise-shell band that held it from her face, back over her head, across her shoulders, cascading all the way down to the small of her back.

Her coral lips pursed as if she could not help the smile that now brightened her face. "Yes," she said softly, musically, "you are truly surprised."

"I'm sorry," I said. "Am I staring?" I gave an unnatural laugh. Of course I was staring. I could not stop.

"Perhaps you are weary from your climb. Would you like some food now? A cool drink to refresh you?"

"I would like to meet Morodor," I said, breaking my eyes away from her gaze with a concerted effort. She seemed to possess an ability to draw emotion out of me, as if she held the key to channels in myself I did not know existed.

"In time," she said. "You must be patient. There are many pressing matters that need attending to. Only he can see to them. I am certain you understand."

Indeed I did not. To have come this far, to have waited so long . . . all

I felt was frustration. Like a hurt little boy, I had wanted Morodor to greet me at the front door by way of apology for the discourtesy of the utter stillness at the quay when I arrived. But no. There were more important matters for him.

"When I wrote to your brother——"

Marissa had lifted her long pale palms. "Please," she said, smiling. "Be assured that my brother wishes to aid you. I suspect that is because he is a writer himself. There is much time here at Fuego del Aire and lately his contemplation has found this somewhat more physical outlet."

I thought of the grisly stories the ferryboat captain had heaped on me—and others, over time, that had come my way from other loquacious mouths—and felt a chill creeping through my bones at the idea of Morodor's physical outlets.

"It must be fascinating to be able to write novels," Marissa said. "I must confess that I was quite selfishly happy when I learned of your coming. Your writing has given me much pleasure." She touched the back of my hand as if I might be a sculpture of great artistry. "This extraordinary talent must make you very desirable in . . . your world."

"You mean literary circles . . . entertainment. . . ."

"Circles, yes. You are quite special. My brother doubtless divined this from your letter." She took her fingertips from me. "But now it is late and I am certain you are tired. May I show you to your room? Food and drink are waiting for you there."

That night there was no moon. Or rather no moon could be seen. Nor the stars nor even the sky itself. Peering out the window of my turret room, I could see nothing but the whiteness of the mist. It was as if the rest of the world had vanished.

Gripping the edge of the windowsill with my fingers, I leaned out as far as I dared, peering into the night in an attempt to pick up any outline, any shape. But not even the tops of the enormous pines could poke their way through the pall.

I strained to hear the comforting hiss and suck of the ocean spending itself on the rocky shore so far below me. There was nothing of that, only the odd intermittent whistling of the wind through the stiff-fingered turrets of the castle.

At length, I went back to bed, but for the longest time I could not fall asleep. I had waited so long for Morodor's reply to my letter, had traveled for so many days just to be here now, it seemed impossible to relax enough for sleep to overtake me.

I was itchy with anticipation. Oh more. I was burning. . . . In the days after I had received his affirmative answer, the thought of coming here, of talking to him, of learning his secrets had, more and more, come to stand for my own salvation.

It is perhaps difficult enough for any author to be blocked in his work. But for me . . . I lived to write. Without it, there seemed no reason at all to live, for I had found during this blocked time that the days and nights passed like months, years, centuries, as ponderous as old elephants. They had become my burden.

I had been like a machine, feverishly turning out one book after another—one a year—for . . . how many years now? Fifteen? Twenty? You see, the enfant terrible has lost count already. Mercifully.

Until this year when there was nothing, a desert of paper, and I grew increasingly desperate, sitting home like a hermit, traveling incessantly, bringing smiling girls home, abstaining, swinging from one extreme to the other like a human pendulum in an attempt to get the insides in working order again.

Nothing.

And then one drunken night I had heard the first of the stories about Fuego del Aire and, even through the vapors of my stupor, *something* had penetrated. An idea, perhaps or, more accurately at that point, the ghost of an idea. Of lost love, betrayal and the ultimate horror. As simple as that. And as complex. But I knew that imagination was no longer enough, that I would have to seek out this place myself. I had to find Morodor and somehow persuade him to see me. . . .

Sleep. I swear to you it finally came, although, oddly, it was like no slumber I had ever had, for I dreamed that I was awake and trying desperately to fall asleep. I knew that I was to see Morodor in the morning, that I had to be sharp and that, sleepless, I would fall far short of that.

In the dream I lay awake, clutching the bedspread up around my chest, staring at the ceiling with such intensity that I suspected at any minute I would be able to see right through it.

I opened my eyes. Or closed them and opened them again to find the dawnlight streaming through the tall narrow window. I had forgotten to close the curtains before going to bed.

For just an instant I had the strangest sensation in my body. It was as if my legs had gone dead, all the strength flowing out of my muscles and into the wooden floor of my room. But the paralysis had somehow freed my upper torso so that I felt an enormous outpouring of energy.

A brief stab of fear rustled through my chest and my heart fluttered. But as soon as I sat up, the sensation went away. I rose, washed, dressed and went down to breakfast.

Food was waiting in steaming array along the length of an immense wooden table. In fact, now that I had my first good look at Fuego del Aire in the light of day, I saw that everything was of wood: the paneled walls, the floor where you could see it between the series of dark patterned carpets, the cathedral ceilings; door handles, windowsills, even the lighting fixtures. If I had not seen the outside of the castle myself, I would have sworn the place had been built entirely of wood.

Two formal settings were laid out, one at the head of the table and the other by its left side. Assuming the first was for Morodor, I settled into the side chair and began to help myself.

But it was not Morodor who came down the wide staircase; it was Marissa. She was, that morning, a sight to make the heart pound. It was as if the sun had detached itself from its prescribed route across the heavens and had descended to earth. She wore a sky-blue tunic, wrapped criss-cross between her breasts and around her narrow waist with a deep green satin sash. On her feet she wore rope sandals. I saw that one of her toes was girdled by a tiny gold ring.

Her smile as she approached had the warmth of summer itself. And her hair! How can I adequately describe the way her hair shone in the daylight, sparking and glittering as if each strand were itself some mysterious source of light. Those waves of golden honey acted as if they had a life of their own.

"Good morning," she said easily. "Did you sleep well?"

"Yes," I lied. "Perfectly." I lifted a bowl of green figs. "Fruit?"

"Yes, please. Just a bit." But even with that she left more on her plate than she ate.

"I was hoping to find your brother already awake," I said, finishing up my meal.

She smiled sweetly. "Unfortunately, he is not an early riser. Be patient. All will be well." She rose. "If you are finished, I imagine you are quite curious about Fuego del Aire. There is much here to see."

We went out of the main hall, through corridors and chambers one after another, so filled, so disparate that I soon became dizzied with wonder. The place seemed to go on forever.

At length we emerged into a room that, judging by its accouterments, must once have been a scullery. We crossed it quickly and went through a small door I did not see until Marissa pulled it open.

The mist of last night had gone completely and above was only an enormous cerulean sky clear of cloud or bird. I could hear the distant sea hurling itself with ceaseless abandon at the jagged base of the mount. But lowering my gaze I saw only foliage.

"The garden," Marissa breathed, slipping her hand into mine. "Come on." She took me past a field of tiger lilies, rows of flowering woodbine; through a rose garden of such humbling perfection, it took my breath away.

Beyond, we came upon a long sculptured hedge half again as tall as I stand. There was a long narrow opening through which she led me and immediately we were surrounded by high walls of hedges. They were lushly verdant and immaculately groomed so that it was impossible to say where one left off and another began, seamless on and on and——

"What is this place?" I said.

But Marissa did not answer until, after many twistings and turning, we were deep within. Then she faced me and said, "This is the Labyrinth. My brother had it constructed for me when I was just a child. Perhaps he thought it would keep me out of trouble."

"There *is* a way out," I said uneasily, looking around me at the dark-green screens looming up on every side.

"Oh yes." She laughed, a bell-like silvery tone. "It is up here." And tapped the side of her head with a slender forefinger. "This is where I come to think, when I am sad or distraught. It is so peaceful and still and no one can find me here if I choose to remain hidden, not even Morodor. This is my domain."

She began to lead me onward, through switchbacks, past cul-de-sacs, moving as unerringly as if she were a magnet being drawn toward the North Pole. And I followed her silently; I was already lost.

"My brother used to say to me, 'Marissa, this labyrinth is unique in all the world for I have made it from the blueprint of your mind. All these intricate convolutions . . . the pattern corresponds to the eddies and whorls of your own brain."

She stared at me with those huge mocking eyes, so blue it seemed as if the noonday sky were reflected there. The hint of a smile played at the corners of her lips. "But of course I was only a child then and always trying to do what he did . . . to be like him." She shrugged. "He was most likely trying to make me feel special . . . don't you think?"

"He wouldn't need this place to do that," I said. "How on earth do you find your way out of here?" Nothing she had said had lessened my uneasiness.

"The years," she said seriously, "have taken care of that."

She pulled at me and we sat, our torsos in the deep shade of the hedges, out stretched-out legs in the buttery warmth of the sunlight. Somewhere, close at hand, a bumblebee buzzed fatly, contentedly.

I put my head back and watched the play of light and shadow on the hedge opposite us. Ten thousand tiny leaves moved minutely in the soft breeze as if I were watching a distant crowd fluttering lifted handkerchiefs at the arrival of some visiting emperor. A kind of dreamy warmth stole over me and at once my uneasiness was gone.

"Yes," I told her. "It *is* peaceful here."

"I am glad," she said. "You feel it too. Perhaps that is because you are a writer. A writer feels things more deeply, is that not so?"

I smiled. "Maybe some, yes. We're always creating characters for our stories so we have to be adept at pulling apart the people we meet. We have to be able to get beyond the world and, like a surgeon, expose their workings."

"And you're never frightened of such things?"

"Frightened? Why?"

"Of what you'll find there."

"I've discovered many things there over the years. How could all of them be pleasant? Why should I want them to be? I sometimes think that many of my colleagues live off the *un*pleasant traits they find beneath the surface." I shrugged. "In any event, nothing seems to work well without the darkness of conflict. In life as well as in writing."

Her eyes opened and she looked at me sideways. "Am I wrong to think that knowledge is very important to you?"

"What could be more important to a writer? I sometimes think there is a finite amount of knowledge—not to be assimilated—but that can be used."

"And that is why you have come here."

"Yes."

She looked away. "You have never married. Why is that?"

I shrugged while I thought about that for a moment. "I imagine it's because I've never fallen in love."

She smiled at that. "Never ever. Not in all the time——"

I laughed. "Now wait a minute! I'm not that old. Thirty-seven is hardly ancient."

"Thirty-seven," she mouthed softly, as if she were repeating words alien to her. "Thirty-seven. Really?"

"Yes." I was puzzled. "How old are you?"

"As old as I look." She tossed her hair. "I told you last night. Time means very little here."

"Oh yes, day to day. But I mean you must——"

"No more talk now," she said, rising and pulling at my hand. "There is too much to see."

We left the labyrinth by a simple enough path, though, left to myself, I undoubtedly would have wandered around in there until someone had the decency to come and get me.

Presently we found ourselves at a stone parapet beyond which the peak dropped off so precipitously that it seemed as if we were standing on the verge of a rift in the world.

This was the western face of the island, one that I had not seen on my journey here. Far below us—certainly more than a thousand feet—the sea creamed and sucked at the jagged rocks, iced at their base by shining pale-gray barnacles. Three or four large lavender and white gulls dipped and wheeled through the foaming spray as they searched for food.

"Beautiful, isn't it?" Marissa said.

But I had already turned from the dark face of the sea to watch the planes and hollows of her own shining face, lit by the soft summer light, all rose and golden, radiating a warmth. . . .

It took me some time to understand the true nature of that heat. It stemmed from the same spot deep inside me from which had leaped that sharp momentary anger.

"Marissa," I breathed, saying her name as if it were a prayer.

And she turned to me, her cornflower blue eyes wide, her full lips slightly parted, shining. I leaned over her, coming closer inch by inch until I had to shut my eyes or cross them. Then I felt the rush of her lips against mine, so incredibly soft, at first cool and fragrant, then quickly warming to blood-heat.

"No," she said, her voice muffled by our flesh. "Oh, don't." But her lips opened under mine and I felt her hot tongue probing into my mouth.

My arms went around her, pulling her to me as gently as I would handle a stalk of wheat. I could feel the hard press of her breasts, the round softness of her stomach, and the heat. The heat rising. . . .

And with the lightning comes the rain. That's from an old poem my mother used to sing to me late at night when the storms woke me up. I cannot remember any more of it. Now it's just a fragment of truth, an artifact unearthed from the silty riverbed of my mind. And I the archeologist of this region as puzzled as everyone else at what I sometimes find. But that, after all, is what has kept me writing, year after year. An engine of creation.

The night is impenetrable with cloud and the hissing downpour. But still I stand at my open window, high up above the city, at the very edge of heaven.

I cannot see the streets below me—the one or two hurrying people beneath their trembling umbrellas or the lights of the cars, if indeed there are any out at this ungodly hour—just the spectral geometric patterns, charcoal-gray on black, of the buildings' tops closest to mine. But not as high. None of them is as high.

Nothing exists now but this tempest and its fury. The night is alive with it, juddering and crackling. Or am I wrong? Is the night alive with something else? I know. *I know.*

I hear the sound of them now. . . .

The days passed like the most intense of dreams. The kind where you can recall every single detail any time you wish, producing its emotions again and again with a conjurer's facility.

Being with Marissa, I forgot about my obsessive desire to seek out

Morodor. I no longer asked her where he was or when I would get to see him. In fact, I hoped I never would, for, if there were any truth to the legends of Fuego del Aire, they most assuredly must stem from his dark soul and not from this creature of air and light who never left my side.

In the afternoons we strolled through the endless gardens—for she was ill at ease indoors—and holding her hand seemed infinitely more joyous than looking upon the castle's illimitable marvels. I fully believe that if we had chanced upon a griffin during one of those walks I would have taken no more notice of it than I would an alley cat.

However, no such fabled creature made its appearance, and as the time passed I became more and more convinced that there was no basis at all to the stories that had been told and re-told over the years. The only magical power Marissa possessed was the one that enabled her to cut to the very core of me with but one word or the merest touch of her flesh against mine.

"I lied to you," I told her one day. It was late afternoon. Thick dark sunlight slanted down on our shoulders and backs, as slow-running as honey. The cicadas wailed like beaten brass and butterflies danced like living jewels in and out of the low bushes and the blossoms as if they were a flock of children playing tag.

"About what?"

"When I said that I had never been in love." I turned over on my back, staring up at a fleecy cloud piled high, a castle in the sky. "I was. Once."

I took her hand, rubbed my thumb over the delicate bones ribbing the back. "It was when I was in college. We met in a child psychology class and fell in love without even knowing it."

For a moment there was a silence between us and I thought perhaps I had made a mistake in bringing it up.

"But you did not marry her."

"No."

"Why not?"

"We were from different . . . backgrounds." I turned to see her face peering at me, seeming as large as the sun in the sky. "I think it would be difficult to explain to you, Marissa. It had something to do with religion."

"Religion." Again she rolled a word off her tongue as if trying to get the taste of a new and exotic food. "I am not certain that I understand."

"We believed in different things—or, more accurately, she believed and I didn't."

"And there was no room for . . . compromise?"

"In this, no. But the ironic part of all of it is that now I have begun to believe, if just a little bit; and she, I think, has begun to disbelieve some of what she had always held sacred."

"How sad," Marissa said. "Will you go back to her?"

"Our time has long passed."

Something curious had come into her eyes. "Then you believe that love has a beginning and an end, always."

I could no longer bear to have those fantastic eyes riveting me. "I had thought so."

"Why do you look away?"

"I——" I watched the sky. The cloud-castle had metamorphosed into a great humpbacked bird. "I don't know."

Her eyes were very clear, piercing though the natural light was dusky. "We are explorers," she said, "at the very precipice of time." Something in her voice drew me. "Can there really be a love without end?"

Now she began to search my face in detail as if she were committing it to memory, as if she might never see me again. And that wild thought brought me fully out of my peaceful dozing.

"Do you love me?"

"Yes," I whispered with someone else's voice. Like a dry wind through sere reeds. And pulled her down to me.

At night we seemed even closer. It was as if I had taken a bit of the sun to bed with me: she was as radiant at night as she was during the day, light and supple and so eager to be held, to be caressed. To be loved.

"Feel how I feel," she whispered, trembling, "when I am close to you." She stretched herself over me. "The mouth can lie with words but the body cannot. This heat is real. All love flows out through the body, do you know that?"

I was beyond being able to respond verbally.

She moved her fingertips on me, then the petal softness of her palms. "I feel your body. How you respond to me. Its depth. As if I were the moon and you the sea." Her lips were at my ear, her esses sibilant. "It is important. More important than you know."

"Why?" I sighed.

"Because only love can mend my heart."

I wondered at the scar there. I moved against her, opening her legs.

"Darling!"

I met Morodor on the first day of my second week at Fuego del Aire. And then it seemed quite by chance.

It was just after breakfast and Marissa had gone back to her room to change. I was strolling along the second floor balustrade when I came across a niche in the wall that I had missed before.

I went through it and found myself on a parapet along the jutting north side of the castle. It was like hanging in mid-air and I would have been utterly stunned by the vista had I not almost immediately run into a dark towering shape.

Hastily I backed up against the stone wall of the castle, thinking I had inadvertently run into another outcropping of this odd structure.

Then, quite literally, it seemed as if a shadow had come to life. It detached itself from the edge of the parapet and now I can see that it was the figure of a man.

He must have been nearly seven feet tall and held about him a great ebon cape, thick and swirling, that rushed down his slender form so that it hissed against the stone floor when he moved.

He turned toward me and I gasped. His face was long and narrow, as bony as a corpse's, his skin fully as pale. His eyes, beneath darkly furred brows, were bits of bituminous matter as if put there to plug a pair of holes into his interior. His nose was long and thin to the point of severity but his lips were full and rubicund, providing the only bit of color to his otherwise deathly pallid face.

His lips opened infinitesimally and he spoke my name. Involuntarily, I shuddered and immediately saw something pass across his eyes: not anger or sorrow but rather a weary kind of resignation.

"How do you do."

The greeting was so formal that it startled me and I was tongue-tied. After all this time, he had faded from my mind and now I longed only to be with Marissa. I found myself annoyed with him for intruding upon us.

"Morodor," I said. I had the oddest impulse to tell him that what he needed most was a good dose of sunshine. That almost made me giggle. Almost.

"Pardon me for saying this but I thought . . . that is, to see you up and around, outside in the daylight——" I stopped, my cheeks burning, unable to go on. I had done it anyway. I cursed myself for the fool that I was.

But Morodor took no offense. He merely smiled—a perfectly ghastly sight—and inclined his head a fraction. "A rather common misconception," he said in his disturbing, rumbling voice. "It is in fact *direct* sunlight that is injurious to my health. I am like a fine old print." His dark hair brushed against his high forehead. "I quite enjoy the daytime, otherwise."

"But surely you must sleep sometime."

He shook his great head. "Sleep is unknown to me. If I slept, I would dream and this is not allowed me." He took a long hissing stride along the parapet. "Come," he said. "Let us walk." I looked back the way I had come and he said, "Marissa knows we are together. Do not fear. She will be waiting for you when we are finished."

Together we walked along the narrow parapet. Apparently, it girdled the entire castle, for I saw no beginning to it and no end.

"You may wonder," Morodor said in his booming, vibratory voice, "why I granted you this interview." His great cape swept around him like the coils of a midnight sea so that it seemed as if he kept the night around him wherever he went. "I sensed in your writing a certain desperation." He turned to me. "And desperation is an emotion with which I can empathize."

"It was kind of you to see me."

"Kind, yes."

"But I must confess that things have . . . changed since I wrote that letter."

"Indeed." Was that a vibratory warning?

"Yes," I plunged onward. "In fact, since I came here, I——" I paused, not knowing how to continue. "The change has come since I arrived at Fuego del Aire."

Morodor said nothing and we continued our perambulation around the perimeter of the castle. Now I could accurately judge just how high up we were. Perhaps that mist I had seen the first night had been a cloud

passing us as if across the face of the moon. And why not? All things
seemed possible here. It struck me as ridiculous that just fifty miles from
here there were supertankers and express trains, Learjets and paved
streets lined with shops dispensing sleekly packaged products manufactured by multinational corporations. Surely all those modern artifacts
were part of a fading dream I once had.

The sea was clear of sails for as far as the horizon. It was a flat and
glittering pool there solely for the pleasure of this man.

"I'm in love with your sister." I had blurted it out and now I stood
stunned, waiting, I suppose, for the full brunt of his wrath.

But instead, he stopped and stared at me. Then he threw his head back
and laughed, a deep booming sound like thunder. Far off, a gull
screeched, perhaps in alarm.

"My dear sir," he said. "You really are the limit!"

"And she's in love with me."

"Oh oh oh. I have no doubt that she is."

"I don't——"

His brows gathered darkly like stormclouds. "You believe your race
to be run." He moved away. "But fear, not love, ends it." Through another niche, he slid back inside the castle. It was as if he had passed
through the wall.

"If I had known that today was the day," Marissa said, "I would have
prepared you."

"For what?"

We were sitting in a bower on a swing-chaise. Above our heads
arched brilliant hyacinth and bougainvillea, wrapped around and around
a white wooden trellis. It was near dusk and the garden was filled with
a deep sapphire light that was almost luminescent. A westerly wind
brought us the rich scent of the sea.

"For him. We are not . . . very much alike. At least, superficially."

"Marissa," I said, taking her hand, "are you certain that you *are*
Morodor's sister?"

"Of course I am. What do you mean?"

"Well, it's obvious, isn't it?" But when she looked at me blankly, I
was forced to go on. "What I mean it, he's precisely . . . what he's supposed to be. At least the way the legends describe . . . what he is."

Her eyes grew dark and she jerked her hand away. She gave me a basilisk stare. "I should have known." Her voice was filled with bitter contempt. "You're just like the rest. And why shouldn't you be?" She stood. "You think he's a monster. Yes, admit it. A monster!"

Her eyes welled up with tears. "And that makes me a monster too, doesn't it. Well, to hell with you!" And she whirled away.

"Marissa!" I cried in anguish. "That's not what I meant at all."

And I ran after her knowing that it was a lie, that it was what I had meant after all. Morodor was all the legends had said he should be. And more. My God but he was hideous. Pallid and cold as the dead. An engine of negative energy, incapable of any real feeling; of crying or true humor. Or love.

Only love can mend my heart.

I *had* meant it. How could this golden girl of air and sunlight bear any family ties to that great looming figure of darkness? Where was the sense in it? The rationality? She had feelings. She laughed and cried, felt pleasure and pain. And she loved. She loved.

"Marissa!" I called again, running. "Marissa, come back!" But she had vanished into the labyrinth and I stood there on the threshold, the scent of roses strong in my nostrils, and peered within. I called out her name over and over again but she did not appear and, unguided, I could not bring myself to venture farther.

Instead, I stormed back to the castle, searching for Morodor. It was already dark and the lights had been lit. As if by magic. In just the same way that the food was prepared, the wine bottles uncorked, my bed turned down in the evening and made in the morning, my soiled clothes washed, pressed and laid out with the professional's precision. And all done without my seeing a soul.

I found Morodor in the library. It was a room as large as a gallery: at least three floors of books, rising upward until the neat rows were lost in the haze of the distance. Narrow wooden walkways circled the library at various levels, connected by a complex network of wide wooden ladders.

He was crouched on one of these, three or four steps off the floor. It seemed an odd position for a man of his size.

He was studying a book as I came in but he quietly closed it when he heard me approach.

"What," I said, rather nastily, "no leather bindings?"

His hard ebon eyes regarded me without obvious emotion. "Leather," he said softly, "would mean the needless killing of animals."

"Oh, I see." My tone had turned acid. "It's only humans who need fear you."

He stood up and I backed away, abruptly fearful as he unfolded upward and upward until he stood over me in all his monstrous height.

"Humans," he said, "fear me only because they choose to fear me."

"You mean you haven't given them any cause to fear you?"

"Don't be absurd." He was as close to being annoyed as I had seen him. "I cannot help being what I am. Just as you cannot. We are both carnivores."

I closed my eyes and shuddered. "But with what a difference!"

"To some I have been a god."

"Such a dark god." My eyes flew open.

"There is a need for that, too." He put the book away. "Yet I am a man for all that."

"A man who can't sleep, who doesn't dream."

"Who cannot die."

"Not even if I drive a stake through your heart?" I did not know whether or not I was serious.

He went across the room to where a strip of wooden paneling intervened between two bookshelves. His hand merged from the folds of his voluminous cape and for the first time I saw the long talon-like nails exposed. I shivered as I saw them dig into the wood with ferocious strength. But not in any hot animal way. The movement was as precise as a surgeon peeling back a patient's peritoneum.

Morodor returned with a shard of wood perhaps eighteen inches in length. It was slightly tapered at one end, not needle sharp but pointed enough to do its work. He thrust it into my hands. "Here," he said harshly. "Do it now."

For an instant, I intended to do just that. But then something inside me cooled. I threw the stake from me. "I'll do no such thing."

He actually seemed disappointed. "No matter. That part of the legend, as others, is incorrect." He went back to his perch on the ladder, his long legs drawn up tightly beneath the cape, the outline of his bony knees like a violent set of punctuation marks on a blank page.

"Legends," he said, "are like funerals. They both serve the same purpose. They give comfort without which the encroachment of terrifying entropy would snuff out man's desire—his absolute hunger—for life."

He looked from his long nails up into my face. "Legends are created to set up their own kind of terror. But it is a terror very carefully bounded by certain limitations: the werewolf can be killed by a silver bullet, the medusa by seeing her own reflection in a mirror.

"You see? Always there is a way out for the intrepid. It is a necessary safety valve venting the terror that lurks within all mankind—atavistic darkness, the unconscious. And death."

He rested his long arms in his lap. "How secure do you imagine mankind would feel if all of them out there knew the reality of it? That there is no escape for me. No stake through the heart."

"But you said direct sunlight——"

"Was injurious to me. Like the flu, nothing more." He smiled wanly. "A week or two in bed and I am fit again." He laughed sardonically.

"Assuming I believe you, why are you telling me this? By your own admission, mankind could not accept the knowledge."

"Then you won't tell them, will you?"

"But *I* know."

He took a deep breath and for the first time his eyes seemed to come to life, sparking and dancing within their deep fleshless sockets. "Why did you wish to come here, my friend?"

"Why, I told you in the letter. I was blocked, out of ideas."

"And now?"

I stared at him quizzically while it slowly began to wash over me. "I can tell them, can't I?"

He smiled sphinx-like. "You are a writer. You can tell them anything you wish."

"When I told you before that I was a man, I meant it."

I was sitting with Morodor high up in one of the castle's peaks, in what he called the cloud room. Like all the other chambers I had been in here, it was paneled in wood.

"I have a hunger to live just like all the rest of the masses." He leaned back in his chair, shifting about as if he were uncomfortable. To his left and right, enormous windows stood open to the starry field of the night.

There were no shutters, no curtains; they could not be closed. A sharp, chill wind blew in, ruffling his dark hair but he seemed oblivious to the caress. "But do not mistake my words. I speak not as some plutocrat bloated on wealth. It is only that I am . . . special."

"What happened?"

His eyes flashed and he shifted again. "In each case, it is different. In mine . . . well, let us say that my hunger for life outweighed my caution." He smiled bleakly. "But then I have never believed that caution was a desirable trait."

"Won't you tell me more."

He looked at me in the most avuncular fashion. "I entered into a wager with . . . someone."

"And you won."

"No. I lost. But it was meant that I should lose. Otherwise, I would not be here now." His eyes had turned inward and in so doing had become almost wistful. "I threw the dice one time, up against a wall of green baize."

"You crapped out."

"No. I entered into life."

"And became *El Amor Brujo*. That's what you're sometimes called: the love sorcerer."

"Because of my . . . hypnotic effect on women." He moved minutely and his cape rustled all about him like a copse of trees stirred by a midnight wind. "A survival trait. Like seeing in the dark or having built-in radar."

"Then there's nothing magical——"

"There is," he said, "magic involved. One learns . . . many arts over the years. I have time for everything."

I shivered, pulled my leather jacket closer about me. He might not mind the chill, but I did. I pointed to the walls. "Tell me something. The outside of Fuego del Aire is pure stone. But here, inside, there is only wood. Why is that?"

"I prefer wood, my friend. I am not a creature of the earth and so stone insults me; its density inhibits me. I feel more secure with the wood." His hand lifted, fluttered, dropped back into his lap. "Trees." He said it almost as if it were a sacred word.

In the ensuing silence, I began to sweat despite the coldness. I knew what I at least was leading up to. I rubbed my palms down the fabric of my trousers. I cleared my throat.

"Morodor. . . ."

"Yes." His eyes were half-shut as if he were close to sleep.

"I really do love Marissa."

"I know that." But there seemed no kindness in his voice.

I took a deep breath. "We had a row. She thinks I see you as a monster."

He did not move, his eyes did not open any wider, for which I was profoundly grateful. "In a world where so many possibilities exist, this is true. Yet I am also a man. And I am Marissa's brother. I am friend . . . foe; master . . . servant. It is all in the perception." Still he did not move. "What do *you* see, my friend?"

I wished he'd stop calling me that. I said nothing.

"If you are not truthful with me, I shall know it." His ruby lips seemed to curve upward at their corners. "Something else you may add to the new legend . . . if you choose to write about it."

"I've no wish to deceive you, Morodor. I'm merely trying to sort through my own feelings." I thought he nodded slightly.

"I confess . . . to finding your appearance . . . startling."

"I appreciate your candor."

"Oh, hell, I thought you were hideous."

"I see."

"You hate me now."

"Why should I hate you? Because you take the world view?"

"But that was at first. Already you've changed before my eyes. God knows I've tried but now I don't even find your appearance odd."

As if divining my thoughts, he said, "And this disturbs you."

"It does."

He nodded his head again. "Quite understandable. It will pass." He looked at me. "But you are afraid of that too."

"Yes," I said softly.

"Soon you shall meet my sister again."

I shook my head. "I don't understand."

"Of course you don't." Now his voice sounded softer. "Have patience, my friend. You are young enough still to rush headlong over the precipice merely to discover what is beyond it."

"That's why I came here."

"I know. But that time has passed. Now life has you by the throat and it will be a struggle to the end." His eyes flew open, seeming as hot as burning coals. "And who shall be the victor, my friend? When you have the answer to that, you shall understand it all."

I ate dinner alone that night. I had spent hours searching the castle for Marissa but it was as if she had vanished. Weary at last, I returned to the dining hall and availed myself of vast quantities of the hot food.

I was terrified and I thought that this would act as an inhibitor on my appetite. But, strangely, just the opposite was happening. I ate and ate as if this alone could assuage my fear.

It was Morodor I was terrified of, I knew that. But was it because I feared him or liked him?

Afterward, it was all I could do to drag myself up the staircase. I stumbled down the hallway and into bed without even removing my clothes.

I slept a deep dreamless sleep but when I opened my eyes it was still dark out. I turned over, about to return to sleep, when I heard a sound. I sat bolt upright, the short hairs at the back of my neck stiff and quivering.

Silence.

And out of the silence a weird, thin cry. I got off the bed about to open the door to the hallway when it came again and I turned. It was coming from outside in the blackness of the night.

I threw open the shutters wide and leaned out just as I had on my first night here. This time there was no mist. Stars shone intermittently through the gauzy cloud cover with a fierce cold light, blinking on and off as if they were silently appealing for help.

At first I saw nothing, hearing only the high soughing of the wind through the pines. Then, off to my left, so high up that I mistook it for another cloud, something moved.

I turned my head in that direction and saw a shape a good deal darker than a cloud. It blossomed with sickening speed, blacker even than the night. Wraith or dream, which was it? The noise of the flapping wings, leathery, horned and, what?, scabbed, conjured up in my mind the image of a giant bat.

Precariously, I leaned farther out, saw that it was heading for the open apertures of the cloud room. I hurled myself across the room and out the door, heading up the stairs in giant bounds.

Consequently, I was somewhat out of breath by the time I launched myself through the open doorway to the aerie and there found only Morodor.

He turned quickly from his apparent contemplation of the sky. "You should be asleep," he said. But something in his tone told me that I had been expected.

"Something woke me."

"Not a nightmare, I trust."

"A sound from the night. It was nothing to do with me."

"It is usually quite still here. What kind of sound?"

"It sounded like a scream . . . a terrible cry."

Morodor only stared at me, unblinking, until I was forced to go on. "I went to the window and looked out. I . . . saw a shape I could not clearly identify; I heard the awful sound of bat wings."

"Oh," Morodor said, "that's quite impossible. We have none here, I've seen to that. Bats are boring, really. As with octopi, I'm afraid their ferocious reputation has been unjustly thrust upon them."

"Just what the hell did I see then?"

Morodor's hand lifted, fell, the arch of a great avian wing. "Whatever it was, it brought you up here."

"Then there *was* something there!" I said in triumph. "You admit it."

"I admit," said Morodor carefully, "that I wanted to see you. The fact is you are here."

"You and I," I said. "But what of Marissa? I have been looking for her all evening. I must see her."

"Do you think it wise to see her now, to . . . continue what has begun, knowing what you do about me?"

"But she is nothing like you. You two are the shadow and the light."

Morodor's gaze was unwavering. "Two sides of the coin, my friend. The same coin."

I was fed up with his oblique answers. "Perhaps," I said sharply, "it's just that you don't want me to see her. After all, I'm an outsider. I don't belong at Fuego del Aire. But if that's the case, let me warn you, I won't be balked!"

"That's the spirit!" His hand clenched into a fist. "Forget all about that which you saw from your bedroom window. It has nothing to do with you." His tone was mocking.

"A bird," I said uncertainly. "That's all it was."

"My friend," he said calmly, "there is no bird as large as the one you saw tonight."

And he reached out for the first time. I felt his chill touch as his long fingers gripped my shoulder with a power that made me wither inside. "Come," he commanded. "Over here at the windowledge."

I stood there, dazed with shock as he let go of me and leaped out into the night.

I screamed, reaching out to save him, thinking that, after all, his apparent melancholy signaled a wish to die. Then I saw his great ebon cape ballooning out like a sail, drawn upward by the cross-currents and, for the first time, I saw what had been hidden beneath its voluminous folds.

I had thought he wore the thing as an affectation, because it was part of the legend. But now I understood. What care had he for legends? He wore the cape for practical reasons.

For now from under it spread a pair of the most extraordinary wings I had ever seen. They were glossy and pitch black, as far away from bat's wings as you could get. For one thing, they were feathered or at least covered in long silky strips that had the appearance of feathers. For another, they were as supple as a hummingbird's and quite as beautiful. And made even more so by the thick, muscular tendons by which they were attached to his back. It was like seeing the most beautifully developed torso: hard muscle tone combined with sleek line. And yet. And yet there was more, in the most literal sense, because more musculature was required in order for those massive wings to support the weight of the rest of the body.

Those wings! Sharply angled and hard, delicate as brushstrokes, they beat at the air like heroic engines. They were a magnificent creation, nothing less than a crowning achievement, an evolutionary pinnacle of the Creator.

But out of the wonder came terror and I thought: Marissa! My God! My God! He means to turn her into this. *El Amor Brujo.*

Without a word, I turned and bolted from the room. Taking the steps three at a time, I returned to the second floor and there found Marissa asleep in her own bed.

My heart beating like a triphammer, I brought a light close to her face. But no. An exhalation hissed from my mouth. There was no change. But still I feared Morodor and what he could do to her.

"Marissa!" I whispered urgently. "Marissa! Wake up!" I shook her but she would not waken. Hurling the light aside, I bent and scooped her up in my arms. Turning, I kicked the door wide and hurried down the stairs. Where I thought to go at that moment remains a mystery to me still. All I know was that I had to get Marissa away from that place.

The way to the disused scullery I knew and this was the route I took. Outside, the wind ruffled my hair but Marissa remained asleep.

I carried her through the field of tiger lilies and the woodbine, down the center aisle of the vast rose garden, to the verge of the labyrinth. Without thinking, I took her inside.

It was dark there. Darker than the night with the high ebon walls, textured like stucco, looming up on every side. I stumbled down the narrow pathways, turing now left or right at random until I knew that I was truly lost. But at least Morodor could not find us and I had with me this place's only key.

Panting, my muscles aching, I knelt on the grass and set Marissa down beside me. I looked around. All I could hear was the faroff whistle of the wind as if diminished by time. Even the booming surf was beyond hearing now.

I sat back and wiped my brow, staring down at that golden face, so innocent in repose, so shockingly beautiful. I could not allow——

Marissa's eyes opened and I helped her to sit up.

"What has happened?"

"I was awakened by a strange sound," I told her. "I saw your brother outside the castle. I thought at first it was a bird but when I went to find out, I saw him."

She looked at me but said nothing.

I gripped her shoulders. I had begun sweating again. "Marissa," I said hoarsely. "He was flying."

Her eyes brightened and she leaned toward me, kissed me hard on the lips. "Then it's happened! The time is here."

"Time," I echoed her stupidly. "Time for what?"

"For the change," she said as if talking to a slow-witted child.

"Yes," I said. "I suspected as much. That's why I've brought you into the labyrinth. We're safe here."

Her brows furrowed. "Safe? Safe from what?"

"From Morodor," I said desperately. "He can't touch you here. Now he cannot change you. You'll stay like this forever. You'll never have to look like him."

For the first time, I saw fright in her eyes. "I don't understand." She shivered. "Didn't he tell you?"

"Tell me what?" I hung on to her. "I ran out of there as soon as I saw him——"

"Oh no!" she cried. "It's all destroyed now. All destroyed!" She put her face in her hands, weeping bitterly.

"Marissa," I said softly, holding her close. "Please don't cry. I can't bear it. I've saved you. Why are you crying?"

She shook me off and stared wide-eyed at me. Even tear-streaked she was exquisitely beautiful. It did not matter that she was filled with pain. No emotion could alter those features. Not even, it seemed, time itself. Only Morodor, her haunted brother.

"He was supposed to tell you. To prepare you," she said between sobs. "Now it has all gone wrong."

"Marissa," I said, stroking her, "don't you know I love you? I've said it and I meant it. Nothing can change that. As soon as we get out of here, we'll——"

"Tell me, how deep is your love for me?" She was abruptly icily calm.

"How deep can any emotion be? I don't think it can be measured."

"Do not be so certain of that," she whispered, "until you've heard me out." She put her hands up before her body, steepling them as if they were a church's spire. "It is not Morodor who will work the change. It is you."

"Me?"

"And it has already begun."

My head was whirling and I put the flat of my hand against the ground as if to balance myself. "What are you saying?"

"The change comes only when we are in love and that love is re-turned. When we find a mate. The emotion and its reflection releases some chemical catalyst hidden deep inside our DNA helices which has remained dormant until triggered."

Her fingers twined and untwined anxiously. "This is not a . . . state that can be borne alone; it is far too lonely. So this is how it is handled. An imperative of nature."

"No!" I cried. "No no no! What you're telling me is impossible. It's madness!"

"It is life, and life only."

"Your life! Not mine!"

I stood up, stumbled, but I could not escape the gaze of her lambent eyes. I stared at her in mounting horror. "Liar!" I cried. "Where is Morodor's mate if this is true?"

"Away," she said calmly. "Feeding."

"My God!" I whirled away. "My God!" And slammed into the prickly wall of a hedge.

"Can love hold so much terror for you?" she asked. "You have a responsibility. To yourself as well as to me. Isn't that what love is?"

But I could no longer think clearly. I only knew that I must get away from them both. *The change has already begun,* she had said. I do not think that I wanted to see the fruits of that terrible metamorphosis. Not after having known her and loved her like this, all air and sunlight.

Two sides of the coin. Wasn't that what I had said to Morodor? How he must have laughed at that. Yes. Two sides. But of the same coin.

"Don't you see?" I heard her voice but could no longer see her. "You have nothing to fear. It is your destiny——*our* destiny, together."

Howling, I clawed my way from her, staggering, tripping as I ran through the labyrinth. My only coherent thought was to somehow get to the sea and then to hurl myself into its rocking embrace.

To swim. To swim. And if I were lucky I would at last be thrown up onto the soft sand of some beach far, far away.

But the night had come alive with shadows drenched in my own terror. And, like a mirror, they threw up to me the ugly writhing apparitions from the very bottom of my soul, thrusting them rudely into the light for me to view.

And above me the sound of. . . .

Wings.

Even through the horrendous tattoo of the storm I can make out that sound. It's the same sound that reached down into my heavy slumber that night in Fuego del Aire and wrenched me awake. I did not know it then but I know it now.

But I know many things now that I did not then. I have had time to think. To think and to write. Sometimes they are one and the same. Like tonight.

Coming to terms. I have never been able to do that. I have never *wanted* to do that. My writing kept me fluid, moving in and out as the spirit took me. New York today, Capri the next. The world was my oyster.

But what of *me*?

The sound is louder now: that high keening whistle like the wind through the pines. It buzzes through my brain like a downed bottle of vintage champagne. I feel lightheaded but more than that. Light-bodied. Because I know. *I know.*

There is nothing but excitement inside me now. All the fear and the horror I felt in the labyrinth leached away from me. I have had six months to contemplate my destiny. Morodor was right: For each one, it is different. The doorway metamorphoses to suit the nature of the individual.

For me it is love. I denied that when Marissa confronted me with the process of her transmogrificaiton. Such beauty! How could I lose that? I thought. It took me all of this time to understand that it was not her I feared losing but myself. Marissa will always be Marissa.

But what of me? Change is what we fear above all else and I am no different.

Was no different. I have already forgotten the golden creature of Fuego del Aire: she haunts my dreams still but I remember only her inner self. It is somehow like death, this acceptance of life. Perhaps this is where the legends began.

All around me the city sleeps on, safe and secure, wrapped in the arms of the myths of its own creation. Shhh! Don't bother to disturb it. No one would listen anyway.

The beating of the wings is very loud now, drowning out even the heavy pulsing of the rain. It reverberates in my mind like a heartbeat, dimming sight, taste, touch, smell. It dominates me in a way I thought only my writing could.

My shutters are open wide. I am drenched by the rain, buffeted by the chill wind. I am buoyed up by them both. I tremble at the thought. I love. *I love*. Those words a river of silver turning my bones hollow.

And now I lift my head to the place where last night the full moon rode calm and clear, a ghostly idiogram written upon the air, telling me that it is time for me to let go of all I know, to plunge inward toward the center of my heart. Six months have passed and it is time. *I know*. For now the enormous thrumming emanates from that spot. Beat-beat. Beat-beat. Beat-beat.

The heart-sound.

At last. There in the night, I see her face as she comes for me.

Dayblood

by Roger Zelazny

I crouched in the corner of the collapsed shed behind the ruined church. The dampness soaked through the knees of my jeans, but I knew that my wait was just about ended. Picturesquely, a few tendrils of mist rose from the soaked ground, to be stirred feebly by predawn breezes. How Hollywood of the weather. . . .

I cast my gaze about the lightening sky, guessing correctly as to the direction of arrival. Within a minute I saw them flapping their way back—a big, dark one and a smaller, pale one. Predictably, they entered the church through the opening where a section of the roof had years before fallen in. I suppressed a yawn as I checked my watch. Fifteen minutes from now they should be settled and dozing as the sun spills morning all over the east. Possibly a little sooner, but give them a bit of leeway. No hurry yet.

I stretched and cracked my knuckles. I'd rather be home in bed. Nights are for sleeping, not for playing nursemaid to a couple of stupid vampires.

Yes, Virginia, there really are vampires. Nothing to get excited about, though. Odds are you'll never meet one. There just aren't that many around. In fact, they're damn near an endangered species—which is entirely understandable, considering the general level of intelligence I've encountered among them.

Take this guy Brodsky as an example. He lives—pardon me, resides—near a town containing several thousand people. He could have visited a different person each night for years without ever repeating himself, leaving his caterers (I understand that's their in-term these days) with little more than a slight sore throat, a touch of temporary anemia, and a couple of soon-to-be-forgotten scratches on the neck.

But no. He took a fancy to a local beauty—one Elaine Wilson, ex-majorette. Kept going back for more. Pretty soon she entered the customary coma and underwent the *nosferatu* transformation. All right, I know I said there aren't that many of them around—and personally I do feel that the world could use a few more vampires. But it's not a population-pressure thing with Brodsky, just stupidity and greed. No real finesse, no planning. While I applaud the creation of another member of the undead, I am sufficiently appalled by the carelessness of his methods to consider serious action. He left a trail that just about anyone could trace here; he also managed to display so many of the traditional signs and to leave such a multitude of clues that even in these modern times a reasonable person could become convinced of what was going on.

Poor old Brodsky—still living in the Middle Ages and behaving just as he did in the days of their population boom. It apparently never occurred to him to consider the mathematics of that sort of thing. He drains a few people he becomes particularly attracted to and they become *nosferatu*. If they feel the same way and behave the same way, they go out and recruit a few more of their caterers. And so on. It's like a chain letter. After a time, everyone would be *nosferatu* and there wouldn't be any caterers left. Then what? Fortunately, nature has ways of dealing with population explosions, even at this level. Still, a sudden rash of recruits in this mass-media age could really mess up the underground ecosystem.

So much for philosophy. Time to get inside and beat the crowd.

I picked up my plastic bag and worked my way out of the shed, cursing softly when I bumped against a post and brought a shower down over me. I made my way through the field then and up to the side door of the old building. It was secured by a rusty padlock, which I snapped and threw into the distant cemetery.

Inside, I perched myself on the sagging railing of the choir section and opened my bag. I withdrew my sketchbook and the pencil I'd brought along. Light leaked in through the broken window to the rear. What it fell upon was mostly trash. Not a particularly inspiring scene. Whatever . . . I began sketching it. It's always good to have a hobby that can serve as an excuse for odd actions, as an icebreaker . . .

Ten minutes, I guessed. At most.

Six minutes later, I heard their voices. They weren't particularly noisy, but I have exceptionally acute hearing. There were three of them, as I'd guessed there would be.

They entered through the side door also, slinking, jumpy—looking all about and seeing nothing. At first they didn't even notice me creating art where childish voices had filled Sunday mornings with off-key praise in years gone by.

There was old Dr. Morgan, several wooden stakes protruding from his black bag (I'll bet there was a hammer in there, too—I guess the Hippocratic Oath doesn't extend to the undead—*primum, non nocere,* etc.); and Father O'Brien, clutching his Bible like a shield, crucifix in his other hand; and young Ben Kelman (Elaine's fiancé), with a shovel over his shoulder and a bag from which I suspected the sudden odor of garlic to have its origin.

I cleared my throat, and all three of them stopped, turned, bumped into each other.

"Hi, Doc," I said. "Hi, Father. Ben . . ."

"Wayne!" Doc said. "What are you doing here?"

"Sketching," I said. "I'm into old buildings these days."

"The hell you are!" Ben said. "Excuse me, Father . . . You're just after a story for your damned newspaper!"

I shook my head.

"Really I'm not."

"Well, Gus'd never let you print anything about this, and you know it."

"Honest," I said. "I'm not here for a story. But I know why you're here, and you're right—even if I wrote it up, it would never appear. You really believe in vampires?"

Doc fixed me with a steady gaze.

"Not until recently," he said. "But, son, if you'd seen what we've seen, you'd believe."

I nodded my head and closed my sketchpad.

"All right," I replied. "I'll tell you. I'm here because I'm curious. I wanted to see it for myself, but I don't want to go down there alone. Take me with you."

They exchanged glances.

"I don't know . . ." Ben said.

"It won't be anything for the squeamish," Doc told me.

Father O'Brien just nodded.

"I don't know about having anyone else in on this," Ben added.

"How many more know about it?" I asked.

"It's just us, really," Ben explained. "We're the only ones who actually saw him in action."

"A good newspaperman knows when to keep his mouth shut," I said, "but he's also a very curious creature. Let me come along."

Ben shrugged and Doc nodded. After a moment Father O'Brien nodded too.

I replaced my pad and pencil in the bag and got down from the railing.

I followed them across the church, out into a short hallway, and up to an open, sagging door. Doc flicked on a flashlight and played it upon a rickety flight of stairs leading down into darkness. Slowly then, he began to descend. Father O'Brien followed him. The stairs groaned and seemed to move. Ben and I waited till they had reached the bottom. Then Ben stuffed his bag of pungent groceries inside his jacket and withdrew a flashlight from his pocket. He turned it on and stepped down. I was right behind him.

I halted when we reached the foot of the stair. In the beams from their lights I beheld the two caskets set up on sawhorses, also the thing on the wall above the larger one.

"Father, what is that?" I pointed.

Someone obligingly played a beam of light upon it.

"It looks like a sprig of mistletoe tied to the figure of a little stone deer," he said.

"Probably has something to do with black magic," I offered.

He crossed himself, went over to it and removed it.

"Probably so," he said, crushing the mistletoe and throwing it across the room, shattering the figure on the floor and kicking the pieces away.

I smiled. I moved forward then.

"Let's get the things open and have a look," Doc said.

I lent them a hand.

When the caskets were open, I ignored the comments about paleness, reservation, and bloody mouths. Brodsky looked the same as he always did—dark hair, heavy dark eyebrows, sagging jowls, a bit of a paunch. The girl was lovely, though. Taller than I'd thought, however, with a very faint pulsation at the throat and an almost bluish cast to her skin.

Father O'Brien opened his Bible and began reading, holding the flashlight above it with a trembling hand. Doc placed his bag upon the floor and fumbled about inside it.

Ben turned away, tears in his eyes. I reached out then and broke his neck quietly while the others were occupied. I lowered him to the floor and stepped up beside Doc.

"What—?" he began, and that was his last word.

Father O'Brien stopped reading. He stared at me across his Bible.

"You work for *them?*" he said hoarsely, darting a glance at the caskets.

"Hardly," I said, "but I need them. They're my life's blood."

"I don't understand . . ."

"Everything is prey to something else, and we do what we must. That's ecology. Sorry, Father."

I used Ben's shovel to bury the three of them beneath an earthen section of the floor toward the rear—garlic, stakes, and all. Then I closed the caskets and carried them up the stairs.

I checked around as I hiked across a field and back up the road after the pickup truck. It was still relatively early, and there was no one about.

I loaded them both in back and covered them with a tarp. It was a thirty-mile drive to another ruined church I knew of.

Later, when I had installed them safely in their new quarters, I penned a note and placed it in Brodsky's hand:

Dear B,

Let this be a lesson to you. You are going to have to stop acting like Bela Lugosi. You lack his class. You are lucky to be waking up at all this night. In the future be more circumspect in your activities or I may retire you myself. After all, I'm not here to serve you.

Yours truly,

W

P.S. The mistletoe and the statue of Cernunnos don't work anymore. Why did you suddenly get superstitious?

I glanced at my watch as I left the place. It was eleven fifteen. I stopped at a 7–11 a little later and used their outside phone.

"Hi, Kiela," I said when I heard her voice. "It's me."

"Werdeth," she said. "It's been a while."

"I know. I've been busy."

"With what?"

"Do you know where the old Church of the Apostles out off Route 6 is?"

"Of course. It's on my backup list, too."

"Meet me there at twelve thirty and I'll tell you about it over lunch."

The Man Who Loved the Vampire Lady

by Brian Stableford

*A man who loves a vampire lady may not die young, but cannot
live forever.* (Walachian proverb)

It was the thirteenth of June in the Year of Our Lord 1623. Grand
Normandy was in the grip of an early spell of warm weather, and
the streets of London bathed in sunlight. There were crowds everywhere, and the port was busy with ships, three having docked that very
day. One of the ships, the *Freemartin*, was from the Moorish enclave and
had produce from the heart of Africa, including ivory and the skins of
exotic animals. There were rumors, too, of secret and more precious
goods: jewels and magical charms; but such rumors always attended the
docking of any vessel from remote parts of the world. Beggars and street
urchins had flocked to the dockland, responsive as ever to such whis-
perings, and were plaguing every sailor in the streets, as anxious for gossip as for copper coins. It seemed that the only faces not animated by
excitement were those worn by the severed heads that dressed the spikes
atop the Southwark Gate. The Tower of London, though, stood quite
aloof from the hubbub, its tall and forbidding turrets so remote from the
streets that they belonged to a different world.

Edmund Cordery, mechanician to the court of the Archduke Girard, tilted the small concave mirror on the brass device that rested on his workbench, catching the rays of the afternoon sun and deflecting the light through the system of lenses.

He turned away and directed his son, Noell, to take his place. "Tell me if all is well," he said tiredly. "I can hardly focus my eyes, let alone the instrument."

Noell closed his left eye and put his other to the microscope. He turned the wheel that adjusted the height of the stage. "It's perfect," he said. "What is it?"

"The wing of a moth." Edmund scanned the polished tabletop, checking that the other slides were in readiness for the demonstration. The prospect of Lady Carmilla's visit filled him with a complex anxiety that he resented in himself. Even in the old days, she had not come to his laboratory often. But to see her here—on his own territory, as it were—would be bound to awaken memories that were untouched by the glimpses that he caught of her in the public parts of the Tower and on ceremonial occasions.

"The water slide isn't ready," Noell pointed out.

Edmund shook his head. "I'll make a fresh one when the time comes," he said. "Living things are fragile, and the world that is in a water drop is all too easily destroyed."

He looked farther along the bench-top, and moved a crucible, placing it out of sight behind a row of jars. It was impossible—and unnecessary—to make the place tidy, but he felt it important to conserve some sense of order and control. To discourage himself from fidgeting, he went to the window and looked out at the sparkling Thames and the strange gray sheen on the slate roofs of the houses beyond. From this high vantage point, the people were tiny; he was higher even than the cross on the steeple of the church beside the Leathermarket. Edmund was not a devout man, but such was the agitation within him, yearning for expression in action, that the sight of the cross on the church made him cross himself, murmuring the ritual devotion. As soon as he had done it, he cursed himself for childishness.

I am forty-four years old, he thought, *and a mechanician. I am no longer the boy who was favored with the love of the lady, and there is no need for this stupid trepidation.*

He was being deliberately unfair to himself in this private scolding. It was not simply the fact that he had once been Carmilla's lover that made him anxious. There was the microscope, and the ship from the Moorish country. He hoped that he would be able to judge by the lady's reaction how much cause there really was for fear.

The door opened then, and the lady entered. She half turned to indicate by a flutter of her hand that her attendant need not come in with her, and he withdrew, closing the door behind him. She was alone, with no friend or favorite in tow. She came across the room carefully, lifting the hem of her skirt a little, though the floor was not dusty. Her gaze flicked from side to side, to take note of the shelves, the beakers, the furnace, and the numerous tools of the mechanician's craft. To a commoner, it would have seemed a threatening environment, redolent with unholiness, but her attitude was cool and controlled. She arrived to stand before the brass instrument that Edmund had recently completed, but did not look long at it before raising her eyes to look fully into Edmund's face.

"You look well, Master Cordery," she said calmly. "But you are pale. You should not shut yourself in your rooms now that summer is come to Normandy."

Edmund bowed slightly, but met her gaze. She had not changed in the slightest degree, of course, since the days when he had been intimate with her. She was six hundred years old—hardly younger than the archduke—and the years were impotent as far as her appearance was concerned. Her complexion was much darker than his, her eyes a deep liquid brown, and her hair jet black. He had not stood so close to her for several years, and he could not help the tide of memories rising in his mind. For her, it would be different: his hair was gray now, his skin creased; he must seem an altogether different person. As he met her gaze, though, it seemed to him that she, too, was remembering, and not without fondness.

"My lady," he said, his voice quite steady, "may I present my son and apprentice, Noell."

Noell bowed more deeply than his father, blushing with embarrassment.

The Lady Carmilla favored the youth with a smile. "He has the look of you, Master Cordery," she said—a casual compliment. She returned her attention then to the instrument.

"The designer was correct?" she asked.

"Yes, indeed," he replied. "The device is most ingenious. I would dearly like to meet the man who thought of it. A fine discovery—though it taxed the talents of my lens grinder severely. I think we might make a better one, with much care and skill; this is but a poor example, as one must expect from a first attempt."

The Lady Carmilla seated herself at the bench, and Edmund showed her how to apply her eye to the instrument, and how to adjust the focusing wheel and the mirror. She expressed surprise at the appearance of the magnified moth's wing, and Edmund took her through the series of prepared slides, which included other parts of insects' bodies, and sections through the stems and seeds of plants.

"I need a sharper knife and a steadier hand, my lady," he told her. "The device exposes the clumsiness of my cutting."

"Oh no, Master Cordery," she assure him politely. "These are quite pretty enough. But we were told that more interesting things might be seen. Living things too small for ordinary sight."

Edmund bowed in apology and explained about the preparation of water slides. He made a new one, using a pipette to take a drop from a jar full of dirty river water. Patiently, he helped the lady search the slide for the tiny creatures that human eyes were not equipped to perceive. He showed her one that flowed as if it were semiliquid itself, and tinier ones that moved by means of cilia. She was quite captivated, and watched for some time, moving the slide very gently with her painted fingernails.

Eventually she asked: "Have you looked at other fluids?"

"What kind of fluids?" he asked, though the question was quite clear to him and disturbed him.

She was not prepared to mince words with him. "Blood, Master Cordery," she said very softly. Her past acquaintance with him had taught her respect for his intelligence, and he half regretted it.

"Blood clots very quickly," he told her. "I could not produce a satisfactory slide. It would take unusual skill."

"I'm sure that it would," she replied.

"Noell has made drawings of many of the things we *have* looked at," said Edmund. "Would you like to see them?"

She accepted the change of subject, and indicated that she would. She moved to Noell's station and began sorting through the drawings, occasionally looking up at the boy to compliment him on his work. Edmund stood by, remembering how sensitive he once had been to her moods and desires, trying hard to work out now exactly what she was thinking. Something in one of her contemplative glances at Noell sent an icy pang of dread into Edmund's gut, and he found his more important fears momentarily displaced by what might have been anxiety for his son, or simply jealously. He cursed himself again for his weakness.

"May I take these to show the archduke?" asked the Lady Carmilla, addressing the question to Noell rather than to his father. The boy nodded, still too embarrassed to construct a proper reply. She took a selection of the drawings and rolled them into a scroll. She stood and faced Edmund again.

"We are most interested in this apparatus," she informed him. "We must consider carefully whether to provide you with new assistants, to encourage development of the appropriate skills. In the meantime, you may return to your ordinary work. I will send someone for the instrument, so that the archduke can inspect it at his leisure. Your son draws very well, and must be encouraged. You and he may visit me in my chambers on Monday next; we will dine at seven o'clock, and you may tell me about all your recent work."

Edmund bowed to signal his acquiescence—it was, of course, a command rather than an invitation. He moved before her to the door in order to hold it open for her. The two exchanged another brief glance as she went past him.

When she had gone, it was as though something taut unwound inside him, leaving him relaxed and emptied. He felt strangely cool and distant as he considered the possibility—stronger now—that his life was in peril.

When the twilight had faded, Edmund lit a single candle on the bench and sat staring into the flame while he drank dark wine from a flask. He did not look up when Noell came into the room, but when the boy brought another stool close to his and sat down upon it, he offered the flask. Noell took it, but sipped rather gingerly.

"I'm old enough to drink now?" he commented dryly.

"You're old enough," Edmund assured him. "But beware of excess, and never drink alone. Conventional fatherly advice, I believe."

Noell reached across the bench so that he could stroke the barrel of the microscope with slender fingers.

"What are you afraid of?" he asked.

Edmund sighed. "You're old enough for that, too, I suppose?"

"I think you ought to tell me."

Edmund looked at the brass instrument and said: "It were better to keep things like this dark secret. Some human mechanician, I daresay, eager to please the vampire lords and ladies, showed off his cleverness as proud as a peacock. Thoughtless. Inevitable, though, now that all this play with lenses has become fashionable."

"You'll be glad of eyeglasses when your sight begins to fail," Noell told him. "In any case, I can't see the danger in this new toy."

Edmund smiled. "New toys," he mused. "Clocks to tell the time, mills to grind the corn, lenses to aid human sight. Produced by human craftsmen for the delight of their masters. I think we've finally succeeded in proving to the vampires just how very clever we are—and how much more there is to know than we know already."

"You think the vampires are beginning to fear us?"

Edmund gulped wine from the flask and passed it again to his son. "Their rule is founded in fear and superstition," he said quietly. "They're long-lived, suffer only mild attacks of diseases that are fatal to us, and have marvelous powers of regeneration. But they're not immortal, and they're vastly outnumbered by humans. Terror keeps them safe, but terror is based in ignorance, and behind their haughtiness and arrogance, there's a gnawing fear of what might happen if humans ever lost their supernatural reverence for vampirekind. It's very difficult for them to die, but they don't fear death any the less for that."

"There've been rebellions against vampire rule. They've always failed."

Edmund nodded to concede the point. "There are three million people in Grand Normandy," he said, "and less than five thousand vampires. There are only forty thousand vampires in the entire imperium of Gaul, and about the same number in the imperium of Byzantium—no telling how many there may be in the khanate of Walachia and Cathay, but not so very many more. In Africa the vampires must be outnumbered three or four thousand to one. If people no longer saw them as demons and demi-gods, as unconquerable forces of evil, their empire would be fragile. The centuries through which they live give them wisdom, but longevity seems to be inimical to creative thought—they learn, but they don't *invent*. Humans remain the true masters of art and science, which are forces of change. They've tried to control that—to turn it to their advantage—but it remains a thorn in their side."

"But they do have power," insisted Noell. "They *are* vampires."

Edmund shrugged. "Their longevity is real—their powers of regeneration, too. But is it really their magic that makes them so? I don't know for sure what merit there is in their incantations and rituals, and I don't think even *they* know—they cling to their rites because they dare not abandon them, but where the power that makes humans into vampires really comes from, no one knows. From the devil? I think not. I don't believe in the devil—I think it's something in the blood. I think vampirism may be a kind of disease—but a disease that makes men stronger instead of weaker, insulates them against death instead of killing them. If that *is* the case—do you see now why the Lady Carmilla asked whether I had looked at blood beneath the microscope?"

Noell stared at the instrument for twenty seconds or so, mulling over the idea. Then he laughed.

"If we could *all* become vampires," he said lightly, "we'd have to suck one another's blood."

Edmund couldn't bring himself to look for such ironies. For him, the possibilities inherent in discovering the secrets of vampire nature were much more immediate, and utterly bleak.

"It's not true that they *need* to suck the blood of humans," he told the boy. "It's not nourishment. It gives them . . . a kind of pleasure that we can't understand. And it's part of the mystique that makes them so terrible . . . and hence so powerful." He stopped, feeling embarrassed. He did not know how much Noell knew about his sources of information. He and his wife never talked about the days of his affair with the Lady Carmilla, but there was no way to keep gossip and rumor from reaching the boy's ears.

Noell took the flask again, and this time took a deeper draft from it. "I've heard," he said distantly, "that humans find pleasure, too . . . in their blood being drunk."

"No," replied Edmund calmly. "That's untrue. Unless one counts the small pleasure of sacrifice. The pleasure that a human man takes from a vampire lady is the same pleasure that he takes from a human lover. It might be different for the girls who entertain vampire men, but I suspect it's just the excitement of hoping that they may become vampires themselves."

Noell hesitated, and would probably have dropped the subject, but Edmund realized suddenly that he did not want the subject dropped. The boy had a right to know, and perhaps might one day *need* to know.

"That's not entirely true," Edmund corrected himself. "When the Lady Carmilla used to taste my blood, it did give me pleasure, in a way. It pleased me because it pleased *her*. There *is* an excitement in loving a vampire woman . . . even though the chance that a vampire lady's lover may himself become a vampire is so remote as to be inconsiderable."

Noell blushed, not knowing how to react to this acceptance into his father's confidence. Finally he decided that it was best to pretend a purely academic interest.

"Why are there so many more vampire women than men?" he asked.

"No one knows for sure," Edmund said. "No humans, at any rate. I can tell you what I believe, from hearsay and from reasoning, but you must understand that it is a dangerous thing to think about, let alone to speak about."

Noell nodded.

"The vampires keep their history secret," said Edmund, "and they try to control the writing of human history, but the following facts are probably true. Vampirism came to western Europe in the fifth century, with the vampire-led horse of Attila. Attila must have known well enough how to make more vampires—he converted both Aëtius, who became ruler of the imperium of Gaud, and Theodosius II, the emperor of the east who was later murdered. Of all the vampires that now exist, the vast majority must be converts. I have heard reports of vampire children born to vampire ladies, but it must be an extremely rare occurrence. Vampire men seem to be much less virile than human men—it is said that they couple very rarely. Nevertheless, they frequently take human consorts, and these consorts often become vampires. Vampires usually claim that this is a gift, bestowed deliberately by magic, but I am not so sure they can control the process. I think the semen of vampire men carries some kind of seed that communicates vampirism much as the semen of humans makes women pregnant—and just as haphazardly. That's why the male lovers of vampire ladies don't become vampires."

Noell considered this, and then asked: "Then where do vampire lords come from?"

"They're converted by other male vampires," Edmund said. "Just at

Attila converted Aëtius and Theodosius." He did not elaborate, but waited to see whether Noell understood the implication. An expression of disgust crossed the boy's face and Edmund did not know whether to be glad or sorry that his son could follow the argument through.

"Because it doesn't always happen," Edmund went on, "it's easy for the vampires to pretend that they have some special magic. But some women never become pregnant, though they lie with their husbands for years. It is said, though, that a human may also become a vampire by drinking vampire's blood—if he knows the appropriate magic spell. That's a rumor the vampires don't like, and they exact terrible penalties if anyone is caught trying the experiment. The ladies of our own court, of course, are for the most part onetime lovers of the archduke or his cousins. It would be indelicate to speculate about the conversion of the archduke, though he is certainly acquainted with Aëtius."

Noell reached out a hand, palm downward, and made a few passes above the candle flame, making it flicker from side to side. He stared at the microscope.

"*Have* you looked at blood?" he asked.

"I have," replied Edmund. "And semen. Human blood, of course—and human semen."

"And?"

Edmund shook his head. "They're certainly not homogenous fluids," he said, "but the instrument isn't good enough for really detailed inspection. There are small corpuscles—the ones in semen have long, writhing tails—but there's more . . . much more . . . to be seen, if I had the chance. By tomorrow this instrument will be gone—I don't think I'll be given the chance to build another."

"You're surely not in danger! You're an important man—and your loyalty has never been in question. People think of you as being almost a vampire yourself. A black magician. The kitchen girls are afraid of me because I'm your son—they cross themselves when they see me."

Edmund laughed, a little bitterly. "I've no doubt they suspect me of intercourse with demons, and avoid my gaze for fear of the spell of the evil eye. But none of that matters to the vampires. To them, I'm only a human, and for all that they value my skills, they'd kill me without a thought if they suspected that I might have dangerous knowledge."

Noell was clearly alarmed by this. "Wouldn't. . . ." He stopped, but saw Edmund waiting for him to ask, and carried on after only a brief pause. "The Lady Carmilla . . . wouldn't she . . . ?"

"Protect me?" Edmund shook his head. "Not even if I were her favorite still. Vampire loyalty is to vampires."

"She was human once."

"It counts for nothing. She's been a vampire for nearly six hundred years, but it wouldn't be any different if she were no older than I."

"But . . . she did love you?"

"In her way," said Edmund sadly. "In her way." He stood up then, no longer feeling the urgent desire to help his son to understand. There were things the boy could find out only for himself and might never have to. He took up the candle tray and shielded the flame with his hand as he walked to the door. Noell followed him, leaving the empty flask behind.

Edmund left the citadel by the so-called Traitor's Gate, and crossed the Thames by the Tower Bridge. The houses on the bridge were in darkness now, but there was still a trickle of traffic, even at two in the morning, the business of the great city did not come to a standstill. The night had clouded over, and a light drizzle had begun to fall. Some of the oil lamps that were supposed to keep the thoroughfare lit at all times had gone out, and there was not a lamplighter in sight. Edmund did not mind the shadows, though.

He was aware before he reached the south bank that two men were dogging his footsteps, and he dawdled in order to give them the impression that he would be easy to track. Once he entered the network of streets surrounding the Leathermarket, though, he gave them the slip. He knew the maze of filthy streets well enough—he had lived here as a child. It was while he was apprenticed to a local clockmaker that he had learned the cleverness with tools that had eventually brought him to the notice of his predecessor, and had sent him on the road to fortune and celebrity. He had a brother and a sister still living and working in the district, though he saw them very rarely. Neither one of them was proud to have a reputed magician for a brother, and they had not forgiven him his association with the Lady Carmilla.

He picked his way carefully through the garbage in the dark alleys, unperturbed by the sound of scavenging rats. He kept his hands on the pommel of the dagger that was clasped to his belt, but he had no need to draw it. Because the stars were hidden, the night was pitch-dark, and few of the windows were lit from within by candlelight, but he was able to keep track of his progress by reaching out to touch familiar walls every now and again.

He came eventually to a tiny door set three steps down from a side street, and rapped upon it quickly, three times and then twice. There was a long pause before he felt the door yield beneath his fingers, and he stepped inside hurriedly. Until he relaxed when the door clicked shut again, he did not realize how tense he had been.

He waited for a candle to be lit.

The light, when it came, illuminated a thin face, crabbed and wrinkled, the eyes very pale and the wispy white hair gathered imperfectly behind a linen bonnet.

"The lord be with you," he whispered.

"And with you, Edmund Cordery," she croaked.

He frowned at the use of his name—it was a deliberate breach of etiquette, a feeble and meaningless gesture of independence. She did not like him, though he had never been less than kind to her. She did not fear him as so many others did, but she considered him tainted. They had been bound together in the business of the Fraternity for nearly twenty years, but she would never completely trust him.

She led him into an inner room, and left him there to take care of his business.

A stranger stepped from the shadows. He was short, stout, and bald, perhaps sixty years old. He made the special sign of the cross, and Edmund responded.

"I'm Cordery," he said.

"Were you followed?" The older man's tone was deferential and fearful.

"Not here. They followed me from the Tower, but it was easy to shake them loose."

"That's bad."

"Perhaps—but it has to do with another matter, not with our business. There's no danger to you. Do you have what I asked for?"

The stout man nodded uncertainly. "My masters are unhappy," he said. "I have been asked to tell you that they do not want you to take risks. You are too valuable to place yourself in peril."

"I am in peril already. Events are overtaking us. In any case, it is neither your concern nor that of your . . . masters. It is for me to decide."

The stout man shook his head, but it was a gesture of resignation rather than a denial. He pulled something from beneath the chair where he had waited in the shadows. It was a large box, clad in leather. A row of small holes was set in the longer side, and there was a sound of scratching from within that testified to the presence of living creatures.

"You did exactly as I instructed?" asked Edmund.

The small man nodded, then put his hand on the mechanician's arm, fearfully. "Don't open it, sir, I beg you. Not here."

"There's nothing to fear," Edmund assured him.

"You haven't been in Africa, sir, as I have. Believe me, *everyone* is afraid—and not merely humans. They say that vampires are dying, too."

"Yes, I know," said Edmund distractedly. He shook off the older man's restraining hand and undid the straps that sealed the box. He lifted the lid, but not far—just enough to let the light in, and to let him see what was inside.

The box contained two big gray rats. They cowered from the light.

Edmund shut the lid again and fastened the straps.

"It's not my place, sir," said the little man hesitantly, "but I'm not sure that you really understand what you have there. I've seen the cities of West Africa—I've been in Corunna, too, and Marseilles. They remember other plagues in those cities, and all the horror stories are emerging again to haunt them. Sir, if any such thing ever came to London. . . ."

Edmund tested the weight of the box to see whether he could carry it comfortably. "It's not your concern," he said. "Forget everything that has happened. I will communicate with your masters. It is in my hands now."

"Forgive me," said the other, "but I must say this: there is naught to be gained from destroying vampires, if we destroy ourselves, too. It would be a pity to wipe out half of Europe in the cause of attacking our oppressors."

Edmund stared at the stout man coldly. "You talk too much," he said. "Indeed, you talk a *deal* too much."

"I beg your pardon, sire."

Edmund hesitated for a moment, wondering whether to reassure the messenger that his anxiety was understandable, but he had learned long ago that where the business of the Fraternity was concerned, it was best to say as little as possible. There was no way of knowing when this man would speak again of this affair, or to whom, or with what consequence.

The mechanician took up the box, making sure that he could carry it comfortably. The rats stirred inside, scrabbling with their small clawed feet. With his free hand, Edmund made the sign of the cross again.

"God go with you," said the messenger, with urgent sincerity.

"And with thy spirit," replied Edmund colorlessly.

Then he left, without pausing to exchange a ritual farewell with the crone. He had no difficulty in smuggling his burden back into the Tower, by means of a gate where the guard was long practiced in the art of turning a blind eye.

When Monday came, Edmund and Noell made their way to the Lady Carmilla's chambers. Noell had never been in such an apartment before, and it was a source of wonder to him. Edmund watched the boy's reactions to the carpets, the wall hangings, the mirrors and ornaments, and could not help but recall the first time *he* had entered these chambers. Nothing had changed here, and the rooms were full of provocations to stir and sharpen his faded memories.

Younger vampires tended to change their surroundings often, addicted to novelty, as if they feared the prospect of being changeless themselves. The Lady Carmilla had long since passed beyond this phase of her career. She had grown used to changelessness, had transcended the kind of attitude to the world that permitted boredom and ennui. She had adapted herself to a new aesthetic of existence, whereby her personal space became an extension of her own eternal sameness, and innovation was confined to tightly controlled areas of her life—including the irregular shifting of her erotic affections from one lover to another.

The sumptuousness of the lady's table was a further source of astonishment to Noell. Silver plates and forks he had imagined, and crystal goblets, and carved decanters of wine. But the lavishness of provision for just three diners—the casual waste—was something that obviously set him aback. He had always known that he was himself a member of a privileged elite, and that by the standards of the greater world, Master Cordery and his family ate well; the revelation that there was a further order of magnitude to distinguish the private world of the real aristocracy clearly made its impact upon him.

Edmund had been very careful in preparing his dress, fetching from his closet finery that he had not put on for many years. On official occasions he was always concerned to play the part of mechanician, and dressed in order to sustain that appearance. He never appeared as a courtier, always as a functionary. Now, though, he was reverting to a kind of performance that Noell had never seen him play, and though the boy had no idea of the subtleties of his father's performance, he clearly understood something of what was going on; he had complained acidly about the dull and plain way in which his father had made *him* dress.

Edmund ate and drank sparingly, and was pleased to note that Noell did likewise, obeying his father's instructions despite the obvious temptations of the lavish provision. For a while the lady was content to exchange routine courtesies, but she came quickly enough—by her standards—to the real business of the evening.

"My cousin Girard," she told Edmund, "is quite enraptured by your clever device. He finds it most interesting."

"Then I am pleased to make him a gift of it," Edmund replied. "And I would be pleased to make another, as a gift of Your Ladyship."

"That is not our desire," she said coolly. "In fact, we have other matters in mind. The archduke and his seneschal have discussed certain tasks that you might profitably carry out. Instructions will be communicated to you in due time, I have no doubt."

"Thank you, my lady," said Edmund.

"The ladies of the court were pleased with the drawings that I showed to them," said the Lady Carmilla, turning to look at Noell. "They marveled at the thought that a cupful of Thames water might contain thousands of tiny living creatures. Do you think that our bodies, too, might be the habitation of countless invisible insects?"

Noell opened his mouth to reply, because the question was addressed to him, but Edmund interrupted smoothly.

"There are creatures that may live upon our bodies," he said, "and worms that may live within. We are told that the macrocosm reproduces in essence the microcosm of human beings; perhaps there is a small microcosm within us, where our natures are reproduced again, incalculably small. I have read . . ."

"I have read, Master Cordery," she cut in, "that the illnesses that afflict humankind might be carried from person to person by means of these tiny creatures."

"The idea that diseases were communicated from one person to another by tiny seeds was produced in antiquity," Edmund replied, "but I do not know how such seeds might be recognized, and I think it very unlikely that the creatures we have seen in river water could possibly be of that character."

"It is a disquieting thought," she insisted, "that our bodies might be inhabited by creatures of which we can know nothing, and that every breath we take might be carrying into us seeds of all kinds of change, too small to be seen or tasted. It makes me feel uneasy."

"But there is no need," Edmund protested. "Seeds of corruptibility take root in human flesh, but yours is inviolate."

"You know that is not so, Master Cordery," she said levelly. "You have seen me ill yourself."

"That was a pox that killed many humans, my lady—yet it gave to you no more than a mild fever."

"We have reports from the imperium of Byzantium, and from the Moorish enclave, too, that there is a plague in Africa, and that it has now reached the southern regions of the imperium of Gaul. It is said that this plague makes little distinction between human and vampire."

"Rumors, my lady," said Edmund soothingly. "You know how news becomes blacker as it travels."

The Lady Carmilla turned again to Noell, and this time addressed him by name so that there could be no opportunity for Edmund to usurp the privilege of answering her. "Are you afraid of me, Noell?" she asked.

The boy was startled, and stumbled slightly over his reply, which was in the negative.

"You must not lie to me," she told him. "You *are* afraid of me, because I am a vampire. Master Cordery is a skeptic, and must have told you that vampires have less magic than is commonly credited to us, but he must also have told you that I can do you harm if I will. Would you like to be a vampire yourself, Noell?"

Noell was still confused by the correction, and hesitated over his reply, but he eventually said: "Yes, I would."

"Of course you would," she purred. "All humans would be vampires if they could, no matter how they might pretend when they bend the knee in church. And men *can* become vampires; immortality is within our gift. Because of this, we have always enjoyed the loyalty and devotion of the greater number of our human subjects. We have always rewarded that devotion in some measure. Few have joined our ranks, but the many have enjoyed centuries of order and stability. The vampires rescued Europe from a Dark Age, and as long as vampires rule, barbarism will always be held in check. Our rule has not always been kind, because we cannot tolerate defiance, but the alternative would have been far worse. Even so, there are men who would destroy us—did you know that?"

Noell did not know how to reply to this, so he simply stared, waiting for her to continue. She seemed a little impatient with his gracelessness, and Edmund deliberately let the awkward pause go on. He saw a certain advantage in allowing Noell to make a poor impression.

"There is an organization of rebels," the Lady Carmilla went on. "A secret society, ambitious to discover the secret way to which vampires are made. They put about the idea that they would make all men immortal, but this is a lie, and foolish. The members of this brotherhood seek power for themselves."

The vampire lady paused to direct the clearing of one set of dishes and the bringing of another. She asked for a new wine, too. Her gaze wandered back and forth between the gauche youth and his self-assured father.

"The loyalty of your family is, of course, beyond question," she eventually continued. "No one understands the workings of society like a mechanician, who knows well enough how forces must be balanced and how the different parts of a machine must interlock and support one another. Master Cordery knows well how the cleverness of rulers resembles the cleverness of clockmasters, do you not?"

"Indeed, I do, my lady," replied Edmund.

"There might be a way," she said, in a strangely distant tone, "that a good mechanician might earn a conversion to vampirism."

Edmund was wise enough not to interpret this as an offer or a promise. He accepted a measure of the new wine and said: "My lady, there are matters that it would be as well for us to discuss in private. May I send my son to his room?"

The Lady Carmilla's eyes narrowed just a little, but there was hardly any expression in her finely etched features. Edmund held his breath, knowing that he had forced a decision upon her that she had not intended to make so soon.

"The poor boy has not quite finished his meal," she said.

"I think he has had enough, my lady," Edmund countered. Noell did not disagree, and, after a brief hesitation, the lady bowed to signal her permission. Edmund asked Noell to leave, and, when he was gone, the Lady Carmilla rose from her seat and went from the dining room into an inner chamber. Edmund followed her.

"You were presumptuous, Master Cordery," she told him.

"I was carried away, my lady. There are too many memories here."

"The boy is mine," she said, "if I so choose. You do know that, do you not?"

Edmund bowed.

"I did not ask you here tonight to make you witness the seduction of your son. Nor do you think that I did. This matter that you would discuss with me—does it concern science or treason?"

"Science, my lady. As you have said yourself, my loyalty is not in question."

Carmilla laid herself upon a sofa and indicated that Edmund should take a chair nearby. This was the antechamber to her bedroom, and the air was sweet with the odor of cosmetics.

"Speak," she bade him.

"I believe that the archduke is afraid of what my little device might reveal," he said. "He fears that it will expose to the eye such seeds as carry vampirism from one person to another, just as it might expose the seeds that carry disease. I think that the man who devised the instrument may have been put to death already, but I think you know well enough that a discovery once made is likely to be made again and again. You are uncertain as to what course of action would best serve your ends, because you cannot tell whence the greater threat to your rule might come. There is the Fraternity, which is dedicated to your destruction; there is plague in Africa, from which even vampires may die; and there is the new sight, which renders visible what previously lurked unseen. Do you want my advice, Lady Carmilla?"

"Do you *have* any advice, Edmund?"

"Yes. Do not try to control by terror or persecution the things that are happening. Let your rule be unkind *now*, as it has been before, and it will open the way to destruction. Should you concede power gently, you might live for centuries yet, but if you strike out . . . your enemies will strike back."

The vampire lady leaned back her head, looking at the ceiling. She contrived a small laugh.

"I cannot take advice such as that to the archduke," she told him flatly.

"I thought not, my lady," Edmund replied very calmly.

"You humans have your own immortality," she complained. "Your faith promises it, and you all affirm it. Your faith tells you that you must not covet the immortality that is ours, and we do no more than agree with you when we guard it so jealously. You should look to your Christ for fortune, not to us. I think you know well enough that we could not convert the world if we wanted to. Our magic is such that it can be used only sparingly. Are you distressed because it has never been offered to you? Are you bitter? Are you becoming our enemy because you cannot become our kin?"

"You have nothing to fear from me, my lady," he lied. Then he added, not quite sure whether it was a lie or not: "I loved you faithfully. I still do."

She sat up straight then, and reached out a hand as though to stroke his cheek, though he was too far away for her to reach.

"That is what I told the archduke," she said, "when he suggested to me that you might be a traitor. I promised him that I could test your loyalty more keenly in my chambers than his officers in theirs. I do not think you could delude me, Edmund. Do you?"

"No, my lady," he replied.

"By morning," she told him gently, "I will know whether or not you are a traitor."

"That you will," he assured her. "That you will, my lady."

He woke before her, his mouth dry and his forehead burning. He was not sweating—indeed, he was possessed by a feeling of desiccation, as though the moisture were being squeezed out of his organs. His head was aching, and the light of the morning sun that streamed through the unshuttered window hurt his eyes.

He pulled himself up to a half-sitting position, pushing the coverlet back from his bare chest.

So soon! he thought. He had not expected to be consumed so quickly, but he was surprised to find that his reaction was one of relief rather than fear or regret. He had difficulty collecting his thoughts, and was perversely glad to accept that he did not need to.

He looked down at the cuts that she had made on his breast with her little silver knife; they were raw and red, and made a strange contrast with the faded scars whose crisscross pattern still engraved the story of unforgotten passions. He touched the new wounds gently with his fingers, and winced at the fiery pain.

She woke up then, and saw him inspecting the marks.

"Have you missed the knife?" she asked sleepily. "Were you hungry for its touch?"

There was no need to lie now, and there was a delicious sense of freedom in that knowledge. There was a joy in being able to face her, at last, quite naked in his thoughts as well as his flesh.

"Yes, my lady," he said with a slight croak in his voice. "I had missed the knife. Its touch . . . rekindled flames in my soul."

She had closed her eyes again, to allow herself to wake slowly. She laughed. "It is pleasant, sometimes, to return to forsaken pastures. You can have no notion how a particular *taste* may stir memories. I am glad to have seen you again, in this way. I had grown quite used to you as the gray mechanician. But now . . ."

He laughed, as lightly as she, but the laugh turned to a cough, and something in the sound alerted her to the fact that all was not as it should be. She opened her eyes and raised his head, turning toward him.

"Why, Edmund," she said, "you're as pale as death!"

She reached out to touch his cheek, and snatched her hand away again as she found it unexpectedly hot and dry. A blush of confusion spread across her own features. He took her hand and held it, looking steadily into her eyes.

"Edmund," she said softly. "What have you done?"

"I can't be sure," he said, "and I will not live to find out, but I have tried to kill you, my lady."

He was pleased by the way her mouth gaped in astonishment. He watched disbelief and anxiety mingle in her expression, as though fighting for control. She did not call out for help.

"This is nonsense," she whispered.

"Perhaps," he admitted. "Perhaps it was also nonsense that we talked last evening. Nonsense about treason. Why did you ask me to make the microscope, my lady, when you knew that making me a party to such a secret was as good as signing my death warrant?"

"Oh Edmund," she said with a sigh. "You could not think that it was my own idea? I tried to protect you, Edmund, from Girard's fear and suspicions. It was because I was your protector that I was made to bear the message. What have you done, Edmund?"

He began to reply, but the words turned into a fit of coughing.

She sat upright, wrenching her hand away from his enfeebled grip, and looked down at him as he sank back upon the pillow.

"For the love of God!" she exclaimed, as fearfully as any true believer. "It is the plague—the plague out of Africa!"

He tried to confirm her suspicion, but could do so only with a nod of his head as he fought for breath.

"But they held the *Freemartin* by the Essex coast for a full fortnight's quarantine," she protested. "There was no trace of plague aboard."

"The disease kills men," said Edmund in a shallow whisper. "But animals can carry it, in their blood, without dying."

"You cannot know this!"

Edmund managed a small laugh. "My lady," he said, "I am a member of that Fraternity that interests itself in everything that might kill a vampire. The information came to me in good time for me to arrange delivery of the rats—though when I asked for them, I had not in mind the means of using them that I eventually employed. More recent events. . . ." Again he was forced to stop, unable to draw sufficient breath even to sustain the thin whisper.

The Lady Carmilla put her hand to her throat, swallowing as if she expected to feel evidence already of her infection.

"You would destroy me, Edmund?" she asked, as though she genuinely found it difficult to believe.

"I would destroy you all," he told her. "I would bring disaster, turn the world upside down, to end your rule. . . . We cannot allow you to stamp out learning itself to preserve your empire forever. Order must be fought with chaos, and chaos is come, my lady."

When she tried to rise from the bed, he reached out to restrain her, and though there was no power left in him, she allowed herself to be checked. The coverlet fell away from her, to expose her breasts as she sat upright.

"The boy will die for this, Master Cordery," she said. "His mother, too."

"They're gone," he told her. "Noell went from your table to the custody of the society that I serve. By now they're beyond your reach. The archduke will never catch them."

She stared at him, and now he could see the beginnings of hate and fear in her stare.

"You came here last night to bring me poisoned blood," she said. "In the hope that this new disease might kill even me, you condemned yourself to death. What did you do, Edmund?"

He reached out again to touch her arm, and was pleased to see her flinch and draw away: that he had become dreadful.

"Only vampires live forever," he told her hoarsely. "But anyone may drink blood, if they have the stomach for it. I took full measure from my two sick rats . . . and I pray to God that the seed of this fever is raging in my blood . . . and in my semen, too. You, too, have received full measure, my lady . . . and you are in God's hands now like any common mortal. I cannot know for sure whether you will catch the plague, or whether it will kill you, but I—an unbeliever—am not ashamed to pray. Perhaps you could pray, too, my lady, so that we may know how the Lord favors one unbeliever over another."

She looked down at him, her face gradually losing the expressions that had tugged at her features, becoming masklike in its steadiness.

"You could have taken our side, Edmund. I trusted you, and I could have made the archduke trust you, too. You could have become a vampire. We could have shared the centuries, you and I."

This was dissimulation, and they both knew it. He had been her lover, and had ceased to be, and had grown older for so many years that now she remembered him as much in his son as in himself. The promises were all too obviously hollow now, and she realized that she could not even taut him with them.

From beside the bed she took up the small silver knife that she had used to let his blood. She held it now as if it were a dagger, not a delicate instrument to be used with care and love.

"I thought you still loved me," she told him. "I really did."

That, at least, he thought, might be true.

He actually put his head farther back, to expose his throat to the expected thrust. He wanted her to strike him—angrily, brutally, passionately. He had nothing more to say, and would not confirm or deny that he did still love her.

He admitted to himself now that his motives had been mixed, and that he really did not know whether it was loyalty to the Fraternity that had made him submit to this extraordinary experiment. It did not matter.

She cut his throat, and he watched her for a few long seconds while she stared at the blood gouting from the wound. When he saw her put stained fingers to her lips, knowing what she knew, he realized that after her own fashion, she still loved him.

The Cookie Lady

by Philip K. Dick

W here you going, Bubber?" Ernie Mill shouted from across the street, fixing papers for his route.

"No place," Bubber Surle said.

"You going to see your lady friend?" Ernie laughed and laughed. "What do you go visit that old lady for? Let us in on it!"

Bubber went on. He turned the corner and went down Elm Street. Already, he could see the house, at the end of the street, set back a little on the lot. The front of the house was overgrown with weeds, old dry weeds that rustled and chattered in the wind. The house itself was a little gray box, shabby and unpainted, the porch steps sagging. There was an old weather-beaten rocking chair on the porch with a torn piece of cloth hanging over it.

Bubber went up the walk. As he started up the rickety steps he took a deep breath. He could smell it, the wonderful warm smell, and his mouth began to water. His heart thudding with anticipation, Bubber turned the handle of the bell. The bell grated rustily on the other side of the door. There was silence for a time, then the sounds of someone stirring.

Mrs. Drew opened the door. She was old, very old, a little dried-up old lady, like the weeds that grew along the front of the house. She smiled down at Bubber, holding the door wide for him to come in.

"You're just in time," she said. "Come on inside, Bernard. You're just in time—they're just now ready."

Bubber went to the kitchen door and looked in. He could see them, resting on a big blue plate on top of the stove. Cookies, a plate of warm, fresh cookies right out of the oven. Cookies with nuts and raisins in them.

"How do they look?" Mrs. Drew said. She rustled past him, into the kitchen. "And maybe some cold milk, too. You like cold milk with them." She got the milk pitcher from the window box on the back porch. Then she poured a glass of milk for him and set some of the cookies on a small plate. "Let's go into the living room," she said.

Bubber nodded. Mrs. Drew carried the milk and the cookies in and set them on the arm of the couch. Then she sat down in her own chair, watching Bubber plop himself down by the plate and begin to help himself.

Bubber ate greedily, as usual, intent on the cookies, silent except for chewing sounds. Mrs. Drew waited patiently, until the boy had finished, and his already ample sides bulged that much more. When Bubber was done with the plate he glanced toward the kitchen again, at the rest of the cookies on the stove.

"Wouldn't you like to wait until later for the rest?" Mrs. Drew said.

"All right," Bubber agreed.

"How were they?"

"Fine."

"That's good." She leaned back in her chair. "Well, what did you do in school today? How did it go?"

"All right."

The little old lady watched the boy look restlessly around the room. "Bernard," she said presently, "won't you stay and talk to me for awhile?" He had some books on his lap, some school books. "Why don't you read to me from your books? You know, I don't see too well any more and it's a comfort to me to be read to."

"Can I have the rest of the cookies after?"

"Of course."

Bubber moved over toward her, to the end of the couch. He opened his books, World Geography, Principles of Arithmetic, Hoyte's Speller. "Which do you want?"

She hesitated. "The geography?"

Bubber opened the big blue book at random. PERU. "Peru is bounded on the north by Eucador and Colombia, on the south by Chile, and on the east by Brazil and Bolivia. Peru is divided into three main sections. These are, first—"

The little old lady watched him read, his fat cheeks wobbling as he read, holding his finger next to the line. She was silent, watching him, studying the boy intently as he read, drinking in each frown of concentration, every motion of his arms and hands. She relaxed, letting herself sink back in her chair. He was very close to her, only a little way off. There was only the table and lamp between them. How nice it was to have him come; he had been coming for over a month, now, ever since the day she had been sitting on her porch and seen him go by and thought to call to him, pointing to the cookies by her rocker.

Why had she done it? She did not know. She had been alone so long that she found herself saying strange things and doing strange things. She saw so few people, only when she went down to the store, or the mailman came with her pension check. Or the garbage men.

The boy's voice droned on. She was comfortable, peaceful and relaxed. The little old lady closed her eyes and folded her hands in her lap. And as she sat, dozing and listening, something began to happen. The little old lady was beginning to change, her gray wrinkles and lines dimming away. As she sat in the chair she was growing younger, the thin fragile body filling out with youth again. The gray hair thickened and darkened, color coming to the wispy strands. Her arms filled, too, the mottled flesh turning a rich hue as it had been once, many years before.

Mrs. Drew breathed deeply, not opening her eyes. She could feel *something* happening; but she did not know just what. *Something* was going on; she could feel it, and it was good. But what it was she did not exactly know. It had happened before, almost every time the boy came and sat by her. Especially of late, sine she had moved her chair nearer to the couch. She took a deep breath. How good it felt, the warm fullness, a breath of warmth inside her cold body for the first time in years!

In her chair the little old lady had become a dark-haired matron of perhaps thirty, a woman with full cheeks and plump arms and legs. Her lips were red again, her neck even a little too fleshy, as it had been once in the long forgotten past.

Suddenly the reading stopped. Bubber put down his book and stood up. "I have to go," he said. "Can I take the rest of the cookies with me?"

She blinked, rousing herself. The boy was in the kitchen, filling his pockets with cookies. She nodded, dazed, still under the spell. The boy took the last cookies. He went across the living room to the door. Mrs. Drew stood up. All at once the warmth left her. She looked down at her hands. Wrinkled, thin.

"Oh!" she murmured. Tears blurred her eyes. It was gone, gone again as soon as he moved away. She tottered to the mirror above the mantel and looked at herself. Old faded eyes stared back, eyes deep-set in a withered face. Gone, all gone, as soon as the boy had left her side.

"I'll see you later," Bubber said.

"Please," she whispered. "Please come back again. Will you come back?"

"Sure," Bubber said listlessly. He pushed the door open. "Good-bye." He went down the steps. In a moment she heard his shoes against the sidewalk. He was gone.

"Bubber, you come in here!" May Surle stood angrily on the porch. "You get in here and sit down at the table."

"All right." Bubber came slowly up on the porch, pushing inside the house.

"What's the matter with you?" She caught his arm. "Where have you been? Are you sick?"

"I'm tired." Bubber rubbed his forehead.

His father came through the living room with the newspapers, in his undershirt. "What's the matter?" he said.

"Look at him," May Surle said. "All worn out. What you been doing, Bubber?"

"He's been visiting that old lady," Ralf Surle said. "Can't you tell? He's always washed out after he's been visiting her. What do you go there for, Bub? What goes on?"

"She gives him cookies," May said. "You know how he is about things to eat. He'd do anything for a plate of cookies."

"Bub," his father said, "listen to me. I don't wan you hanging around that crazy old lady any more. Do you hear me? I don't care how many cookies she gives you. You come home too tired! No more of that. You hear me?"

Bubber looked down at the floor, leaning against the door. His heart beat heavily, labored. "I told her I'd come back," he muttered.

"You can go once more," May said, going into the dining room, "but only once more. Tell her you won't be able to come back again, though. You make sure you tell her nice. Now go upstairs and get washed up."

"After dinner better have him lie down," Ralf said, looking up the stairs, watching Bubber climb slowly, his hand on the banister. He shook his head. "I don't like it," he murmured. "I don't want him going there any more. There's something strange about that old lady."

"Well, it'll be the last time," May said.

Wednesday was warm and sunny. Bubber strode along, his hands in his pockets. He stopped in front of McVane's drug store for a minute, looking speculatively at the comic books. At the soda fountain a woman was drinking a big chocolate soda. The sight of it made Bubber's mouth water. That settled it. He turned and continued on his way, even increasing his pace a little.

A few minutes later he came up on the gray sagging porch and rang the bell. Below him the weeds blew and rustled with the wind. It was almost four o'clock; he could not stay too long. But then, it was the last time anyhow.

The door opened, Mrs. Drew's wrinkled face broke into smiles. "Come in, Bernard. It's good to see you standing there. It made me feel so young again to have you come visit."

He went inside, looking around.

"I'll start the cookies. I didn't know if you were coming." She padded into the kitchen. "I'll get them started right away. You sit down on the couch."

Bubber went over and sat down. He noticed that the table and lamp were gone; the chair was right up next to the couch. He was looking at the chair in perplexity when Mrs. Drew came rustling back into the room.

"They're in the oven. I had the batter all ready. Now." She sat down in the chair with a sigh. "Well, how did it go today? How was school?"

"Fine."

She nodded. How plump he was, the little boy, sitting just a little distance from her, his cheeks red and full! She could touch him, he was so close. Her aged heart thumped. Ah, to be young again. Youth was so much. It was everything. What did the world mean to the old? *When all the world is old, lad. . . .*

"Do you want to read to me, Bernard?" she asked presently.

"I didn't bring any books."

"Oh." She nodded. "Well, I have some books," she said quickly. "I'll get them."

She got up, crossing to the bookcase. As she opened the doors, Bubber said, "Mrs. Drew, my father says I can't come here any more. He says this is the last time. I thought I'd tell you."

She stopped, standing rigid. Everything seemed to leap around her, the room twisting furiously. She took a harsh, frightened breath. "Bernard, you're—you're not coming back?"

"No, my father says not to."

There was silence. The old lady took a book at random and came slowly back to her chair. After a while she passed the book to him, her hands trembling. The boy took it without expression, looking at its cover.

"Please read, Bernard. Please."

"All right." He opened the book. "Where'll I start?"

"Anywhere. Anywhere, Bernard."

He began to read. It was something by Trollope; she only half heard the words. She put her hand to her forehead, the dry skin, brittle and thin, like old paper. She trembled with anguish. The last time?

Bubber read on, slowly, monotonously. Against the window a fly buzzed. Outside the sun began to set, the air turning cool. A few clouds came up, and the wind in the trees rushed furiously.

The old lady sat, close by the boy, closer than ever, hearing him read, the sound of his voice, sensing him close by. Was this really the last time? Terror rose up in her and she pushed it back. The last time! She gazed at him, the boy sitting so close to her. After a time she reached out her thin, dry hand. She took a deep breath. He would never be back. There would be no more times, no more. This was the last time he would sit there.

She touched his arm.

Bubber looked up. "What is it?" he murmured.

"You don't mind if I touch your arm, do you?"

"No, I guess not." He went on reading. The old lady could feel the youngness of him, flowing between her fingers through her arm. A pulsating, vibrating youngness, so close to her. It had never been that close, where she could actually touch it. The feel of life made her dizzy, unsteady.

And presently it began to happen, as before. She closed her eyes, letting it move over her, filling her up, carried into her by the sound of the voice and the feel of the arm. The change, the glow, was coming over her, the warm, rising feeling. She was blooming again, filling with life, swelling into richness, as she had been, once, long ago.

She looked down at her arms. Rounded, they were, and the nails clear. Her hair. Black again, heavy and black against her neck. She touched her cheek. The wrinkles had gone, the skin pliant and soft.

Joy filled her, a growing, bursting joy. She stared around her, at the room. She smiled, feeling her firm teeth and gums, red lips, strong white teeth. Suddenly she got to her feet, her body secure and confident. She turned a little, lithe, quick circle.

Bubber stopped reading. "Are the cookies ready?" he said.

"I'll see." Her voice was alive, deep with a quality that had dried out many years before. Now it was there again, *her* voice, throaty and sensual. She walked quickly to the kitchen and opened the oven. She took out the cookies and put them on top of the stove.

"All ready," she called gaily. "Come and get them."

Bubber came past her, his gaze fastened on the sight of the cookies. He did not even notice the woman by the door.

Mrs. Drew hurried from the kitchen. She went into the bedroom, closing the door after her. Then she turned, gazing into the full-length mirror on the door. Young—she was young again, filled out with the sap of vigorous youth. She took a deep breath, her steady bosom swelling. Her eyes flashed, and she smiled. She spun, her skirts flying. Young and lovely.

And this time it had not gone away.

She opened the door. Bubber had filled his mouth and his pockets. He was standing in the center of the livingroom, his face fat and dull, a dead white.

"What's the matter?" Mrs. Drew said.

"I'm going."

"All right, Bernard. And thanks for coming to read to me." She laid her hand on his shoulder. "Perhaps I'll see you again some time."

"My father—"

"I know." She laughed gaily, opening the door for him. "Good-bye, Bernard. Good-bye."

She watched him go slowly down the steps, one at a time. Then she closed the door and skipped back into the bedroom. She unfastened her dress and stepped out of it, the worn gray fabric suddenly distasteful to her. For a brief second she gazed at her full, rounded body, her hands on her hips.

She laughed with excitement, turning a little, her eyes bright. What a wonderful body, bursting with life. A swelling breast—she touched herself. The flesh was firm. There was so much, so many things to do! She gazed about her, breathing quickly. So many things! She started the water running in the bathtub and then went to tie her hair up.

The wind blew around him as he trudged home. It was late, the sun had set and the sky overhead was dark and cloudy. The wind that blew and nudged against him was cold, and it penetrated through his clothing, chilling him. The boy felt tired, his head ached, and he stopped every few minutes, rubbing his forehead and resting, his heart laboring. He left Elm Street and went up Pine Street. The wind screeched around him, pushing him from side to side. He shook his head, trying to clear it. How weary he was, how tired his arms and legs were. He felt the wind hammering at him, pushing and plucking at him.

He took a breath and went on, his head down. At the corner he stopped, holding on to a lamppost. The sky was quite dark, the street lights were beginning to come on. At last he went on, walking as best he could.

"Where is that boy?" May Surle said, going out on the porch for the tenth time. Ralf flicked on the light and they stood together. "What an awful wind."

The wind whistled and lashed at the porch. The two of them looked up and down the dark street, but they could see nothing but a few newspapers and trash being blown along.

"Let's go inside," Ralf said. "He sure is going to get a licking when he gets home."

They sat down at the dinner table. Presently May put down her fork. "Listen! Do you hear something?"

Ralf listened.

Outside, against the front door, there was a faint sound, a tapping sound. He stood up. The wind howled outside, blowing the shades in the room upstairs. "I'll go see what it is," he said.

He went to the door and opened it. Something gray, something gray and dry was blowing up against the porch, carried by the wind. He stared at it, but he could not make it out. A bundle of weeds, weeds and rags blown by the wind, perhaps.

The bundle bounced against his legs. He watched it drift past him, against the wall of the house. Then he closed the door again slowly.

"What is it?" May called.

"Just the wind," Ralf Surle said.

The Miracle Mile

by Robert R. McCammon

T he car died outside Perdido Beach. It was a messy death, a wheeze of oil and a clatter of cylinders, a dark tide spreading across the sun-cracked pavement. When it was over, they sat there for a few minutes saying nothing, just listening to the engine tick and steam, but then the baby began to cry and it came to them that they had to get moving. Kyle got the suitcase, Allie took the bag of groceries in one arm and the baby in the other, Tommy laced up his sneakers and took the thermos of water, and they left the old dead car on the roadside and started walking south to the Gulf.

Kyle checked his watch again. It was almost three o'clock. The sun set late, in midsummer. July heat crushed them, made the sweat ooze from their pores and stick the clothes to their flesh. The road, bordered by pine woods, was deserted. This season there would be no tourists. This season thee would be no lights or laughter on the Miracle Mile.

They kept walking, step after step, into the steamy haze of heat. Kyle took the baby for a while, and they stopped for a sip of water and a rest in the shade. Flies buzzed around their faces, drawn to the moisture. Then Kyle said, "I guess we'd better go on," and his wife and son got up again, the baby cradled in Kyle's arm. Around the next curve of the long road they saw a car off in a drainage ditch on the left-hand side. The car's red paint had faded, the tires were flat, and the driver's door was open. Of the car's occupants there was no sigh. Allie walked a little closer to Kyle as they passed the car; their arms touched, wet flesh against wet flesh, and Kyle noted she looked straight ahead with that thousand-yard stare he'd seen on his own face as he'd shaved in the mirror this morning at dawn.

"When are we gonna get there?" Tommy asked. He was twelve years old, his patience wearing thin. It occurred to Kyle that Tommy asked that question every year, from his seat in the back of the car: *Hey, Dad, when are we gonna get there?*

"Soon," Kyle answered. "It's not far." His stock reply. They'd never walked the last few miles into Perdido Beach, not once in all the many years they'd been coming here for summer vacation. "We ought to see the water pretty soon."

"Hot," Allie said, and she wiped her forehead with the back of her arm. "Hot out here."

Over a hundred, Kyle figured. The sun reflecting off the pavement was brutal. The road shimmered ahead, between the thin pines. A black snake slid across in front of them, and up against the blue, cloudless sky hawks searched for currents. "Soon," Kyle said, and he licked his dry lips. "It's not far at all now."

It was four o'clock when the pine woods fell away and they saw the first wreckage from Hurricane Jolene. A motel with pink walls had most of its roof ripped away. A twisted sign lay in the parking lot amid abandoned cars. Curtains, cigarette butts, deck chairs, and other debris floated in the swimming pool. "Can we get out of the sun for a few minutes?" Allie asked him, and he nodded and led his family toward the pink ruins.

Some of the doors remained, but most of them had been torn from their hinges by the storm. The first unit, without a door, had a bed with a bloodstained sheet and the flies spun above it in a dark, roiling cloud. He opened the door of the next unit, number eight, and they went into a room where the heat had been trapped but the sun and the flies turned away. The room's bed had been stripped to the mattress and a lamp with flamingoes on the shade had been overturned, but it looked safe. He opened the blinds and the windows, and in his inhalation of air he thought he could smell the Gulf's salt. Allie sat down on the bed with the baby and took a squeeze tube of sun block from the grocery bag. She began to paint the infant's face with it, as the baby's pink fingers grasped at the air. Then she covered her own face and arms with the sun block.

"I'm already burning," she said as she worked the stuff into her skin. "I didn't used to burn so fast. Want some?"

"Yeah." The back of Kyle's neck was stinging. He stood over his wife and looked at the baby, as Tommy sprawled on the bed and stared at the ceiling. "She needs a name," Kyle said.

"Hope," Allie answered, and she looked up at her husband with heat-puffed eyes. "Hope would be a good name, don't you think?"

It would be a cruel name, he decided. A name not suited for these times or this world. But saying no would be just as cruel, wouldn't it? He saw how badly Allie wanted it, so he said, "I think that's fine," and as soon as he said it he felt the rage surge in him like a bitter flood tide and he had to turn away before she saw it in his face. The infant couldn't be more than six months old. Why had it fallen to him, to do this thing?

He took the thermos and went into the bathroom, where there was a sink and a shower stall and a tub with a sliding door of smoked plastic. He pulled the blind up and opened the small window in there too, and then he turned on the sink's tap and waited for the rusty water to clear before he refilled the thermos.

Something moved, there in the bathroom. Something moved with a long, slow, and agonized stretching sound.

Kyle looked at the smoked plastic door for a moment, a pulse beating in his skull, and then he reached out and slid it open.

It was lying in the tub. Like a fat cocoon, it was swaddled in bed sheets and tacky beach towels covered with busty cartoon bathing beauties and studs swigging beer. It was impossible to determine where the head and feet were, the arms bound to its sides and the hands hidden. The thing in its shroud of sheets and towels trembled, a hideous involuntary reaction of nerves and muscles, and Kyle thought, *It smells me.*

"Kill it."

He looked back at Allie, who stood in the doorway behind him with the baby in her arms. Her face was emotionless, her eyes vacant as a dreamer's. "Kill it, Kyle," she said. "Please kill it."

"Tom?" he called. He heard his voice crack. "Take your mother outside, will you?" The boy didn't respond, and when Kyle peered out from the bathroom he saw his son sitting up on the bed. Tommy was staring at him, with the same dead eyes as his mother. Tommy's mouth was half-open, a silver thread of saliva hanging down. "Tom? Listen up!" He said

it sharply, and Tommy's gaze cleared. "Go outside with your mother. Do
you hear me?"

"Yes sir," Tommy said, and he did as he was told. When he was alone,
Kyle opened his suitcase, reached beneath the socks and underwear and
found the .38 pistol hidden there. He loaded it from a box of shells,
cocked the gun, and walked back into the bathroom where the wrapped-
up thing at the bottom of the tub awaited.

Kyle tried to get a grip on the towels and pull them loose, but they
were held so tightly they wouldn't give. When he pulled with greater de-
termination, the shape began thrashing back and forth with terrible
strength, and Kyle let go and stepped back. The thing's thrashing ceased,
and it lay still again. Kyle had once seen one that had grown a hard skin,
like a roach. He had seen one with a flat, cobralike head on an elongated
neck. Their forms were changing, a riot of evolution gone insane. In
these times, in this world, even the fabric of nature had been ripped
asunder.

He didn't have time to waste. He aimed the gun at the thing's mid-
section and squeezed the trigger. The noise of the shots was thunderous
in the little bathroom. When he was through shooting, there were six
holes in the towels and sheets but no blood.

"Chew on those," Kyle said.

There was a wet, splitting noise. Reddish black liquid soaked the towels and began to stream toward the drain. Kyle thought of a leech that
had just burst open. He clenched his teeth, got out of the bathroom and
closed the door behind him, and then he put the pistol back into the suitcase and snapped the suitcase shut.

His wife, son, and the baby called Hope were waiting for him, outside
in the hot yellow sunshine.

Kyle checked the cars in the motel's parking lot. One had keys in the
ignition, though its windshield was shattered. He got in and tried the engine; the dead battery wouldn't even give out a gasp. They started walking again, toward the south, as the sun moved into the west and the
afternoon shadows began to gather.

Tommy saw them first: sand dunes rising between the palmettos. He
cried out with joy and ran for the beach, where the Gulf's waves rolled
up in lathery foam and gulls skimmed the blue water. He took off his
sneakers and socks, threw them aside and rushed into the sea, and be-

hind him came his father and mother, footsore and drenched with sweat. Kyle and Allie both took off their shoes and waded into the water, the baby in Allie's arms, and as the waves rolled around them onto the sand Kyle inhaled a chestful of salt air and cleansed his senses. Then he looked down the beach, is crescent curving toward the east, and the motels that stood at the edge of the Gulf.

They were alone.

Gulls darted in, screaming. Two of them fought over a crab that had been flipped onto its back. Broken shells glittered where the sand turned brown and hard. And all along the beach the motels—the blocky violet, sea green, periwinkle, and cream-colored buildings that had stood there since Kyle and Allie were teenagers—were without life, like the structures of an ancient civilization. Hurricane Jolene had done its damage; some of the motels—the Spindrift, the Sea Anchor, the Coral Reef—had been reduced to hulks, their signs battered and dangling, their windows broken out, whole walls washed away. A hundred yards down the beach, a cabin cruiser lay on its side, its hull ripped open like a fish's belly. Where Kyle recalled the sight of a hundred sunbathers tanning on their towels, there was nothing but white emptiness. The lifeguard's station was gone. There was no aroma of coconut-scented tanning butter, no blare of radios, no volleyball games, nobody tossing a Frisbee to a dog in the surf. The gulls strutted around, fat and happy in the absence of humanity.

Kyle had expected this, but the reality gnawed at his heart. He loved this place; he had been young here, had met and courted Allie here. They'd come to Perdido Beach on their honeymoon, sixteen years ago. And they'd come back, every year since. What was summer, without a vacation at the beach? Without sand in your shoes, the sun on your shoulders, the sound of young laughter, and the smell of the Gulf? What was life worth, without such as that?

A hand slid into his.

"We're here," Allie said. She was smiling, but when she kissed him he tasted a tear.

They were going to cook, out in this sun. They needed to find a room. Check in, stow the suitcase and the groceries. Think about the future.

Kyle watched the waves coming in. Tommy went underwater, clothes and all, and rose up sputtering and yelling for the sake of it. Allie's hand squeezed Kyle's, and Kyle thought, *We're standing on the edge of what used to be, and there's nowhere left to run.*

Nowhere.

"I love you," Kyle told his wife, and he drew her tightly against him. He could feel the heat of her skin. She was going to have a bad sunburn. Hope's cheeks were red. Pick up some Solarcaine somewhere. God knows *they* don't need it.

Nowhere.

He walked out of the water. The wet sand sucked around his ankles, trying to hold him, but he broke free and trudge up across the hard sand, leaving footprints all the way to where he'd left his suitcase. Allie was following him, with the red-cheeked Hope. "Tom?" Kyle called. "Tommy, let's go!" The boy splashed and romped for a moment more, gulls spinning around his head either in curiosity or thinking he was a rather large fish, and then Tommy came out of the water and picked up his socks and sneakers.

They began to walk eastward on the beach toward the Miracle Mile. A skeleton lay half-buried in the sand just past the wrecked cabin cruiser. A child's orange pail was caught by the surf, pulled out and thrust onto shore again, the sea playing a game with the dead. The sun was getting lower, the shadows growing. The suitcase was heavy, so Kyle changed hands. The tires of a dune buggy jutted up from the waves, and farther on a body with some flesh on it was drifting in the shallow water. The gulls had been at work; it was not pretty.

Kyle watched his wife, her shadow going before her. The baby began to cry, and Allie gently shushed her. Tommy threw shells into the water, trying to get a skimmer. They had found the infant in a gas station south of Montgomery, Alabama, near nine o'clock this morning. There had been an abandoned station wagon outside at the pumps, and the child had been on the floor in the women's room. On the driver's seat of the station wagon was a great deal of dried blood. Tommy had thought the blotch looked like the state of Texas. There had been dried blood on the door-knob of the women's room too, but what had happened at that gas station was unknown. Was the mother attacked? Had she planned to come back for the baby? Had she crawled off into the woods and died? They'd searched around the gas station, but found no corpses.

Well, life was a mystery, wasn't it? Kyle had agreed to take the baby with them, on their vacation to the beach. But he cursed God for doing this to him, because he'd finally got things right in his soul.

Hope. It had to be a cosmic joke. And if God and the devil were at war over this spinning ball of black sorrows, it was terribly clear who had control of the nuclear weapons.

Biological incident.

That was the first of it. How the government tried to explain. A biological incident, at some kind of secret—up until then—testing center in North Dakota. That was six years ago. The biological incident was worse than they'd let on. They had created something from their stew of gene manipulation and bacteriological tampering that had sent their ten test subjects out into the world with a vengeance. The ten had multiplied into twenty, the twenty to forty, the forty to eighty, and on and on. They had the wrath of Hell in their blood, a contamination that made AIDS look like a common cold. The germ boys had learned how to create—by accident, yes—weapons that walked on two legs. What foreign power were we going to unleash that taint upon? No matter; it had come home to live.

Biological incident.

Kyle shifted the suitcase again. *Call them what they are,* he thought. They craved blood like addicts used to crave heroin and crack. They wrapped themselves up and hid in closets and basements and any hole they could winnow into. Their skin burst and oozed and they split apart at the seams like old suits in the sunlight. Call them what they are, damn it.

They were everywhere now. They had everything. The television networks, the corporations, the advertising agencies, the publishing houses, the banks, the law. Everything. Once in a while a pirate station broke in on the cable, human beings pleading for others not to give up hope. Hope. There it was again, the cosmic joke. Those bastards were as bad as fundamentalist preachers; their role models were Jim Bakker and Jerry Falwell, seen through a dark glass. They wanted to convert everybody on earth, make them see the "truth," and if you didn't choose to join the fold they battered you in like a weak door and chewed the faith into you.

It wasn't just America. It was everywhere: Canada, the Soviet Union, Japan, Germany, Norway, Africa, England, South America, and Spain. Everywhere. The contamination—the "faith"—knew no racial nor national boundaries. It was another cosmic joke, with a hideous twist: The world was moving toward a true brotherhood.

Kyle watched his shadow loom before him, its darkness merging with Allie's. If a man couldn't take a vacation in the sun with his family, he thought, then what the hell good was living?

"Hey, Dad!" Tommy said. "There it is!"

Kyle looked to where his son was pointing. The motel had stucco walls painted pale blue, its roof of red slate. Some of the roof had collapsed, the walls and windows broken. The motel's sign had survived the hurricane, and said THE DRIFTWOOD.

It was where Kyle and Allie had spent their honeymoon, and where they'd stayed—cabana number five, overlooking the Gulf—every summer vacation for sixteen years. "Yes," Kyle answered. "That's the place." He turned his back to the sea and walked toward the concrete steps that led up to the Driftwood, and Allie followed with Hope and the grocery bag. Tommy paused to bend down and examine a jellyfish that had washed up and been caught by the sun at low tide, and then he came on too.

The row of oceanview cabanas had been demolished. Number five was a cavern of debris, its roof caved in. "Watch the glass," Kyle cautioned them, and he continued on around the brackish swimming pool and the deck that caught the afternoon's sea breeze. He climbed another set of stairs from the pool's deck to the major portion of the Driftwood, his wife and son behind him, and he stood facing a warren of collapsed rooms and wreckage.

Summer could be a heartless thing.

For a few seconds he almost lost it. Tears burned his eyes, and he thought he was going to choke on a sob. It had been important, so vitally important, that they come to Perdido Beach again, and see this place where life had been fresh and good and all the days were ahead of them. Now, more than anything, Kyle could see that it was over. But then Allie said, in a terribly cheerful voice, "It's not so bad," and Kyle laughed instead of cried. His laughter spiralled up, was taken by the Gulf breeze and broken like the walls of the Driftwood. "We can stay right here," Allie said, and she walked past her husband into an opening where a door used to be.

The room's walls were cracked, the ceiling blotched with water stains. The furniture—bed, chest of drawers, chairs, lamps, all ticky-tacky when they were new—had been whirled around and smashed to kindling. Pipes stuck up where the sink had been in the bathroom, but the toilet remained and the shower stall—empty of intruders—was all right. Kyle tried the tap and was amazed to hear a rumbling down in the Driftwood's guts. A thin trickle of rusty water flowed from the shower head. Kyle turned the tap off and the rumbling died.

"Clear this stuff away," Allie told Tommy. "Let's get this mattress out from underneath."

"We can't stay here," Kyle said.

"Why can't we?" Her eyes were vacant again. "We can make do. We've been making do at home. We can make do on vacation too."

"No. We've got to find somewhere else."

"We've always stayed at the Driftwood." A childlike petulance rose up in her voice, and she began to rock the baby. "Always. We can stay right here, like we do every summer. Can't we, Tommy?"

"I guess so," he said, and he nudged the shattered television set with his foot.

Kyle and Allie stared at each other. The breeze came in around them through the doorway and then left again.

"We can stay here," Allie said.

She's out of it, he thought. Who could blame her? Her systems were shutting down, a little tighter day after day. "All right." He touched her hair and smoothed it away from her face. "The Driftwood it is."

Tommy went to find a shovel and broom, because there was a lot of glass on the linoleum-tiled floor. As Allie unpacked the groceries, the baby laid to rest on a pillow, Kyle checked the rooms on either side. Nothing sleeping in them, nothing folded up and waiting. He checked as many rooms as he could get into. There was something bad—neither skeleton nor fully fleshed, but bloated and dark as a slug—wearing a flower-print shirt and red shorts in a room nearer the pool, but Kyle could tell it was a dead human being and not one of them. A Gideon's Bible lay close at hand, and also the broken beer bottle with which the sunlover had slashed his wrists. On a countertop, next to the stub of a burned-out candle, was a wallet, some change, and a set of car keys. Kyle didn't look at the wallet, but he took the keys. Then he put the shower curtain over the corpse and continued his search of the Driftwood's rooms. He walked through a breezeway, past the Driftwood's office and to the front of the motel, and there he found a half-dozen cars in the parking lot. Across the street was Nick's Pancake House, its windows blown in. Next to it, the Goofy Golf place and the Go-Kart track, both deserted, their concession stands shuttered and storm ravaged. Kyle began to check the cars, as gulls cried out overhead and sailed in lazy circles.

The keys fit the ignition of a blue Toyota with a Tennessee license tag. Its engine, cranky at first, finally spat black smoke and awakened. The gas gauge's needle was almost to the E, but there were plenty of gas stations on the Strip. Kyle shut the engine off and got out, and that was when he looked toward the Miracle Mile.

It was a beautifully clear afternoon. He could see all the way to the amusement park, where the Ferris wheel and the roller coaster rose up, where the Sky Needle loomed over the Hang Out dance pavilion and the Super Water Slide stood next to the Beach Arcade.

His eyes stung. He heard ghosts on the wind, calling in young voices from the dead world. He had to look away from the Miracle Mile before his heart cracked, and he walked back the way he'd come, the keys gripped in his palm.

Tommy was at work clearing away debris. The mattress had been swept free of glass. A chair had been salvaged, and a table on which a lamp had sat. Allie had put on her swimsuit—the one with aquamarine fish on it that she'd found in a Sears store last week—and she wore sandals so her feet wouldn't be cut. The flesh of her arms and face were blushed with Florida sun. It dawned on Kyle how much weight Allie had lost. She was as skinny as she'd been their first night together, here at the Driftwood a long, long time ago.

"I'm ready for the beach," she told him. "How do I look?" She turned around for him to appreciate the swimsuit.

"Nice. Really nice."

"We shouldn't waste the sunshine, should we?"

She'd had enough sun for one day. But he smiled tightly and said, "No."

Beneath one of the yellow beach umbrellas, Kyle sat beside his wife while she fed Hope from a jar of Gerber's mixed fruit. The groceries had come from a supermarket in the same area they'd found the baby, and Allie had stocked up on items she hadn't even thought about since Tommy was an infant. Out in the Gulf, Tommy splashed and swam as the sun sparkled golden on the waves.

"Don't go too far!" Kyle cautioned, and Tommy waved his *don't worry* wave and swam out a little farther. There was a boy for you, Kyle thought. Always testing his limits. Like me, when I was his age. Kyle lay down on the sand, his hands cupped behind his head. He had been coming to Perdido Beach since he was five years old. One of his first memories was of his father and mother dancing at the pavilion, to "Stardust" or some other old tune. He recalled a day when his father had taken him on every ride on the Miracle Mile: the Ferris wheel, roller coaster, mad mouse, tiltawhirl, scrambler, and octopus. He remembered his father's square brown face and white teeth, clenched in a grin as the mad mouse shot them heavenward. They had feasted on popcorn, cotton candy, candied apples, and corn dogs. They had thrown balls at milk jugs and rings at spindles and come away empty-handed but wiser in the ways of the Miracle Mile.

It had been one of the happiest days of his life.

After Kyle's mother had died of cancer eight years ago, his father had moved out to Arizona to live near his younger brother and his wife. A little over a week past, a midnight call had come from that town in Arizona, and through the static-hissing phone line the voice of Kyle's father had said, *I'm coming to visit you, son. Coming real soon. Me and your uncle Alan and aunt Patti Ann. I feel so much better now, son. My joints don't ache anymore. Oh, it's a wonderful life, this is! I sure do look forward to seeing my sweet grandboy....*

They had left their house the next morning and found another house in a town ten miles away. There were still some humans left, in the little towns. But some of them were crazy with terror, and others had made fortresses out of their homes. They put bars on the windows and slept in the daylight, surrounded by guns and barbed wire.

Kyle sat up and watched his son throwing himself against the waves, the glittering water splashing high. He saw himself out there; he hadn't changed so much, but the world had. The rachet gears of God's machine had slipped, and from here on out the territory was treacherous and uncharted.

He had decided he couldn't live behind bars and barbed wire. He couldn't live without the sun, or Perdido Beach in July, or without Tommy and Allie. If those things got hold of him—if they got hold of any of his family—then what would life be? A scuttling in the dark? A moan from gore-wet lips? He couldn't think about this anymore, and he blanked his mind: a trick he'd learned, out of necessity.

He watched his wife feeding the baby. The sight of Allie cradling the child made him needful; the need was on him before he could think about it. Allie was skinny, sure, but she looked good in her new swimsuit, and her hair was light brown and pretty in the reflected sunlight and her gray eyes had the shine of life in them again, for a little while. He said, "Allie?" and when she looked at him she saw the need in his face. He touched her shoulder, and she leaned over and kissed him on the lips. The kiss lingered, grew soft and wet and his tongue found hers. She smiled at him, her eyes hazy, and she put the child down on a beach towel.

Kyle didn't care if Tommy saw. They were beyond the need for privacy. A precious moment could not be turned aside. Kyle and Allie lay together under the yellow umbrella, their bodies damp and entwined, their hearts beating hard, and out in the waves Tommy pretended not to see and went diving for sand dollars. He found ten.

The sun was sinking. It made the Gulf of Mexico turn the color of fire, and way out past the shallows dolphins played.

"It'll be getting dark soon," Kyle said at last. The moon was coming out, a slice of silver against the east's darkening blue. "I've got somebody's car keys. Want to ride up to the Miracle Mile?"

Allie said that would be fine, and she held Hope against her breasts.

The wind had picked up. It blew stinging sand against their legs as they walked across the beach. Tommy stopped to throw a shell. "I got a skimmer, Dad!" he shouted.

In the room, Allie put on a pair of white shorts over her wet suit. Tommy wore a T-shirt with the computer image of a rock band on the front, and baggy orange cutoffs. Kyle dry-shaved with his razor, then dressed in a pair of khaki trousers and a dark blue pullover shirt. As he was lacing up his sneakers, he gave Tommy the car keys. "It's a blue Toyota. Tennessee tag. Why don't you go start her up?"

"You mean it? Really?"

"Why not?"

"Allll *right!*"

"Wait a minute!" Kyle cautioned before Tommy could leave. "Allie, why don't you go with him? I'll be up in a few minutes."

She frowned, reading his mood. "What's wrong?"

THE MIRACLE MILE   103

"Nothing. I just want to sit here and think. I'll be there by the time you get the car ready."

Allie took the baby, and she and Tommy went around to the parking lot. In the gathering dark, Kyle sat on the mattress and stared at the cracks in the wall. This was their honeymoon motel. It had once seemed like the grandest place on earth. Maybe it still was.

When Kyle opened the Toyota's door and Tommy slid into the back seat, he was wearing his poplin windbreaker, zipped up to his chest. He got behind the wheel, and he said, "Let's go see it."

Theirs was the only car that moved on the long, straight road called the Strip. Kyle turned on the headlights, but it wasn't too dark to see the destruction on either side of them. "We ate there last summer," Tommy said, and pointed at a heap of rubble that used to be a Pizza Hut. They drove past T-Shirt City, the Shell Shack, and the Dixie Hot Shoppe, where a cook named Pee Wee used to make the best grouper sandwiches Kyle had ever eaten. All those places were dark hulks now. He kept going at a slow, steady speed. "Cruising the Strip," he and his buddies used to call it, when they came looking for girls and good times on spring break. His first roaring drunk was in a motel called the Surf's Inn. His first poker game had been played at Perdido Beach. He'd lost his first real fight behind a bar here, and ended up with a busted nose. He'd met the first girl he'd . . . well, there had been a lot of first at Perdido Beach.

God, there were ghosts here.

"Sun's almost gone," Tommy said.

Kyle turned the car to a place where they could watch the sunset over a motel's ruins. It was going down fast, the Gulf streaked with dark gold, orange, and purple. Allie's hand found her husband's; it was the hand with her wedding ring on it. The baby cried a little, and Kyle knew how she felt. The sun went away in a last scarlet flash, and then it was gone toward the other side of the world and the night was closing in.

"It was pretty, wasn't it?" Allie asked. "Sunsets are always so pretty at the beach."

Kyle started driving again, taking them to the Miracle Mile. His heart was beating hard, his palms damp on the wheel. Because there it was, the paradise of his memories. He pulled the car to the side of the road and stopped.

The last of the light glinted on the rails of the roller coaster. The Ferris wheel's cars were losing their paint, and rocked in the strengthening wind. Another casualty of Jolene was the mad mouse's maze of tracks. The long red roof of the Hang Out dance pavilion, the underside of which was painted with Day-Glo stars and comets, had been stripped to the boards, but the open-air building still stood. Within the smashed windows of the Beach Arcade, the pinball machines had been overturned. Metal rods dangled down from the Sky Needle, its foundation cracked. The concession stand that used to sell foot-long hot dogs and flavored snow cones had been flattened. The water slide had survived, though, and so had a few of the other mechanical rides. The merry-go-round—a beauty of carved, leaping lions and proud horses—remained almost unscathed. Fit for the junkyard were the haunted house and hall of mirrors, but the fun house with its entrance through a huge red grin was still there.

"We met here," Allie said. She was talking to Tommy. "Right over there." She pointed toward the roller coaster. "Your father was in line behind me. I was with Carol Akins and Denise McCarthy. When it came time for us to get on, I had to sit with him. I didn't know him. I was sixteen, and he was eighteen. He was staying at the Surf's Inn. That's where all the hoods stayed."

"I wasn't a hood,' Kyle said.

"You were what a hood *was* then. You drank and smoked and you were looking for trouble." She stared at the roller coaster, and Kyle watched her face. "We went around four times."

"Five."

"Five," she recalled, and nodded. "The fifth time we rode in the front car. I was so scared I almost wet my pants."

"Aw, Mom!" Tommy said.

"He wrote me a letter. It came a week after I got home. There was sand in the envelope." She smiled, a faint smile, and Kyle had to look somewhere else. "He said he hoped we could see each other again. Do you remember that, Kyle?"

"Like yesterday," he answered.

"I dreamed about the Miracle Mile, for a long time after that. I dreamed we would be together. I was a silly thing when I was sixteen."

"You're still that way," Tommy said.

"Amen," Kyle added.

They sat there for a few more minutes, staring down the darkening length of the Miracle Mile. Many lives had crossed here, many had come and gone, but this place belonged to them. They knew it, in their hearts. It was theirs, forever. Their linked initials cut into a wooden railing of the Hang Out said so. It didn't matter that there might be ten thousand more initials carved in the pavilion; they had returned here, and where were the others?

The wind made the Ferris wheel's cars creak, but otherwise silence reigned. Kyle broke it. "We ought to go to the pier. That's what we ought to do."

The long fishing pier just past the Miracle Mile, where the bait used to be cut and reeled out every hour of the day and night. He and his father used to go fishing there, while his mother stretched out on a folding chair and read the forms from the dog track up the highway.

"I'm going to need some Solarcaine," Allie said as they drove past the Miracle Mile. "My arms are stinging."

"And I'm thirsty," Tommy said. "Can we get something to drink?"

"Sure. We'll find something."

The pier—LONGEST PIER ON THE PANHANDLE, the battered metal sign said—was a half mile past the amusement park. Kyle parked in front of it, in a deserted lot. A soft drink machine stood inside the pier's admission gate, but without electricity it was useless. Tommy got his arm up inside it and grasped a can but he couldn't pull it out. Kyle turned the machine over and tried to break it open. Its lock held, a last grip of civilization.

"Damn," Tommy said, and kicked the machine.

Next door to the pier, across the lot, was a rubble of what had been a seafood restaurant. The sign remained, a swordfish riding a surfboard. "Why don't we try over there?" Kyle asked, placing his hand on his son's shoulder. "Maybe we can find some cans. Allie, we'll be right back."

"I'll go with you."

"No," he said. "You wait on the pier."

Allie stood very still. In the deepening gloom, Kyle could only see the outline of her face. "I want to talk to Tommy," Kyle told her. She didn't move; it seemed to him she was holding her breath. "Man talk," he said.

Silence.

Finally, she spoke. "Come right back. Okay?"

"Okay."

"And don't step on a nail. Be careful. Okay?"

"We will be. Watch where you walk too." He guided Tommy toward the ruins, and the wind shrilled around them.

They were almost there when Tommy asked what he wanted to talk about. "Just some stuff," Kyle answered. He glanced back. Allie was on the pier, facing away from them. Maybe she was looking at the sea, or maybe at the Miracle Mile. It was hard to tell.

"I got too much sun. My neck's burning."

"Oh," Kyle said, "you'll be all right."

The stars were coming out. It was going to be a beautiful night. He kept his hand on Tommy's shoulder, and together they walked into the wreckage beneath the surfing swordfish. They kept going, over glass and planks, until Kyle had the remnant of a cinder block wall between them and Allie.

"Dad, how're we going to find anything in here? It's so dark."

"Hold it. See that? There beside your right foot? Is that a can?"

"I can't see it."

Kyle unzipped his windbreaker. "I think it is." A lump had lodged in his throat, and he could hardly speak. "Can you see it?"

"Where?"

Kyle placed one hand against the top of his son's head. It was perhaps the most difficult movement of flesh and bone he had ever made in his life. "Right there," he said, as he drew the .38 from his waistband with his other hand. *Click.*

"What was that, Dad?"

"You're my good boy," Kyle croaked, and he put the barrel against Tommy's skull.

No. This was the most difficult movement of flesh and bone.

A spasm of his finger on the trigger. A terrible *crack* that left his eardrums ringing.

It was done.

Tommy slid down, and Kyle wiped his hand on the leg of his trousers. *Oh Jesus,* he thought. A sense of panic swelled inside him. *Oh Jesus, I should've found him something to drink before I did it.*

He staggered, tripped over a pile of boards and cinder blocks and went down on his knees in the dark, the after sound of the shot still echoing. *My God, he died thirsty. Oh my God, I just killed my son.* He shivered and

moaned, sickness burning in his stomach. It came to him that he might
have only wounded the boy, and Tommy might be lying there in agony.
"Tommy?" he said. "Can you hear me?" No, no; he'd shot the boy right
in the back of the head, just as he'd planned. If Tommy wasn't dead, he
was dying and he knew nothing. It had been fast and unexpected and
Tommy hadn't had a chance to even think about death.

"Forgive me," Kyle whispered, tears streaking down his face. "Please
forgive me."

It took him a while to find the strength to stand. He put the pistol away
and zipped his windbreaker up again, and then he wiped his face and left
the ruins where his son's body lay. Kyle walked toward the pier, where
Allie stood with the baby in the deep purple dark.

"Kyle?" she called before he reached her.

"Yes."

"I heard a noise."

"Some glass broke. It's all right."

"Where's Tommy, Kyle?"

"He'll be here in a few minutes," Kyle said, and he stopped in front of
her. He could feel the sea moving below him, amid the pier's concrete
pilings. "Why don't we walk to the end?"

Allie didn't speak. Hope was sleeping, her head against Allie's shoulder.

Kyle looked up at the sky full of stars and the silver slice of moon. "We
used to come out here together. Remember?"

She didn't answer.

"We used to come out and watch the fishermen at night. I asked you to
marry me at the end of the pier. Do you remember?"

"Yes." A quiet voice.

"Then when you said yes I jumped off. Remember that?"

"I thought you were crazy," Allie said.

"I was. I am. Always will be."

He saw her tremble, violently. "Tommy?" she called into the night.
"Tommy, come on now!"

"Walk with me. All right?"

"I can't . . . I can't . . . think, Kyle. I can't . . ."

Kyle took her hand. Her fingers were cold. "There's nothing to think
about. Everything's under control. Do you understand?"

"We can . . . stay right here," she said. "Right here. It's safe here."

"There's only one place that's safe," Kyle said. "It's not here."

"*Tommy?*" she called, and her voice broke.

"Walk with me. Please." He gripped her hand tighter. She went with him.

Jolene had bitten off the last forty feet of the pier. It ended on a jagged edge, and below them the Gulf surged against the pilings. Kyle put his arm around his wife and kissed her cheek. Her skin was hot and damp. She leaned her head against his shoulder, as Hope's head was against her own. Kyle unzipped his windbreaker.

"It was a good day, wasn't it?" he asked her, and she nodded.

The wind was in their faces, coming in hard off the sea. "I love you," Kyle said.

"I love you," she answered.

"Are you cold?"

"Yes."

He gave her his windbreaker, and zipped it up around her shoulders and the baby. "Look at those stars!" he said. "You can't see so many stars anywhere else but the beach, can you?"

She shook her head.

Kyle kissed her temple and put a bullet into it.

Then he let her go.

Allie and the baby fell off the pier. Kyle watched her body go down and splash into the Gulf. The waves picked her up, closed over her, turned her on her stomach and made her hair float like an opening fan. Kyle looked up at the sky. He took a deep breath, cocked the pistol again and put the barrel into his mouth, pointed upward toward his brain.

God forgive me there is no Hell there is no—

He heard a low humming sound. The noise, he realized, of machinery at work.

Lights came on, a bright shock in the sky. The stars faded. Multicolored reflections scrawled across the moving waves.

Music. The sound of a distant pipe organ.

Kyle turned around, his bones freezing.

The Miracle Mile.

The Miracle Mile was coming to life.

Lights rimmed the Ferris wheel and the roller coaster's rails. Floods glared over the Super Water Slide. The merry-go-round was lit up like a birthday cake. A spotlight had been pointed upward, and combed the night above the Miracle Mile like a call to celebration.

Kyle's finger was on the trigger. He was ready.

The Ferris wheel began to turn: a slow, groaning process. He could see figures in the gondolas. The center track of the roller coaster started moving with a clanking of gears, and then the roller coaster cars were cranked up to the top of the first incline. There were people in the cars. No, not people. Not human beings. Them.

They had taken over the Miracle Mile.

Kyle heard them scream with delight as the roller coarser's cars went over the incline like a long, writhing snake.

The merry-go-round was turning. The pipe organ music, a scratchy recording, was being played from speakers at the carousel's center. Kyle watched the riders going around, and he pulled the pistol's barrel from his mouth. Light bulbs had blinked on in the Hang Out, and now the sound of rock music spilled out from a jukebox. Kyle could see them in the pavilion, a mass of them pressed together and dancing at the edge of the sea.

They had taken everything. The night, the cities, the towns, freedom, the law, the world.

And now the Miracle Mile.

Kyle grinned savagely, as tears ran down his cheeks.

The roller coaster rocketed around. The Ferris wheel was turning faster.

They had hooked up generators, of course, there in the amusement part. They'd gotten gasoline to run the generators from a gas station on the Strip.

You could make bombs out of gasoline and bottles.

Find those generators. Pull the plug on the Miracle Mile.

He had four bullets in the gun. The extras had been in case he screwed up and wounded instead of killed. Four bullets. The car keys had been in the windbreaker. *Sleep well, my darling,* he thought.

I will be joining you.

But not yet. Not yet.

Maybe he could find a way to make the roller coaster's cars jump the tracks. Maybe he could blow up the Hang Out, with all of them mashed up together inside. They would make a lovely bonfire, on this starry summer night. He gritted his teeth, his guts full of rage. They might take the world, but they would not take his family. And they would pay for taking the Miracle Mile, if he could do anything about it.

He was insane now. He knew it. But the instant of knowing was pulled away from him like Allie's body in the waves, and he gripped the pistol hard and took the first step back along the pier toward shore.

Careful. Keep to the darkness. Don't let them see you. Don't let them smell *you.*

Screams and laughter soared over the Miracle Mile, as a solitary figure walked back with a gun in his hand and flames in his mind.

It came to Kyle that his vacation was over.

Something had to Be Done

by David Drake

h e was out in the hall just a minute ago, sir," the pinched-faced
WAC said, looking up from her typewriter in irritation. "You
can't mistake his face."

Captain Richmond shrugged and walked out of the busy office. Blinking in the dim marble were a dozen confused civilians, bussed in for
their pre-induction physicals. No one else was in the hallway. The thick-
waisted officer frowned, then thought to open the door of the men's
room. "Sergeant Morzek?" he called.

Glass clinked within one of the closed stalls and a deep voice with a
catch in it grumbled, "Yeah, be right with you." Richmond thought he
smelled gin.

"You the other ghoul?" the voice questioned as the stall swung open.
Any retort Richmond might have made withered when his eyes took in
the cadaverous figure in ill-tailored greens. Platoon sergeants's chevrons
on the sleeves, and below them a longer row of service stripes than the
captain remembered having seen before. God, this walking corpse might
have served in World War II! Most of the ribbons ranked above the
sergeant's breast pockets were unfamiliar, but Richmond caught the little V for valor winking in the center of a silver star. Even in those medal-
happy days in Southeast Asia they didn't toss many of those around.

The sergeant's cheeks were hollow, his fingers grotesquely thin where they rested on top of the door or clutched the handles of his zipped AWOL bag. Where no moles squatted, his skin was as white as a convict's; but the moles were almost everywhere, hands and face, dozens and scores of them, crowding together in welted obscenity.

The sergeant laughed starkly. "Pretty, aren't I? The docs tell me I got too much sun over there and it gave me runaway warts. Hell, four years is enough time for it to."

"Umm," Richmond grunted in embarrassment, edging back into the hall to have something to do. "Well, the car's in back . . . if you're ready, we can see the Lunkowskis."

"Yeah, Christ," the sergeant said, "that's what I came for, to see the Lunkowskis." He shifted his bag as he followed the captain and it clinked again. Always before, the other man on the notification team had been a stateside officer like Richmond himself. He had heard that a few low-casualty outfits made a habit of letting whoever knew the dead man best accompany the body home, but this was his first actual experience with the practice. He hoped it would be his last.

Threading the green Ford through the heavy traffic of the city center, Richmond said, "I take it Private Lunkowski was one of your men?"

"Yeah, Stevie-boy was in my platoon for about three weeks," Morzek agreed with a chuckle. "Lost six men in that time and he was the last. Six out of twenty-nine, not very damn good, was it?"

"You were under heavy attack?"

"Hell, no, mostly the dinks were letting us alone for a change. We were out in the middle of War Zone C, you know, most Christ-bitten stretch of country you ever saw. No dinks, no trees—they'd all been defoliated. Not a damn thing but dust and each other's company."

"Well, what did happen?" Richmond prompted impatiently. Traffic had thinned somewhat among the blocks of old buildings and he began to look for house numbers.

"Oh, mostly they just died." Morzek said. He yawned alcoholically. "Stevie, now, he got blown to hell by a grenade."

Richmond had learned when he was first assigned to notification duty not to dwell on the way his . . . missons had died. The possibilities varied from unpleasant to ghastly. He studiously avoided saying anything more to the sergeant beside him until he found the number he wanted. "One-sixteen. This must the the Lunkowskis."

Morzek got out on the curb side, looking more skeletal than before in the dappled sunlight. He still held his AWOL bag.

"You can leave that in the car," Richmond suggested. "I'll lock up."

"Naw, I'll take it in," the sergeant said as he waited for Richmond to walk around the car. "You know, this is every damn thing I brought from Nam? They didn't bother to open it at Travis, just asked me what I had in it. 'A quart of gin,' I told 'em, 'but I won't have it long.' and they waved me through to make my connections. One advantage to this kind of trip."

A bell chimed far within the house when Richmond pressed the button. It was cooler than he had expected on the pine-shaded porch. Miserable as these high, dark old houses were to heat, the design made a world of sense in the summer.

A light came on inside. The stained-glass window left of the door darkened and a latch snicked open. "Please to come in," invited a soft-voiced figure hidden by the dark oak panel. Morzek grinned inappropriately and led the way into the hall, brightly lighted by an electric chandelier.

"Mr. Lunkowski?" Richmond began to the wispy little man who had admitted them. "We are—"

"But yes, you are here to tell us when Stefan shall come back, are you not?" Lunkowski broke in. "Come into the sitting room, please. Anna and my daughter Rose are there."

"Ah, Mr. Lunkowski," Richmond tried to explain as he followed, all too conscious of the sardonic grin on Morzek's face. "You have been informed by telegram that Private Lunkowski was—"

"Was killed, yes," said the younger of the two red-haired women as she got up from the sofa. "But his body will come back to us soon, will he not? The man on the telephone said . . ."

She was gorgeous, Richmond thought, cool and assured, half smiling as her hair cascaded over her left shoulder like a thick copper conduit. Disconcerted as he was by the whole situation, it was a moment before he realized that Sergeant Morzek was saying, "Oh, the coffin's probably at the airport now, but there's nothing in it but a hundred and fifty pounds of gravel. Did the telegram tell you what happened to Stevie?"

"Sergeant!" Richmond shouted. "You drunken—"

"Oh, calm down, Captain," Morzek interrupted bleakly. "The Lunkowskis, they understand. They want to hear the whole story, don't they?"

"Yes." There was a touch too much sibilance in the word as it crawled from the older woman, Stefan Lunkowski's mother. Her hair was too grizzled now to have more than a touch of red in it, enough to rust the tight ringlets clinging to her skull like a helmet of mail. Without quiet appreciating its importance, Richmond noticed that Mr. Lunkowski was standing in front of the room's only door.

With perfect nonchalance, Sergeant Morzek sat down on an over-stuffed chair, laying his bag across his knees. "Well," he said, "there was quite a report on that one. We told them how Stevie was trying to booby-trap a white phosphorous grenade—fix it to go off as soon as some dink pulled the pin instead of four seconds later. And he goofed."

Mrs. Lunkowski's breath whistled out very softly. She said nothing. Morzek waited for further reaction before he smiled horribly and added. "He burned. A couple pounds of willie pete going blooie, well . . . it keeps burning all the way through you. Like I said, the coffin's full of gravel."

"My god, Morzek," the captain whispered. It was not the sergeant's savage grin that froze him but the icy-eyed silence of the three Lunkowskis.

"The grenade, that was real," Morzek concluded. "The rest of the re-port was a lie."

Rose Lunkowski reseated herself gracefully on a chair in front of the heavily draped windows. "Why don't you start at the beginning Sergeant?" she said with a thin smile that did not show her teeth. "There is much we would like to know before you are gone."

"Sure," Morzek agreed, tracing a mottled forefinger across the pig-mented callosities on his face. "Not much to tell. The night after Stevie got assigned to my platoon, the dinks hit us. No big thing. Had one fel-low dusted off with brass in his ankle from his machine gun blowing up, that was all. But a burst of AK fire knocked Stevie off his tank right at the start."

"What's all this about?" Richmond complained. "If he was killed by rifle fire, why say a grenade—"

"Silence!" The command crackled like heel plates on concrete.

Sergeant Morzek nodded. "Why, thank you, Mr. Lunkowski. You see, the captain there doesn't know the bullets didn't hurt Stevie. He told us his flak jacket had stopped them. It couldn't have and it didn't. I saw it that night, before he burned it—five holes to stick your fingers through, right over the breast pocket. But Stevie was fine, not a mark on him. Well, Christ, maybe he'd had a bandolier or ammo under the jacket. I had other things to think about."

Morzek paused to glance around his audience. "All this Well, Christ, maybe he'd had a bandolier of ammo under the Federal Building."

"You won't be long," the girl hissed in reply.

Morzek grinned. "They broke up the squadron, then," he rasped on, "gave each platoon a sector of War Zone C to cover to stir up the dinks. There's more life on the moon than there was on the stretch we patrolled. Third night out, one of the gunners died. They flew him back to Saigon for an autopsy but damned if I know what they found. Galloping malaria, we figured.

"Three nights later another guy died. Dawson on three-six . . . Christ, the names don't matter. Some time after midnight his track commander woke up, heard him moaning. We got him back to Quan Loi to a hospital, but he never came out of it. The lieutenant thought he got wasp stung on the neck—here, you know?" Morzek touched two fingers to his jugular. "Like he was allergic. Well, it happens."

"But what about Stefan?" Mrs. Lunkowski asked. "The others do not matter."

"Yes, finish it quickly, Sergeant," the younger woman said, and this time Richmond did catch the flash of her teeth.

"We had a third death," Morzek said agreeably, stroking the zipper of his AWOL bag back and forth. "We were all jumpy by then. I doubled the guard, two men awake on every track. Three nights later and nobody in the platoon remembered anything from twenty-four hundred hours till Riggs's partner blinked at ten of one and found him dead.

"In the morning, one of the boys came to me. He'd seen Stevie slip over to Riggs, he said; but he was zonked out on grass and didn't think it really had happened until he woke up in the morning and saw Riggs under a poncho. By then, he was scared enough to tell the whole story. Well, we were all jumpy."

"You killed Stefan." It was not a question but a flat statement.

"Oh, hell, Lunkowski," Morzek said absently, "what does it matter who rolled the grenade into his bunk? The story got around and . . . something had to be done."

"Knowing what you know, you came here?" Mrs. Lunkowski murmured liquidly. "You must be mad."

"Naw, I'm not crazy, I'm just sick." The sergeant brushed his left hand over his forehead. "Malignant melonoma, the docs told me. Twenty-six years in the goddamn army and in another week or two I'd be *warted* to death.

"Captain," he added, turning his cancerous face toward Richmond, "you better leave through the window."

"Neither of you will leave!" snarled Rose Lunkowski as she stepped toward the men.

Morzek lifted a fat gray cylinder from his bag. "Know what this is, honey?" he asked conversationally.

Richmond screamed and leaped for the window. Rose ignored him, slashing her hand out for the phosphorous grenade. Drapery wrapping the captain's body shielded him from glass and splintered window frame as he pitched out into the yard.

He was still screaming there when the blast of white fire bulged the walls of the house.

Valentine from a Vampire

🦇 🦇 🦇

by Daniel Ransom

1

There was only one way to do it, twenty-six-year-old Sam McBride told himself that gray February afternoon, and that was to plain and simple do it:

Pick her up in his Checker cab as he usually did at six o'clock and then, after she'd been riding a few blocks, say casually as possible, "You know, Ms. Ames, there's something I think you should know about the man you're going out with. He's a vampire."

So all afternoon, transporting fat old ladies and skinny old men and rude businessmen and fickle suburban housewives, Sam rehearsed his lines pretty much the way he'd memorized his part in the eighth grade play nearly fourteen years earlier (he'd played a Pilgrim)—by saying them over and over again until they'd lost all meaning. He tried variations on them, of course, trying to minimize the shock they would have on her—"Say, have you noticed your boyfriend's teeth?" or "Is this the first vampire you've ever gone out with?" or "Was that catsup all over your friend's mouth last night?"—so she wouldn't hate him for saying it. (Because hating him was the exact opposite of what he wanted her to do.)

But really, when you came right down to it, there wasn't any grace-

ful way to say it. Because when you came right down to it, calling
somebody a vampire was a pretty serious accusation.

Sam sighed and kept driving, thinking over his lonely womanless life
and what an odd business life was, the older you got. Sam, six foot,
slender, still gangly despite a deep voice and a need to shave twice a
day, had come to the city five years ago after finishing junior college
with an associate degree in retail. Unfortunately, his arrival coincided
with the recession and so he'd drifted into hacking, working for a man
who'd had his larynx removed and who now had to talk through one of
those buzzer jobbies that sounded like bad sci-fi sound effects. The
hack owner spoke just clearly enough for Sam to know he was a cheap-
skate.

The vampire, a man handsome as a screen star of the forties (complete with hair sleek as black ice), was named Karl Richards. Sam had
met him four years ago while hauling a young woman named Debbie
out to Richards's Dracula-like estate. He'd seen the way Debbie had
gone into the place—a real live American girl given to lots of chitchat
and some flirtiness—and how she'd come out. Debbie, pale, soft-spo-
ken now, was never the same again. He took her out there several times
afterward and then one day she stayed permanently, or at least she
didn't call in for a ride back to the city. He had no idea what had happened to her. Not then, anyway. All he knew for sure was that on Valentine's Day of that year her personality underwent a most curious
transformation.

Then came the next two Valentine's Days and two more women—one
named Janice, who had eyes soft as a young animal's, and one named
Stacey, who had remarkable legs—went in one way and came out the
other.

But even then Sam hadn't allowed himself to use the word. He just
said to himself that there were some weird doings involving drugs or
hypnotism or maybe even UFOs going on inside the vast walled estate.
Because even alien creatures with pop-eyes and no voice boxes were
easier to believe than—

—than vampires.

Then one night, cruising past the estate late with a drunken fare, Sam
had glimpsed something truly eerie at the gate of the place.

One moment Karl Richards had been standing there and the next moment . . . Karl Richards was gone.

Sam didn't know if he'd turned into a bat or a slug or an Avon lady, but he sure went somewhere and there was only one semihuman creature who could do anything like that and that was—

—a vampire.

Sam spent the next month sitting up nights recording all this material on his Sony recorder. He had vague notions of maybe going to the police but every morning that he got up with that thought on his mind, he started thinking of the cops he'd met through hacking and what hard cynical bastards they were and how they'd respond to somebody who told them there was a vampire living in the mansion on the southeastern edge of this Midwestern city.

Right.

Then this year, three weeks before Valentine's, Felicia Ames got in his cab and asked to be taken to the mansion, and just like that, Sam fell in love. She was a glowing blond model given to deep (and, he imagined, poetic) sighing and long blue gazes out the cab window at wintry trees and snow-capped waves slamming the concrete piers.

Every twenty minutes since meeting her he had mentally proposed. Every thirty minutes he thought about their having a child (he wanted a kid even if he wasn't quite sure what the hell he was going to do with the little bugger).

And every forty minutes he faced up to the terrible fact that on this Valentine's Day, tonight, sleazy Karl Richards was going to convert one more unwitting American girl into a creature of eternal darkness (or whatever they always said on those great Hammer films WTBS always ran at 2:00 A.M. every Friday night).

He was going to turn Felicia Ames into a vampire.

Or he thought he was, anyway.

But a hack driver named Sam McBride had different ideas.

2

"Hi, Sam."

"Hi, Ms. Ames."

"Gosh."

"What?"

"You think you'll ever stop?"

"Stop what?"

"Calling me 'Ms. Ames.' "

He flushed. "Oh. Right. I forgot. Felicia. I'm supposed to call you 'Felicia.' "

"Please."

So she sat back and he aimed the Checker into traffic, making the ride smooth as he could for her.

"Boy."

"What?" he asked.

"Long day. Whoever says modeling is a glamorous profession just doesn't know."

"Tired, huh?"

"Exhausted."

"Great."

"What?"

"I said, 'Late.' "

"Late?"

"I meant—after a long day, it's late. Maybe you shouldn't go to the mansion tonight. Maybe I should turn the cab around and take you to your apartment house. Maybe you're coming down with something, Felicia, and should go straight to bed." He said all this in a rush. He was hopeful she'd agree and he'd flip the cab around and race to her apartment and then stand guard all night to make sure that Richards didn't get in.

But now she laughed. "Oh, no. I'd never be too tired for tonight."

"Tonight?"

"Valentine's Day. Karl has promised me a very special gift."

Sam gulped. "You have any idea what it is?"

She laughed again, more softly this time. "No, but you can bet when

Karl Richards says a gift is going to be special, it's going to be *very* special."

He watched her in the rearview. Outside, gray night had fallen, the only lights red and blue and green neon reflected in dirty city snow. But in the rearview her face positively radiated. For a moment he did a dangerous thing—closed his eyes to say a silent prayer for courage.

The time had come.

She'd left him no choice.

He had to tell her the truth about Karl Richards.

"Gosh, Sam, look out!"

Snapping his eyes open, he saw that he was about to sideswipe a city bus that moved through the gloom like a giant electric caterpillar.

"Sam, are you all right?"

"Yes," he said. "But you're not."

"What?"

"I said you're not all right."

"Well, that's not a very nice thing to say."

"Oh, I didn't mean you're not all right OK. I meant you're not all right—you're in danger."

"Danger?"

"Felicia, would you let me buy you a cup of coffee?"

"But, Sam, I told Karl—"

He turned around and said, "Felicia, there's something you should know about Karl."

"Oh, Sam, I know what you're going to say." She sounded young and disappointed. "That he's a playboy. That he'll drop me as soon as he's bored and it won't be long before that happens." She touched him on the shoulder and a wonderful warmth spread through his entire body. She'd never touched him this way before. "It's just a storybook fling, the only one I've ever allowed myself. Really. In high school I didn't have time because I was always a cheerleader and trotting off to games. In college I didn't have time because my parents were poor and I had to work my way through. And during my first five years of modeling I didn't have time because I had to take every job that was offered me. Don't you see, Sam, this is my one chance at really having a good time. That's all."

Sam pulled into the parking lot of a McDonald's. Against the gray

night it looked like a big colorful toy box filled with tiny people walking around inside.

"Felicia, there's something I've got to tell you and I guess I have to
do it right here, without even waiting to go inside, right in front of
Ronald McDonald and everything."

"Gosh, Sam, what's so urgent?"

"Karl."

"Karl's urgent?"

"No," Sam said, "Karl's a vampire."

3

They got Cokes and Sam got french fries and they took the most isolated
table they could find, right on a plastic outsize Egg McMuffin who had
two red eyes and kept winking at Sam.

"Vampire," Felicia said. "Gosh, Sam, that's really the most original
one I've heard yet."

"Original what?"

"Oh," she said, "line, I guess you'd call it. I mean, I'm flattered." She
startled him by putting her hand over his and gazing blue into his eyes.
"You're a very nice guy, Sam, and over the past few weeks, we've really gotten to know each other in a strange way. And if Karl wasn't in
the picture—" She withdrew her hand and shook her wonderful blond
head and laughed. "But to be honest, Sam, calling him a vampire is
going overboard, don't you think? How about a drug dealer? Or Com-
munist spy? Or even a pornographer? But a vampire?" Then the smile
faded from her eyes. "Sam, you don't really believe in vampires, do
you?"

"I didn't."

"Didn't?"

"Till I took Debbie and Janice and Stacey out to his mansion on
Valentine's Day and they changed."

"Changed?"

"Yes," Sam said, "changed."

So he told her, in detail, how they'd changed. The chalky skin. The dead eyes. The sullen silence. "Vampires," Sam said.

She took one of his french fries and nibbled at it. She'd explained to him once that she always nibbled at food. To keep her weight for the camera, that was the most pleasure she could allow herself—nibbling.

"Have you ever been heartbroken, Sam? Wanted somebody you couldn't have?"

He stared at her. "Uh, yes."

"Do you remember how you acted?"

"Acted?"

"The depression, the weight loss, the long silences? That's what you're describing here, Sam, nothing more. Karl decided it was time to get rid of these women and move on to new ones, so he dropped them and that was how they reacted."

"Then why would they keep going back to the mansion?"

"Why, to plead their cases. Beg him to reconsider." She had another french fry. "You've been heartbroken before, haven't you, Sam? You do know what I'm talking about?"

Without hesitation, he said it, "Felicia, I'm heartbroken right now."

"You are?"

"Yes. Over you."

She blushed. For all her beauty and sophistication, Sam had found Felicia to be not only modest about her looks but just as socially vulnerable as he was himself. "Oh, Sam." She put her hand back on his. "That's really sweet and I really appreciate it but—right now there's Karl."

"Please let me take you back to your apartment tonight, Felicia. Just till after Valentine's Day passes. He's got something about Valentine's Day."

"Sam, listen, please." She sat back in the seat. "As I've tried to explain, I know this is just a fling and nothing more. But I'm enjoying it. I like being in a grand house where there are servants out of the nineteenth century and where classical music is always playing and where you sit on Louis XVI furniture and where you sip French wine from huge goblets in front of a roaring fireplace and where your tall, dark, handsome lover wears a red silk dinner jacket and speaks to you in a

voice that gives you goose bumps." She laughed. "For a girl whose father ran a corner grocery store, Sam, that's pretty heady stuff."

So Sam, seeing the odds he had to overcome, said it: "He disappeared."

"What?"

"Vanished. Did you ever see the original *Dracula?*"

She sighed. "Oh, Sam, please. It isn't fun anymore. This vampire
thing, I mean. It really isn't."

"He did, Felicia." He raised his hand like a Boy Scout. "On my love
for you, I swear it. One second, he was in my rearview and then he just
disappeared. Vanished. The only people who can do that are vampires."

A certain pity had come into her eyes now. "Sam, would you take me
out to the mansion—and would you do me a favor?"

"Anything. You know that."

"Just don't talk about this anymore, please. Because I am starting to
get scared—but not for myself—for you. I hope you're just saying all
this because you love me and want to start seeing me. I hope you're not
saying it because—" And here, for the first time, she looked uncomfortable. "Because you truly believe it, because then—"

"Then what?"

"Then I'd say you needed to see a shrink or something."

4

Gates of black iron covered the entrance to the mansion. Ground fog
shone silver in the light of a half-moon. Beyond the massive stone walls
light from mullioned windows spread yellow across the snow.

"I guess I should go in now."

They'd been sitting in his cab for twenty minutes now—the radio
tuned low to an FM station playing some soft Stanley Clarke songs—
and really not talking much at all.

It was just that every time she started to put her hand on the door handle, he turned around and said, "Please, Felicia, please don't go."

He's said it four times now and four times she had complied.

But he knew this time—hand on the door, a kind of pity in her eyes—
that she would go.

"Felicia, I—"

"I really do have to go."

"He's a vampire, Felicia. Honest and truly."

"You're sweet, Sam. You really are. You care about me so much
and—"

Then she startled him by leaning forward and kissing him gently on
the lips.

His mind literally spun; his heart was a wild animal.

"Felicia, please—"

But then the back door opened and the dome light went on, exposing
the shabby insides of the cab, the battered dash and the smudged seat
covers and the big red, white, and blue thermos he carried coffee in. This
was his life—the life of a shabby hack in a shabby cab. He guessed he
couldn't blame her (his eyes rising to see the imposing mansion against
the gray night sky) for wanting the type of life Karl Richards offered.

Except Karl Richards was a vampire.

"Felicia—"

This time she touched a finger to her lips and then touched that same
finger to his lips and then she was gone, lost in fog, the gates opening
automatically now that she'd inserted the access card Richards provided
all his women.

Debbie.

Janice.

Stacey.

Gone.

"Felicia!" he cried but already the gates were creaking open and then
creaking closed and she was lost to him forever.

5

His were the particular pleasures of the lonely. He could eat what he
wanted (Snickers, Fritos, Good 'N Plentys) and watch what he wanted.
(Tonight, unable to sleep, thinking of what was happening to Felicia,

he started watching *Twins of Evil* but switched channels as soon as the vampire theme started getting oppressive, and then tuned into the Home Shoppers Channel, a subculture even more fascinating than professional wrestling or professional religion. Who waned to buy a George Washington clock that recited the names of the first thirteen colonies over and over again? Apparently thousands of people did, and at $48.31 apiece. He had purchased only one thing from the Shoppers Channel, a genuine longbow with quiver and arrows. Over the past six months the bow had become his sole hobby. He was reasonably good with it.) Finally, fitfully, he slept on the couch of his drab efficiency apartment.

Then it was morning, the sky a light shade of gray. He shaved, showered, ate his bran, did his sit-ups, and then said an Our Father and three Hail Marys for Felicia. This was around 7:30. Around 8:30 he called the modeling agency where she worked, and said he was her brother (did she even have a brother?) and asked if he could find out where she was working today and, after only a teensy bit of hesitation, the woman gave him the address and even the phone number where Felicia could be found so her brother (in from Egypt; what the hell—if you lie, lie big) could surprise her.

So he promptly called the photography studio where she was on location today and was surprised to learn that she was there.

She hadn't called in sick.

She hadn't just mysteriously vanished.

She was there.

Working.

Could he possibly speak to her?

"Afraid not. We're in the middle of a bitch of a production problem here and she's really tied up. If you'd care to leave your number, though, we could have her call you back."

Baffled, Sam said, "No thanks. Thank you." And hung up.

The rest of the morning, before he had to start hacking (you had to average seventy hours a week behind the wheel if you wanted to reach even the official poverty level of income), he went to the laundromat and to the supermarket and to the video rental store and then to the submarine place where he got this salami hogie that could have fed a Third World nation.

Somewhere in the middle of all this, he had started to whistle and the rest of the day he whistled his ass off because she'd proved him wrong and there was nothing he'd wanted more than to be proved wrong.

Karl Richards might be a jerk-off but he wasn't a vampire.

And eventually he'd dump her and then she'd go through a period of heartbreak and then she'd entrust the rest of her life to Sam.

At least, that was the notion that got Sam to whistling and kept him whistling all day.

Around two he went down to the cab company, to the underground garage that always stank of wet concrete, and said a few words to the man without a voice box and then got in his cab and started his workday.

The first two hours went slowly. There was a chatty plump woman going to the hospital to see her herniated husband. There was a somber priest who made a magnificent sign of the cross whenever they passed a Catholic church. And there was a very tiny woman who smoked those 100 mm. cigarettes and coughed so hard she jumped around on the backseat.

Then came February dusk, lights up in stores, people slanting into the bitter wind running to garages and bus stops, and then he thought of a wonderful idea.

He knew just where Felicia was.

Knew roughly what time she'd get off.

Why not go wait for her there?

Which is what he did, still whistling all the time, shaping the words of his apology, getting ready to laugh a lot about his stupid notion that Karl Richards was a vampire.

The studio was on the northwest part of town, in a forlorn section of the city. He was parked at the curb for nearly an hour before he began to think that maybe the session had ended early and she'd gone home.

Ten minutes later he sat up and was all ready to go when he saw her in the rearview coming out of the door.

Behind him, suddenly a yellow cab pulled up.

She'd phoned for somebody else.

He jumped from the car and over the roof and yelled, "Felicia! Tell him to go on and let me give you a ride!"

She saw him, of course, and recognized him. But she started to get into the yellow cab anyway.

He ran over to her, grabbed her slender wrist before she could close the door.

"I'll take her," Sam said to the angry-looking cabbie. Sam flung a ten-dollar bill at the man. Then he tugged on Felicia's arm and said, "Come on. Please. All right?"

She sighed, looked embarrassed that the cabman was watching them, and then said softly, "All right."

So she got out of one cab and got in another, and then Sam ran around and got behind the wheel and had them in traffic in moments.

"You going home or to the mansion tonight?"

"The mansion."

He shook his head and said, laughing at himself, "I don't want you to hold it against me."

"Hold what against you?"

"Come on, Felicia. You know—my theory about Karl Richards being a vampire."

"That's the trouble," Felicia said and began suddenly and madly to sob. "You were right. He *is* a vampire."

6

For the next two hours they drove through every part of the city imaginable. Past glum slums and palaces; through shopping districts and industrial zones; and along the river where ice shone like glass in moonlight.

Sometimes she talked, though little of it made sense, but mostly she alternated between sniffling and sobbing and staring out the window.

Then she slept.

The radio off, the cab gliding along two-lane asphalt, the only man-made object in sight a radio tower with a single red warning line at its top—in this silence her snoring was reassuring because he thought, She can't be a vampire: vampires don't sleep at night.

Karl Richards might have hypnotized her, or voodoo'd her, or drugged her, but he hadn't turned her into a vampire.

He drove and was hungry suddenly and thought of how good a big slice of double cheese pizza would taste along with a cold mug of beer.

"Have you looked in your rearview mirror yet?" she asked, sounding muzzy with sleep.

"Huh?"

"Your mirror. You still don't believe me, do you, Sam? So look back at me and then look in your mirror."

So he did. Turned around and saw her looking beautiful if slightly mussed in the backseat. Then turned around and looked for her image in the rearview.

And saw nothing.

"My God."

"Pretty crazy, huh?"

"My God," he said again.

"Imagine how I feel," she said, and started sniffling again.

"Then he really did bite you on the—"

"On the arm."

"the arm?"

"It's harder to see the puncture wound on the arm. He laughed about it afterwards. He said the whole world would know there were vampires if all these women walked around with big blue holes in their necks. Here."

She pushed her lovely right arm over the front seat and then pulled up her sleeve and, after pulling up a Band-Aid, showed it to him. By now the teeth marks had scabbed over into what appeared to be a very bad infection of some kind.

"So that," she said, "was my very special Valentine's gift."

"Why does he do it on Valentine's Day?"

"Because that's when he became a vampire. Four hundred years ago. In London. He's sentimental about the day." She sighed. "I have to admit that part was fascinating."

"What part?"

"Hearing about London four hundred years ago."

"He talked to you?"

"Oh, sure. I mean, after I woke up from the bite—it put me out an hour or so—and after he got me calmed down, we had a pretty regular night. He made dinner—we had shrimp with black bean sauce; he's a great cook—an then we listened to his big band records and then we talked. Except now he was free to tell the truth about himself, including

what London was like in those days." Then suddenly she broke into sobs
again.

"Why are you crying? Except for getting turned into a vampire, it
sounds like a pretty wonderful night." He heard jealousy in his voice.

"Because I haven't told you everything."

"What's everything?"

"That I'm part of his entourage now. Forever."

"His entourage?"

She had to stop crying to tell him. He took a small box of Kleenex
from the front seat and handed it back to her. He looked in the rearview
again just in case the first time had been a fluke.

It hadn't been.

"He has more than thirty women living there at the mansion. They're
pretty regular women, for the most part—everything considered, I mean.
He keeps them healthy and beautiful and he uses them for sustenance and
he uses them for sex and everything's fine as long as he gradually re-
plenishes the supply by adding a new one very Valentine's Day. It's really not a bad life if you like total security—but I hate it, Sam. Already I
hate it."

"He has a harem."

"Yes," she said, "that's exactly what it is, Sam, a harem. He's the ultimate male chauvinist. He calls us vampirettes."

"But I thought vampires—"

"Skulked around alleys? Preyed on young women in the fog? Perched
on window ledges disguised as bats?"

"But the night I saw him disappear—"

"It's because you looked in your rearview mirror. The thing about
turning yourself into a bat is strictly comic-book stuff. Anyway, he's
very squeamish about bugs and rodents and such. Unnaturally so." She
paused and stared out the window at the silver hills again.

"I'm going to help you," he said.

"Sam, that's sweet, it really is. But you can't help me."

"There's got to be something—"

"What? Go to the authorities? Even if you did prove to their satisfaction he was a vampire, you'd be dooming me the rest of my life—and
it's going to be a long one, Sam, it really is—to being kept in a prison
somewhere by the authorities. No, Sam." She leaned up and touched his

shoulder. "Please don't do anything. You'd probably only make it worse." She paused. "Do you know what time it is?"

"Eight thirty-five."

"Gosh, you'd better get me back to the mansion."

"I thought maybe we could have something to eat. A pizza or something."

"I'd like to but he's very strict about hours."

"Hours?"

"He runs the place like a dorm. We all keep our jobs—sleeping all day is another myth—but we have to be back at the mansion by nine or we get demerits."

"You're kidding."

"No, he's got this big chart in his den. He puts stars by your name—gold if you've been great, blue if you've been good, black if you've been bad."

"What happens if you get black?"

"I don't know and I'm afraid to find out."

So, not wanting her to get a black star, he broke speed limits getting back to the mansion.

It was 8:57 when he pulled up in front of the iron gates.

He said, "God, Felicia, I've got to see you again. I do."

"Even though I'm a vampire?"

"Felicia, you could be a werewolf and I wouldn't care. I really wouldn't."

"Oh, Sam," she said, and brought her face to his and kissed him tenderly on the cheek. She felt a few degrees cooler than most human beings, but that was about the only difference.

She looked up at the mansion's spires against the gold disc of moon. "Gosh," she said, "I wish we could go back to my apartment. We could order in a pizza and snuggle up on the couch and—" She started crying again. "If only I'd listened to you, Sam."

"You'd better hurry, Felicia," he said. "I don't want you to get a black star."

Miserably, she nodded. "You're right."

As she got out of the car and the dome light came on, he took her arm and said, "I love you, Felicia."

And she said what he'd waited so long to hear in return. "The weird thing is, as soon as I came to last night, the first person I thought about

was you, Sam. Even before I thought about my parents or my cats or my
lovebirds." She smiled sadly. "I guess that must mean I love you, too."
Then she was gone.

7

The next day he called the modeling agency to find out where she was
working this time, but the woman on the other end said, "Is this her
brother again?"

"Uh, yes."

"I checked her files. She doesn't have a brother."

"Oh."

She hung up.

He spent the two hours before work at the library riffling through
books on vampires—they had a surprising number of such volumes—
but soon discovered that most of them did little more than promote
myths. In books, vampires skulked in alleys, preyed on fog-en-
shrouded young women, turned themselves into bats. They didn't—
unlike the only vampire Sam knew—cook gourmet meals, play
Tommy Dorsey records and give his thirty girl friends black stars for
bad behavior.

He left the library and raced to a pay phone. He got the modeling
agency on the phone again—the same woman. As she answered, he slid a
handkerchief across the receiver and said, "This is Lieutenant Carstairs
from the Fourth Precinct. We need to get in touch with one of your models. A Miss—" He paused, pretending to be looking at a notepad. "A
Miss—"

"It's you again, isn't it?"

"Huh?"

"You. The so-called brother. The pest. We've got enough creeps both-
ering our girls. We don't need any more."

She slammed down the receiver.

8

That night he sat in front of the mansion, watching the ground fog wrap itself around the turrets and spires of the great stone house, hoping she'd try to make some kind of escape and would come rushing out to the gate.

She didn't and Sam just sat there drinking Diet Pepsis, and then getting out of the cab and taking a pee in thick mulberry bushes where the occupants of passing cars couldn't see him, and then getting back inside the cab for more of his lonely vigil.

Two hours later he ended up on his couch eating Ding-Dongs with skim milk and watching *The Tall T* with Randolph Scott. He fell asleep with a box of Cracker Jacks on his stomach.

In the morning, exhausted, he put on the only tie he owned and went up to the modeling agency where Felicia worked. He also brought a small spiral tablet. A 35 mm. camera was slung over his tan corduroy jacket.

The woman was about what he'd expected—short, overly made-up, with a dark-eyed gaze that could melt diamonds. "Yes?" she snapped when he went to take his place at the reception counter.

"I'm Bryant from the *Times*. I'm supposed to interview one of your models: Felicia Ames."

"The *Times?* The *New York Times?*"

He smiled. "I wish my paper was that important. No, I'm afraid I'm with *Modeling Times*." He hoped that his self-effacing smile would convince her he was telling the truth.

"Never heard of it."

"That's because we haven't published our first issue yet."

Then the woman did something odd. She sat back in her chair, closed her eyes, and put her fingertips to her temples. "Say something."

"What?"

"Say something."

"What do you want me to—"

"It's you!" she said. "The fake brother. The phoney cop. Now, you get out of here!"

She stood up and pointed to the door, and he had no choice but to comply.

The rest of the day he drove his cab, taking every chance to cruise by the three studios where she normally worked, but finding no sign of her.

That night he took up his vigil at the mansion again. Around midnight he thought he heard a scream, faint behind the fog, but he couldn't be sure if it was only his imagination and his exhaustion.

On the couch he watched *This Island Earth* with Jeff Morrow and a woman who'd been a real babe named Faith Domergue, and fell asleep with a box of Screaming Yellow Zonkers on his chest.

He didn't wake till nearly noon and was therefore in a hurry, shaving while he peed, ironing a shirt while he ate his bran.

He was fifteen minutes late starting his shift. The man without the voice box laid some very angry sci-fi effects on him.

There were skinny people, black people, white people, pudgy people, straight people, gay people, nice-looking people, repellent people, pleasant people, surly people—it was one of those inexplicably busy days. He didn't really get an opportunity to buzz past the studios where she generally worked and it was nearly eleven o'clock before he got to the mansion where he sat for twenty minutes and dozed off.

The stress of the past three days, plus the late hours, had drained him.

He went home and lay on the couch again, the movie tonight being one of his favorites, *D.O.A.* with Edmond O'Brien, who'd been the chunkiest leading man Sam had ever seen, but he was asleep even before the doomed Edmond realized he'd been fatally poisoned. A sack of chip-dip–flavored Lay's potato chips next to his head.

The pounding started around 4:00 A.M. At first he thought it was part of a nightmare he couldn't wake up from.

Pounding.

Finally, still thinking he was acting out a role in a nightmare, he got up and stumbled to the door, clumsily taking off the three security locks, and at last seeing who stood there.

Felicia.

Tears streaming down her face.

A small overnight bag in her left hand.

"Sam," she sobbed. "Sam, may I move in with you?"

9

Two hours later, over a pepperoni pizza delivered steaming hot, she said, "I don't blame you if you're scared of me."

"Why would I be scared of you?"

"Well . . ." she said, and stopped eating.

"Felicia—" he began, and put his hand out to her.

But she stopped him. "There's a very good possibility I'm a vampire."

"But you look fine. You look wonderful, in fact."

"I'm pale."

"Sure you're pale. But you've also been under a great strain."

"And this pizza is the first thing I've eaten in two days."

"It's just the stress really. I read a magazine article on stress and—"

"I don't want to—"

He stared at her. "To what?"

"To get you involved in this any more than you are already."

"But, Felicia, I love you and you love me."

She started sniffling again. "But maybe it's not enough."

He sprang to the couch and sat next to her. "I know this isn't much." His hand swept the drab apartment, the dated posters from the seventies, the collection of sci-fi and horror paperbacks in orange crates, and the longbow and its attendant paraphernalia. "But we'll move. Arizona. New Mexico. Oregon. Someplace, Felicia—someplace where we can get started on a new life. And—"

She put her head on his shoulder and drew him into her. "But I'm a vampire."

"Everybody's got things wrong with them, Felicia. Everybody."

"But being a vampire is more than just something wrong."

So he kissed her because it was the only way to keep her quiet. In the course of the kiss, he realized how much he loved her. It was frightening—far more than vampires could ever be.

"I'll go to the bank tomorrow and draw out my savings and then we'll go to the bus depot and we'll leave for New Mexico. He'll never find us there."

She sighed. "That's what scares me."

"What?"

"I don't think he'll give up so easily."

"Felicia, I promise. He won't even remember you."

"Oh, Sam," she said, drawing closer to him for another kiss, "I sure hope you're right."

"I am right, Felicia, I promise." Then he paused and gulped and said, "Felicia, I—"

She smiled at him. "I know. Me too." Then she said, "Do you really think we're going to be together, Sam?"

"Always."

"You're not just saying that?"

"I promise you, Felicia. I promise you."

For purposes of lovemaking and sleep, Sam decided to give her the royal treatment. He turned the sofa into a bed and dug out his only set of clean sheets from a cardboard box filled with a reasonably complete collection of Jonah Hex comic books.

The lovemaking was tender, and immediately afterward, she fell asleep in his embrace, there in the long shadows of the tiny apartment, the nimbus of streetlight like faded gold against the cracked west window, traffic sounds faint in the night.

Sam wondered: Could it really end this happily? This easily? Karl Richards just handing her over to him?

But eventually, no matter how compelling his doubts, he fell asleep, too, as crazy in love as he'd ever been, the woman in his arms all the things a woman was capable of being—lover, friend, sister, partner, conspirator.

His last waking thought was of how wonderful life could be.

He was asleep maybe twenty minutes before a sound woke him. Through one groggily opened eye, he saw Felicia in silhouette at the window. She was putting her clothes on.

"Felicia—what's wrong?"

Nothing. She said nothing. Just continued to dress.

"Felicia?"

He threw the covers back and went over to her. He wore nothing but jockey shorts.

He got around in front of her and put both his hands on her shoulders and started shaking her. He forced her face up so he could see her expression in the deep night shadows.

Her eyes were dark vacuums. All he could think of was some kind of hypnosis or mind control or—

Then he moved over to the window rimed with silver frost around the edges and looked down into the street. A long black limousine sat beneath the streetlight. A tall, slender man dressed in a black topcoat stood outside the limo. He stared directly up at Sam's apartment.

The man was Karl Richards.

"No, Felicia!" Sam screamed. "Don't go with him! Don't go with him!"

He dashed to the sink, soaked a towel in cold water, came back to her, and pressed the icy cloth against her face.

Dimly, he saw recognition in her eyes.

"Felicia?"

"Yes." She sounded robotic.

"If you go with him, you'll never be free again. Do you understand, Felicia?"

"Yes."

"Then fight back. Resist the thoughts he's sending out." He shook her hard. "Fight back, Felicia. You want to stay here with me. We'll leave for New Mexico in just a few hours. You'll be safe and happy and loved and—"

And then she let out an animal roar that paralyzed him.

He could not imagine such a sound coming from this beautiful woman.

Nor could he imagine a woman—or a man, for that matter—possessing the sheer physical strength she displayed: she took him by the shoulder and flung him across the room, slamming him into the wall where the longbow hung.

The back of his head cracked against the plaster hard enough that a darkness even deeper than the night began to spread before his eyes and . . .

Just before tumbling into unconsciousness, he heard the terrible animal roar she'd made earlier . . . and then he heard his apartment door flung back . . . footsteps down the creaking wooden steps and . . .

And then, despite every effort, he felt himself pulled inevitably down into the waiting gloom that was not unlike death.

When he woke, his teeth were chattering from the cold. His head hurt him worse than the worst hangover he'd ever had.

The window was purple-gold with dawn glowing through the frost.

The room, always a mess, was now a shambles, evidence of the strength she'd suddenly shown.

He needed clothes and he needed coffee and he needed to very carefully think through—

If he hadn't been right next to the fallen longbow, maybe the idea would never have come to him. But as he started to push himself to his feet, his fingers touched the sleek wood, the curving bow, and right then—right there in his jockey shorts and needing very badly to pee— he got the idea.

And it was a wonderful idea, and he knew it was a wonderful idea as soon as he had it.

It was the idea that was going to win him Felicia back once and for all.

10

"Peace," Albert Carney said when Sam entered his carpentry shop three hours later. Albert, a fat and unkempt man with wild hair and beard turning gray these days, wiped pudgy fingers on his bib overalls and flashed Sam the V sign for peace, the way people used to greet others back in the sixties. He looked as if he hadn't shaved, bathed, or slept for several months.

Sam always thought of Albert as the last of the hippies, the one person he knew who would never give up the flower-power era. For instance, now the air was being stirred by the slashing sounds of Jefferson Airplane singing "White Rabbit" on the cassette deck. The shop, which was really a large, converted garage that smelled sweetly of wood shavings, was decorated with posters of people such as Ken Kesey, Allen Ginsberg, and Jerry Rubin. Nobody could ever accuse Albert Carney of giving up the faith.

Albert picked up a tiny marijuana roach, lit it, toked deep and true, then offered the clip to Sam.

Sam shook his head. "How's business?"

Albert nodded to various pieces of cabinetry in various stages of carpentering or staining. "Enough to last me a couple lifetimes." He smiled with teeth that would have required two dentists to get clean and then said, "Say—you're goin' to be haulin' me around Saturday night. Big sixties festival down at the Freak."

The Freak was a beer and wine bar near the railroad depot, where once a month they had a sixties night. Albert, who didn't want to get busted for drunk driving, always had Sam haul him back and forth in the cab. That's how they'd met.

"Be glad to, Albert."

Albert had another toke. "So what brings you here, man? Especially with that bow. That mother looks fierce!"

"It is fierce, Albert. Very fierce. And that's why I need to talk to you. I need to make it even fiercer."

"How you gonna do that?"

"With your help, I'm going to make a very special kind of arrow."

"What kind would that be, Sam?"

"It's got to be a wooden stake that I can notch in my bow and shoot."

"A wooden stake?" Albert laughed, taking the final toke. "What you gonna hunt—vampires?"

Sam laughed right along with him. "You think you can do it?"

Albert shrugged. "Probably."

"It would have to be able to pierce—armor."

"That's why the English invented the longbow. So it could do just that." He took the bow, examined it. "That shouldn't be any problem."

"How long?"

"How long?"

"Yeah, how long will it take?"

"Well, I'd have to use the lathe and then fire-harden it and—"

"Albert, I need this arrow by six o'clock tonight."

"You're kidding."

"I'm not, Albert."

"God."

"Albert, it's life and death."

Albert looked him over. "You look real strung out, man."

"I wish I could tell you."

Albert looked at him and said, "OK, man. The number of times you've kept me out of the drunk tank, I guess this is the least I can do

for you." He nodded to the lathe. "You come back here at six tonight and
I'll have it ready for you."

Sam put his hand on Albert's shoulder. "I wish there was some way I
could repay you."

"There is, man."

"What's that?"

"Tell me the truth about why you want this arrow."

Sam laughed again, though the sound was obviously strained. "Like
you said, I'm going to go hunting vampires."

But this time Albert didn't laugh. "You know, man, I'm beginning to
wonder if you're not serious."

11

Sam spent the afternoon taking care of passengers. It seemed important
to him to stay calm. What lay before him tonight required not only skill
and luck but steady nerves.

Whether talking to the rich dowager who always told him about her
son-in-law the songwriter ("Kenny Rogers calls him all the time just to
talk") or taking Mr. Gunderson to his doctor's appointment ("I'm eighty-
two and they want to know why I don't feel so good—and that's why I
don't feel so good, because I'm eighty-two that's why, the stupid
bastids")—whatever he did, his mind remained on the plan, or, as his
mind thought of it. The Plan.

Last night, summoned to the waiting limo by Karl Richards, Felicia
had forgotten her purse in which resided the electronic access card that
would let whoever possessed it inside the walled estate.

The card now rested in Sam's shirt pocket.

Four dragged by; five to six crawled: it was time to go to Albert's.

This time the cassette machine played Neil Young singing "My Old
Man" and Albert had himself a much more formidable joint than the little roach he'd sported before.

This one was fat enough to last for a couple hours of watching a light
show.

"Here you go," Albert said, toking up.

What he handed Sam looked like a small tree that had been shaved down to the size of a baseball bat.

"Sure hope that bow of yours can handle this," Albert said.

"No problem," Sam said, holding the huge arrow. The feathers near the end of the nock were bright yellow.

"Though I'd kind of dress it up," Albert said. "What do you think of the point?"

Pure wood, the point pricked Sam's finger at the slightest touch. A drop of blood appeared.

"Kind of heavy duty, wouldn't you say?"

"Sam, if I was into kissing guys, I'd plant a big one on your cheek." He dug into his back pocket for his wallet. "What do I owe you?"

"I already told you."

"The cab ride?"

"Right."

"You got it."

Now so intent on his mission that he even forgot to say good-bye, Sam took the arrow and started to leave the garage.

"Hey," Albert said.

Sam turned around. "Oh, yeah. sorry. Shoulda said good-bye."

"No, not that," Albert said.

"What then?"

"Put the tip of it up by your nose."

Sam angled the long, pointed shaft of fire-hardened wood to his nose.

Immediately, he pulled the arrow away from his nostrils. "Whew. What'd you dip it in, anyway? Sheep dung?"

Albert looked very proud of himself. "What else? Garlic."

12

There was an electronic buzz and then the black grillwork of the gates parted and Sam went inside.

In the silver fog that lay across the land so heavily all he could see of the mansion was a single spire silhouetted against the round yellow disc of moon, Sam moved cautiously to the house.

Now that the gates had been opened, Karl Richards would be expecting somebody. Probably one of the women, done with her day's work.

Sam had to move quickly, and did, his feet making sucking sounds in the damp grass, the sound of his heart huge in his ears.

After ten minutes, he reached what appeared to be a large screened-in veranda. He tried the door—locked.

From his pocket he took a switchblade, clicked it open. He tore a four-foot gash in the screening and then went inside, carrying his longbow carefully in one hand, the arrow carefully in the other.

He crossed a flagstone walkway filled with summer furniture that looked dirty and cold on this winter's night. He went up three steps to a door that would take him inside. He put his hand on the knob and then whispered a prayer before turning it. If it was only open—

Locked.

Glancing wildly around, he saw a window three feet off the veranda floor. He went over to it, pulling a deck chair with him. Standing on the tarpaulin seat, he peeked through the window. What he saw was a shadowy hallway at the far end of which appeared to be a vast living room filled with Victorian antiques.

He said the same prayer he'd said before. This time his luck was better. The window eased open and he dropped inside the mansion.

He lay in the shadows, smelling furniture polish and floor wax and the remnants of a dinner that had included some kind of spaghetti sauce. Only after ten minutes did he make his move.

The living room—vast with a vaulted ceiling and huge fireplace—proved empty, as did an adjacent room which was filled with what looked like original oils by Degas and Chagall.

Carefully, he made his way through the first floor: dining room; kitchen; sewing room; den. Nothing.

Then from upstairs he heard the scream.

Racing to the bottom of a staircase that fanned wider as it stretched in carpeted splendor to the second level, Sam gulped and prepared himself for the confrontation that had been inevitable since the first time he'd dropped Felicia off at the mansion.

He crept up the stairs, the sound of an angry male voice growing louder the higher he went.

A wide corridor with walls of flocked red wallpaper; a large flattering portrait of Karl Richards himself decked out in a black suit and high white collar (eyes glistening as blackly as his hair); a partially opened door through which the man's voice came—these were the first things Sam saw.

Hefting the wooden crossbow, he got up on tiptoe and edged to the door.

Inside he saw a large group of women, dressed in everything from baby doll pajamas to diaphanous negligees, gathered in a circle in the center of a huge room appointed, as the living room was, with Victorian furnishings.

Pacing back and forth before the women was a tall man in a red silk dinner jacket and black slacks. He was flawlessly handsome and flawlessly angry.

"I want obedience!" he snapped. "Not mere compliance!" He paused and said in a lower yet curiously more menacing tone, "None of you can escape me—so why not obey me!"

"We're people, too," a strawberry blond with wonderful breasts said. "We have rights."

"You are *not* people," Karl Richards said. "You are vampires."

"So you're not even going to listen to our petition about forming a committee to change some of the rules?"

"I am the absolute master!" Richards screamed. "Not only the master of darkness—but the master of this house."

It was then that Sam saw Felicia. She sat near the back. She wore a modest blue cotton nightgown that made her look little-girlish and all the more beautiful.

She chose that moment to look up and when she did so, she saw Sam.

He held up the bow and arrow for her to see and then touched a finger to his lips, sshhhing her.

"There will be no more talk about committees or changing the rules or anything!" Karl Richards said. "And to prove it, I want all of you girls in bed within fifteen minutes—with the lights out."

Sam gulped.

The moment was here.

He notched the arrow, gulped, said another silent prayer, kicked the door open, and pulled back on the bowstring.

Karl Richards did just what Sam had hoped he would. Startled by the door's flying open, the vampire turned around to face Sam.

And Sam let go the stake that had been shaved into an arrow.

Richards, seeing what was about to happen, grabbed a nearly naked woman who had been standing a few inches from him—and pushed her into the path of the arrow.

She twisted as the stake went deep into her heart. The noise she made was nearly intolerable to Sam.

Then Karl Richards went crazy.

Teeth the size of wolf fangs appeared in the corners of his mouth, and his lips began to drip silver saliva.

"Oh gosh, Sam, now he'll get you for sure!" he heard Felicia shout.

The idea had occurred to Sam.

As Richards moved forward, hands turning into talons now, Sam backed up against the staircase until there was no place he could go unless he jumped the considerable distance to the first floor.

"You have enraged me long enough!" shouted Richards, his face distorted by rage and spittle.

Behind Richards, Sam could see the fallen woman, the arrow sticking up out of her bloody chest like a lance.

He shouted to Felicia: "Pull the arrow out and bring it to me!"

It was then that Richards's talons shredded through Sam's cheeks.

Sam spent the next two minutes dodging the taller and more athletic man, running down the hallway, only to be tripped—then pinned down, only to squirm free at the last moment.

He did not notice Felicia until Richards had backed him up against a corner.

"Here, Sam!" she called and threw him the arrow.

It fell two feet short of Sam's grasp.

Richards, cursing, bent to pick up the arrow. "I'll break it in half and then I'll do the same to you!"

But as he stooped, Sam sprang from the corner and kicked him hard on the side of the face, sending Richards awkwardly to his knees.

Sam snatched up the arrow and notched it for the second time in the bowstring. It was sticky with the woman's blood.

Then Sam let go the giant arrow. It ripped through the vampire's heart with such force that it emerged from the beast's back, dripping blood and entrails.

The master of darkness was dead as hell.

13

"Good-bye," said the brunet, embracing Felicia in the vestibule downstairs.

The brunet wore a gabardine business suit and carried a large gray piece of American Tourister luggage and had a tan London Fog draped over her arm. She sure didn't look like a vampire.

"Where will you go?" Felicia asked.

"My uncle owns a travel agency in Cleveland. I'll probably give that a try first."

"We should have a get-together once a year."

"Yes, a picnic or something," the brunet said. Then she put out her hand to Sam. "I owe you a lot more than I can say."

He looked at Felicia and smiled. "I had selfish reasons."

Quite seriously, the lovely brunet said, "I'll always be a vampire but now at least I'm my own person."

An airport limo pulled up and honked.

"Well," the brunet said, "good-bye."

Then she walked outside to the sunlight that was almost white. The grass was brilliant green. As usual in the Midwest, spring had simply shown up one morning, like a lover one had almost forgotten.

Sam said, "Well, that's the last of them."

"Yes," Felicia said, smiling. "Every one of the women packed and away from this place." She leaned over and kissed him on the cheek. "Oh, Sam. We all owe you so much."

"You know I don't want gratitude, Felicia. I did it because I love you." He nodded upstairs. "Now why don't you go upstairs and pack? Then we can get out of here, too."

She kissed him again. "It won't take long."

She went up the broad stairs. He entertained himself by walking through the room with the Chagall and Degas oils. It was warm in here.

The furnace in the basement was roaring. He had put Karl Richards's corpse in it.

She was back, an overnight bag in her hand, a few minutes later.

"Ready?" he said.

"Oh, Sam, if you could only know how ready I am."

"Good. Then let's lock this place up and never think about it again."

She giggled. "Let's."

So they went outside to the brilliant day and he put the key in the lock and started to turn it and that was when a rough piece of wood scraped the knuckle of his left thumb.

And several small bubbles of blood appeared.

He laughed. "Mr. Graceful strikes again," he said.

He finished locking the door and then turned around to look at her.

The fangs didn't alter her face all that much. And she wasn't spitting all over the place. And her eyes weren't psychotic and crazed.

She was a vampire, OK, but at least she was a very pretty and feminine one.

She started sobbing instantly and fell into his arms.

An hour later they had completed their second lap around the huge estate. They had seen dogs, they had seen horses, they had seen deer; they had seen oak, they had seen maple, they had seen elm; they had seen rock and grass and lake.

And they had faced a terrible truth.

Now, sitting on a porch swing in the park pavilion: "We can't be together, Sam."

"Don't say that anymore. Please."

"It's true. The mere sight of blood—I'm a vampire. My teeth—"

"You didn't bite me. You're not some terrible beast. You're—"

"As vampires go, I'm probably pretty OK," Felicia said, watching the course of a jay as it flew up to a tree limb. "I mean, I was a decent human being, so I'll probably be a decent vampire. But that sill doesn't mean we can be together."

"Oh please, Felicia. Please don't say that anymore."

She stood up, then bent down to take his hands and pull him up, too. Her eyes were wet with her tears. "I love you more than I've ever loved anybody, Sam. But it won't work and you know it and I know it."

"But it's no different from my marrying a Polynesian woman. There'll be some cultural differences at first but—"

"Yes. I don't cast a reflection, my whole body surges when I see blood, and I'm probably going to live to be a few thousand years old. But other than that I'll just be a typical suburban housewife, right, Sam?"

"Felicia, I—"

She put her lips to his. Their kiss was long and tender and halfway through, Sam recognized the kiss for what it was:

Good-bye.

She entwined her hand in his and together they walked out of the estate, the grillwork gates closing behind them.

They stood on the curb and Sam said, "What will you do?"

She tried a smile but it was mostly sad. "Right now I'm not thinking very clearly, Sam. I guess I don't have any idea at all what I'll do. Just whatever comes along, I guess."

Then she waved good-bye to him and started walking away, a beautiful, retreating figure, until she rounded a corner and was out of sight.

Gone.

Forever.

14

During the next year he saw a shrink who tried to convince him that none of it had ever happened, a priest who accused him of being a satanist, a minister who wanted him to come on his TV talk show and discuss how even vampires could become good Christians.

He also tried singles bars, dating services, and old girl friends.

But no matter what he tried, there were still the lasting memories of Felicia, and of their plans, and of how much he'd loved her and loved her still.

Spring became summer became autumn became winter. A new cable channel appeared, one that played a lot of Monogram films, including the best of the Charlie Chans and Bowery Boys, and that helped some,

and scores of new types of junk food came along, and that helped a little bit, too.

But mostly there was just driving the cab and lying on the couch
thinking about Felicia. Thinking uselessly about Felicia. He had tried all
the agencies and all the studios, but there was no word of her. Obviously
she had moved away.

He contented himself with cable and food that only a chemist could
love.

He had only a vague idea of what day it was, that overcast February
Tuesday.

He'd had his usual afternoon-load of people he liked and people he
disliked.

Now it was dusk and the dispatcher had just sent him to an address
near the downtown area.

He pulled up and waited in front of an aged brick building.

A woman in a fashionable felt hat, one whose rim obscured her face,
walked gracefully from the building and got in the car. She smelled wonderfully of perfume and womanness.

He was halfway down the block before he said, "I forgot to ask, where
would you like to go?"

All she said was, "Why don't you look in your mirror, Sam?"

He didn't have to look in the mirror. He knew the voice.

"My God," he said.

"It's Valentine's Day," she said.

"My God," he said.

"It's selfish of me, Sam, but I just had to see you—"

"My God," he said.

"I've missed you so much and—" She whipped off her felt hat and let
her lovely blond hair tumble free.

Finally, he was able to speak coherently. "I've looked everywhere for
you. For a year."

"That's so sweet—"

"To tell you something."

"Tell me what?"

"That I have a plan."

"What plan?"

"There's a park up ahead."

"All right."

"And I'm going to pull into that park."

"All right."

"And then I'm going to ask you to sit up in the front seat with me."

For the first time she sounded a bit hesitant, suspicious. "All right."

He pulled into the park. At night the only illumination was the nimbus of electric light off dirty snow.

They parked next to a pavilion. "OK," he said. "Get up front."

"What's going to happen, Sam?"

"You'll see. Please, Felicia. Just get up front."

So she got up front.

As soon as she was in the front seat, he did it: grabbed the church key he kept on the dash and cut a deep gash on his hand.

In the shadows, he saw her entire body begin to tremble, saw the fangs begin to form in the corners of her mouth.

"I should have thought of this that day we walked around the mansion," Sam said, holding out his hand. "I can't turn you back into a human but you can turn me into a vampire."

"Sam, are you sure you want to—"

Sam laughed. "Make me your valentine, Felicia. Make me your valentine right now."

Mama Gone

by Jane Yolen

Mama died four nights ago, giving birth to my baby sister Ann. Bubba cried and cried, "Mama gone," in his little-boy voice, but I never let out a single tear.

There was blood red as any sunset all over the bed from that birthing, and when Papa saw it he rubbed his head against the cabin wall over and over and over and made little animal sounds. Sukey washed Mama down and placed the baby on her breast for a moment. "Remember," she whispered.

"Mama gone," Bubba wailed again.

But I never cried.

By all rights we should have buried her with garlic in her mouth and her hands and feet cut off, what with her being vampire kin and all. But Papa absolutely refused.

"Your Mama couldn't stand garlic," he said when the sounds stopped rushing out of his mouth and his eyes had cleared. "It made her come all over with rashes. She had the sweetest mouth and hands."

And that was that. Not a one of us could make him change his mind, not even Granddad Stokes or Pop Wilber or any other of the men who came to pay their last respects. And as Papa is a preacher, and a brimstone man, they let it be. The onliest thing he would allow was for us to tie red ribbons round her ankles and wrists, a kind of sign like a line of blood. Everybody hoped that would do.

But on the next day, she rose from out her grave and commenced to prey upon the good folk of Taunton.

Of course she came to our house first, that being the dearest place she knew. I saw her outside my window, gray as a gravestone, her dark eyes like the holes in a shroud. When she stared in, she didn't know me, though I had always been her favorite.

"Mama, be gone," I said and waved my little cross at her, the one she had given me the very day I'd been born. "Avaunt." The old Bible word sat heavy in my mouth.

She put her hand up on the window frame, and as I watched, the gray fingers turned splotchy pink from all the garlic I had rubbed into the wood.

Black tears dropped from her black eyes, then. But I never cried.

She tried each window in turn and not a person awake in the house but me. But I had done my work well and the garlic held her out. She even tried the door, but it was no use. By the time she left, I was so sleepy, I dropped down right by the door. Papa found me there at cockcrow. He never did ask what I was doing, and if he guessed, he never said.

Little Joshua Greenough was found dead in his crib. The doctor took two days to come over the mountains to pronounce it. By then the garlic around his little bed to keep him from walking, too, had mixed with the death smells. Everybody knew. Even the doctor, and him a city man. It hurt his mama and papa sore to do the cutting. But it had to be done.

The men came to our house that very noon to talk about what had to be. Papa kept shaking his head all through their talking. But even his being preacher didn't stop them. Once a vampire walks these mountain hollars, there's nary a house or barn that's safe. Nighttime is lost time. And no one can afford to lose much stock.

So they made their sharp sticks out of green wood, the curling shavings littering our cabin floor. Bubba played in them, not understanding. Sukey was busy with the baby, nursing it with a bottle and a sugar teat. It was my job to sweep up the wood curls. They felt slick on one side, bumpy on the other. Like my heart.

Papa said, "I was the one let her turn into a night walker. It's my business to stake her out."

No one argued. Specially not the Greenoughs, their eyes still red from weeping.

"Just take my children," Papa said. "And if anything goes wrong, cut off my hands and feet and bury me at Mill's Cross, under the stone. There's garlic hanging in the pantry. Mandy Jane will string me some."

So Sukey took the baby and Bubba off to the Greenoughs' house, that seeming the right thing to do, and I stayed the rest of the afternoon with Papa, stringing garlic and pressing more into the windows. But the strand over the door he took down.

"I have to let her in somewhere," he said. "And this is where I'll make my stand." He touched me on the cheek, the first time ever. Papa never has been much for show.

"Now you run along to the Greenoughs', Mandy Jane," he said. "And remember how much your mama loved you. This isn't her, child. Mama's gone. Something else has come to take her place. I should have remembered that the Good Book says, 'The living know that they shall die; but the dead know not anything.' "

I wanted to ask him how the vampire knew to come first to our house, then, but I was silent, for Papa had been asleep and hadn't seen her.

I left without giving him a daughter's kiss, for his mind was well set on the night's doing. But I didn't go down the lane to the Greenoughs' at all. Wearing my triple strand of garlic, with my cross about my neck, I went to the burying ground, to Mama's grave.

It looked so raw against the greening hillside. The dirt was red clay, but all it looked like to me was blood. There was no cross on it yet, no stone. That would come in a year. Just a humping, a heaping of red dirt over her coffin, the plain pinewood box hastily made.

I lay facedown in that dirt, my arms opened wide. "Oh, Mama," I said, "the Good Book says you are not dead but sleepeth. Sleep quietly, Mama, sleep well." And I sang to her the lullaby she had always sung to me and then to Bubba and would have sung to Baby Ann had she lived to hold her.

> *"Blacks and bays,*
> *Dapples and grays,*
> *All the pretty little horses."*

And as I sang I remembered Papa thundering at prayer meeting once, "Behold, a pale horse: and his name that sat on him was Death." The rest of the song just stuck in my throat then, so I turned over on the grave and stared up at the setting sun.

It had been a long and wearying day, and I fell asleep right there in the burying ground. Any other time fear might have overcome sleep. But I just closed my eyes and slept.

When I woke, it was dead night. The moon was full and sitting between the horns of two hills. There was a sprinkling of stars overhead. And Mama began to move the ground beneath me, trying to rise.

The garlic strands must have worried her, for she did not come out of the earth all at once. It was the scrabbling of her long nails at my back that woke me. I leaped off that grave and was wide awake.

Standing aside the grave, I watched as first her long gray arms reached out of the earth. Then her head, with its hair that was once so gold now gray and streaked with black and its shroud eyes, emerged. And then her body in its winding sheet, stained with dirt and torn from walking to and fro upon the land. Then her bare feet with blackened nails, though alive Mama used to paint those nails, her one vanity and Papa allowed it seeing she was so pretty and otherwise not vain.

She turned toward me as a hummingbird toward a flower, and she raised her face up and it was gray and bony. Her mouth peeled back from her teeth and I saw that they were pointed and her tongue was barbed.

"Mama gone," I whispered in Bubba's voice, but so low I could hardly hear it myself.

She stepped toward me off that grave, lurching down the hump of dirt. But when she got close, the garlic strands and the cross stayed her.

"Mama."

She turned her head back and forth. It was clear she could not see with those black shroud eyes. She only sensed me there, something warm, something alive, something with the blood running like satisfying streams through the blue veins.

"Mama," I said again. "Try and remember."

That searching awful face turned toward me again, and the pointy teeth were bared once more. Her hands reached out to grab me, then pulled back.

"Remember how Bubba always sucks his thumb with that funny little noise you always said was like a little chuck in its hole. And how Sukey hums through her nose when she's baking bread. And how I listened to your belly to hear the baby. And how Papa always starts each meal with the blessing on things that grow fresh in the field."

The gray face turned for a moment toward the hills, and I wasn't even sure she could hear me. But I had to keep trying.

"And remember when we picked the blueberries and Bubba fell down the hill, tumbling head-end over. And we laughed until we heard him, and he was saying the same six things over and over till long past bed."

The gray face turned back toward me and I thought I saw a bit of light in the eyes. But it was just reflected moonlight.

"And the day Papa came home with the new ewe lamb and we fed her on a sugar teat. You stayed up all the night and I slept in the straw by your side."

It was as if stars were twinkling in those dead eyes. I couldn't stop staring, but I didn't dare stop talking either.

"And remember the day the bluebird stunned itself on the kitchen window and you held it in your hands. You warmed it to life, you said. To life, Mama."

Those stars began to run down the gray cheeks.

"There's living, Mama, and there's dead. You've given so much life. Don't be bringing death to these hills now." I could see that the stars were gone from the sky over her head; the moon was setting.

"Papa loved you too much to cut your hands and feet. You gotta return that love, Mama. You gotta."

Veins of red ran along the hills, outlining the rocks. As the sun began to rise, I took off one strand of garlic. Then the second. Then the last. I opened my arms. "Have you come back, Mama, or are you gone?"

The gray woman leaned over and clasped me tight in her arms. Her head bent down toward mine, her mouth on my forehead, my neck, the outline of my little gold cross burning across her lips.

She whispered, "Here and gone, child, here and gone," in a voice like wind in the coppice, like the shaking of willow leaves. I felt her kiss on my cheek, a brand.

Then the sun came between the hills and hit her full in the face, burning her as red as earth. She smiled at me and then there was only dust motes in the air, dancing. When I looked down at my feet, the grave dirt was hardly disturbed but Mama's gold wedding band gleamed atop it.

I knelt down and picked it up, and unhooked the chain holding my cross. I slid the ring into the chain, and the two nestled together right in the hollow of my throat. I sang:

> *"Blacks and bays,*
> *Dapples and grays . . . "*

and from the earth itself, the final words sang out.

> *All the pretty little horses.*

That was when I cried, long and loud, a sound I hope never to make again as long as I live.

Then I went back down the hill and home, where Papa still waited by the open door.

Beyond Any Measure

by Karl Edward Wagner

1

I n the dream I find myself alone in a room. I hear musical chimes—
a sort of music-box tune—and I look around to see where the sound
is coming from.

"I'm in a bedroom. Heavy curtains close off the windows, and it's
quite dark, but I can sense that the furnishings are entirely antique—late
Victorian, I think. There's a large four-poster bed, with its curtains
drawn. Beside the bed is a small night table upon which a candle is burning. It is from here that the music seems to be coming.

"I walk across the room toward the bed, and as I stand beside it I see
a gold watch resting on the night table next to the candlestick. The
music-box tune is coming from the watch, I realize. It's one of those old
pocket-watch affairs with a case that opens. The case is open now, and I
see that the watch's hands are almost at midnight. I sense that on the inside of the watchcase there will be a picture, and I pick up the watch to
see whose picture it is.

"The picture is obscured with a red smear. It's fresh blood.

"I look up in sudden fear. From the bed, a hand is pulling aside the
curtain.

"That's when I wake up."

"Bravo!" applauded someone.

Lisette frowned momentarily, then realized that the comment was directed toward another of the chattering groups crowded into the gallery. She sipped her champagne; she must be a bit tight, or she'd never have started talking about the dreams.

"What do you think, Dr. Magnus?"

It was the gala reopening of Covent Garden. The venerable fruit, flower and vegetable market, preserved from the demolition crew, had been renovated into an airy mall of expensive shops and galleries: "London's new shopping experience." Lisette thought it an unhappy hybrid of born-again Victorian exhibition hall and trendy "shoppes." Let the dead past bury its dead. She wondered what they might make of the old Billingsgate fish market, should SAVE win its fight to preserve that landmark, as now seemed unlikely.

"Is this dream, then, a recurrent one, Miss Seyrig?"

She tried to read interest or skepticism in Dr. Magnus' pale blue eyes. They told her nothing.

"Recurrent enough."

To make me mention it to Danielle, she finished in her thoughts. Danielle Borland shared a flat—she'd stopped terming it an apartment even in her mind—with her in a row of terrace houses in Bloomsbury, within an easy walk of London University. The gallery was Maitland Reddin's project; Danielle was another. Whether Maitland really thought to make a business of it, or only intended to showcase his many friends' not always evident talents was not open to discussion. His gallery in Knightsbridge was certainly successful, if that meant anything.

"How often is that?" Dr. Magnus touched his glass to his blonde-bearded lips. He was drinking only Perrier water, and, at that, was using his glass for little more than to gesture.

"I don't know. Maybe half a dozen times since I can remember. And then, that many again since I came to London."

"You're a student at London University, I believe Danielle said?"

"That's right. In art. I'm over here on fellowship."

Danielle had modelled for an occasional session—Lisette now was certain it was solely from a desire to display her body rather than due to any financial need—and when a muttered profanity at a dropped brush disclosed a common American heritage, the two *émigrés* had rallied at a pub afterward to exchange news and views. Lisette's bed-sit near the

Museum was impossible, and Danielle's roommate had just skipped to
the Continent with two months' owing. By closing time it was settled.

"How's your glass?"

Danielle, finding them in the crowd, shook her head in mock dismay
and refilled Lisette's glass before she could cover it with her hand.

"And you, Dr. Magnus?"

"Quite well, thank you."

"Danielle, let me give you a hand?" Maitland had charmed the two of
them into acting as hostesses for his opening.

"Nonsense, darling. When you see me starting to pant with the heat,
then call up the reserves. Until then, do keep Dr. Magnus from straying
away to the other parties."

Danielle swirled off with her champagne bottle and her smile. The
gallery, christened "Such Things May Be" after Richard Burton (*not*
Liz Taylor's ex, Danielle kept explaining, and got laughs each time),
was ajostle with friends and well-wishers—as were most of the shops
tonight: private parties with evening dress and champagne, only a scattering of displaced tourists, gaping and photographing. She and
Danielle were both wearing slit-to-thigh crepe de Chine evening
gowns and could have passed for sisters: Lisette blonde, green-eyed,
with a dust of freckles; Danielle light brunette, hazel-eyed, acclimated
to the extensive facial makeup London woman favored; both tall without seeming coltish, and close enough of a size to wear each other's
clothes.

"It must be distressing to have the same nightmare over and again,"
Dr. Magnus prompted her.

"There have been others as well. Some recurrent, some not. Similar in
that I wake up feeling like I've been through the sets of some old Hammer film."

"I gather you were not actually troubled with such nightmares until
recently?"

"Not really. Being in London seems to have triggered them. I suppose
it's repressed anxieties over being in a strange city." It was bad enough
that she'd been taking some of Danielle's pills in order to seek dreamless sleep.

"Is this, then, your first time in London, Miss Seyrig?"

"It is." She added, to seem less the typical American student: "Although my family was English."

"Your parents?"

"My mother's parents were both from London. They emigrated to the States just after World War I."

"Then this must have been rather a bit like coming home for you."

"Not really. I'm the first of our family to go overseas. And I have no memory of Mother's parents. Grandmother Keswicke died the morning I was born." Something Mother never was able to work through emotionally, Lisette added to herself.

"And have you consulted a physician concerning these nightmares?"

"I'm afraid your National Health Service is a bit more than I can cope with." Lisette grimaced at the memory of the night she had tried to explain to a Pakistani intern why she wanted sleeping medications.

She suddenly hoped her words hadn't offended Dr. Magnus, but then, he scarcely looked the type who would approve of socialized medicine. Urbane, perfectly at ease in formal evening attire, he reminded her somewhat of a blonde-bearded Peter Cushing. Enter Christopher Lee, in black cape, she mused, glancing toward the door. For that matter, she wasn't at all certain just what sort of doctor Dr. Magnus might be. Danielle had insisted she talk with him, very likely had insisted that Maitland invite him to the private opening: "The man has such *insight!* And he's written a number of books on dreams and the subconscious— and not just rehashes of Freudian silliness!"

"Are you going to be staying in London for some time, Miss Seyrig?"

"At least until the end of the year."

"Too long a time to wait to see whether these bad dreams will go away once you're back home in San Francisco, don't you agree? It can't be very pleasant for you, and you really should look after yourself."

Lisette made no answer. *She* hadn't told Dr. Magnus she was from San Francisco. So then, Danielle had already talked to him about her.

Dr. Magnus smoothly produced his card, discreetly offered it to her. "I should be most happy to explore this further with you on a professional level, should you wish."

"I don't really think it's worth . . ."

"Of course it is, my dear. Why otherwise would we be talking? Perhaps next Tuesday afternoon? Is there a convenient time?"

Lisette slipped his card into her handbag. It nothing else, perhaps he could supply her with some barbs or something. "Three?"

"Three it is, then."

2

The passageway was poorly lighted, and Lisette felt a vague sense of dread as she hurried along it, holding the hem of her nightgown away from the gritty filth beneath her bare feet. Peeling scabs of wallpaper blotched the leprous plaster, and, when she held the candle close, the gouges and scratches that patterned the walls with insane graffiti seemed disquietingly nonrandom. Against the mottled plaster, her figure threw a double shadow: distorted, one crouching forward, the other following.

A full-length mirror panelled one segment of the passageway, and Lisette paused to study her reflection. Her face appeared frightened, her blonde hair in disorder. She wondered at her nightgown—pale, silken, billowing, of an antique mode—not remembering how she came to be wearing it. Nor could she think how it was that she had come to this place.

Her reflection puzzled her. Her hair seemed longer than it should be, trailing down across her breasts. Her finely chiselled features, prominent jawline, straight nose—her face, except the expression, was not hers: lips fuller, more sensual, redder than her lip-gloss, glinted; teeth fine and white. Her green eyes, intense beneath level brows, cat-cruel, yearning.

Lisette released the hem of her gown, raised her fingers to her reflection in wonder. Her fingers passed through the glass, touched the face beyond.

Not a mirror. A doorway. Of a crypt.

The mirror-image fingers that rose to her face twisted in her hair, pulled her face forward. Glass-cold lips bruised her own. The dank breath of the tomb flowed into her mouth.

Dragging herself from the embrace, Lisette felt a scream rip from her throat . . .

. . . And Danielle was shaking her awake.

3

The business card read *Dr. Ingmar Magnus*, followed simply by *Consultations* and a Kensington address. Not Harley Street, at any rate. Lisette considered it for the hundredth time, watching for street names on the corners of buildings as she walked down Kensington Church Street from the Notting Hill Gate station. No clue as to what type of doctor, nor what sort of consultations; wonderfully vague, and just the thing to circumvent licensing laws, no doubt.

Danielle had lent her one of his books to read: *The Self Reborn*, put out by one of those miniscule scholarly publishers clustered about the British Museum. Lisette found it a bewildering mélange of occult philosophy and lunatic-fringe theory—all evidently having something to do with reincarnation—and gave it up after the first chapter. She had decided not to keep the appointment, until her nightmare Sunday night had given force to Danielle's insistence.

Lisette wore a loose silk blouse above French designer jeans and ankle-strap sandal-toe high heels. The early summer heat wave now threatened rain, and she would have to run for it if the grey skies made good. She turned into Holland Street, passed the recently closed Equinox bookshop, where Danielle had purchased various works by Aleister Crowley. A series of back streets—she consulted her map of Central London—brought her to a modestly respectable row of nineteenth-century brick houses, now done over into offices and flats. She checked the number on the brass plaque with her card, sucked in her breath and entered.

Lisette hadn't known what to expect. She wouldn't have been surprised, knowing some of Danielle's friends, to have been greeted with clouds of incense, Eastern music, robed initiates. Instead she found a disappointingly mundane waiting room, rather small but expensively furnished, where a pretty Eurasian receptionist took her name and spoke into an intercom. Lisette noted that there was no one else—patients? clients?—in the waiting room. She glanced at her watch and noticed she was several minutes late.

"Please do come in, Miss Seyrig." Dr. Magnus stepped out of his office and ushered her inside. Lisette had seen a psychiatrist briefly a few years before, at her parents' demand, and Dr. Magnus's office suggested the same—from the tasteful, relaxed decor, the shelves of scholarly books, down to the traditional psychoanalyst's couch. She took a chair beside the modern, rather carefully arranged desk, and Dr. Magnus seated himself comfortably in the leather swivel chair behind it.

"I almost didn't come," Lisette began, somewhat aggressively.

"I'm very pleased that you did decide to come." Dr. Magnus smiled reassuringly. "It doesn't require a trained eye to see that something is troubling you. When the unconscious tries to speak to us, it is foolhardy to attempt to ignore its message."

"Meaning that I may be cracking up?"

"I'm sure that must concern you, my dear. However, very often dreams such as yours are evidence of the emergence of a new level of self-awareness—sort of growing pains of the psyche, if you will—and not to be considered a negative experience by any means. They distress you only because you do not understand them—even as a child kept in ignorance through sexual repression is frightened by the changes of puberty. With your cooperation, I hope to help you come to understand the changes of your growing self-awareness, for it is only through a complete realization of one's self that one can achieve personal fulfillment and thereby true inner peace."

"I'm afraid I can't afford to undergo analysis just now."

"Let me begin by emphasizing to you that I am not suggesting psychoanalysis; I do not in the least consider you to be neurotic, Miss Seyrig. What I strongly urge is an *exploration* of your unconsciousness—a discovery of your whole self. My task is only to guide you along the course of your self-discovery, and for this privilege I charge no fee."

"I hadn't realized the National Health Service was this inclusive."

Dr. Magnus laughed easily. "It isn't, of course. My work is supported by a private foundation. There are many others who wish to learn certain truths of our existence, to seek answers where mundane science has not yet so much as realized there are questions. In that regard I am simply another paid researcher, and the results of my investigations are made available to those who share with us this yearning to see beyond the stultifying boundaries of modern science."

He indicated the book-lined wall behind his desk. Much of one shelf appeared to contain books with his own name prominent upon their spines.

"Do you intend to write a book about me?" Lisette meant to put more of a note of protest in her voice.

"It is possible that I may wish to record some of what we discover together, my dear. But only with scupulous discretion, and, needless to say, only with your complete permission."

"My dreams." Lisette remembered the book of his that she had tried to read. "Do you consider them to be evidence of some previous incarnation?"

"Perhaps. We can't be certain until we explore them further. Does the idea of reincarnation smack too much of the occult to your liking, Miss Seyrig? Perhaps we should speak in more fashionable terms of Jungian archetypes, genetic memory or mental telepathy. The fact that the phenomenon has so many designations is ample proof that dreams of a previous existence are a very real part of the unconscious mind. It is undeniable that many people have experienced, in dreams or under hypnosis, memories that cannot possibly arise from their personal experience. Whether you believe that the immortal soul leaves the physical body at death to be reborn in the living embryo, or prefer to attribute it to inherited memories engraved upon DNA, or whatever explanation—this is a very real phenomenon and has been observed throughout history.

"As a rule, these memories of past existence are entirely buried within the unconscious. Almost everyone has experienced *déjà vu*. Subjects under hypnosis have spoken in languages and archaic dialects of which their conscious mind has no knowledge, have recounted in detail memories of previous lives. In some cases these submerged memories burst forth as dreams; in these instances, the memory is usually one of some emotionally laden experience, something too potent to remain buried. I believe that this is the case with your nightmares—the fact that they are recurrent being evidence of some profound significance in the events they recall."

Lisette wished for a cigarette; she'd all but stopped buying cigarettes with British prices, and from the absence of ashtrays here, Dr. Magnus was a nonsmoker.

"But why have these nightmares only lately become a problem?"

"I think I can explain that easily enough. Your forebears were from London. The dreams became a problem after you arrived in London. While it is usually difficult to define any relationship between the subject and the remembered existence, the timing and the force of your dream regressions would seem to indicate that you may be the reincarnation of someone—an ancestress, perhaps—who lived here in London during this past century."

"In that case, the nightmares should go away when I return to the States."

"Not necessarily. Once a doorway to the unconscious is opened, it is not so easily closed again. Moreover, you say that you had experienced these dreams on rare occasions prior to your coming here. I would suggest that what you are experiencing is a natural process—a submerged part of your self is seeking expression, and it would be unwise to deny this shadow-stranger within you. I might further argue that your presence here in London is hardly coincidence—that your decision to study here was determined by that part of you who emerges in these dreams."

Lisette decided she wasn't ready to accept such implications just now. "What do you propose?"

Dr. Magnus folded his hands as neatly as a bishop at prayer. "Have you ever undergone hypnosis?"

"No." She wished she hadn't made that sound like two syllables.

"It has proved to be extraordinarily efficacious in a great number of cases such as your own, my dear. Please do try to put from your mind the ridiculous trappings and absurd mumbo-jumbo with which the popular imagination connotes hypnotism. Hypnosis is no more than a technique through which we may release the entirety of the unconscious mind to free expression, unrestricted by the countless artificial barriers that make us strangers to ourselves."

"You want to hypnotize me?" The British inflection came to her, turning her statement into both question and protest.

"With your fullest cooperation, of course. I think it best. Through regressive hypnosis we can explore the significance of these dreams that trouble you, discover the shadow stranger within your self. Remember—this is a part of *you* that cries out for conscious expression. It is only through the full realization of one's identity, of one's total self, that true inner tranquillity may be achieved. Know thyself, and you will find peace."

"Know myself?"

"Precisely. You must put aside this false sense of guilt, Miss Seyrig. You are not possessed by some alien and hostile force. These dreams, these memories of another existence—this is *you*."

4

"Some bloody weirdo made a pass at me this afternoon," Lisette confided.

"On the tube, was it?" Danielle stood on her toes, groping along the top of their bookshelf. Freshly showered, she was wearing only a lace-trimmed teddy—cami-knickers, they called them in the shops here—and her straining thigh muscles shaped her buttocks nicely.

"In Kensington, actually. After I had left Dr. Magnus's office." Lisette was lounging in an old satin slip she'd found at a stall in Church Street. They were drinking Bristol Cream out of brandy snifters. It was an intimate sort of evening they loved to share together, when not in the company of Danielle's various friends.

"I was walking down Holland Street, and there was this seedy-looking creep all dressed out in punk regalia, pressing his face against the door where that Equinox bookshop used to be. I made the mistake of glancing at him as I passed, and he must have seen my reflection in the glass, because he spun right around, looked straight at me, and said: 'Darling! What a lovely surprise to see you!' "

Lisette sipped her sherry. "Well, I gave him my hardest stare, and would you believe the creep just stood there smiling like he knew me, and so I yelled, 'Piss off!' in my loudest American accent, and he just froze there with his mouth hanging open."

"Here it is," Danielle announced. "I'd shelved it beside Roland Franklyn's *We Pass from View*—that's another you ought to read. I must remember someday to return it to that cute Liverpool writer who lent it to me."

She settled cozily beside Lisette on the couch, handed her a somewhat

smudged paperback, and resumed her glass of sherry. The book was en-
titled *More Stately Mansions: Evidences of the Infinite* by Dr. Ingmar
Magnus, and bore an affectionate inscription from the author to
Danielle. "This is the first. The later printings had two of his studies
deleted; I can't imagine why. But these are the sort of sessions he was
describing to you."

"He wants to put *me* in one of his books," Lisette told her with an extravagant leer. "Can a woman trust a man who writes such ardent in-
scriptions to place her under hypnosis?"

"Dr. Magnus is a perfect gentleman," Danielle assured her, somewhat
huffily. "He's a distinguished scholar and is thoroughly dedicated to his
research. And besides, I've let him hypnotize me on a few occasions."

"I didn't know that. Whatever for?"

"Dr. Magnus is always seeking suitable subjects. I was fascinated by
his work, and when I met him at a party I offered to undergo hypnosis."

"What happened?"

Danielle seemed envious. "Nothing worth writing about, I'm afraid.
He said I was either too thoroughly integrated, or that my previous lives
were too deeply buried. That's often the case, he says, which is why absolute proof of reincarnation is so difficult to demonstrate. After a few
sessions I decided I couldn't spare the time to try further."

"But what was it like?"

"As adventurous as taking a nap. No caped Svengali staring into my
eyes. No lambent girasol ring. No swirling lights. Quite dull, actually.
Dr. Magnus simply lulls you to sleep."

"Sounds safe enough. So long as I don't get molested walking back
from his office."

Playfully, Danielle stroked her hair. "You hardly look the punk rock
type. You haven't chopped off your hair with garden shears and dyed the
stubble green. And not a single safety pin through your cheek."

"Actually I suppose he may not have been a punk rocker. Seemed a
bit too old, and he wasn't garish enough. It's just that he was wearing a
lot of black leather, and he had gold earrings and some sort of medallion."

"In front of the Equinox, did you say? How curious."

"Well, I think I gave him a good start. I glanced in a window to see

whether he was trying to follow me, but he was just standing there looking stunned."

"*Might* have been an honest mistake. Remember the old fellow at
Midge and Fiona's party who kept insisting he knew you?"

"And who was pissed out of his skull. Otherwise he might have been
able to come up with a more original line."

Lisette paged through *More Stately Mansions* while Danielle selected
a Tangerine Dream album from the stack and placed it on her stereo at
low volume. The music seemed in keeping with the grey drizzle of the
night outside and the coziness within their sitting room. Seeing she was
busy reading, Danielle poured sherry for them both and stood studying
the bookshelves—a hodgepodge of occult and metaphysical topics
stuffed together with art books and recent paperbacks in no particular
order. Wedged between Aleister Crowley's *Magick in Theory and Practice* and *How I Discovered My Infinite Self* by "An Initiate," was Dr.
Magnus's most recent book, *The Shadow Stranger*. She pulled it down,
and Dr. Magnus stared thoughtfully from the back of the dust jacket.

"Do you believe in reincarnation?" Lisette asked her.

"I do. Or rather, I do some of the time." Danielle stood behind the
couch and bent over Lisette's shoulder to see where she was reading.
"Midge Vaughn assures me that in a previous incarnation I was hanged
for witchcraft."

"Midge should be grateful she's living in the twentieth century."

"Oh, Midge says we were sisters in the same coven and were hanged
together; that's the reason for our close affinity."

"I'll bet Midge says that to all the girls."

"Oh, I like Midge." Danielle sipped her sherry and considered the
rows of spines. "Did you say that man was wearing a medallion? Was it
a swastika or that sort of thing?"

"No. It was something like a star in a circle. And he wore rings on
every finger."

"Wait! Kind of greasy black hair slicked back from a widow's peak to
straight over his collar in back? Eyebrows curled up into points like
they've been waxed?"

"That's it."

"Ah, Mephisto!"

"Do you know him, then?"

"Not really. I've just seen him a time or two at the Equinox and a few other places. He reminds me of some ham actor playing Mephistopheles. Midge spoke to him once when we were by there, but I gather he's not part of her particular coven. Probably hadn't heard that the Equinox had closed. Never impressed me as a masher; very likely he actually did mistake you for someone."

"Well, they do say that everyone has a double. I wonder if mine is walking somewhere about London, being mistaken for me?"

"And no doubt giving some unsuspecting classmate of yours a resounding slap on the face."

"What if I met her suddenly?"

"Met your double—your *Doppelgänger*? Remember William Wilson? Disaster, darling—*disaster!*"

5

There really wasn't much to it; no production at all. Lisette felt nervous, a bit silly, and perhaps a touch cheated.

"I want you to relax," Dr. Magnus told her. "All you have to do is just relax."

That's what her gynecologist always said, too, Lisette thought with a sudden tenseness. She lay on her back on Dr. Magnus's analyst's couch: her head on a comfortable cushion, legs stretched primly out on the leather upholstery (she'd deliberately worn jeans again), fingers clenched damply over her tummy. A white gown instead of jeans, and I'll be ready for my coffin, she mused uncomfortably.

"Fine. That's it. You're doing fine, Lisette. Very fine. Just relax. Yes, just relax, just like that. Fine, that's it. Relax."

Dr. Magnus's voice was a quiet monotone, monotonously repeating soothing encouragements. He spoke to her tirelessly, patiently, slowly dissolving her anxiety.

"You feel sleepy, Lisette. Relaxed and sleepy. Your breathing is slow and relaxed, slow and relaxed. Think about your breathing now, Lisette. Think how slow and sleepy and deep each breath comes. You're breathing deeper, and you're feeling sleepier. Relax and sleep, Lisette, breathe and sleep. Breathe and sleep . . ."

She *was* thinking about her breathing. She counted the breaths; the slow monotonous syllables of Dr. Magnus' voice seemed to blend into her breathing like a quiet, tuneless lullaby. She *was* sleepy, for that matter, and it was very pleasant to relax here, listening to that dim, droning murmur while he talked on and on. How much longer until the end of the lecture . . .

"You are asleep now, Lisette. You are asleep, yet you can still hear my voice. Now you are falling deeper, deeper, deeper into a pleasant, relaxed sleep, Lisette. Deeper and deeper asleep. Can you still hear my voice?"

"Yes."

"You are asleep, Lisette. In a deep, deep sleep. You will remain in this deep sleep until I shall count to three. As I count to three, you will slowly arise from your sleep until you are fully awake once again. Do you understand?"

"Yes."

"But when you hear me say the word *amber*, you will again fall into a deep, deep sleep, Lisette, just as you are asleep now. Do you understand?"

"Yes."

"Listen to me as I count, Lisette. One. Two. Three."

Lisette opened her eyes. For a moment her expression was blank, then a sudden confusion. She looked at Dr. Magnus seated beside her, then smiled ruefully. "I was asleep, I'm afraid. Or was I . . . ?"

"You did splendidly, Miss Seyrig." Dr. Magnus beamed reassurance. "You passed into a simple hypnotic state, and as you can see now, there was no more cause for concern than in catching an afternoon nap."

"But I'm sure I just dropped off." Lisette glanced at her watch. Her appointment had been for three, and it was now almost four o'clock.

"Why not just settle back and rest some more, Miss Seyrig. That's it, relax again. All you need is to rest a bit, just a pleasant rest."

Her wrist fell back onto the cushions, as her eyes fell shut.

"Amber."

Dr. Magnus studied her calm features for a moment. "You are asleep now, Lisette. Can you hear me?"

"Yes."

"I want you to relax, Lisette. I want you to fall deeper, deeper, deeper into sleep. Deep, deep sleep. Far, far, far into sleep."

He listened to her breathing, then suggested: "You are thinking of your childhood now, Lisette. You are a little girl, not even in school yet. Something is making you very happy. You remember how happy you are. Why are you so happy?"

Lisette made a childish giggle. "It's my birthday party, and Ollie the Clown came to play with us."

"And how old are you today?"

"I'm five." Her right hand twitched, extended fingers and thumb.

"Go deeper now, Lisette. I want you to reach farther back. Far, far back into your memories. Go back to a time before you were a child in San Francisco. Far, farther back, Lisette. I want you to go back to the time of your dreams."

He studied her face. She remained in a deep hypnotic trance, but her expression registered sudden anxiousness. It was as if she lay in normal sleep—reacting to some intense nightmare. She moaned.

"Deeper, Lisette. Don't be afraid to remember. Let your mind flow back to another time."

Her features still showed distress, but she seemed less agitated as his voice urged her deeper.

"Where are you?"

"I'm . . . I'm not certain." Her voice came in a well-bred English accent. "It's quite dark. Only a few candles are burning. I'm frightened."

"Go back to a happy moment," Dr. Magnus urged her, as her tone grew sharp with fear. "You are happy now. Something very pleasant and wonderful is happening to you."

Anxiety drained from her features. Her cheeks flushed; she smiled pleasurably.

"Where are you now?"

"I'm dancing. It's a grand ball to celebrate Her Majesty's Diamond Jubilee, and I've never seen such a throng. I'm certain Charles means to propose to me tonight, but he's ever so shy, and now he's simply fuming that Captain Stapledon has the next two dances. He's so dashing in his uniform. Everyone is watching us together."

"What is your name?"

"Elisabeth Beresford."

"Where do you live, Miss Beresford?"

"We have a house in Chelsea. . . ."

Her expression abruptly changed. "It's dark again. I'm all alone. I can't see myself, although surely the candles shed sufficient light. There's something there in the candlelight. I'm moving closer."

"One."

"It's an open coffin." Fear edged her voice.

"Two."

"God in Heaven!"

"Three."

6

"We," Danielle announced grandly, "are invited to a party."

She produced an engraved card from her bag, presented it to Lisette, then went to hang up her damp raincoat.

"Bloody English summer weather!" Lisette heard her from the kitchen. "Is there any more coffee made? Oh, fantastic!"

She reappeared with a cup of coffee and an opened box of cookies— Lisette couldn't get used to calling them biscuits. "Want some?"

"No, thanks. Bad for my figure."

"And coffee on an empty tummy is bad for the nerves," Danielle said pointedly.

"*Who* is Beth Garrington?" Lisette studied the invitation.

"Um." Danielle tried to wash down a mouthful of crumbs with too-hot coffee. "Some friend of Midge's. Midge dropped by the gallery this afternoon and gave me the invitation. A costume revel. Rock stars to royalty among the guests. Midge promises that it will be super fun; said the last party Beth threw was unbridled debauchery—there was cocaine being passed around in an antique snuff box for the guests. Can you imagine that much coke!"

"And how did Midge manage the invitation?"

"I gather the discerning Ms. Garrington had admired several of my drawings that Maitland has on display—yea, even unto so far as to pur-

chase one. Midge told her that she knew me and that we two were ornaments for any debauchery."

"The invitation is in both our names."

"Midge *likes* you."

"Midge despises me. She's jealous as a cat."

"Then she must have told our depraved hostess what a lovely couple
we make. Besides, Midge is jealous of everyone—even dear Maitland,
whose interest in me very obviously is not of the flesh. But don't fret
about Midge—English women are naturally bitchy toward 'foreign'
women. They're oh-so proper and fashionable, but they never shave
their legs. That's why I love mah fellow Americans."

Danielle kissed her chastely on top of her head, powdering Lisette's
hair with biscuit crumbs. "And I'm cold and wet and dying for a shower.
How about you?"

"A masquerade?" Lisette wondered. "What sort of costume? Not
something that we'll have to trot off to one of those rental places for,
surely?"

"From what Midge suggests, anything goes so long as it's wild. Just
create something divinely decadent, and we're sure to knock them
dead." Danielle had seen *Cabaret* half a dozen times. "It's to be in some
back alley stately old home in Maida Vale, so there's no danger that the
tenants downstairs will call the cops."

When Lisette remained silent, Danielle gave her a playful nudge.
"Darling, it's a party we're invited to, not a funeral. What is it—didn't
your session with Dr. Magnus go well?"

"I suppose it did." Lisette smiled without conviction. "I really can't
say; all I did was doze off. Dr. Magnus seemed quite excited about it,
though. I found it all . . . well, just a little bit scary."

"I thought you said you just dropped off. *What* was scary?"

"It's hard to put into words. It's like when you're starting to have a
bad trip on acid: there's nothing wrong that you can explain, but somehow your mind is telling you to be afraid."

Danielle sat down beside her and squeezed her arm about her shoulders. "That sounds to me like Dr. Magnus is getting somewhere. I felt
just the same sort of free anxiety the first time I underwent analysis. It's
a good sign, darling. It means you're beginning to understand all those
troubled secrets the ego keeps locked away."

"Perhaps the ego keeps them locked away for some perfectly good reason."

"Meaning hidden sexual conflicts, I suppose." Danielle's fingers gently massaged Lisette's shoulders and neck. "Oh, Lisette. You mustn't be shy about getting to know yourself. *I* think it's exciting."

Lisette curled up against her, resting her cheek against Danielle's breast while the other girl's fingers soothed the tension from her muscles. She supposed she was overreacting. After all, the nightmares were what distressed her so; Dr. Magnus seemed completely confident that he could free her from them.

"Which of your drawings did our prospective hostess buy?" Lisette asked, changing the subject.

"Oh, didn't I tell you?" Danielle lifted up her chin. "It was that charcoal study I did of you."

Lisette closed the shower curtains as she stepped into the tub. It was one of those long, narrow, deep tubs beloved of English bathrooms that always made her think of a coffin for two. A Rube Goldberg plumbing arrangement connected the hot and cold faucets, and from the common spout was affixed a rubber hose with a shower head which one might either hang from a hook on the wall or hold in hand. Danielle had replaced the ordinary shower head with a shower massager when she moved in, but she left the previous tenant's shaving mirror—a bevelled glass oval in a heavily enameled antique frame—hanging on the wall above the hook.

Lisette glanced at her face in the steamed-over mirror. "I shouldn't have let you display that at the gallery."

"But why not?" Danielle was shampooing, and lather blinded her as she turned about. "Maitland thinks it's one of my best."

Lisette reached around her for the shower attachment. "It seems a bit personal somehow. All those people looking at me. It's an invasion of privacy."

"But it's thoroughly modest, darling. Not like some topless billboard in Soho."

The drawing was a charcoal and pencil study of Lisette, done in what Danielle described as her David Hamilton phase. In sitting for it, Lisette had piled her hair in a high chignon and dressed in an antique cotton camisole and drawers with lace insertions that she'd found at a shop in Westbourne Grove. Danielle called it *Dark Rose*. Lisette had thought it made her look fat.

Danielle grasped blindly for the shower massage, and Lisette placed it in her hand. "It just seems a bit too personal to have some total stranger owning my picture." Shampoo coursed like seafoam over Danielle's breasts. Lisette kissed the foam.

"Ah, but soon she won't be a total stranger," Danielle reminded her, her voice muffled by the pulsing shower spray.

Lisette felt Danielle's nipples harden beneath her lips. The brunette still pressed her eyes tightly shut against the force of the shower, but the other hand cupped Lisette's head encouragingly. Lisette gently moved her kisses downward along the other girl's slippery belly, kneeling as she did so. Danielle murmured, and when Lisette's tongue probed her drenched curls, she shifted her legs to let her knees rest beneath the blonde girl's shoulders. The shower massage dropped from her fingers.

Lisette made love to her with a passion that surprised her—spontaneous, suddenly fierce, unlike their usual tenderness together. Her lips and tongue pressed into Danielle almost ravenously, her own ecstasy even more intense than that which she was drawing from Danielle. Danielle gasped and clung to the shower rail with one hand, her other fist clenched upon the curtain, sobbing as a long orgasm shuddered through her.

"Please, darling!" Danielle finally managed to beg. "My legs are too wobbly to hold me up any longer!"

She drew away. Lisette raised her face.

"Oh!"

Lisette rose to her feet with drugged movements. Her wide eyes at last registered Danielle's startled expression. She touched her lips and turned to look in the bathroom mirror.

"I'm sorry," Danielle put her arm about her shoulder. "I must have started my period. I didn't realize . . ."

Lisette stared at the blood-smeared face in the fogged shaving mirror.

Danielle caught her as she started to slump.

7

She was conscious of the cold rain that pelted her face, washing from her nostrils the too-sweet smell of decaying flowers. Slowly she opened her eyes onto darkness and mist. Rain fell steadily, spiritlessly, glueing her white gown to her drenched flesh. She had been walking in her sleep again.

Wakefulness seemed forever in coming to her, so that only by slow degrees did she become aware of herself, of her surroundings. For a moment she felt as if she were a chess piece arrayed upon a board in a darkened room. All about her, stone monuments crowded together, their weathered surfaces streaming with moisture. She felt neither fear nor surprise that she stood in a cemetery.

She pressed her bare arms together across her breasts. Water ran over her pale skin as smoothly as upon the marble tombstones, and though her flesh felt as cold as the drenched marble, she did not feel chilled. She stood barefoot, her hair clinging to her shoulders above the low-necked cotton gown that was all she wore.

Automatically, her steps carried her through the darkness, as if following a familiar path through the maze of glistening stone. She knew where she was: this was Highgate Cemetery. She could not recall how she knew that, since she had no memory of ever having been to this place before. No more could she think how she knew her steps were taking her deeper into the cemetery instead of toward the gate.

A splash of color trickled onto her breast, staining its paleness as the rain dissolved it into a red rose above her heart.

She opened her mouth to scream, and a great bubble of unswallowed blood spewed from her lips.

"Elisabeth! Elisabeth!"
"Lisette! Lisette!"
Whose voice called her?
"Lisette! You can wake up now, Lisette."
Dr. Magnus' face peered into her own. Was there sudden concern behind that urbane mask?
"You're awake now, Miss Seyrig. Everything is all right."

Lisette stared back at him for a moment, uncertain of her reality, as if suddenly awakened from some profound nightmare.

"I . . . I thought I was dead." Her eyes still held her fear.

Dr. Magnus smiled to reassure her. "Somnambulism, my dear. You remembered an episode of sleepwalking from a former life. Tell me, have you yourself ever walked in your sleep?"

Lisette pressed her hands to her face, abruptly examined her fingers. "I don't know. I mean, I don't think so."

She sat up, searched in her bag for her compact. She paused for a moment before opening the mirror.

"Dr. Magnus, I don't think I care to continue these sessions." She stared at her reflection in fascination, not touching her makeup, and when she snapped the case shut, the frightened strain began to relax from her face. She wished she had a cigarette.

Dr. Magnus sighed and pressed his fingertips together, leaning back in his chair; watched her fidget with her clothing as she sat nervously on the edge of the couch.

"Do you really wish to terminate our exploration? We have, after all, made excellent progress during these last few sessions."

"Have we?"

"We have, indeed. You have consistently remembered incidents from the life of one Elisabeth Beresford, a young English lady living in London at the close of the last century. To the best of your knowledge of your family history, she is not an ancestress."

Dr. Magnus leaned forward, seeking to impart his enthusiasm. "Don't you see how important this is? If Elisabeth Beresford was not your ancestress, then there can be no question of genetic memory being involved. The only explanation must therefore be reincarnation—proof of the immortality of the soul. To establish this I must first confirm the existence of Elisabeth Beresford, and from that demonstrate that no familial bond exists between the two of you. We simply must explore this further."

"Must we? I meant, what progress have we made toward helping me, Dr. Magnus? It's all very good for you to be able to confirm your theories of reincarnation, but that doesn't do anything for me. If anything, the nightmares have grown more disturbing since we began these sessions."

"Then perhaps we dare not stop."

"What do you mean?" Lisette wondered what he might do if she suddenly bolted from the room.

"I mean that the nightmares will grow worse regardless of whether you decide to terminate our sessions. Your unconscious self is struggling to tell you some significant message from a previous existence. It will continue to do so no matter how stubbornly you will yourself not to listen. My task is to help you listen to this voice, to understand the message it must impart to you—and with this understanding and self-awareness, you will experience inner peace. Without my help . . . Well, to be perfectly frank, Miss Seyrig, you are in some danger of a complete emotional breakdown."

Lisette slumped back against the couch. She felt on the edge of panic and wished Danielle were here to support her.

"Why are my memories always nightmares?" Her voice shook, and she spoke slowly to control it.

"But they aren't always frightening memories, my dear. It's just that the memory of some extremely traumatic experience often seeks to come to the fore. You would expect some tremendously emotional laden memory to be a potent one."

"Is Elisabeth Beresford . . . dead?"

"Assuming she was approximately twenty years of age at the time of Queen Victoria's Diamond Jubilee, she would have been past one hundred today. Besides, Miss Seyrig, her soul has been born again as your own. It must therefore follow . . ."

"Dr. Magnus. I don't *want* to know how Elisabeth Beresford died."

"Of course," Dr. Magnus told her gently. "Isn't that quite obvious?"

8

"For a wonder, it's forgot to rain tonight."

"Thank god for small favors," Lisette commented, thinking July in London had far more to do with monsoons than the romantic city of fogs celebrated in song. "All we need is to get these rained on."

She and Danielle bounced about on the back seat of the black Austin taxi, as their driver democratically seemed as willing to challenge lorries as pedestrians for right-of-way on the Edgeware Road. Feeling a bit self-conscious, Lisette tugged at the hem of her patent leather trench coat. They had decided to wear brightly embroidered Chinese silk lounging pyjamas that they'd found at one of the vintage clothing shops off the Portobello Road—gauzy enough for stares, but only a demure trouser-leg showing beneath their coats. "We're going to a masquerade party," Lisette had felt obliged to explain to the driver. Her concern was need-less, as he hadn't given them a second glance. Either he was used to the current Chinese look in fashion, or else a few seasons of picking up cou-ples at discos and punk rock clubs had inured him to any sort of cos-tume.

The taxi turned into a series of side streets off Maida Vale and even-tually made a neat U-turn that seemed almost an automotive pirouette. The frenetic beat of a new wave rock group clattered past the gate of an enclosed courtyard: something Mews—the iron plaque on the brick wall was too rusted to decipher in the dark—but from the lights and noise it must be the right address. A number of expensive-looking cars—Lisette recognized a Rolls or two and at least one Ferrari—were among those crowded against the curb. They squeezed their way past them and made for the source of the revelry, a brick-fronted townhouse of three or more storeys set at the back of the courtyard.

The door was opened by a girl in an abbreviated maid's costume. She checked their invitation while a similarly clad girl took their coats, and a third invited them to select from an assortment of masks and indicated where they might change. Lisette and Danielle chose sequined domino masks that matched the dangling scarves they wore tied low across their brows.

Danielle withdrew an ebony cigarette holder from her bag and con-sidered their reflections with approval. "Divinely decadent," she drawled, gesturing with her black-lacquered nails. "All that time for my eyes, and just to cover them with a mask. Perhaps later—when it's cock's-crow and all unmask . . . Forward, darling."

Lisette kept at her side, feeling a bit lost and out of place. When they passed before a light, it was evident that they wore nothing beneath the silk pyjamas, and Lisette was grateful for the strategic brocade. As they came upon others of the newly arriving guests, she decided there was no danger of outraging anyone's modesty here. As Midge had promised, anything goes so long as it's wild, and while their costumes might pass for street wear, many of the guests needed avail themselves of the changing rooms upstairs.

A muscular young man clad only in a leather loincloth and a sword belt with broadsword descended the stairs leading a buxom girl by a chain affixed to her wrists; aside from her manacles, she wore a few scraps of leather. A couple in punk rock gear spat at them in passing; the girl was wearing a set of panties with dangling razor blades for tassels and a pair of black latex tights that might have been spray paint. Two girls in vintage Christian Dior New Look evening gowns ogled the semi-nude swordsman from the landing above; Lisette noted their pronounced shoulders and Adam's apples and felt a twinge of jealousy that hormones and surgery could let them show a better cleavage than she could.

A new wave group called the Needle was performing in a large first-floor room—Lisette supposed it was an actual ballroom, although the house's original tenants would have considered tonight's ball a *danse macabre*. Despite the fact that the decibel level was well past the threshold of pain, most of the guests were congregated here, with smaller, quieter parties gravitating into other rooms. Here, about half were dancing, the rest standing about trying to talk. Marijuana smoke was barely discernible within the harsh haze of British cigarettes.

"There's Midge and Fiona," Danielle shouted in Lisette's ear. She waved energetically and steered a course through the dancers.

Midge was wearing an elaborate medieval gown—a heavily brocaded affair that ran from the floor to midway across her nipples. Her blonde hair was piled high in some sort of conical headpiece, complete with flowing scarf. Fiona waited upon her in a page boy's costume.

"Are you just getting here?" Midge asked, running a deprecative glance down Lisette's costume. "There's champagne over on the sideboard. Wait, I'll summon one of the cute little French maids."

Lisette caught two glasses from a passing tray and presented one to Danielle. It was impossible to converse, but then she hadn't anything to talk about with Midge, and Fiona was no more than a shadow.

"Where's our hostess?" Danielle asked.

"Not down yet," Midge managed to shout. "Beth always waits to make a grand entrance at her little dos. You won't miss her."

"Speaking of entrances . . ." Lisette commented, nodding toward the couple who were just coming onto the dance floor. The woman wore a Nazi SS officer's hat, jackboots, black trousers and braces across her bare chest. She was astride the back of her male companion, who wore a saddle and bridle in addition to a few other bits of leather harness.

"I can't decide whether that's kinky or just tacky," Lisette said.

"Not like your little sorority teas back home, is it?" Midge smiled.

"Is there any coke about?" Danielle interposed quickly.

"There was a short while ago. Try the library—that's the room just down from where everyone's changing."

Lisette downed her champagne and grabbed a refill before following Danielle upstairs. A man in fish-net tights, motorcycle boots and a vest comprised mostly of chain and bits of Nazi medals caught at her arm and seemed to want to dance. Instead of a mask, he wore about a pound of eye shadow and black lipstick. She shouted an inaudible excuse, held a finger to her nostril and sniffed, and darted after Danielle.

"That was Eddie Teeth, lead singer for the Trepans, whom you just cut," Danielle told her. "Why didn't he grab *me!*"

"You'll get your chance," Lisette told her. "I think he's following us."

Danielle dragged her to a halt halfway up the stairs.

"Got toot right here, loves." Eddie Teeth flipped the silver spoon and phial that dangled amidst the chains on his vest.

"Couldn't take the noise in there any longer," Lisette explained.

"Needle's shit." Eddie Teeth wrapped an arm about either waist and propelled them up the stairs. "You gashes sisters? I can dig incest."

The library was pleasantly crowded—Lisette decided she didn't want to be cornered with Eddie Teeth. A dozen or more guests stood about, sniffing and conversing energetically. Seated at a table, two of the ubiquitous maids busily cut lines onto mirrors and set them out for the guests, whose number remained more or less constant as people wandered in and left. A cigarette box offered tightly rolled joints.

"That's Thai." Eddie Teeth groped for a handful of the joints, stuck one in each girl's mouth, the rest inside his vest. Danielle giggled and fitted hers to her cigarette holder. Unfastening a silver tube from his vest, he snorted two thick lines from one of the mirrors. "Toot your eyeballs out, loves," he invited them.

One of the maids collected the mirror when they had finished and replaced it with another—a dozen lines of cocaine neatly arranged across it's surface. Industriously she began to work a chunk of rock through a sifter to replenish the empty mirror. Lisette watched in fascination. This finally brought home to her the wealth this party represented: all the rest simply seemed to her like something out of a movie, but dealing out coke to more than a hundred guests was an extravagance she could relate to.

"Danielle Borland, isn't it?"

A man dressed as Mephistopheles bowed before them. "Adrian Tregannet. We've met at one of Midge Vaughn's parties, you may recall."

Danielle stared at the face below the domino mask. "Oh, yes. Lisette, it's Mephisto himself."

"Then this is Miss Seyrig, the subject of your charcoal drawing that Beth so admires." Mephisto caught Lisette's hand and bent his lips to it. "Beth is so much looking forward to meeting you both."

Lisette retrieved her hand. "Aren't you the . . ."

"The rude fellow who accosted you in Kensington some days ago," Tregannet finished apologetically. "Yes, I'm afraid so. But you really must forgive me for my forwardness. I actually did mistake you for a very dear friend of mine, you see. Won't you let me make amends over a glass of champagne?"

"Certainly." Lisette decided that she had had quite enough of Eddie Teeth, and Danielle was quite capable of fending for herself if she grew tired of having her breasts squeezed by a famous pop star.

Tregannet quickly returned with two glasses of champagne. Lisette finished another two lines and smiled appreciatively as she accepted a glass. Danielle was trying to shotgun Eddie Teeth through her cigarette holder, and Lisette thought it a good chance to slip away.

"Your roommate is tremendously talented," Tregannet suggested. "Of course, she chose so charming a subject for her drawing."

Slick as snake oil, Lisette thought, letting him take her arm. "How very nice of you to say so. However, I really feel a bit embarrassed to think that some stranger owns a portrait of me in my underwear."

"Utterly chaste, my dear—as chaste as the *Dark Rose* of its title. Beth chose to hang it in her boudoir, so I hardly think it is on public display. I suspect from your garments in the drawing that you must share Beth's appreciation for the dress and manners of this past century."

Which is something I'd never suspect of our hostess, judging from this party, Lisette considered. "I'm quite looking forward to meeting her. I assume then that Ms. is a bit too modern for one of such quiet tastes. Is it Miss or Mrs. Garrington?"

"Ah, I hadn't meant to suggest an impression of a genteel dowager. Beth is entirely of your generation—a few years older than yourself, perhaps. Although I find Ms. too suggestive of American slang, I'm sure Beth would not object. However, there's no occasion for such formality here."

"You seem to know her well, Mr. Tregannet."

"It is an old family. I know her aunt, Julia Weatherford, quite well through our mutual interest in the occult. Perhaps you, too . . . ?"

"Not really; Danielle is the one you should chat with about that. My field is art. I'm over here on fellowship at London University." She watched Danielle and Eddie Teeth toddle off for the ballroom and jealously decided that Danielle's taste in her acquaintances left much to be desired. "Could I have some more champagne?"

"To be sure. I won't be a moment."

Lisette snorted a few more lines while she waited. A young man dressed as an Edwardian dandy offered her his snuff box and gravely demonstrated its use. Lisette was struggling with a sneezing fit when Tregannet returned.

"You needn't have gone to all the bother," she told him. "These little French maids are dashing about with trays of champagne."

"But those glasses have lost the proper chill," Tregannet explained. "To your very good health."

"Cheers." Lisette felt lightheaded, and promised herself to go easy for a while. "Does Beth live here with her aunt, then?"

"Her aunt lives on the Continent; I don't believe she's visited London for several years. Beth moved in about ten years ago. Theirs is not a large family, but they are not without wealth, as you can observe. They travel a great deal as well, and it's fortunate that Beth happened to be in London during your stay here. Incidently, just how long will you be staying in London?"

"About a year is all." Lisette finished her champagne. "Then it's back to my dear, dull family in San Francisco."

"Then there's no one here in London . . . ?"

"Decidedly not, Mr. Tregannet. And now if you'll excuse me, I think
I'll find the ladies'."

Cocaine might well be the champagne of drugs, but cocaine and
champagne didn't seem to mix well, Lisette mused, turning the bathroom over to the next frantic guest. Her head felt really buzzy, and she
thought she might do better if she found a bedroom somewhere and lay
down for a moment. But then she'd most likely wake up and find some
man on top of her, judging from this lot. She decided she'd lay off the
champagne and have just a line or two to shake off the feeling of having
been sandbagged.

The crowd in the study had changed during her absence. Just now it
was dominated by a group of guests dressed in costumes from *The
Rocky Horror Show*, now closing out its long run at the Comedy Theatre
in Piccadilly. Lisette had grown bored with the fad the film version had
generated in the States, and pushed her way past the group as they vig-
orously danced the Time Warp and bellowed out songs from the show.

" 'Give yourself over to absolute pleasure,' " someone sang in her ear
as she industriously snorted a line from the mirror. " 'Erotic nightmares
beyond any measure,' " the song continued.

Lisette finished a second line, and decided she had had enough. She
straightened from the table and broke for the doorway. The tall trans-
vestite dressed as Frankie barred her way with a dramatic gesture,
singing ardently: " 'Don't dream it—be it!' "

Lisette blew him a kiss and ducked around him. She wished she could
find a quiet place to collect her thoughts. Maybe she should find
Danielle first—if she could handle the ballroom that long.

The dance floor was far more crowded than when they'd come in. At
least all these jostling bodies seemed to absorb some of the decibels
from the blaring banks of amplifiers and speakers. Lisette looked in vain
for Danielle amidst the dancers, succeeding only in getting champagne
sloshed on her back. She caught sight of Midge, recognizable above the
mob by her conical medieval headdress, and pushed her way toward her.

Midge was being fed caviar on bits of toast by Fiona while she talked
with an older woman who looked like the pictures Lisette had seen of
Marlene Dietrich dressed in men's formal evening wear.

"Have you seen Danielle?" Lisette asked her.

"Why, not recently, darling," Midge smiled, licking caviar from her lips with the tip of her tongue. "I believe she and that rock singer were headed upstairs for a bit more privacy. I'm sure she'll come collect you once they're finished."

"Midge, you're a cunt," Lisette told her through her sweetest smile. She turned away and made for the doorway, trying not to ruin her exit by staggering. Screw Danielle—she needed to have some fresh air.

A crowd had gathered at the foot of the stairway, and she had to push through the doorway to escape the ballroom. Behind her, the Needle mercifully took a break. "She's coming down!" Lisette heard someone whisper breathlessly. The inchoate babel of the party fell to a sudden lull that made Lisette shiver.

At the top of the stairway stood a tall woman, enveloped in a black velvet cloak from her throat to her ankles. Her blonde hair was piled high in a complex variation of the once-fashionable French twist. Strings of garnets entwined in her hair and edged the close-fitting black mask that covered the upper half of her face. For a hushed interval she stood there, gazing imperiously down upon her guests.

Adrian Tregannet leapt to the foot of the stairway. He signed to a pair of maids, who stepped forward to either side of their mistress.

"Milords and miladies!" he announced with a sweeping bow. "Let us pay honor to our bewitching mistress whose feast we celebrate tonight! I give you the lamia who haunted Adam's dreams—Lilith!"

The maids smoothly swept the cloak from their mistress' shoulders. From the multitude at her feet came an audible intake of breath. Beth Garrington was attired in a strapless corselette of gleaming black leather, laced tightly about her waist. The rest of her costume consisted only of knee-length, stiletto-heeled tight boots, above-the-elbow gloves, and a spiked collar around her throat—all of black leather that contrasted starkly against her white skin and blonde hair. At first Lisette thought she wore a bull-whip coiled about her body as well, but then the coils moved, and she realized that it was an enormous black snake.

"Lilith!" came the shout, chanted in a tone of awe. "Lilith!"

Acknowledging their worship with a sinuous gesture, Beth Garrington descended the staircase. The serpent coiled from gloved arm to gloved arm, entwining her cinched waist, its eyes considered the revellers imperturbably. Champagne glasses lifted in a toast to Lilith, and the chattering voice of the party once more began to fill the house.

Tregannet touched Beth's elbow as she greeted her guests at the foot of the stairway. He whispered into her ear, and she smiled graciously and moved away with him.

Lisette clung to the staircase newel, watching them approach. Her head was spinning, and she desperately needed to lie down in some fresh air, but she couldn't trust her legs to carry her outside. She stared into the eyes of the serpent, hypnotized by its flickering tongue.

The room seemed to surge in and out of focus. The masks of the guests seemed to leer and gloat with the awareness of some secret jest; the dancers in their fantastic costumes became a grotesque horde of satyrs and wanton demons, writhing about the ballroom in some witches' sabbat of obscene mass copulation. As in a nightmare, Lisette willed her legs to turn and run, realized that her body was no longer obedient to her will.

"Beth, here's someone you've been dying to meet," Lisette heard Tregannet say. "Beth Garrington, allow me to present Lisette Seyrig."

The lips beneath the black mask curved in a pleasurable smile. Lisette gazed into the eyes behind the mask, and discovered that she could no longer feel her body. She thought she heard Danielle cry out her name.

The eyes remained in her vision long after she slid down the newel and collapsed upon the floor.

9

The Catherine Wheel was a pub on Kensington Church Street. They served good pub lunches there, and Lisette liked to stop in before walking down Holland Street for her sessions with Dr. Magnus. Since today was her final such session, it seemed appropriate that they should end the evening here.

"While I dislike repeating myself," Dr. Magnus spoke earnestly, "I really do think we should continue."

Lisette drew on a cigarette and shook her head decisively. "No way, Dr. Magnus. My nerves are shot to hell. I mean, look—when I freak out at a costume party and have to be carted home to bed by my roommate! It was like when I was a kid and got hold of some bad acid: the whole world was some bizarre and sinister freak show for weeks. Once I got my head back on, I said: No more acid."

"That was rather a notorious circle you were travelling in. Further, you were, if I understand you correctly, overindulging a bit that evening."

"A few glasses of champagne and a little toot never did anything before but make me a bit giggly and talkative." Lisette sipped her half of lager; she'd never developed a taste for English bitter, and at least the lager was chilled. They sat across from each other at a table the size of a hubcap; she in the corner of a padded bench against the wall, he at a chair set out into the room, pressed in by a wall of standing bodies. A foot away from her on the padded bench, three young men huddled about a similar table, talking animatedly. For all that, she and Dr. Magnus might have been all alone in the room. Lisette wondered if the psychologist who had coined the faddish concept of "space" had been inspired in a crowded English pub.

"It isn't just that I fainted at the party. It isn't just the nightmares." She paused to find words. "It's just that everything somehow seems to be drifting out of focus, out of control. It's . . . well, it's frightening."

"Precisely why we must continue."

"Precisely why we must not." Lisette sighed. They'd covered this ground already. It had been a moment of weakness when she agreed to allow Dr. Magnus to buy her a drink afterward instead of heading back to the flat. Still, he had been so distressed when she told him she was terminating their sessions.

"I've tried to cooperate with you as best I could, and I'm certain you are entirely sincere in your desire to help me." Well, she wasn't all *that* certain, but no point in going into that. "However, the fact remains that since we began these sessions, my nerves have gone to hell. You say they'd be worse without the sessions, I say the sessions have made them worse, and maybe there's no connection at all—it's just that my nerves have gotten worse, so now I'm going to trust my intuition and try life without these sessions. Fair enough?"

Dr. Magnus gazed uncomfortably at his barely tasted glass of sherry. "While I fully understand your rationale, I must in all conscience beg you to reconsider, Lisette. You are running risks that . . ."

"Look. If the nightmares go away, then terrific. If they don't, I can always pack up and head back to San Francisco. That way I'll be clear of whatever it is about London that disagrees with me, and if not, I'll see my psychiatrist back home."

"Very well, then." Dr. Magnus squeezed her hand. "However, please bear in mind that I remain eager to continue our sessions at any time, should you change your mind."

"That's fair enough, too. And very kind of you."

Dr. Magnus lifted his glass of sherry to the light. Pensively, he remarked: "Amber."

10

"Lisette?"

Danielle locked the front door behind her and hung up her inadequate umbrella in the hallway. She considered her face in the mirror and grimaced at the mess of her hair. "Lisette? Are you here?"

No answer, and her rain things were not in the hallway. Either she was having a late session with Dr. Magnus, or else she'd wisely decided to duck under cover until this bloody rain let up. After she'd had to carry Lisette home in a taxi when she passed out at the party, Danielle was starting to feel real concern over her state of health.

Danielle kicked off her damp shoes as she entered the living room. The curtains were drawn against the greyness outside, and she switched on a lamp to brighten the flat a bit. Her dress clung to her like a clammy fish-skin; she shivered, and thought about a cup of coffee. If Lisette hadn't returned yet, there wouldn't be any brewed. She'd have a warm shower instead, and after that she'd see to the coffee—if Lisette hadn't returned to set a pot going in the meantime.

"Lisette?" Their bedroom was empty. Danielle turned on the overhead light. Christ, it was gloomy! So much for long English summer evenings—with all the rain, she couldn't remember when she'd last seen the sun. She struggled out of her damp dress, spread it flat across her bed with the vague hope that it might not wrinkle too badly, then tossed her bra and tights onto a chair.

Slipping into her bathrobe, Danielle padded back into the living room.

Still no sign of Lisette, and it was past nine. Perhaps she'd stopped off at a pub. Crossing to the stereo, Danielle placed the new Blondie album on the turntable and turned up the volume. Let the neighbors complain—at least this would help dispel the evening's gloom.

She cursed the delay needed to adjust the shower temperature to satisfaction, then climbed into the tub. The hot spray felt good, and she stood under it contentedly for several minutes—initially revitalized, then lulled into a delicious sense of relaxation. Through the rush of the spray, she could hear the muffled beat of the stereo. As she reached for the shampoo, she began to move her body with the rhythm.

The shower curtain billowed as the bathroom door opened. Danielle risked a soapy squint around the curtain—she knew the flat was securely locked, but after seeing *Psycho* . . . It was only Lisette, already undressed, her long blonde hair falling over her breasts.

"Didn't hear you come in with the stereo going," Danielle greeted her. "Come on in before you catch cold."

Danielle resumed lathering her hair as the shower curtain parted and the other girl stepped into the tub behind her. Her eyes squeezed shut against the soap, she felt Lisette's breasts thrust against her back, her flat belly press against her buttocks. Lisette's hands came around her to cup her breasts gently.

At least Lisette had gotten over her silly tiff about Eddie Teeth. She'd explained to Lisette that she'd ditched that greasy slob when he'd tried to dry hump her on the dance floor, but how do you reason with a silly thing who faints at the sight of a snake?

"Jesus, you're chilled to the bone!" Danielle complained with a shiver. "Better stand under the shower and get warm. Did you get caught in the rain?"

The other girl's fingers continued to caress her breasts, and instead of answering, her lips teased the nape of Danielle's neck. Danielle made a delighted sound deep in her throat, letting the spray rinse the lather from her hair and over their embraced bodies. Languidly she turned about to face her lover, closing her arms about Lisette's shoulders for support.

Lisette's kisses held each taut nipple for a moment, teasing them almost painfully. Danielle pressed the other girl's face to her breasts, sighed as her kisses nibbled upward to her throat. She felt weak with arousal, and only Lisette's strength held her upright in the tub. Her lover's lips upon her throat tormented her beyond enduring; Danielle gasped and lifted Lisette's face to meet her own.

Her mouth was open to receive Lisette's red-lipped kiss, and it opened wider as Danielle stared into the eyes of her lover. Her first emotion was one of wonder.

"You're not Lisette!"

It was nearly midnight when Lisette unlocked the door to their flat and quietly let herself in. Only a few lights were on, and there was no sign of Danielle—either she had gone out, or, more likely, had gone to bed.

Lisette hung up her raincoat and wearily pulled off her shoes. She'd barely caught the last train. She must have been crazy to let Dr. Magnus talk her into returning to his office for another session that late, but then he was quite right: as serious as her problems were, she really did need all the help he could give her. She felt a warm sense of gratitude to Dr. Magnus for being there when she so needed his help.

The turntable had stopped, but a light on the amplifier indicated that the power was still on. Lisette cut it off and closed the lid over the turntable. She felt too tired to listen to an album just now.

She became aware that the shower was running. In that case, Danielle hadn't gone to bed. She supposed she really ought to apologize to her for letting Midge's bitchy lies get under her skin. After all, she had ruined the party for Danielle; poor Danielle had had to get her to bed and had left the party without ever getting to meet Beth Garrington, and she was the one Beth had invited in the first place.

"Danielle? I'm back." Lisette called through the bathroom door. "Do you want anything?"

No answer. Lisette looked into their bedroom, just in case Danielle had invited a friend over. No, the beds were still made up; Danielle's clothes were spread out by themselves.

"Danielle?" Lisette raised her voice. Perhaps she couldn't hear over the noise of the shower. "Danielle?" Surely she was all right.

Lisette's feet felt damp. She looked down. A puddle of water was seeping beneath the door. Danielle must not have the shower curtains closed properly.

"Danielle! You're flooding us!"

Lisette opened the door and peered cautiously within. The curtain was closed, right enough. A thin spray still reached through a gap, and the shower had been running long enough for the puddle to spread. It occurred to Lisette that she should see Danielle's silhouette against the translucent shower curtain.

"Danielle!" She began to grow alarmed. "Danielle! Are you all right?"

She pattered across the wet tiles and drew aside the curtain. Danielle lay in the bottom of the tub, the spray falling on her upturned smile, her flesh paler than the porcelain of the tub.

11

It was early afternoon when they finally allowed her to return to the flat. Had she been able to think of another place to go, she probably would have gone there. Instead, Lisette wearily slumped onto the couch, too spent to pour herself the drink she desperately wanted.

Somehow she had managed to phone the police, through her hysteria make them understand where she was. Once the squad car arrived, she had no further need to act out of her own initiative; she simply was carried along in the rush of police investigation. It wasn't until they were questioning her at New Scotland Yard that she realized she herself was not entirely free from suspicion.

The victim had bled to death, the medical examiner ruled, her blood washed down the tub drain. A safety razor used for shaving legs had been opened, its blade removed. There were razor incisions along both wrists, directed lengthwise, into the radial artery, as opposed to the shallow, crosswise cuts utilized by suicides unfamiliar with human anatomy. There was, in addition, an incision in the left side of the throat. It was either a very determined suicide, or a skillfully concealed murder. In view of the absence of any signs of forced entry or of a struggle, more likely the former. The victim's roommate did admit to a recent quarrel. Laboratory tests would indicate whether the victim might have been drugged or rendered unconscious through a blow. After that, the inquest would decide.

Lisette had explained that she had spent the evening with Dr. Magnus. The fact that she was receiving emotional therapy, as they interpreted it, caused several mental notes to be made. Efforts to reach Dr. Magnus by telephone proved unsuccessful, but his secretary did confirm that Miss Seyrig had shown up for her appointment the previous afternoon. Dr. Magnus would get in touch with them as soon as he returned to his office. No, she did not know why he had cancelled today's appointments, but it was not unusual for Dr. Magnus to dash off suddenly when essential research demanded immediate attention.

After a while they let Lisette make phone calls. She phoned her parents, then wished she hadn't. It was still the night before in California, and it was like turning back the hands of time to no avail. They urged her to take the next flight home, but of course it wasn't all that simple, and it just wasn't feasible for either of them to fly over on a second's notice, since after all there really was nothing they could do. She phoned Maitland Reddin, who was stunned at the news and offered to help in any way he could, but Lisette couldn't think of any way. She phoned Midge Vaughn, who hung up on her. She phoned Dr. Magnus, who still couldn't be reached. Mercifully, the police took care of phoning Danielle's next of kin.

A physician at New Scotland Yard had spoken with her briefly and had given her some pills—a sedative to ease her into sleep after her ordeal. They had driven her back to the flat after impressing upon her the need to be present at the inquest. She must not be concerned should any hypothetical assailant yet be lurking about, inasmuch as the flat would be under surveillance.

Lisette stared dully about the flat, still unable to comprehend what had happened. The police had been thorough—measuring, dusting for fingerprints, leaving things in a mess. Bleakly, Lisette tried to convince herself that this was only another nightmare, that in a moment Danielle would pop in and find her asleep on the couch. Christ, what was she going to do with all of Danielle's things? Danielle's mother was remarried and living in Colorado; her father was an executive in a New York investment corporation. Evidently he had made arrangements to have the body shipped back to the States.

"Oh, Danielle." Lisette was too stunned for tears. Perhaps she should check into a hotel for now. No, she couldn't bear being all alone with her thoughts in a strange place. How strange to realize now that she really had no close friends in London other than Danielle—and what friends she did have were mostly people she'd met through Danielle.

She'd left word with Dr. Magnus's secretary for him to call her once he came in. Perhaps she should call there once again, just in case Dr. Magnus had missed her message. Lisette couldn't think what good Dr. Magnus could do, but he was such an understanding person, and she felt much better whenever she spoke with him.

She considered the bottle of pills in her bag. Perhaps it would be best to take a couple of them and sleep around the clock. She felt too drained just now to have energy enough to think.

The phone began to ring. Lisette stared at it for a moment without comprehension, then lunged up from the couch to answer it.

"Is this Lisette Seyrig?"

It was a woman's voice—one Lisette didn't recognize. "Yes. Who's calling, please?"

"This is Beth Garrington, Lisette. I hope I'm not disturbing you."

"That's quite all right."

"You poor dear! Maitland Reddin phoned to tell me of the tragedy. I can't tell you how shocked I am. Danielle seemed such a dear from our brief contact, and she had such a great talent."

"Thank you. I'm sorry you weren't able to know her better." Lisette sensed guilt and embarrassment at the memory of that brief contact.

"Darling, you can't be thinking about staying in that flat alone. Is there someone there with you?"

"No, there isn't. That's all right. I'll be fine."

"Don't be silly. Listen, I have enough empty bedrooms in this old barn to open a hotel. Why don't you just pack a few things and come straight over?"

"That's very kind of you, but I really couldn't."

"Nonsense! It's no good for you to be there all by yourself. Strange as this may sound, but when I'm not throwing one of these invitational riots, this is a quiet little backwater and things are dull as church. I'd love the company, and it will do you a world of good to get away."

"You're really very kind to invite me, but I . . ."

"Please Lisette—be reasonable. I have guest rooms here already made up, and I'll send the car around to pick you up. All you need do is say yes and toss a few things into your bag. After a good night's sleep, you'll feel much more like coping with things tomorrow."

When Lisette didn't immediately reply, Beth added carefully: "Besides, Lisette. I understand the police haven't ruled out the possibility of murder. In that event, unless poor Danielle simply forgot to lock up, there is a chance that whoever did this has a key to your flat."

"The police said they'd watch the house."

"He might also be someone you both know and trust, someone Danielle invited in."

Lisette stared wildly at the sinister shadows that lengthened about the flat. Her refuge had been violated. Even familiar objects seemed tainted and alien. She fought back tears. "I don't know what to think." She realized she'd been clutching the receiver for a long, silent interval.

"Poor dear! There's nothing you need think about! Now listen. I'm at my solicitor's tidying up some property matters for Aunt Julia. I'll phone right now to have my car sent around for you. It'll be there by the time you pack your toothbrush and pyjamas, and whisk you straight off to bucolic Maida Vale. The maids will plump up your pillows for you, and you can have a nice nap before I get home for dinner. Poor darling, I'll bet you haven't eaten a thing. Now, say you'll come."

"Thank you. It's awfully good of you. Of course I will."

"Then it's done. Don't worry about a thing, Lisette. I'll see you this evening."

12

Dr. Magnus hunched forward on the narrow seat of the taxi, wearily massaging his forehead and temples. It might not help his mental fatigue, but maybe the reduced muscle tension would ease his headache. He glanced at his watch. Getting on past ten. He'd had no sleep last night, and it didn't look as if he'd be getting much tonight. If only those girls would answer their phone!

It didn't help matters that his conscience plagued him. He had broken a sacred trust. He should never have made use of posthypnotic suggestion last night to persuade Lisette to return for a further session. It went against all principles, but there had been no other course: the girl was adamant, and he had to know—he was so close to establishing final proof. If only for one final session of regressive hypnosis . . .

Afterward he had spent a sleepless night, too excited for rest, at work in his study trying to reconcile the conflicting elements of Lisette's released memories with the historical data his research had so far compiled. By morning he had been able to pull together just enough facts to deepen the mystery. He had phoned his secretary at home to cancel all his appointments, and had spent the day at the tedious labor of delving through dusty municipal records and newspaper files, working feverishly as the past reluctantly yielded one bewildering clue after another.

By now Dr. Magnus was exhausted, hungry and none too clean, but he had managed to establish proof of his theories. He was not elated. In doing so he had uncovered another secret, something undreamt of in his philosophies. He began to hope that his life work was in error.

"Here's the address, sir."

"Thank you, driver." Dr. Magnus awoke from his grim revery and saw that he had reached his destination. Quickly, he paid the driver and hurried up the walk to Lisette's flat. Only a few lights were on, and he rang the bell urgently—a helpless sense of foreboding making his movements clumsy.

"Just one moment, sir!"

Dr. Magnus jerked about at the voice. Two men in plain clothes approached him briskly from the pavement.

"Stand easy! We're police."

"Is something the matter, officers?" Obviously, something was.

"Might we ask what your business here is, sir?"

"Certainly. I'm a friend of Miss Borland and Miss Seyrig. I haven't been able to reach them by phone, and as I have some rather urgent matters to discuss with Miss Seyrig, I thought perhaps I might try reaching her here at her flat." He realized he was far too nervous.

"Might we see some identification, sir?"

"Is there anything wrong, officers?" Magnus repeated, producing his wallet.

"Dr. Ingmar Magnus." The taller of the pair regarded him quizzically. "I take it you don't keep up with the news, Dr. Magnus."

"Just what is this about!"

"I'm Inspector Bradley, Dr. Magnus, and this is Detective Sergeant Wharton. CID. We've been wanting to ask you a few questions, sir, if you'll just come with us."

It was totally dark when Lisette awoke from troubled sleep. She stared wide-eyed into the darkness for a moment, wondering where she was. Slowly memory supplanted the vague images of her dream. Switching on a lamp beside her bed, Lisette frowned at her watch. It was close to midnight. She had overslept.

Beth's Rolls had come for her almost before she had had time hastily to pack her overnight bag. Once at the house in Maida Vale, a maid— wearing a more conventional uniform than those at her last visit—had shown her to a spacious guest room on the top floor. Lisette had taken a sedative pill and gratefully collapsed onto the bed. She'd planned to catch a short nap, then meet her hostess for dinner. Instead she had slept for almost ten solid hours. Beth must be convinced she was a hopeless twit after this.

As so often happens after an overextended nap, Lisette now felt restless. She wished she'd thought to bring a book. The house was completely silent. Surely it was too late to ring for a maid. No doubt Beth had meant to let her sleep through until morning, and by now would have retired herself. Perhaps she should take another pill and go back to sleep herself.

On the other hand, Beth Garrington hardly seemed the type to make it an early night. She might well still be awake, perhaps watching television where the noise wouldn't disturb her guest. In any event, Lisette didn't want to go back to sleep just yet.

She climbed out of bed, realizing that she'd only half undressed before falling asleep. Pulling off bra and panties, Lisette slipped into the antique nightdress of ribbons and lace she'd brought along. She hadn't thought to pack slippers or a robe, but it was a warm night, and the white cotton gown was modest enough for a peek into the hall.

There was a ribbon of light edging the door of the room at the far end of the hall. The rest of the hallway lay in darkness. Lisette stepped quietly from her room. Since Beth hadn't mentioned other guests, and the servants' quarters were elsewhere, presumably the light was coming from her hostess' bedroom and indicated she might still be awake.

Lisette decided she really should make the effort to meet her hostess while in a conscious state.

She heard a faint sound of music as she tiptoed down the hallway. The door to the room was ajar, and the music came from within. She was in luck; Beth must still be up. At the doorway she knocked softly.

"Beth? Are you awake? It's Lisette."

There was no answer, but the door swung open at her touch.

Lisette started to call out again, but her voice froze in her throat. She recognized the tune she heard, and she knew this room. When she entered the bedroom, she could no more alter her actions than she could control the course of her dreams.

It was a large bedroom, entirely furnished in the mode of the late Victorian period. The windows were curtained, and the room's only light came from a candle upon a night table beside the huge four-poster bed. An antique gold pocket watch lay upon the night table also, and the watch was chiming an old music-box tune.

Lisette crossed the room, praying that this was no more than another vivid recurrence of her nightmare. She reached the night table and saw that the watch's hands pointed toward midnight. The chimes stopped. She picked up the watch and examined the picture that she knew would be inside the watchcase.

The picture was a photograph of herself.

Lisette let the watch clatter onto the table, stared in terror at the four-poster bed.

From within, a hand drew back the bed curtains.

Lisette wished she could scream, could awaken.

Sweeping aside the curtains, the occupant of the bed sat up and gazed at her.

And Lisette stared back at herself.

"Can't you drive a bit faster than this?"

Inspector Bradley resisted the urge to wink at Detective Sergeant Wharton. "Sit back, Dr. Magnus. We'll be there in good time. I trust you'll have rehearsed some apologies for when we disrupt a peaceful household in the middle of the night."

"I only pray such apologies will be necessary," Dr. Magnus said, continuing to sit forward as if that would inspire the driver to go faster.

It hadn't been easy, Dr. Magnus reflected. He dare not tell them the truth. He suspected that Bradley had agreed to making a late night call on Beth Garrington more to check out his alibi than from any credence he gave to Magnus's improvised tale.

Buried all day in frenzied research, Dr. Magnus hadn't listened to the news, had ignored the tawdry London tabloids with their lurid headlines: "Naked Beauty Slashed in Tub" "Nude Model Slain in Bath" "Party Girl Suicide or Ripper's Victim?" The shock of learning of Danielle's death was seconded by the shock of discovering that he was one of the "important leads" police were following.

It had taken all his powers of persuasion to convince them to release him—or, at least, to accompany him to the house in Maida Vale. Ironically, he and Lisette were the only ones who could account for each other's presence elsewhere at the time of Danielle's death. While the CID might have been skeptical as to the nature of their late night session at Dr. Magnus's office, there were a few corroborating details. A barman at the Catherine Wheel had remembered the distinguished gent with the beard leaving after his lady friend had dropped off of a sudden. The cleaning lady had heard voices and left his office undisturbed. This much they'd already checked, in verifying Lisette's whereabouts that night. Half a dozen harassed records clerks could testify as to Dr. Magnus's presence for today.

Dr. Magnus grimly reviewed the results of his research. There was an Elisabeth Beresford, born in London in 1879, of a well-to-do family who lived in Cheyne Row on the Chelsea Embankment. Elisabeth Beresford married a Captain Donald Stapledon in 1899 and moved to India with her husband. She returned to London, evidently suffering from consumption contracted while abroad, and died in 1900. She was buried in Highgate Cemetery. That much Dr. Magnus had initially learned with some difficulty. From that basis he had pressed on for additional corroborating details, both from Lisette's released memories and from research into records of the period.

It had been particularly difficult to trace the subsequent branches of the family—something he must do in order to establish that Elisabeth Beresford could not have been an ancestress of Lisette Seyrig. And it disturbed him that he had been unable to locate Elisabeth Stapledon nee Beresford's tomb in Highgate Cemetery.

Last night he had pushed Lisette as relentlessly as he dared. Out of her resurfacing visions of horror he finally found a clue. These were not images from nightmare, not symbolic representations of buried fears. They were literal memories.

Because of the sensation involved and the considerable station of the families concerned, public records had discreetly avoided reference to the tragedy, as had the better newspapers. The yellow journals were less reticent, and here Dr. Magnus began to know fear.

Elisabeth Stapledon had been buried alive.

At her final wishes, the body had not been embalmed. The papers suggested that this was a clear premonition of her fate, and quoted passages from Edgar Allan Poe. Captain Stapledon paid an evening visit to his wife's tomb and discovered her wandering in a dazed condition about the graves. This was more than a month after her entombment.

The newspapers were full of pseudo-scientific theories, spiritualist explanations and long accounts of Indian mystics who had remained in a state of suspended animation for weeks on end. No one seems to have explained exactly how Elisabeth Stapledon escaped from both coffin and crypt, but it was supposed that desperate strength had wrenched loose the screws, while providentially the crypt had not been properly locked after a previous visit.

Husband and wife understandably went abroad immediately afterward, in order to escape publicity and for Elisabeth Stapledon to recover from her ordeal. This she very quickly did, but evidently the shock was more than Captain Stapledon could endure. He died in 1902, and his wife returned to London soon after, inheriting his extensive fortune and properties, including their house in Maida Vale. When she later inherited her own family's estate—her sole brother fell in the Boer War—she was a lady of great wealth.

Elisabeth Stapledon became one of the most notorious hostesses of the Edwardian era and on until the close of the First World War. Her beauty was considered remarkable, and men marvelled while her rivals bemoaned that she scarcely seemed to age with the passing years. After the War she left London to travel about the exotic East. In 1924 news came of her death in India.

Her estate passed to her daughter, Jane Stapledon, born abroad in 1901. While Elisabeth Stapledon made occasional references to her daughter, Jane was raised and educated in Europe and never seemed to have come to London until her arrival in 1925. Some had suggested that the mother had wished to keep her daughter pure from her own Bohemian life style, but when Jane Stapledon appeared, it seemed more likely that her mother's motives for her seclusion had been born of jealousy. Jane Stapledon had all her mother's beauty—indeed, her older admirers vowed she was the very image of Elisabeth in her youth. She also had inherited her mother's taste for wild living; with a new circle of friends from her own age group, she took up where her mother had left off. The newspapers were particularly scandalized by her association with Aleister Crowley and others of his circle. Although her dissipations bridged the years of Flaming Youth to the Lost Generation, even her enemies had to admit she carried her years extremely well. In 1943 Jane Stapledon was missing and presumed dead after an air raid levelled and burned a section of London where she had gone to dine with friends.

Papers in the hands of her solicitor left her estate to a daughter living in America, Julia Weatherford, born in Miami in 1934. Evidently her mother had enjoyed a typical whirlwind resort romance with an American millionaire while wintering in Florida. Their marriage was a secret one, annulled following Julia's birth, and her daughter had been left with her former husband. Julia Weatherford arrived from the States early in 1946. Any doubts as to the authenticity of her claim were instantly banished, for she was the very picture of her mother in her younger days. Julia again seemed to have the family's wild streak, and she carried on the tradition of wild parties and bizarre acquaintances through the Beat Generation to the Flower Children. Her older friends thought it amazing that Julia in a minidress might easily be mistaken as being of the same age group as her young, pot-smoking, hippie friends. But it may have been that at last her youth began to fade, because since 1967 Julia Weatherford had been living more or less in seclusion in Europe, occasionally visited by her niece.

Her niece, Beth Garrington, born in 1950, was the orphaned daughter of Julia's American half-sister and a wealthy young Englishman from Julia's collection. After her parents' death in a plane crash in 1970, Beth had become her aunt's protegée, and carried on the mad life in London. It was apparent that Beth Garrington would inherit her aunt's property as well. It was also apparent that she was the spitting image of her Aunt

Julia when the latter was her age. It would be most interesting to see the two of them together. And that, of course, no one had ever done.

At first Dr. Magnus had been unwilling to accept the truth of the dread secret he had uncovered. And yet, with the knowledge of Lisette's released memories, he knew there could be no other conclusion.

It was astonishing how thoroughly a woman who thrived on notoriety could avoid having her photographs published. After all, changing fashions and new hair styles, careful adjustments with cosmetics, could only do so much, and while the mind's eye had an inaccurate memory, a camera lens did not. Dr. Magnus did succeed in finding a few photographs through persistent research. Given a good theatrical costume and makeup crew, they all might have been taken of the same woman on the same day.

They might also all have been taken of Lisette Seyrig.

However, Dr. Magnus knew that it *would* be possible to see Beth Garrington and Lisette Seyrig together.

And he prayed he would be in time to prevent this.

With this knowledge tormenting his thoughts, it was a miracle that Dr. Magnus had held onto sanity well enough to persuade New Scotland Yard to make this late night drive to Maida Vale—desperate, in view of what he knew to be true. He had suffered a shock as severe as any that night when they told him at last where Lisette had gone.

"She's quite all right. She's staying with a friend."

"Might I ask where?"

"A chauffered Rolls picked her up. We checked registration, and it belongs to a Miss Elisabeth Garrington in Maida Vale."

Dr. Magnus had been frantic then, had demanded that they take him there instantly. A telephone call informed them that Miss Seyrig was sleeping under sedation and could not be disturbed; she would return his call in the morning.

Controlling his panic, Dr. Magnus had managed to contrive a disjointed tangle of half-truths and plausible lies—anything to convince them to get over to the Garrington house as quickly as possible. They already knew he was one of those occult kooks. Very well, he assured them that Beth Garrington was involved in a secret society of drug fiends and satanists (all true enough), that Danielle and Lisette had been lured to their most recent orgy for unspeakable purposes. Lisette had been secretly drugged, but Danielle had escaped to carry her roommate home before they could be used for whatever depraved rites awaited them—perhaps ritual sacrifice. Danielle had been murdered—either to shut her up or as part of the ritual—and now they had Lisette in their clutches as well.

All very melodramatic, but enough of it was true. Inspector Bradley knew of the sex and drugs orgies that took place there, but there was firm pressure from higher up to look the other way. Further, he knew enough about some of the more bizarre cult groups in London to consider that ritual murder was quite feasible, given the proper combination of sick minds and illegal drugs. And while it hadn't been made public, the medical examiner was of the opinion that the slashes to the Borland girl's throat and wrists had been an attempt to disguise the fact that she had already bled to death from two deep punctures through the jugular vein.

A demented killer, obviously. A ritual murder? You couldn't discount it just yet. Inspector Bradley had ordered a car.

"Who are you, Lisette Seyrig, that you wear my face?"

Beth Garrington rose sinuously from her bed. She was dressed in an off-the-shoulder nightgown of antique lace, much the same as that which Lisette wore. Her green eyes—the eyes behind the mask that had so shaken Lisette when last they'd met—held her in their spell.

"When first faithful Adrian swore he'd seen my double, I thought his brain had begun to reel with final madness. But after he followed you to your little gallery and brought me there to see your portrait, I knew I had encountered something beyond even my experience."

Lisette stood frozen with dread fascination as her nightmare came to life. Her twin paced about her, appraising her coolly as a serpent considers its hypnotized victim.

"Who are you, Lisette Seyrig, that yours is the face I have seen in my dreams, the face that haunted my nightmares as I lay dying, the face that I thought was my own?"

Lisette forced her lips to speak. "*Who* are you?"

"My name? I change that whenever it becomes prudent for me to do so. Tonight I am Beth Garrington. Long ago I was Elisabeth Beresford."

"How can this be possible?" Lisette hoped she was dealing with a madwoman, but knew her hope was false.

"A spirit came to me in my dreams and slowly stole away my mortal life, in return giving me eternal life. You understand what I say, even though your reason insists that such things cannot be."

She unfastened Lisette's gown and let it fall to the floor, then did the same with her own. Standing face to face, their nude bodies seemed one a reflection of the other.

Elisabeth took Lisette's face in her hands and kissed her full on the lips. The kiss was a long one; her breath was cold in Lisette's mouth. When Elisabeth released her lips and gazed longingly into her eyes, Lisette saw the pointed fangs that now curved downward from her upper jaw.

"Will you cry out, I wonder? If so, let it be in ecstasy and not in fear. I shan't drain you and discard you as I did your silly friend. No, Lisette, my new-found sister. I shall take your life in tiny kisses from night to night—kisses that you will long for with your entire being. And in the end you shall pass over to serve me as my willing chattel—as have the few others I have chosen over the years."

Lisette trembled beneath her touch, powerless to break away. From the buried depths of her unconscious mind, understanding slowly emerged. She did not resist when Elisabeth led her to the bed and lay down beside her on the silken sheets. Lisette was past knowing fear.

Elisabeth stretched her naked body upon Lisette's warmer flesh, lying between her thighs as would a lover. Her cool fingers caressed Lisette; her kisses teased a path from her belly across her breasts and to the hollow of her throat.

Elisabeth paused and gazed into Lisette's eyes. Her fangs gleamed with a reflection of the inhuman lust in her expression.

"And now I give you a kiss sweeter than any passion your mortal brain dare imagine, Lisette Seyrig—even as once I first received such a kiss from a dream-spirit whose eyes stared into mine from my own face. Why have you haunted my dreams, Lisette Seyrig?"

Lisette returned her gaze silently, without emotion. Nor did she flinch when Elisabeth's lips closed tightly against her throat, and the only sound was a barely perceptible tearing, like the bursting of a maidenhead, and the soft movement of suctioning lips.

Elisabeth suddenly broke away with an inarticulate cry of pain. Her lips smeared with scarlet, she stared down at Lisette in bewildered fear. Lisette, blood streaming from the wound on her throat, stared back at her with a smile of unholy hatred.

"*What* are you, Lisette Seyrig?"

"I am Elisabeth Beresford." Lisette's tone was implacable. "In another lifetime you drove my soul from my body and stole my flesh for your own. Now I have come back to reclaim that which once was mine."

Elisabeth sought to leap away, but Lisette's arms embraced her with sudden, terrible strength—pulling their naked bodies together in a horrid imitation of two lovers at the moment of ecstasy.

The scream that echoed into the night was not one of ecstasy.

At the sound of the scream—afterward they never agreed whether it was two voices together or only one—Inspector Bradley ceased listening to the maid's outraged protests and burst past her into the house.

"Upstairs! On the double!" He ordered needlessly. Already Dr. Magnus had lunged past him and was sprinting up the stairway.

"I think it came from the next floor up! Check inside all the rooms!" Later he cursed himself for not posting a man at the door, for by the time he was again able to think rationally, there was no trace of the servants.

In the master bedroom at the end of the third-floor hallway, they found two bodies behind the curtains of the big four-poster bed. One had only just been murdered; her nude body was drenched in the blood from her torn throat—seemingly far too much blood for one body. The other body was a desiccated corpse, obviously dead for a great many years. The dead girl's limbs obscenely embraced the mouldering cadaver that lay atop her, and her teeth, in final spasm, were locked in the lich's throat. As they gaped in horror, clumps of hair and bits of dried skin could be seen to drop away.

Detective Sergeant Wharton looked away and vomited on the floor.

"I owe you a sincere apology, Dr. Magnus." Inspector Bradley's face was grim. "You were right. Ritual murder by a gang of sick degenerates. Detective Sergeant! Leave off that, and put out on all-points bulletin for Beth Garrington. And round up anyone else you find here! Move, man!"

"If only I'd understood in time," Dr. Magnus muttered. He was obviously to the point of collapse.

"No, *I* should have listened to you sooner," Bradley growled. "We might have been in time to prevent this. The devils must have fled down some servants' stairway when they heard us burst in. I confess I've bungled this badly."

"She was a vampire, you see," Dr. Magnus told him dully, groping to explain. "A vampire loses its soul when it becomes one of the undead. But the soul is deathless; it lives on even when its previous incarnation has become a soulless demon. Elisabeth Beresford's soul lived on, until Elisabeth Beresford found reincarnation in Lisette Seyrig. Don't you see? Elisabeth Beresford met her own reincarnation, and that meant destruction for them both."

Inspector Bradley had been only half listening. "Dr. Magnus, you've done all you can. I think you should go down to the car with Detective Sergeant Wharton now and rest until the ambulance arrives."

"But you must see that I was right!" Dr. Magnus pleaded. Madness danced in his eyes. "If the soul is immortal and infinite, then time has no meaning for the soul. Elisabeth Beresford was haunting herself."

Red as Blood

by Tanith Lee

A fairy tale! A fairy tale! And finally one with bite.

The beautiful Witch Queen flung open the ivory case of the magic
mirror. Of dark gold the mirror was, dark gold as the hair of the
Witch Queen that poured down her back. Dark gold the mirror
was, and ancient as the seven stunted black trees growing beyond the
pale blue glass of the window.

"*Speculum, speculum,*" said the Witch Queen to the magic mirror.
"*Dei gratia.*"

"*Volente Deo. Audio.*"

"Mirror," said the Witch Queen. "Whom do you see?"

"I see you, mistress," replied the mirror. "And all in the land. But
one."

"Mirror, mirror, who is it you do not see?"

"I do not see Bianca."

The Witch Queen crossed herself. She shut the case of the mirror and,
walking slowly to the window, looked out at the old trees through the
panes of pale blue glass.

Fourteen years ago, another woman had stood at this window, but she
was not like the Witch Queen. The woman had black hair that fell to her
ankles; she had a crimson gown, the girdle worn high beneath her
breasts, for she was far gone with child. And this woman had thrust open

the glass casement on the winter garden, where the old trees crouched in the snow. Then, taking a sharp bone needle, she had thrust it into her finger and shaken three bright drops on the ground. "Let my daughter have," said the woman, "hair black as mine, black as the wood of these warped and arcane trees. Let her have skin like mine, white as this snow. And let her have my mouth, red as my blood." And the woman had smiled and licked at her finger. She had a crown on her head; it shone in the dusk like a star. She never came to the window before dusk; she did not like the day. She was the first Queen, and she did not possess a mirror.

The second Queen, the Witch Queen, knew all this. She knew how, in giving birth, the first Queen had died. Her coffin had been carried into the cathedral and masses had been said. There was an ugly rumor—that a splash of holy water had fallen on the corpse and the dead flesh had smoked. But the first Queen had been reckoned unlucky for the kingdom. There had been a strange plague in the land since she came there, a wasting disease for which there was no cure.

Seven years went by. The King married the second Queen, as unlike the first as frankincense to myrrh.

"And this is my daughter," said the King to his second Queen.

There stood a little girl child, nearly seven years of age. Her black hair hung to her ankles, her skin was white as snow. Her mouth was red as blood, and she smiled with it.

"Bianca," said the King, "you must love your new mother."

Bianca smiled radiantly. Her teeth were bright as sharp bone needles.

"Come," said the Witch Queen, "come, Bianca. I will show you my magic mirror."

"Please, Mama," said Bianca softly, "I do not like mirrors."

"She is modest," said the King. "And delicate. She never goes out by day. The sun distresses her."

That night, the Witch Queen opened the case of her mirror.

"Mirror, whom do you see?"

"I see you, mistress. And all in the land. But one."

"Mirror, mirror, who is it you do not see?"

"I do not see Bianca."

The second Queen gave Bianca a tiny crucifix of golden filigree. Bianca would not accept it. She ran to her father and whispered: "I am afraid. I do not like to think of Our Lord dying in agony on His cross. She means to frighten me. Tell her to take it away."

The second Queen grew wild white roses in her garden and invited Bianca to walk there after sundown. But Bianca shrank away. She whispered to her father: "The thorns will tear me. She means me to be hurt."

When Bianca was twelve years old, the Witch Queen said to the King, "Bianca should be confirmed so that she may take Communion with us."

"This may not be," said the King. "I will tell you, she has not even been christened, for the dying word of my first wife was against it. She begged me, for her religion was different from ours. The wishes of the dying must be respected."

"Should you not like to be blessed by the church," said the Witch Queen to Bianca. "To kneel at the golden rail before the marble altar. To sing to God, to taste the ritual bread and sip the ritual wine."

"She means me to betray my true mother," said Bianca to the King. "When will she cease tormenting me?"

The day she was thirteen, Bianca rose from her bed, and there was a red stain there, like a red, red flower.

"Now you are a woman," said her nurse.

"Yes," said Bianca. And she went to her true mother's jewel box, and out of it she took her mother's crown and set it on her head.

When she walked under the old black trees in the dusk, the crown shone like a star.

The wasting sickness, which had left the land in peace for thirteen years, suddenly began again, and there was no cure.

The Witch Queen sat in a tall chair before a window of pale green and dark white glass, and in her hands she held a Bible bound in rosy silk.

"Majesty," said the huntsman, bowing very low.

He was a man, forty years old, strong and handsome, and wise in the hidden lore of the forests, the occult lore of the earth. He would kill too, for it was his trade, without faltering. The slender fragile deer he could kill, and the moonwinged birds, and the velvet hares with their sad, foreknowing eyes. He pitied them, but pitying, he killed them. Pity could not stop him. It was his trade.

"Look in the garden," said the Witch Queen.

The hunter looked through a dark white pane. The sun had sunk, and a maiden walked under a tree.

"The Princess Bianca," said the huntsman.

"What else?" asked the Witch Queen.

The huntsman crossed himself.

"By Our Lord, Madam, I will not say."

"But you know."

"Who does not?"

"The King does not."

"Or he does."

"Are you a brave man?" asked the Witch Queen.

"In the summer, I have hunted and slain boar. I have slaughtered wolves in winter."

"But are you brave enough?"

"If you command it, Lady," said the huntsman, "I will try my best."

The Witch Queen opened the Bible at a certain place, and out of it she drew a flat silver crucifix, which had been resting against the words: *Thou shalt not be afraid for the terror by night. . . . Nor for the pestilence that walketh in darkness.*

The huntsman kissed the crucifix and put it about his neck, beneath his shirt.

"Approach," said the Witch Queen, "and I will instruct you in what to say."

Presently, the huntsman entered the garden, as the stars were burning up in the sky. He strode to where Bianca stood under a stunted dwarf tree, and he kneeled down.

"Princess," he said. "Pardon me, but I must give you ill tidings."

"Give them then," said the girl, toying with the long stem of a wan, night-growing flower which she had plucked.

"Your stepmother, that accursed, jealous witch, means to have you slain. There is no help for it but you must fly the palace this very night. If you permit, I will guide you to the forest. There are those who will care for you until it may be safe for you to return."

Bianca watched him, but gently, trustingly.

"I will go with you, then," she said.

They went by a secret way out of the garden, through a passage under the ground, through a tangled orchard, by a broken road between great overgrown hedges.

Night was a pulse of deep, flickering blue when they came to the forest. The branches of the forest overlapped and intertwined like leading in a window, and the sky gleamed dimly through like panes of blue-colored glass.

"I am weary," sighed Bianca. "May I rest a moment?"

"By all means," said the huntsman. "In the clearing there, foxes come to play by night. Look in that direction, and you will see them."

"How clever you are," said Bianca. "And how handsome."

She sat on the turf, and gazed at the clearing.

The huntsman drew his knife silently and concealed it in the folds of his cloak. He stopped above the maiden.

"What are you whispering?" demanded the huntsman, laying his hand on her wood-black hair.

"Only a rhyme my mother taught me."

The huntsman seized her by the hair and swung her about so her white throat was before him, stretched ready for the knife. But he did not strike, for there in his hand he held the dark golden locks of the Witch Queen, and her face laughed up at him and she flung her arms about him, laughing.

"Good man, sweet man, it was only a test of you. Am I not a witch? And do you not love me?"

The huntsman trembled, for he did love her, and she was pressed so close her heart seemed to beat within his own body.

"Put away the knife. Throw away the silly crucifix. We have no need of these things. The King is not one half the man you are."

And the huntsman obeyed her, throwing the knife and the crucifix far off among the roots of the trees. He gripped her to him, and she buried her face in his neck, and the pain of her kiss was the last thing he felt in this world.

The sky was black now. The forest was blacker. No foxes played in the clearing. The moon rose and made white lace through the boughs, and through the backs of the huntsman's empty eyes. Bianca wiped her mouth on a dead flower.

"Seven asleep, seven awake," said Bianca. "Wood to wood. Blood to blood. Thee to me."

There came a sound like seven huge rendings, distant by the length of several trees, a broken road, an orchard, an underground passage. Then a sound like seven huge single footfalls. Nearer. And nearer.

Hop, hop, hop, hop. Hop, hop, hop.

In the orchard, seven black shudderings.

On the broken road, between the high hedges, seven black creepings. Brush crackled, branches snapped.

Through the forest, into the clearing, pushed seven warped, misshapen, hunched-over, stunted things. Woody-black mossy fur, woody-black bald masks. Eyes like glittering cracks, mouths like moist caverns. Lichen beards. Fingers of twiggy gristle. Grinning. Kneeling. Faces pressed to the earth.

"Welcome," said Bianca.

The Witch Queen stood before a window of glass like diluted wine. She looked at the magic mirror.

"Mirror. Whom do you see?"

"I see you, mistress. I see a man in the forest. He went hunting, but not for deer. His eyes are open, but he is dead. I see all in the land. But one."

The Witch Queen pressed her palms to her ears.

Outside the window the garden lay, empty of its seven black and stunted dwarf trees.

"Bianca," said the Queen.

The windows had been draped and gave no light. The light spilled from a shallow vessel, light in a sheaf, like the pastel wheat. It glowed upon four swords that pointed east and west, that pointed north and south.

Four winds had burst through the chamber, and three arch-winds. Cool fires had risen, and parched oceans, and the gray-silver powders of Time.

The hands of the Witch Queen floated like folded leaves on the air, and through dry lips the Witch Queen chanted.

"Pater omnipotens, mittere digneris sanctum Angelum tuum de Infernis."

The light faded, and grew brighter.

There, between the hilts of the four swords, stood the Angel Lucefiel, somberly gilded, his face in shadow, his golden wings spread and blazing at his back.

"Since you have called me, I know your desire. It is a comfortless wish. You ask for pain."

"You speak of pain, Lord Lucefiel, who suffer the most merciless pain of all. Worse than the nails in the feet and wrists. Worse than the thorns and the bitter cup and the blade in the side. To be called upon for evil's sake, which I do not, comprehending your true nature, son of God, brother of The Son."

"You recognize me, then. I will grant what you ask."

And Lucefiel (by some named Satan, Rex Mundi, but nevertheless the left hand, the sinister hand of God's design) wrenched lightning from the ether and cast it at the Witch Queen.

It caught her in the breast. She fell.

The sheaf of light towered and lit the golden eyes of the Angel, which were terrible, yet luminous with compassion, as the swords shattered and he vanished.

The Witch Queen pulled herself from the floor of the chamber, no longer beautiful, a withered, slobbering hag.

Into the core of the forest, even at noon, the sun never shone. Flowers propagated in the grass, but they were colorless. Above, the black-green roof hung down nets of thick, green twilight through which albino butterflies and moths feverishly drizzled. The trunks of the trees were smooth as the stalks of underwater weeds. Bats flew in the daytime, and birds who believed themselves to be bats.

There was a sepulcher, dripped with moss. The bones had been rolled out, had rolled around the feet of seven twisted dwarf trees. They looked like trees. Sometimes they moved. Sometimes something like an eye glittered, or a tooth, in the wet shadows.

In the shade of the sepulcher door sat Bianca, combing her hair.

A lurch of motion disturbed the thick twilight.

The seven trees turned their heads.

A hag emerged from the forest. She was crook-backed and her head was poked forward, predatory, withered, and almost hairless, like a vulture's.

"Here we are at last," grated the hag, in a vulture's voice.

She came closer, and cranked herself down on her knees, and bowed her face into the turf and the colorless flowers.

Bianca sat and gazed at her. The hag lifted herself. Her teeth were yellow palings.

"I bring you the homage of witches, and three gifts," said the hag.

"Why should you do that?"

"Such a quick child, and only fourteen years. Why? Because we fear you. I bring you gifts to curry favor."

Bianca laughed. "Show me."

The hag made a pass in the green air. She held a silken cord worked curiously with plaited human hair.

"Here is a girdle which will protect you from the devices of priests, from crucifix and chalice and the accursed holy water. In it are knotted the tresses of a virgin, and of a woman no better than she should be, and of a woman dead. And here—" a second pass and a comb was in her hand, lacquered blue over green—"a comb from the deep sea, a mermaid's trinket, to charm and subdue. Part your locks with this, and the scent of ocean will fill men's nostrils and the rhythm of the tides their ears, the tides that bind men like chains. Last," added the hag, "that old symbol of wickedness, the scarlet fruit of Eve, the apple red as blood. Bite, and the understanding of sin, which the serpent boasted of, will be made known to you." And the hag made her last pass in the air and extended the apple, with the girdle and the comb, toward Bianca.

Bianca glanced at the seven stunted trees.

"I like her gifts, but I do not quite trust her."

The bald masks peered from their shaggy beardings. Eyelets glinted. Twiggy claws clacked.

"All the same," said Bianca. "I will let her tie the girdle on me, and comb my hair herself."

The hag obeyed, simpering. Like a toad she waddled to Bianca. She tied on the girdle. She parted the ebony hair. Sparks sizzled, white from the girdle, peacock's eye from the comb.

"And now, hag, take a little bite of the apple."

"It will be my pride," said the hag, "to tell my sisters I shared this fruit with you." And the hag bit into the apple, and mumbled the bite noisily, and swallowed, smacking her lips.

Then Bianca took the apple and bit into it.

Bianca screamed—and choked.

She jumped to her feet. Her hair whirled about her like a storm cloud. Her face turned blue, then slate, then white again. She lay on the pallid flowers, neither stirring nor breathing.

The seven dwarf trees rattled their limbs and their bear-shaggy heads, to no avail. Without Bianca's art they could not hop. They strained their claws and ripped at the hag's sparse hair and her mantle. She fled between them. She fled into the sunlit acres of the forest, along the broken road, through the orchard, into a hidden passage.

The hag reentered the palace by the hidden way, and the Queen's chamber by a hidden stair. She was bent almost double. She held her ribs. With one skinny hand she opened the ivory case of the magic mirror.

"*Speculum, speculum. Dei gratia.* Whom do you see?"

"I see you, mistress. And all in the land. And I see a coffin."

"Whose corpse lies in the coffin?"

"That I cannot see. It must be Bianca."

The hag, who had been the beautiful Witch Queen, sank into her tall chair before the window of pale, cucumber green and dark white glass. Her drugs and potions waited, ready to reverse the dreadful conjuring of age the Angel Lucefiel had placed on her, but she did not touch them yet.

The apple had contained a fragment of the flesh of Christ, the sacred wafer, the Eucharist.

The Witch Queen drew her Bible to her and opened it randomly.

And read, with fear, the word: *Resurcat.*

It appeared like glass, the coffin, milky glass. It had formed this way. A thin white smoke had risen from the skin of Bianca. She smoked as a fire smokes when a drop of quenching water falls on it. The piece of Eucharist had stuck in her throat. The Eucharist, quenching water to her fire, caused her to smoke.

Then the cold dews of night gathered, and the colder atmospheres of midnight. The smoke of Bianca's quenching froze about her. Frost formed in exquisite silver scroll-work all over the block of misty ice that contained Bianca.

Bianca's frigid heart could not warm the ice. Nor the sunless, green twilight of the day.

You could just see her, stretched in the coffin, through the glass. How lovely she looked, Bianca. Black as ebony, white as snow, red as blood.

The trees hung over the coffin. Years passed. The trees sprawled about the coffin, cradling it in their arms. Their eyes wept fungus and green resin. Green amber drops hardened like jewels in the coffin of glass.

"Who is that lying under the trees?" the Prince asked, as he rode into the clearing.

He seemed to bring a golden moon with him, shining about his golden head, on the golden armor and the cloak of white satin blazoned with gold and blood and ink and sapphire. The white horse trod on the colorless flowers, but the flowers sprang up again when the hoofs had passed. A shield hung from the saddle-bow, a strange shield. From one side it had a lion's face, but from the other, a lamb's face.

The trees groaned, and their heads split on huge mouths.

"Is this Bianca's coffin?" asked the Prince.

"Leave her with us," said the seven trees. They hauled at their roots. The ground shivered. The coffin of ice-glass gave a great jolt, and a crack bisected it.

Bianca coughed.

The jolt had precipitated the piece of Eucharist from her throat.

Into a thousand shards the coffin shattered, and Bianca sat up. She stared at the Prince, and she smiled.

"Welcome, beloved," said Bianca.

She got to her feet, and shook out her hair, and began to walk toward the Prince on the pale horse.

But she seemed to walk into a shadow, into a purple room, then into a crimson room whose emanations lanced her like knives. Next she walked into a yellow room where she heard the sound of crying, which tore her ears. All her body seemed stripped away; she was a beating heart. The beats of her heart became two wings. She flew. She was a raven, then an owl. She flew into a sparkling pane. It scorched her white. Snow white. She was a dove.

She settled on the shoulder of the Prince and hid her head under her wing. She had no longer anything black about her, and nothing red.

"Begin again now, Bianca," said the Prince. He raised her from his shoulder. On his wrist there was a mark. It was like a star. Once a nail had been driven in there.

Bianca flew away, up through the roof of the forest. She flew in at a delicate wine window. She was in the palace. She was seven years old.

The Witch Queen, her new mother, hung a filigree crucifix around her neck.

"Mirror," said the Witch Queen. "Whom do you see?"

"I see you, mistress," replied the mirror. "And all in the land. I see Bianca."

No Such Thing As a Vampire

by Richard Matheson

I n the early autumn, Madame Alexis Gheria awoke one morning to a sense of utmost torpor. For more than a minute, she lay inertly on her back, her dark eyes staring upward. How wasted she felt. It seemed as if her limbs were sheathed in lead. Perhaps she was ill. Petre must examine her and see.

Drawing in a faint breath, she pressed up slowly on an elbow. As she did, her nightdress slid, rustling, to her waist. How had it come unfastened? she wondered, looking down at herself.

Quite suddenly, Madame Gheria began to scream.

In the breakfast room, Dr. Petre Gheria looked up, startled, from his morning paper. In an instant, he had pushed his chair back, slung his napkin on the table and was rushing for the hallway. He dashed across its carpeted breadth and mounted the staircase two steps at a time.

It was a near hysterical Madame Gheria he found sitting on the edge of her bed looking down in horror at her breasts. Across the dilated whiteness of them, a smear of blood lay drying.

Dr. Gheria dismissed the upstairs maid who stood frozen in the open doorway, gaping at her mistress. He locked the door and hurried to his wife.

"Petre!" she gasped.

"Gently." He helped her lie back across the blood-stained pillow.

"Petre, what *is* it?" she begged.

"Lie still, my dear." His practiced hands moved in swift search over her breasts. Suddenly, his breath choked off. Pressing aside her head, he stared down dumbly at the pinprick lancinations on her neck, the ribbon of tacky blood that twisted downward from them.

"My *throat*," Alexis said.

"No, it's just a——" Dr. Gheria did not complete the sentence. He knew exactly what it was.

Madame Gheria began to tremble. "Oh, my God, my *God*," she said.

Dr. Gheria rose and foundered to the wash basin. Pouring in water, he returned to his wife and washed away the blood. The wound was clearly visible now—two tiny punctures close to the jugular. A grimacing Dr. Gheria touched the mounds of inflamed tissue in which they lay. As he did, his wife groaned terribly and turned her face away.

"Now listen to me," he said, his voice apparently calm. "We will not succumb, immediately, to superstition, do you hear? There are any number of——"

"I'm going to die," she said.

"Alexis, do you hear me?" He caught her harshly by the shoulders.

She turned her head and stared at him with vacant eyes. "You know what it is," she said.

Dr. Gheria swallowed. He could still taste coffee in his mouth.

"I know what it appears to be," he said, "and we shall—not ignore the possibility. However——"

"I'm going to die," she said.

"Alexis!" Dr. Gheria took her hand and gripped it fiercely. *"You shall not be taken from me,"* he said.

Solta was a village of some thousand inhabitants situated in the foothills of Romania's Bihor Mountains. It was a place of dark traditions. People, hearing the bay of distant wolves, would cross themselves without a thought. Children would gather garlic buds as other children gather flowers, bringing them home for the windows. On every door there was a painted cross, at every throat a metal one. Dread of the vampire's blighting was as normal as the dread of fatal sickness. It was always in the air.

Dr. Gheria thought about that as he bolted shut the windows of Alexis' room. Far off, molten twilight hung above the mountains. Soon it would be dark again. Soon the citizens of Solta would be barricaded in their garlic-reeking houses. He had no doubt that every soul of them knew exactly what had happened to his wife. Already the cook and upstairs maid were pleading for discharge. Only the inflexible discipline of the butler, Karel, kept them at their jobs. Soon, even that would not suffice. Before the horror of the vampire, reason fled.

He'd seen the evidence of it that very morning when he'd ordered Madame's room stripped to the walls and searched for rodents or venomous insects. The servants had moved about the room as if on a floor of eggs, their eyes more white than pupil, their fingers twitching constantly to their crosses. They had known full well no rodents or insects would be found. And Gheria had known it. Still, he'd raged at them for their timidity, succeeding only in frightening them further.

He turned from the window with a smile.

"There now," he said, "nothing alive will enter this room tonight."

He caught himself immediately, seeing the flare of terror in her eyes.

"Nothing at *all* will enter," he amended.

Alexis lay motionless on her bed, one pale hand at her breast, clutching at the worn silver cross she'd taken from her jewel box. She hadn't worn it since he'd given her the diamond-studded one when they were married. How typical of her village background that, in this moment of dread, she should seek protection from the unadorned cross of her church. She was such a child. Gheria smiled down gently at her.

"You won't be needing that, my dear," he said, "you'll be safe tonight."

Her fingers tightened on the crucifix.

"No, no, wear it if you will," he said. "I only meant that I'll be at your side all night."

"You'll stay with me?"

He sat on the bed and held her hand.

"Do you think I'd leave you for a moment?" he said.

Thirty minutes later, she was sleeping. Dr. Gheria drew a chair beside the bed and seated himself. Removing his glasses, he massaged the bridge of his nose with the thumb and forefinger of his left hand. Then, sighing, he began to watch his wife. How incredibly beautiful she was. Dr. Gheria's breath grew strained.

"There is no such thing as a vampire," he whispered to himself.

There was a distant pounding. Dr. Gheria muttered in his sleep, his fingers twitching. The pounding increased; an agitated voice came swirling from the darkness. "Doctor!" it called.

Gheria snapped awake. For a moment, he looked confusedly toward the locked door.

"Dr. Gheria?" demanded Karel.

"What?"

"Is everything all right?"

"Yes, everything is——"

Dr. Gheria cried out hoarsely, springing for the bed. Alexis' nightdress had been torn away again. A hideous dew of blood covered her chest and neck.

Karel shook his head.

"Bolted windows cannot hold away the creature, sir," he said.

He stood, tall and lean, beside the kitchen table on which lay the cluster of silver he'd been polishing when Gheria had entered.

"The creature has the power to make of itself a vapor which can pass through any opening however small," he said.

"But the cross!" cried Gheria. "It was still at her throat—untouched! Except by—blood," he added in a sickened voice.

"This I cannot understand," said Karel, grimly. "The cross should have protected her."

"But why did I see nothing?"

"You were drugged by its mephitic presence," Karel said. "Count yourself fortunate that you were not, also, attacked."

"I do not count myself fortunate!" Dr. Gheria struck his palm, a look of anguish on his face. "What am I to do, Karel?" he asked.

"Hang garlic," said the old man. "Hang it at the windows, at the doors. Let there be no opening unblocked by garlic."

Gheria nodded distractedly. "Never in my life have I seen this thing," he said, brokenly. "Now, my own wife . . ."

"I have seen it," said Karel. "I have, myself, put to its rest one of these monsters from the grave."

"The stake——?" Gheria looked revolted.

The old man nodded slowly.

Gheria swallowed. "Pray God you may put this one to rest as well," he said.

"Petre?"

She was weaker now, her voice a toneless murmur. Gheria bent over her. "Yes, my dear," he said.

"It will come again tonight," she said.

"No." He shook his head determinedly. "It cannot come. The garlic will repel it."

"My cross didn't," she said. "You didn't."

"The garlic will," he said. "And see?" He pointed at the bedside table. "I've had black coffee brought for me. I won't sleep tonight."

She closed her eyes, a look of pain across her sallow features.

"I don't want to die," she said. "Please don't let me die, Petre."

"You won't," he said. "I promise you; the monster shall be destroyed."

Alexis shuddered feebly. "But if there is no way, Petre," she murmured.

"There is always a way," he answered.

Outside, the darkness, cold and heavy, pressed around the house. Dr. Gheria took his place beside the bed and began to wait. Within the hour, Alexis slipped into a heavy slumber. Gently, Dr. Gheria released her hand and poured himself a cup of steaming coffee. As he sipped it, hotly bitter, he looked around the room. Door locked, windows bolted, every opening sealed with garlic, the cross at Alexis' throat. He nodded slowly to himself. It will work, he thought. The monster would be thwarted.

He sat there, waiting, listening to his breath.

Dr. Gheria was at the door before the second knock.

"Michael!" He embraced the younger man. "Dear Michael, I was sure you'd come!"

Anxiously, he ushered Dr. Vares toward his study. Outside, darkness was just falling.

"Where on earth are all the people of the village?" asked Vares. "I swear I didn't see a soul as I rode in."

"Huddling, terror-stricken, in their houses," Gheria said, "and all my servants with them save for one."

"Who is that?"

"My butler, Karel," Gheria answered. "He didn't answer the door because he's sleeping. Poor fellow, he is very old and has been doing the work of five." He gripped Vares' arm. "Dear Michael," he said, "you have no idea how glad I am to see you."

Vares looked at him worriedly. "I came as soon as I received your message," he said.

"And I appreciate it," Gheria said. "I know how long and hard a ride it is from Cluj."

"What's wrong?" asked Vares. "Your letter only said——"

Quickly, Gheria told him what had happened in the past week.

"I tell you, Michael, I stumble at the brink of madness," he said. "Nothing works! Garlic, wolfsbane, crosses, mirrors, running water— useless! No, don't say it! This isn't superstition nor imagination! This is *happening*! A vampire is destroying her! Each day she sinks yet deeper into that—deadly torpor from which——"

Gheria clenched his hands. "And yet I cannot understand it," he muttered, brokenly, "I simply cannot understand it."

"Come, sit, sit." Doctor Vares pressed the older man into a chair, grimacing at the pallor of him. Nervously, his fingers sought for Gheria's pulse beat.

"Never mind me," protested Gheria. "It's Alexis we must help." He pressed a sudden, trembling hand across his eyes. "Yet how?" he said.

He made no resistance as the young man undid his collar and examined his neck.

"You, too," said Vares, sickened.

"What does that matter?" Gheria clutched at the younger man's hand. "My friend, my dearest friend," he said, "tell me that it is not I! Do *I* do this hideous thing to her?"

Vares looked confounded. *"You?"* he said. "But——"

"I know, I know," said Gheria, "I, myself, have been attacked. Yet nothing follows, Michael! What breed of horror is this which cannot be impeded? From what unholy place does it emerge? I've had the countryside examined foot by foot, every graveyard ransacked, every crypt inspected! There is no house within the village that has not been subjected to my search. I tell you, Michael, there is nothing! Yet, there *is* something—something which assaults us nightly, draining us of life. The village is engulfed by terror—and I as well! I never see this creature, never hear it! Yet, every morning, I find my beloved wife——"

Vares' face was drawn and pallid now. He stared intently at the older man.

"What am I to do, my friend?" pleaded Gheria. "How am I to save her?"

Vares had no answer.

"How long has she—been like this?" asked Vares. He could not remove his stricken gaze from the whiteness of Alexis' face.

"For days," said Gheria. "The retrogression has been constant."

Dr. Vares put down Alexis' flaccid hand. "Why did you not tell me sooner?" he asked.

"I thought the matter could be handled," Gheria answered, faintly. "I know now that it—cannot."

Vares shuddered. "But, surely——" he began.

"There is nothing left to be done," said Gheria. "Everything has been tried, *everything*!" He stumbled to the window and stared out bleakly into the deepening night. "And now it comes again," he murmured, "and we are helpless before it."

"Not helpless, Petre." Vares forced a cheering smile to his lips and laid his hand upon the older man's shoulder. "I will watch her tonight."

"It's useless."

"Not at all, my friend," said Vares, nervously. "And now you must sleep."

"I will not leave her," said Gheria.

"But you need rest."

"I cannot leave," said Gheria. "I will not be separated from her."

Vares nodded. "Of course," he said. "We will share the hours of watching then."

Gheria sighed. "We can try," he said, but there was no sound of hope in his voice.

Some 20 minutes later, he returned with an urn of steaming coffee which was barely possible to smell through the heavy mist of garlic fumes which hung in the air. Trudging to the bed, Gheria set down the tray. Dr. Vares had drawn a chair up beside the bed.

"I'll watch first," he said. "You sleep, Petre."

"It would do no good to try," said Gheria. He held a cup beneath the spigot and the coffee gurgled out like smoking ebony.

"Thank you," murmured Vares as the cup was handed to him. Gheria nodded once and drew himself a cupful before he sat.

"I do not know what will happen to Solta if this creature is not destroyed," he said. "The people are paralyzed by terror."

"Has it—been elsewhere in the village?" Vares asked him.

Gheria sighed exhaustedly. "Why need it go elsewhere?" he said. "It is finding all it—craves within these walls." He stared despondently at Alexis. "When we are gone," he said, "it will go elsewhere. The people know that and are waiting for it."

Vares set down his cup and rubbed his eyes.

"It seems impossible," he said, "that we, practitioners of a science, should be unable to——"

"What can science effect against it?" said Gheria. "Science which will not even admit its existence? We could bring, into this very room, the foremost scientists of the world and they would say—my friends, you have been deluded. There is no vampire. All is mere trickery."

Gheria stopped and looked intently at the younger man. He said, "Michael?"

Vares' breath was slow and heavy. Putting down his cup of untouched coffee, Gheria stood and moved to where Vares sat slumped in his chair. He pressed back an eyelid, looked down briefly at the sightless pupil, then withdrew his hand. The drug was quick, he thought. And most effective. Vares would be insensible for more than time enough.

Moving to the closet, Gheria drew down his bag and carried it to the bed. He tore Alexis' nightdress from her upper body and, within seconds, had drawn another syringe full of her blood; this would be the last withdrawal, fortunately. Stanching the wound, he took the syringe to Vares and emptied it into the young man's mouth, smearing it across his lips and teeth.

That done, he strode to the door and unlocked it. Returning to Vares, he raised and carried him into the hall. Karel would not awaken; a small amount of opiate in his food had seen to that. Gheria labored down the steps beneath the weight of Vares' body. In the darkest corner of the cellar, a wooden casket waited for the younger man. There he would lie until the following morning when the distraught Dr. Petre Gheria would, with sudden inspiration, order Karel to search the attic and cellar on the remote, nay fantastic possibility that——

Ten minutes later, Gheria was back in the bedroom checking Alexis' pulse beat. It was active enough; she would survive. The pain and torturing horror she had undergone would be punishment enough for her. As for Vares . . .

Dr. Gheria smiled in pleasure for the first time since Alexis and he had returned from Cluj at the end of the summer. Dear spirits in heaven, would it not be sheer enchantment to watch old Karel drive a stake through Michael Vares' damned cuckolding heart!

The Vampire of Mallworld

🦇 🦇 🦇

by S.P. Somtow

Clement barJulian was a quadrillionaire with eyes in the back of his head. I was a reporter for the Holothrills-National Enquirer Syndicate, stiffly snapping at my live turtle soup in the middle of a gourmet restaurant in the middle of a thirty-klick-long shopping center floating in space, trying to get the man to talk about a vampire—and he wasn't talking.

"I hate to presume on our old friendship—" I was saying. Above, a holo-Zeiss projected a shimmering stardome. My turtle swam half-heartedly in its bowl of bluish nutriliquid, and I was only waiting for it to hold still a moment so I could jab it with my fork.

"You presume," said Clement barJulian, "too far. There is no vampire in Mallworld." The candlelight flared up for a moment, playing flicker-shadow with his face. It was, of course, a deliberately contrived effect; I knew that Clement liked to affect a menacing mien. "Go home, Milton. Aren't you supposed to be covering the atrocities of the seven-veiled sect or something?"

"Yes, I was. But they assigned someone else. Got some kind of notion that I'm slipping . . . hell, Clement, you've seen the ratings! I'm only the most popular holovee personality in the solar system! Remember when I covered the time in Mallworld when the mini-demat booths backfired and

left six hundred shoppers minus their heads? Remember when the Selespridon governor of Sol System was molested by a hundred girl scouts
from bible belt? And here I am investigating filler material. Sticking me
with a moderately gory carnival act when I could be covering the war in
Luna or interviewing a Selespridon. . . ." Carefully I maneuvered myself
to get some good shots of barJulian. I was incognito, of course, covered
with mounds of plastiflesh; indeed, the pot belly I'd snapped over my
well-muscled torso was a pouch to carry my camera in, and it was operat-
ing surreptitiously through my navel.

"Always whining, Milton Huang, always whining," said Clement bar-
Julian, as he slurped the last of his Denebian whiteworms. "I know very
well that whenever you get a Mallworld story you come to me first and
whine and hope I'll bail you out—not to mention that I own a not bad
share of the networks. But I've never heard of a vampire in Mallworld,
and I don't even rightly know what one is—some kind of geek, no—and
if anyone would know I would." He was right; his family *owned* Mallworld. He was worth enough to buy Phobos and Deimos and use them for
juggling balls. And yet—he was edgier than I'd ever seen him. He'd always been very cordial with me, though you can't really ever today what
the super-rich have clicking in their minds. But today he was downright
hostile. Was there something going on?

"I'll investigate, of course," I said. My career was slipping and I could
hardly do otherwise.

"That," said Clement portentously, "is life."

It was a relief to step out of the Galaxy Palace restaurant. Clement bar-
Julian owned it, of course. It was the only place in existence where you
could see the stars—the way they used to look, before the Selespridar
came and shunted everything inside the orbit of Saturn into a pocket universe "for your own good"—projected via the last surviving holoZeiss
recording. It's a beautiful restaurant; depressing, too. I'd gotten some good
establishing shots there—only 2D unfortunately, but they could be super-
imposed into a holocollage, very in and arty that year, back at the studio.

Once in the corridor—

Mallworld was as it always was. Crazi-gravi corridors corkscrewing
precariously and mobiustripping around straight corridors liens with
demat booths, and you could look up and see level after level after level
on either side of you, vanishing into infinity, above and below; signs

yelling at you, garish holoads with sensual young men and women selling perfume, airbeds, spacecars, relics of the cross, pet salamanders, laxatives, compact sensuo-surrogates for asteroid miners, rut pills, skating gloves— and the people, streaming by like space truckers' convoys, and the robots weighed down with shopping bags, and the jabbering, the jabbering. . . .

Setting off at random—figured I should do some more establishing shots—I found a courtyard with upside-down fountains. An orchestra of Rigellian semisentients was playing a squeaky music from their synthe- sizing rituals.

Perhaps I've been a little too Machiavellian, going straight to barJu- lian, straight to the top like this— I thought. Resolutely I turned to sum- mon a comsim. Why not try the direct approach?

The comsim landed on my shoulder, a bearded six-inch man in pink.

"Hello. I am computer simulacrum MALLGUIDE 227719," it buzzed. "Can I help you?"

"Yes. Uh, where's the Vampire?"

"Hee!" it snickered, fluttering around my head. "You must be loaded! Show me your thumb."

Satisfied by my creditworthiness, it went on, "Honored sir—" it had suddenly become very obsequious, being programmed to react favorably to well-heeled thumbprints—"I cannot talk. But for one of such a bottom- less expense account. . . ."

"What do you mean, you can't talk?"

"You will be contacted!" And it was gone. I hadn't even been able to turn quickly enough to get a good angle through the camera eye in my navel.

All there was left to do was find a hotel and wait, so I got into a booth and asked for the Gaza Plaza, and in a split second I was walking into the hotel that was a scale model of the Great Pyramid of Khufu. Or perhaps it *was* the Great Pyramid—the ads were deliberately ambiguous there.

I felt a bit strange in the pyramid-shaped room, which was kept at a half-gee for comfort. There was a crazy, queasy feeling in my stomach . . . but wait! It wasn't the gravity!

All right, you can come out now, I subvocalized. My belly ripped open at the command from my throat gizmo, and my camera flopped all over the bed, wires and tentacles and micromikes wriggling like Medusa's head.

"Well," I said. "What do you make of it all?"

"Pretty weird," it said. "I still think it's a hoax, but what do I know."

"Hell," I said, "it's just some guy drinking blood. Why should Clement barJulian get all defensive about it? And what about all this cloak and dagger stuff with the comsims? I don't like it—"

Suddenly all the lights went out. "What the—" I stuttered, thinking, *Uh oh, not a repeat of last season's blackout!*

An eerie green light flickered on, cold and faint as in a dream. Then a comsim matted in: almost a foot tall, hovering in the air, with a dark black cloak that trailed behind him and rippled ever so gently. Its eyes were closed, and its lips were thin, red, sensuous.

"Quick, Clunko, get this on tape!" I murmured.

"Whaddya think I'm doing, dummy?"

I just stared and stared at the comsim. I almost recognized it: it was like a forgotten childhood image, an old story, a racial memory even.

The eyes flashed open. They were bloodshot. I was transfixed. Terror lanced my stomach for a wild moment before I could regain control.

Then—

A horrible cackle reverberated around the room, the mouth opened, the hideous fangs glistened, death-white, the eerie light shifting, darkening, gigantic shadows twisting. . . .

"Good evening," it said. A sinuous, cold voice. "I am a comsim reproduction of Bela Bartok, the most famous Vampire of the ancient earth-myths. If you will kindly follow me, we will demat into the Cellars of doom . . . participation is twelve credits only, observation twelve thousand credits to ensure only the most discriminating clientele . . . and now, the secret Vault of Horror of The Way Out Corporation. Your credit identification, please . . . this way! this way! this way!"

So this was it! I resisted an impulse to clutch Clunko's tentacles; abandoned myself to a deliciously creepy shudder; and followed the comsim through a wall that had begun to shimmer and turn to mist.

TIRED OF LIFE? said the sign in a mellow, farther-image sort of voice. WHY NOT . . . KILL YOURSELF? 300 WAYS POSSIBLE AT *THE WAY OUT CORP!* MOST REVERSIBLE! MONEY BACK GUARANTEE IF STILL ALIVE AFTER PROCESSING!

I noted with some perplexity that The Way Out Corp. was a subsidiary of the Clement barJulian Group. "The plot thickens," I subvoked to Clunko the camera. I'd discarded my pot belly and donned a cloth-of-iridium loinshield; Clunko clattered behind. I still did not dare reveal my true face, of course, since I had some pretty overpowering fans.

Our personal comsim led us inside. Abruptly, a soundscreen cut off the crowd and we were each immersed in our own little silence.

"Your seat, sir," said the comsim resonantly. A dim green light shone on an antique coffin, done up to make a padded couch.

"Yes, but what about the Vam—" He had dematted. I found a piece of paper with writing on it on the couch, programs notes or something: since I can't read, of course, I scrunched it up and threw it behind me. *Okay,* I subvoked. *Spread yourself out and start shooting.* Clunko subdivided into little cells—ah, the miracle of subatomic circuitry!—and began to drift around the place. For holovee you need at least four or five shooting angles or you can't get a good "in-the-round" feeling.

In the dimness I could make some breathing. When my eyes adjusted I saw others in the audience. The bored and rich, all of them. Not since Pope Joan the Fifteenth's funeral had I seen such an array of garish clothing and outlandish, extravagant soma-models: purple skins, vestigial heads and other paraphernalia, grafted-on limbs and appendages, lewd-looking women wearing gilded potato-sacks, and all of them heaving with a sort of vulture-like ecstasy. I even saw a Selespridon, occupying a couch by himself—tall, blue-skinned and magenta-haired and looking decidedly uncomfortable. A subtle, sickly sweet odor pervaded everything. It was so dark there wasn't any scale to it; I mean, there could have been thousands of people here . . . I subvoked an ampli-command to the olfacto track: there's nothing better than a wicked, nasty smell on holovee to really drive a point home. . . .

A voice broke the silence. I came from everywhere at once, as the darkness deepened still more.

"Humans, aliens and semi-sentients," it began, "we are proud to present a genuine reconstruction of the day-to-day life of an ancient mythic Vampire. The Vampire of Earth—whose name has come down to us in various forms as Bella Abzug, Bela Bartok and Clarabelle—was a monstrous alien who devoured . . . human blood.

"Today we have the Vampire of Mallworld. A psychopath of unknown origin, this vampire came to The Way Out Corp. wishing for a release from life. Today, instead, he has earned a permanent place to live out his dread fantasies . . . all his victims are our customers. All the death scenes are genuine, and no victim will be revivified; each has signed an irreversible contract with The Way Out. We warn you—many who have come to watch as members of the audience have eventually found their way onto the stage of death! . . . and we sincerely hope that the desperadoes, the depressed, the schizoid, and the merely bored among you will think of us, when the times come for *you* to seek—*The Way Out!*"

Spotlight on a single coffin on a dais, old and dirty. The audience was quite still. Slowly, agonizingly slowly, the lid creaked open. The sound system was hyperamped to give you the shivers. It creaked . . . creaked . . . and then crashed onto the floor.

Very slowly he stood up. He was tall, over two meters. A black cloak flapped from his shoulders. His face was painted white, unearthly white with a glowing tinge of green. It was a long, bleak face, the black hair merging with the black cape, the lips Mars-red and seductive, the eyes empty, dead. He hardly seemed to notice the audience.

"The first victim," said the announcer. "Miss Emily Smith."

A little old granny tottered onto the stage. She was shaking all over as she crossed the stage's lines of shadow. The Vampire took her into his arms, towering above her. She seemed to see nothing but his compelling eyes.

Teeth glistened. She whimpered once before he ripped her apart, and then she fell to the ground with a crash. A robot dragged off the body.

That's all? I was thinking. I looked around; couples in the audience were intertwined, some shamelessly indulging in erotic little games. *Talk about the rich and bored!* Clunko buzzed in my ear. *Shut up.* I subvoked. *Keep filming.*

A few more victims, mostly women. And then—number ten or eleven, I forget the name, but she was shatteringly beautiful, only a girl . . . she wore a white gown, and her long black hair streamed behind her in the stagewind they had set up for her . . . she just stood there, half in the shadow, deep brown eyes moist and meltingly lovely, and I was on the edge of my seat. So was the audience. A throaty murmur escaped them, was stifled.

"Come, my dear, my little one. . . ." The voice was heard for the first time, and the sound system distorted it into a terrifying, nightmare voice.

She advanced as though hypnotized. The Vampire caressed her face with a large, slender hand that half-glowed with some luminous grease paint; they embraced chastely, then more passionately, and then she was flinging aside her gown and he was biting her all over, and pools of red were spreading all over the white, and her sighs turned into shrieks of terror—

The whole audience cried out all at once. She flopped lifeless to the floor.

A burst of thunderous applause, cheering, the Vampire bowed and de-matted and the lights came blindingly on—

"We hope that you have had a pleasant fright," the announcer said warmly, "and thank you so much for choosing The Way Out Corp. for your entertainment today . . . Good Evening."

I glanced cursorily at the audience. Many were still under the spell. Then I got up to look for the stage door.

This was stupendous! This man had turned a simple geek act into a work of art. I could imagine him wowing them all on the lunchtime news now—the ratings'd put our rivals Astroco in the sanitization club for bankruptcy. Mind you, he *was* a psychotic . . . but one might daydream. He had an air about him. There was no vulgarity here. This had power. This had panache. This had class.

It wasn't just a filler. This had to be a special. Pocket History of Earth's ancient Vampires. Panel of psychologists—human and robot. The works. There was a fortune here, if only I could get the right angle on it.

. . . found a little autodoor that whispered STAGE DOOR, AUTHO-RIZED PERSONNEL ONLY, so I muttered "Holovee, holovee" in that urgent, well-rehearsed tone of voice that I always used to get into forbid-den places. It accordioned open. Then it banged shut behind me and Clunko, and I took a look.

I found the Vampire alone, being helped off with his clothes by a rusty-looking robot. Everything stunk of poverty and degradation in the dress-ing room. Cloaks and props cluttered up every centimeter of the floor. And then I looked at the Vampire's face.

He was standing in front of a mirror. I saw him first in the mirror, a dazed, sad face, a trace of blood on his lips. With a shock, I realized he was only a meter fifty tall or so. He'd been wearing levi-boots.

He had an earnest young face, mousy hair, freckles, a mild, undernour-ished look. . . .

"You the Vampire?" I couldn't believe it.

"I'm the Vampire," he said sadly. The robot had whisked the cloak away and he stood naked in front of me. His soma was emaciated, pitiful. I was still in shock as he went on. "I don't know how you got in—"

"I'm Milton Huang!"

"Who?" The man didn't even watch holovee.

"I'm a holovee personality. I want to do a special on you. You look like you could use the money," I added in a confidential sort of tone. "Listen, what do I call you? Mr. Vampire? Vampey?"

"My name is Federico barJulian," he said emotionlessly, "and my friends usually call me Fred. But then again I have no friends."

I was shaking inside, the way you always do when a terrific humdinger of a story is about to break. "You're . . . a *barJulian?*" How could the scion of one of the richest families in the universe—"

"I told you. My father owns the place. Now leave me alone."

"You're *Clement's* kid?"

"Leave me alone!" I saw his face freeze and a look of deep tragedy come over it. It would be perfect for holovee; this man was a born actor. Lucky he didn't know everything was being committed to tape. "Can't you people leave me in peace?" he said. "You've already turned me into a ridiculous parody, a stage show, forcing me to abase myself because of my terrible hunger. . . ."

"Look, I just want to do some filming. Name your price, for God's sake! Holothrills-National Enquirer is willing to pay any amount within reason. . . ." I walked around him slowly, thinking, *Why does he need to do this? With his kind of credit he could buy up an azroid full of pretty people and bite them all to death.*

As if in answer to my thoughts, he said, "I've been disowned. Father wishes to hush me up completely. I make a living the only way I know how." The pathos was just stunning. Loonies are always good material; they're so unpredictable, so *genuine*. And a quadrillionaire loonie geek was the acme of ratingsworthiness.

He stared me full in the face and said, "I just want to be normal."

"Huh?" I was taken aback. "You can't mean that. Hell, look at what you've got; they all love you out there. Your show has everything an audience could possibly want: a little bit of sex, a little bit of sadism, and a whole lot of archetypal, mythic mystery . . . come on," I said frustratedly, "you can't be *that* psychotic. Money's money."

"But you don't *understand*," he said, practically in tears. Nothing could have been further from the imposing, terrifying figure he had portrayed only a moment before. "I loathe this life. I don't want to be a freak! I want to be normal! Help me! Help me!" And he gripped my arm so tight that it was hurting. Gently I twisted loose. I took a long, stern look at everything I'd seen. Should I cut my losses . . . and lose the most potentially staggering holovee special I'd ever had the chance to make? There was pathos in the way this little man, childlike and torn by uncontrollable desires, was weeping his heart out in the dressing room. There was tragedy, even depth.

Then I got my brainstorm.

"Look here," I said, "we'll *get* you cured! We'll buy you the best psychocomputer in Mallworld. We'll have experts come and root every trauma, every complex. We'll even slip you back into society afterwards; we've got the megacreds to do it, and—"

"There's a price," he said truculently. "There's always a price."

"Let us tape everything."

"Well. . . ." I saw a little gleam in his eye now, and smiled smugly. How well I knew in those days that *everything* has its price.

Taking advantage of his confusion, I went on quickly: "Why, don't you see? As a sensation show it's pretty cool. We could maybe get a thirty-five to forty on the ratings. But as *human interest*—the private anguish of your tormented soul as it finally finds peace—it's incredible! I can see the whole thing," I went on, losing all caution in my enthusiasm, "a three hour feelietape special. We can get the sponsors: hell, the Way Out Corp. will do it for the publicity, maybe even the Vatican! The eyes of billions, in their living rooms, in their spacecars, in their azroid hideouts, eyes, ears, tacto-olfacto electrodes all glued to the holoscreen, from Titan to Mercury . . . 'The Vampire of Mallworld finds truth and meaning, and a new life.' It's warm—it's wonderful—"

"Help me! Oh, help me!" cried the Vampire of Mallworld.

Time passed and the best psychocomps in Mallworld were unable to extract any but the most extraneous information from Fred. We drugged him with every drug we could think of. We had him trussed up in a booth on the fifteenth level of Auntie Annetta's Do-It-Yourself Shrink Shack, alternately pumping him with sensory dep and sensory overload. A biochem-comp stood by, flashing every molecule of his endocrine system on to a strobomanic vidscreen. Even tried some Mediaeval therapy from an old recipe book where you electrocute the victim—patient—half to death . . . I toyed with the idea of getting help from the Selespridar, even. . . .

The best shrink shack in Mallworld was by definition the best shrink shack in the solar system, and this was all it yielded:

Federico barJulian had shown a propensity for bloodletting and other violence from the earliest. He was virgin at twenty-two, twice the normal age. His obsession had crystallized when he watched some ancient two-dimensional tapes of mythological vampire epics from earth: his favorite was a character called Dracula after whom he was later to model his act most consciously. Every six hours, the hunger would come upon him and he would rush down to the suicide parlour for another session. They were certainly milking him for all he was worth, paying him peanuts, and screwing the creditful thumbs of some fairly heavyweight clients . . . the Selespridon, a xeno-anthropologist, for instance, being one of the regulars. The six hours interval between each feeding session was totally reliable. You could tell time by him. In fact, I gave up checking my eyelid calendar completely.

For a person with such a peculiar social problem, he was astonishingly sane: witty, full of tragicomic one-liners, and a great holovee personality. He seemed undaunted at first by the constant failure of the therapy machines. I had a great time with his steadfastness, his courage, his obvious longing to be normal. But it was all wearing thin, and you don't make a good holovee show with failure. The audience has to have a satisfying climax and denoument, or you're stuck with three hours of pathos and gore and sex and human frailty and witty characterization and not a peg to hang the story on. . . .

My boss called me while I was taking a respite in the hotel's automassage-sauna. It was a transmat call; must have cost a fortune, all for the convenience of not having to wait ten minutes in between remarks. The boss materialized right in the middle of my tub of water. It was only a holoimage, but nonetheless unnerving.

"Got anything yet?"

"We're working on it—"

"Now see here, Huang!" The boss began to gyrate wildly around his tripod. "I don't want to catch sight of you in a sauna again, you hear? You've run way over budget and I'm giving you a hundred hours—" Abruptly his twenty seconds were up.

It's hard working for a machine; they have no sense of human dignity.

That was the day some kind of breakthrough happened—

I was too depressed after the boss called, thinking of my career going to seed and my ratings tumbling. After being poked at, prodded by machines, Fred was not feeling too hot either, so we decided to walk through Mallworld. We floated through the corridors in a polo-bubble, because I'd donned my all-too-familiar true somatype and I didn't want to be mobbed by the fans.

"It's not Bela Bartok anyway," he was saying, "it's Bela someone-else. They don't give a damn about accuracy at The Way Out, all they care for is their lousy show."

We turned a corner and sailed past the Galaxy Palace restaurant. We both shuddered, knowing who owned the place. I was becoming quite fond of Fred, even outside my professional capacity. We streaked past a bevy of shopping bags, their wares fairly bursting their seams, sauntering down a slidewalk as if they owned the place. A huge animated tomato demonstrated dance-steps on a whirling dais flanked by twittering comsims. Up a crazi-gravi corridor that gravi-flipflopped so we saw the whole world upside-down—

"Tired of this?" I said.

"Yeah. How about some nature?" We turned into the Earthscape Safari Park.

Striding boldly out of the holographic sea, one of Mallworld's most famous landmarks, the Statue of Limitations, patroness of merchants and thieves. . . .

As we winged down a klomet-wide pathway lined on either side with Grecian columns, with lions (actually leonoids) and tigroids and zebroids and okapoids and crocodiloids acting out the primal drama of nature, and shadows from distant dueling triceratopses blotching the wild wheat-brown savannah, we did not speak much. I saw that Fred was moved by what he saw, I sensed that he felt as they did, was part of this savage world. And then, without warning—

"Mommy!" he shrieked. He crushed me in his arms and tried to bite me, then began to wail like a baby and press hard against my chest, sobbing, "Mommy, Mommy. . . ."

"What's wrong?" I looked ahead and saw nothing but a herd of chimpanzoids, playfully cavorting inside a plastiflesh carcass of an elephant.

"Mommy—"

I was shaken. I mean, I knew he was crazy, but he'd never *acted* crazy before, except for this little quirk of sucking people's blood. I tried to calm him down, but he would not rest until we had gone way past the chimpanzee exhibit, into the aquarium hall where they showed dozens of fish being happily devoured by larger and larger fish. . . .

This new turn of events would keep the studio happy for a day or two. But now we needed results, and fast.

I beckoned to Clunko, who was trotting along behind, and asked for its advice. Meanwhile, Fred was staring at the chains of fish eating fish, smiling happily to himself.

"Maybe he was raised by apes in the jungle—" My camera began.

"Oh, be quiet."

"And acquired carnivorous habits, and when he was adopted back into civilization—"

"Watch enough ancient twodee tapes, you'll soon be as crazy as he is," I snapped. "Besides, he only bites humans. Besides, we found out that he was born right here in Mallworld, at Storkways Inc., in fact, who have never been known to deliver a defective baby—"

"Or so they claim."

"He's never so much as stepped off this thirty-klick hunk of metal! And what place could be safer than Mallworld? Where in hell could he possibly have picked up a chimpanzee-specific mother-surrogate response? I think . . . that it's time for a human psychiatrist, Clunko."

"A witch doctor?"

"Don't be silly. They have had human psychiatrists for centuries—"

"What are you, some kind of back-to-nature ecologizer?"

"You machines are such impossible chauvinists," I said, thinking of my boss.

We spent the day trying to relax: watched lion eat lion, vulture eat vulture, shark eat shark, and, in a rousing climax to the park's entertainments, a passably convincing tyrannosaur eat tyrannosaur . . . and then Fred shambled off to assuage his six-hourly hunger, and I went off to look up

Dr. Emmanuel Varhite. He and I had gone to St. Martin Luther King's Exclusive Strict and Snooty School when we were kids, so presumably he—like Clement barJulian himself—was on the Old Boy Network.

I found him running a psychiatric concession at Gimble and Gamble's Department Store and Feeliepalace on level T67. He'd come down in the world, and had also grown inordinately portly. He accepted the case at once, insisting only on one condition: that Holothrills buy him at least one meal a day at the Galaxy Palace restaurant. That was how low he had sunk, my old schoolmate. It was his own fault for picking such a pointless career, though. As useful to have chosen alchemy or window-washing, or to have learnt how to read.

A few hours later, Emmanuel Varhite was wolfing down Denebian whiteworms with great relish beneath the dome of artificial stars in Clement barJulian's restaurant. We had a table right beneath the starfield, and special wraparound seats that really felt snug. Invisible, too—they were Selespridon force-mechanisms—they made us look as though we were spacing out on Levitol. Clunko was casually disguised among the cutlery. Above, the "stars" shone—fake, but still beautiful. It was a masterstroke, I thought, to film in the Galaxy Palace: the stars were dazzling, and every human being yearns for those outside our space and time. . . .

Here the tables were turned, and we, the underdogs, got served by real people dressed in exotic alien costumes. Probably inaccurate.

I'd settled for the echinoderms stuffed with soft-shell malaprops; Fred, in full Bella Abzug attire, was eating a steak. Rare.

Varhite, whose face resembled a trampled rosebush, was expostulating at the camera. "We know," he said, "that the subject likes to drink blood—preferably killing the victim in the process."

"Come on, Varhite!" I stage-whispered. "Try to sound a little more witch-doctorly . . . our audience can be a little dumb, you know?

"Relaxen Sie . . . I mean, relax, my boy," he said, warming to the image I'd created for him. "There are other clues. For instance, he reacts violently to chimpanzees, calling them 'Mommy, mommy' in a petulant child's voice . . . clearly an anguished plea from the Unconscious.

"He is a product of Storkways Incorporated, the most blue chip, influential baby factory in the Solar System, whose main showroom is, of course, in Mallworld. . . ." as he spoke he never stopped sucking in the whiteworms as they wriggled in their death throes, thus releasing the intoxicating hormone that was the whole secret to their appeal . . . for sheer taste, give me spaghetti. "He first, as it were, concretized his urges when accidentally exposed to an old twodee movie. Now he watches it every day, in between meals, in his little oneroom apartment tucked inside the labyrinthine corridors of The Way Out Corp. And every six hours—"

"They've heard that."

"Now, from these facts, what strange, tortuous, twisted trauma can we glean? Ah—"

"Not much to go on, is there, Doctor?" I said glumly. "Frankly, Doctor—my boss is thinking of dumping this whole project."

"And not cure me?" Fred suddenly looked up from his steak with those hopeless, despairing eyes. . . .

"Come on, kid," I said, patting his hand. "Doctor Varhite and I, we *believe* in you." At that moment, I confess to being moved. He seemed so helpless . . . a baby, really. Trying to look professional, I skewered another echinoderm, watching as it deflated in a messy splat of rheum. "We *will* cure you!" I was almost choking. I'd lived with this thing for days now.

"And yet," said Doctor Varhite, "it seems to be most difficult to isolate the primal trauma. It must be very deep, very deep."

I knew the Doctor was up to something, so I subvoked to my camera. Several forks and spoons levitated to surround the Doctor from all sides. He pulled out something from his armpit pouch and threw it on the table. It was an inflatable hologram. He touched the stud—

A chimpanzee was sitting on the table.

"We've already done this a hundred times, you don't have to be cruel—" I began.

And the Vampire screamed! He tried to clutch me, the empty hologram's throat, tried to bite it, began to sob. I was so involved, subvoking instructions to all my hardware, that it was practically happening to me. And then he sank down on the table, wracked by convulsions, as other diners on their motorized tables swung by to see what all the fuss was about.

"Ah ha!" Doctor Varhite cried. "Positively Pavlovian!"

Abruptly the screaming stopped. Fred pulled himself together, whispered "Mommy" very softly, and gathered his cloak up around himself. He stood erect and tall in his levi-boots, menacing in his deathpale makeup.

His face seemed to shine with a pallid, luminous coldness.

"Blood," he whispered harshly. "Blood, blood, blood!"

Then he swept out of his seat and strode to a demat booth in the middle of the restaurant and disappeared, leaving behind him a giggling audience of diners.

"Well," I sighed, "that's another thing we know."

"Ja," said the Doctor, "regular as clockwork. In the middle of a word, in the middle of an action, when the six hours come, the urge comes. It's uncanny." With a fingertap he deflated his hologram.

"Well, let's go back to the hotel and talk more strategy, eh?" I said. But I wasn't feeling very hopeful.

"What about dessert?" I sighed; the contract was binding, of course, so we ordered. While we were waiting, a six-inch-high hologram of my boss appeared on the table.

"Oh no," I gasped, "not another holo! And this time *I'm* going to get the convulsions."

"Huang!" spluttered the hologram. "Something terrible has happened! Holothrills-National Enquirer had been completely bought up by the Clement barJulian group!"

I could feel my stomach turn. "Does this mean—"

"Yes it does! Now look, you have twenty-four hours to come back to Soaprock, or your expense account is up. Orders from on high say you're fired . . . whatever the cost! Someone in the new administration's after your ass, Huang. Now this is a regular realtime call. I'm not waiting ten minutes just to see you answer, lounging about in a sauna or . . . dining at the Galaxy! I bet that's where you are, isn't it? Now see here—"

He vanished and was replaced by two chocolate sundaes.

I shuddered. There was my whole career, flashing before my eyes. I tried not to think at all, and applied myself greedily to the sundae, an exotic dish made entirely from the blubber of specially cloned whales.

"You see the situation I'm in," I said. "I've raised the kid's hopes sky-high and now I'm to dash them all." Maybe I should have been thinking more about my own career then about Fred the Vampire. But I'd seen his show, I'd been touched by it. The kid had fallen all the way from riches to rags because of his obsession, yet . . . in the moment that he killed, he was a king. I'd seen it, I'd captured it on film, and I was starting to see him as

a martyr symbol of the human race . . . or maybe just falling victim to my
own skillfully worded holoscripts. I don't know.

"We still," Doctor Varhite said kindly, "have twenty-four hours."

"What can we do? We've tried everything!"

"Except . . . confrontation therapy."

"Oh?"

"I have already figured it out. This will be *so* dramatic that you can run
to the competition with it if you have to—"

"BarJulian owns the competition."

"You want to help him, don't you? Regardless."

"Regardless." I knew this was the wrong time for altruism, but I was in
too deep to quit.

"Confrontation therapy was a popular Dark Ages treatment," Varhite
explained as Clunko whirled around the table, "invented by one Marcus
Welby, whose tapes have survived the ages in truncated form. It involves
confronting the patient with the locale, the flavor, the *presence* of his in-
fancy, in order to drive the hidden trauma or *engram* to the surface. Tomorrow, then, we will film at Storkways, Inc.: and the patient will come
to find himself, there, at the very moment of his birth."

"It sounds very far-fetched to me."

"My boy," he said, "what do you know about Storkways Inc.? Did *you*
have the good fortune to be a Storkways child?"

"Of course not! I was born in the regular way, with an android host
mother-surrogate, delivered by Caesarian straight into my mother's arms."

"That's the problem, then. You don't understand the peculiar loneliness,
the *angst*, of a baby factory. I'm sure we can find an answer there . . .
won't you give it a try?"

"What's in it for you, Emmanuel?"

He shrugged. "It's complicated. I guess I want to vindicate us 'witch
doctors' and destroy the ascendancy of the psychocomps. I've been on a
downhill trend lately and I need something. And besides, another day of
the Galaxy Palace's food—"

Just then a waiter slunk up to our table. "Excuse me sir," he said, floun-
dering about in his half-donned fuzzy suit. "Mr. barJulian has asked me to
inform you that you and the Doctor are no longer welcome in this restaurant. A comsim will escort you—"

With a grand gesture Doctor Varhite slung the remainder of his sundae in the waiter's face. He stood dazed for a moment, then toppled into a heap of arms, legs, fur and chocolate sauce.

Clunko had filmed the whole thing. "Bravo!" I said. "Let's get out of here."

"You have no idea," said Doctor Varhite, "how much it cost me to do that."

It was a sorry troupe that matted on the level Y99 an hour or so later; we had just caught the last of Fred's act at The Way Out and he had just done away with a pair of beautiful tangerine-eyed twins. Varhite led the way through a conch-twisty passageway; I followed, not even caring that, even in my normal soma, I was not attracting the attention of any rabid fans . . . Clunko trotted behind and the vampire of Mallworld lagged in the rear. I knew I wouldn't get a chance to see the act again—not at twelve kilocred a throw and no expense account—and so the killings had been tinged with an exquisite sadness. You might wonder why . . . these people have elected, of their own free will, to die, and the exhibitions of suicide parlors are a natural consequence of man's innate commercialism . . . but I found myself thrust into a state of profound longing which no competent newsman should have felt. I began to wonder about myself. Did I really belong in the holothrill trade?

Too soon we reached the lobby of Storkways Inc., a gigantic stylized uterus, painted pain, with transparent walk-levels jutting from the sides, which you approached from below by means of a diagonal slidewalk, through a tubular passageway. The symbolism lent a grave dignity to the proceedings. Storkways was the oldest of the baby production firms, and was known to be incorruptible. No one had ever purchased a faulty baby from Storkways . . . or so they claimed. The primaeval womb would make an excellent final scene, I decided, my spirits lifting a little. I could almost hear the script: *Here, in the very womb of humanity. . . .*

I had to stop and remind myself that I was just doing the day's filming as an empty gesture, an attempt to wring every last microcred from the coffers of the company.

Soon we were greeted by a buxom, human attendant in an oversized diaper and nothing else. She was wearing Storkways' Radiant Motherhood Smile.

"Ah," she said, not at all perturbed by the strange sight of a Vampire in full regalia, a fat little psychoanalyst, a talking camera, and me. "A charming menage you have here, I see! What kind of baby were you interested in, and at what price range?"

I looked a bit indecisive, I suppose, so she quickly went on, "Aquatics are in this season, as are little fuzzies and of course our ever-popular 'normal' model, and—"

She looked at us expectantly. The smile hadn't changed a bit; I knew that it had been soldered on surgically.

"Why don't you nice fellows just browse through our catalogue?" she said. Instantly the air was full of holographic toddlers, solemnly filing past our faces. "Just point to the one you want . . . oh! . . . you're . . . *Milton Huang!*" she shrieked suddenly.

It was the only thing that happened all day. "I'm sure you'll be wanting a custom-made, then," she said thoughtfully. "Are these your husbands?"

"Miss—"

"Could I have your thumbprint, please? Just a formality, credit check you know, and—well actually I wanted it for my collection, I watch your show almost every fourday—"

"We'd like to do some filming here. If you'll just thumb this release—" I fiddled around with spools of minitape from my loinshield.

"O-o-o-o-oh!" She just stared at me, hardly taking in a word, while I explained the situation. "I'll get the manager. Oh, we'd be proud. Very proud indeed." She hopped into demat-booth.

"What do you think?" I whispered to Emmanual.

"Let's be patient," he said. Then, "Oh, look at all the darling babies!"

A seductive voice was saying, in warm, motherly tones, "Number 17 of our 'exotic' line is green-skinned, adapted for Deimos gravity, with a power-steering option for those difficult visits to high-gravity worlds. Choice of three hair colors and two basic personality indexes—'passionate and profound' or 'excitable and extravert.' Actual personality will depend, of course, on environmental factors and your own parental proclivities."

The baby spun round and toddled off in mid-air.

"Number 18. The two heads are perfectly adapted for—"

"Can't we turn this thing off?" I shouted impatiently. Doctor Varhite nudged me gently, and I saw that our friend Fred was gazing, spellbound, at the tot parade.

"Normal . . . normal . . ." he was murmuring, as a charming little number with vestigial wings, four arms and belly-gills drifted by. Poor Fred. I made sure I got a shot of his wistful face. I was in my element now, capturing the very essence of the man for the audience that was never to be. More and more the situation was getting urgent—anyone who'd envy an 'exotic' baby for being normal . . . they're usually intended for Babylon-5, and if you call anything to do with *that* colony normal, you really have flipped your chips.

Miss Perfect Mother came flouncing in with another matriarchal figure, this time in a golden diaper that radiated higher authority. This was Mabel Murray-Pentecost, regional manager of Storkways Inc. She too sported the infamous patent smile.

"Welcome!" she boomed. "I am most honored to be able to conduct you through our venerable halls myself, though I am *sure* that whatever is troubling that poor, poor young man will not be found here. And let me say for the benefit of the audience"—she certainly was making the best of her air time, not knowing that she'd never make it on to the holovee screen— "that Storkways is *dedicated* to the infinite recomplexification of our human gene pool. Why be the same when you can be different? I know it's conservative and old-fashioned of us, but let me say that I *believe* in those values. Here at Storkways Inc. we always say: 'A clone no more!'"

Having said her piece, she beckoned us into a booth.

"Fred has been tranquilized," Varhite was explaining to the Mother, "so that only the most primal memories will precipitate his convulsions." Nevertheless, I noticed that Miss Murray-Pentecost was keeping her distance and even seemed a little leery of Clunko as he clambered after us.

". . . and this is the viewing room," she was saying, "where the little dears all rest and where they can be examined by prospective parents through a sophisticated audio-video-tacto-olfacto projection device in the privacy of their own holoview cubicles."

We were standing in a tremendously long hall lined with float-cribs, five in a row, with narrow lanes between each row, and little comfort-robots whizzing back and forth between the rows. The din was really heady; with some reluctance I resisted the cheap trick of switching up the audio track. I was damn well going to be artistic even if no one was going to experience this show.

"My god!" I exclaimed for the camera. "How many babies do you have here at any one time?"

"Three, four thousand," she said. "We change them every sleep shift."

"But . . . don't they ever get misplaced?" said Doctor Varhite slyly.

"What, sir? Incompetence here at Storkways Inc.? You ask the impossible. Are we not *dedicated* to the preservation of human life? Are we not a byword for ethical behavior throughout the solar system?"

"All right, already!" I said. "Varhite—any luck on the patient?"

Fred was stalking up and down the aisles. He seemed a little restless, with his cloak flying behind him and his hands trembling a bit, but benign enough for now. Every now and then he stopped to croon over one of the babies.

"He won't . . . you know, *eat* one?" asked Mabel Murray-Pentecost anxiously.

"Oh, no. His 'attacks' come very six hours exactly, and he's just been fed," said Doctor Varhite.

"Curious," said the matriarch. "We've just had our feeding too—we run the feeding system every six hours, and it's all computer controlled, obviously—"

Doctor Varhite and I exchanged a quick look. "It's probably fortuitous," I said. "It seems a pretty unlikely connection to me. . . ."

I subvoked Clunko and told him to heel. We had a lot more to squeeze into my last day and I was getting impatient. We weren't going to find a solution anyway . . . Clunko had been having a grand time snapping all the babies—his 'human interest' programming was very deeply ingrained. I had to squeeze to negotiate the aisles, and the manageress' fixed smile had become extremely wearying to look at. The hall was *not* designed for people, but for robots; and the nearest demat booth was a good five hundred meters of squashing and squeezing away.

The next hall was a very murky one. It was two meters across but seemed to stretch forever. The walls were high—about twenty-five meters—and lined with shelves. On each shelf squatted a row of bored-looking chimpanzees, each with a baby in its arms.

"A-*ha!*" said Emmanuel. I saw his point. Now I was sure there was a connection, but what was it? I glanced at Fred, who was shaken but still in one piece—thanks to the massive dose of tranquilizers.

"This," said the guide, "is our feeding room, where our little ones are breast-fed by genetically altered chimpanzees, as you can see. It's ever so hygienic, and you know it's much better psychologically for the child to be able to relate to a living creature."

Now I knew that all the pieces belonged to the same puzzle. But I still couldn't see the answer. Nothing fell into place. What could possibly be traumatic about being breast-fed by a chimpanzee? The idea certainly didn't worry *me*, and I had been a regular baby.

But they gave me a creepy feeling, those rows and rows of apes, each clutching a baby in its arms, each with a dead, glazed look which betrayed . . . what? Genetic tampering? "What now?" I asked Doctor Varhite.

"Is there anything else?" He turned to Miss Murray-Pentecost.

"I don't think so—this represents all the stages that a baby would go through. . . ."

"And yet the patient has exhibited no unusual anxieties, yet." Fred had retreated into his cloak, but was still calm. "You've never discovered—" the doctor began to hem and haw, choosing his words with great care— "any instances of traumatization from these breast feedings?"

"Heaven's, no, Doctor," she said with some revulsion, "our research department—not to mention our discriminating clientele—would never have let us get away with such a thing!"

"And the babies are placed with chimpanzee mother-surrogates immediately after parturition?" said Doctor Varhite.

"Well, yes, of course."

"And if no chimpanzees are available?" I said.

"Well, sometimes it happens, and then we take some of the older babies off the chimpanzee temporarily to make room . . . we have excellent temporary facilities, of course, for the temporarily displaced little ones. . . ."

"Show me," Varhite said grimly.

"You don't ask for much, do you?" she said through her implacable smile. "Come with me." Her golden diaper gleamed in the half-light.

"I do apologize for our lack of demat-booths here," she said, "but we usually only have robots here." A little passageway opened up at our feet, and she motioned us to descend. "We don't usually want any unnecessary infection, you know, and one can't very well put a prospective parent into an autoclave. . . ." She chuckled heartily at her own joke.

The steep passageway was cramped: we had to go single file. Fred and the Doctor lagged; I think Fred was reluctant and had to be coaxed. A strange unease hung in the air. The manageress and I were the first ones to enter the little room. There were perhaps ten circular tables, stacked with hardware.

"On peak seasons," she was saying, "we do sometimes use these."

She indicated one of the round machines on a table, from which half a dozen padded cribs jutted, in some of which babies lay, some gurgling, some asleep. A plastiflesh pacifier extended over the mouth of each infant, and was connected to a vat of milk under the table. Most of the berthlets were empty.

"Seems efficient enough," I said.

She beamed maternally. "It's usually only for a day or so, until a new shipment of fastclone chimps can be transmatted from the farms on Earth."

"What's this here?" I pointed to one of the unoccupied cribs, where a pacifier looked a little odd.

"Why," she said, "I've no idea."

. . . the plastiflesh had broken off, rotted away somehow, revealing the pointed steel of the milk-injector underneath, sharp and ugly. A baby could. . . .

"Are you telling me—" I began.

"Oh, no, our equipment is inspected *daily*. That must be why the crib is unoccupied, you see." I thought I could detect a slight wilting of the permanent smile, even though I knew it was anatomically impossible.

"But isn't it just possible that, if you had a defective pacifier, that a baby could accidentally get assigned to it *before* the daily inspection, and—"

Just then the others came down and crowded around the table. I was just pointing out the faulty pacifier when—

Fred gave a hysterical cry and began to pummel the machine with his fists. Doctor Varhite and I stepped back in shock. He was banging, now his fists were sore and bloody, he was yelling over and over, "Mommy, mommy, mommy, you betrayed me you hurt me you made me drink blood you gave me blood mommy mommy mommy—"

My blood was racing with excitement. I sent the camera flying every which way. Fred was beautiful. The way he clawed at the metal, the way he moaned and shrieked—

"Inspected daily?" I turned to the matriarch grimly.

"I assure you, sir—" she said (without losing her smile for a moment) "your accusations are impossible! We'll sue! We'll sue!"

"Mommy mommy mommy—"

How BIG a story could you get? Incompetence—in *Storkways Incorporated*—within the very bastions of everything we held good in society! I'd shot the show that would undermine the very foundations of our beliefs! No matter that no one would see it—

"I'll sue, you can't go exposing us like this, I can explain!" screamed the matriarch, smiling beautifully and grotesquely the whole time.

Above the tumult I turned to Emmanuel Varhite. "And now let's talk to the expert himself," I said in my suavest holovee voice. "Now that the pieces have come together, what are your conclusions?"

"Dark are the ways of the Unconscious," he began dramatically. (The screaming in the background never stopped. It set the babies off, and *they* were all hollering their lungs out.) "The essence of Confrontation Therapy is truth, sheer truth. Here we have seen an unfortunate trauma: the patient was made to substitute pain and blood for a mother's love and milk. No wonder he felt hostility towards the chimpanzee-mother-surrogate who came too late to aid him from his terrible torment! No wonder he could not forgive! Yes! It was this very womb that the seeds of schizophrenia were sown. . . ."

"Mommy mommy mommy—"

"I'll sue—"

"Waaaaaaagh—"

Seizing the moment, I gathered up my most melodramatic phrases and stood in a heroic poise, full face in front of Clunko. *Go, Clunko, go,* I subvoked, and then began rhetorically: "What have we seen here, friends? We have traced this unfortunate, tragic man's career back to its very roots. We have shown him the source of his terrible inner conflict; and now we have freed him to emerge, a fully *human* being, from the living hell that was his domain. Yes! What we have witnessed today—is Death and Rebirth! Total Catharsis! in a monumental, heartwarming victory for the human spirit!"

I spread out my arms in the famous "crucified" pose that has since made me a household word, held for ten seconds, and turned round to see if I could stop all the screaming.

*   *   *

"... so you see," Clement barJulian was saying to me, "I had to see the finished project. Federico was—is—my son." He downed another glass of angels' tears. "I should have believed that a cure was possible, and yet—and yet—"

"I know." He had wept four times when they showed him the rough edit of the special. He'd rehired me. He'd re-adopted his son. I didn't want to go into all that again—I was trying to ferret out some scandal about his sister-in-law. After a whole year in which I'd become rich, in which Storkways had paid damages through the nose—and hush-up money, too, when a dozen other cases of criminal negligence came to light, and Vampire imitators popped up all over Sol System, and glamorous Fred being chased everywhere by an army of amorous groupies, begging for a gentle nip on the neck in memory of the old days—

Yes. Things certainly turned out right for him. And yet—

"Clement," I said, "I don't like what I do anymore."

He hardly looked up from his main course, a succulent crablike purple thing with splotchy tentacles swimming in a bowl of strawberry jello. I looked away, watching the stars wheel. "Eh?"

"I'm a phony, you know," I said. After a whole year I had to blurt out my heart to someone. "All holovee personalities are. We're really drab. And yet, when I think of when I first watched Fred's show, and saw love and death and beauty and mystery all mingled together, and I knew that this was *Art* . . . nothing *I* do will ever be as beautiful, or as terrifying, or as *real*, as Fred the Vampire's lunacy. Will it?"

"He was crazy!" Clement said. "You cured him, and earned a few creds yourself from the whole thing. You should be happy."

"But I'm scared. I'm scared. I feel like I've destroyed . . . something very personal, something like a soul I suppose. I almost regret it. . . ."

"Come on!" Clement roared. "Here, take your mind off it, let me tell you some juicy gossip—"

I could not bring myself to confess to Clement barJulian that, for a few moments, when his son the Vampire squeezed the life out of a particularly beautiful woman in a passion beyond ecstasy and terror, I would have given anything to feel what he felt . . . for a few seconds that will haunt me forever, I had envied the Vampire of Mallworld.

Child of an Ancient City

by Tad Williams

"**M**erciful Allah! I am as a calf, fatted for slaughter!"

Masrur al-Adan roared with laughter and crashed his goblet down on the polished wood table—once, twice, thrice. A trail of crescent-shaped dents followed his hand. "I can scarce move for gorging."

The fire was banked, and shadows walked the walls. Masrur's table—for he was master here—stood scatter-spread with the bones of small fowl.

Masrur leaned forward and squinted across the table. "A calf," he said. "Fatted." He belched absently and wiped his mouth with wine-stained sleeve.

Ibn Fahad broke off a thin, cold smile. "We have indeed wreaked massacre on the race of pigeons, old friend." His slim hand swept above the littered table-top. "We have also put the elite guard of your wine cellars to flight. And, as usual, I thank you for your hospitality. But do you not sometimes wonder if there is more to life than growing fat in the service of the Caliph?"

"Hah!" Masrur goggled his eyes. "Doing the Caliph's bidding has made me wealthy. I have made *myself* fat." He smiled. The other guests laughed and whispered.

Abu Jamir, a fatter man in an equally stained robe, toppled a small tower erected from the bones of squab. "The night is young, good Masrur!" he cried. "Have someone fetch up more wine and let us hear some stories!"

"Baba!" Masrur bellowed. "Come here, you old dog!"

Within three breaths an old servant stood in the doorway, looking to his sportive master with apprehension.

"Bring us the rest of the wine, Baba—or have you drunk it all?"

Baba pulled at grizzled chin. "Ah . . . ah, but *you* drank it, Master. You and Master Ibn Fahad took the last four jars with you when you went to shoot arrows at the weathercock."

"Just as I suspected," Masrur nodded. "Well, get on across the bazaar to Abu Jamir's place, wake up his manservant, and bring back several jugs. The good Jamir says we must have it now."

Baba disappeared. The chagrined Abu Jamir was cheerfully back-thumped by the other guests.

"A story, a story!" someone shouted. "A tale!"

"Oh, yes, a tale of your travels, Master Masrur!" This was young Hassan, sinfully drunk. No one minded. His eyes were bright, and he was full of innocent stupidity. "Someone said you have traveled to the green lands of the north."

"The north . . . ?" Masrur grumbled, waving his hand as though confronted with something unclean, "No, lad, no . . . that I cannot give to you." His face clouded and he slumped back on his cushions; his tarbooshed head swayed.

Ibn Fahad knew Masrur like he knew his horses—indeed, Masrur was the only human that could claim so much of Ibn Fahad's attention. He had seen his old comrade drink twice this quantity and still dance like a dervish on the walls of Baghdad, but he thought he could guess the reason for this sudden incapacity.

"Oh, Masrur, please!" Hassan had not given up; he was as unshakeable as a young falcon with its first prey beneath its talons. "Tell us of the north. Tell us of the infidels!"

"A good Moslem should not show such interest in unbelievers." Abu Jamir sniffed piously, shaking the last drops from a wine jug. "If Masrur does not wish to tell a tale, let him be."

"Hah!" snorted the host, recovering somewhat, "You only seek to stall me, Jamir, so that my throat shall not be so dry when your wine arrives. No, I have no fear of speaking of unbelievers: Allah would not have given them a place in the world for their own if they had not *some* use. Rather it is . . . certain other things that happened which make me hesitate." He gazed kindly on young Hassan, who in the depths of his drunkenness looked about to cry. "Do not despair, eggling. Perhaps it would do me good to unfold this story. I have kept the details long inside." He emptied the dregs of another jar into his cup. "I still feel it so strongly, though—bitter, bitter times. Why don't *you* tell the story, my good friend?" he said over his shoulder to Ibn Fahad. "You played as much a part as did I."

"No," Ibn Fahad replied. Drunken puppy Hassan emitted a strangled cry of despair.

"But why, old comrade?" Masrur asked, pivoting his bulk to stare in amazement. "Did the experience so chill even *your* heart?"

Ibn Fahad glowered. "Because I know better. As soon as I start you will interrupt, adding details here, magnifying there, then saying: 'No, no, I cannot speak of it! Continue, old friend!' Before I have taken another breath you will interrupt me again. You *know* you will wind up doing all the talking, Masrur. Why do you not start from the beginning and save me my breath?"

All laughed but Masrur, who put on a look of wounded solicitousness. "Of course, old friend," he murmured. "I had no idea that you harbored such grievances. Of course I shall tell the tale." A broad wink was offered to the table. "No sacrifice is too great for a friendship such as ours. Poke up the fire, will you, Baba? Ah, he's gone. Hassan, will you be so kind?"

When the youth was again seated Masrur took a swallow, stroked his beard, and began.

In those days [Masrur said], I myself was but a lowly soldier in the service of Harun al-Rashid, may Allah grant him health. I was young, strong, a man who loved wine more than he should—but what soldier does not?—and a good deal more trim and comely than you see me today.

My troop received a commission to accompany a caravan going north, bound for the land of the Armenites beyond the Caucassian Mountains. A certain prince of that people had sent a great store of gifts as tribute to the Caliph, inviting him to open a route for trade between

his principality and our caliphate. Harun al-Rashid, wisest of wise men
that he is, did not exactly make the camels groan beneath the weight of
the gifts that he sent in return; but he sent several courtiers, including the
under-vizier Walid al-Salameh, to speak for him and to assure this Armenite prince that rich rewards would follow when the route over the
Caucassians was opened for good.

We left Baghdad in grand style, pennants flying, the shields of the soldiers flashing like golden dinars, and the Caliph's gifts bundled onto the
backs of a gang of evil, contrary donkeys.

We followed the banks of the faithful Tigris, resting several days at
Mosul, then continued through the eastern edge of Anatolia. Already as
we mounted northward the land was beginning to change, the clean
sands giving way to rocky hills and scrub. The weather was colder, and
the skies gray, as though Allah's face was turned away from that country, but the men were not unhappy to be out from under the desert sun.
Our pace was good; there was not a hint of danger except the occasional
wolf howling at night beyond the circles of the campfires. Before two
months had passed we had reached the foothills of the Caucassians—
what is called the steppe country.

For those of you who have not strayed far from our Baghdad, I should
tell you that the northern lands are like nothing you have seen. The trees
there grow so close together you could not throw a stone five paces
without striking one. The land itself seems always dark—the trees mask
the sun before the afternoon is properly finished—and the ground is
damp. But, in truth, the novelty of it fades quickly, and before long it
seems that the smell of decay is always with you. We caravaneers had
been over eight weeks a-traveling, and the bite of homesickness was
strong, but we contented ourselves with the thought of the accommodations that would be ours when we reached the palace of the prince, laden
as we were with our Caliph's good wishes—and the tangible proof
thereof.

We had just crossed the high mountain passes and begun our journey
down when disaster struck.

We were encamped one night in a box canyon, a thousand steep feet
below the summit of the tall Caucassian peaks. The fires were not much
but glowing coals, and nearly all the camp was asleep except for two
men standing sentry. I was wrapped in my bedroll, dreaming of how I

would spend my earnings, when a terrible shriek awakened me. Sitting groggily upright, I was promptly knocked down by some bulky thing tumbling onto me. A moment's horrified examination showed that it was one of the sentries, throat pierced with an arrow, eyes bulging with his final surprise. Suddenly there was a chorus of howls from the hillside above. All I could think of was wolves, that the wolves were coming down on us; in my witless state I could make no sense of the arrow at all.

Even as the others sprang up around me the camp was suddenly filled with leaping, whooping shadows. Another arrow hissed past my face in the darkness, and then something crashed against my bare head, filling the nighttime with a great splash of light that illuminated nothing. I fell back, insensible.

I could not tell how long I had journeyed in that deeper darkness when I was finally roused by a sharp boot prodding at my ribcage.

I looked up at a tall, cruel figure, cast by the cloud-curtained morning sun in bold silhouette. As my sight became accustomed I saw a knife-thin face, dark-browed and fierce, with mustachios long as a Tartar herdsman's. I felt sure that whoever had struck me had returned to finish the job, and I struggled weakly to pull my dagger from my sash. This terrifying figure merely lifted one of his pointy boots and trod delicately on my wrist, saying in perfect Arabic: "Wonders of Allah, this is the dirtiest man I have ever seen."

It was Ibn Fahad, of course. The caravan had been of good size, and he had been riding with the Armenite and the under-vizier—not back with the hoi polloi—so we had never spoken. Now you see how we first truly met: me on my back, covered with mud, blood, and spit; and Ibn Fahad standing over me like a rich man examining carrots in the bazaar. Infamy!

Ibn Fahad had been blessed with what I would come later to know as his usual luck. When the bandits—who must have been following us for some days—came down upon us in the night, Ibn Fahad had been voiding his bladder some way downslope. Running back at the sound of the first cries, he had sent more than a few mountain bandits down to Hell courtesy of his swift sword, but they were too many. He pulled together a small group of survivors from the main party and they fought their way free, then fled along the mountain in the darkness listening to the screams echoing behind them, cursing their small numbers and ignorance of the country.

Coming back in the light of day to scavenge for supplies, as well as ascertain the nature of our attackers, Ibn Fahad had found me—a fact he has never allowed me to forget, and for which *I* have never allowed *him* to evade responsibility.

While my wounds and bandit-spites were doctored, Ibn Fahad introduced me to the few survivors of our once-great caravan.

One was Susri al-Din—a cheerful lad, fresh-faced and smooth-cheeked as young Hassan here, dressed in the robes of a rich merchant's son. The soldiers who had survived rather liked him, and called him "Fawn," to tease him for his wide-eyed good looks. There was a skinny wretch of a chief clerk named Abdallah, purse-mouthed and iron-eyed, and an indecently plump young mullah, who had just left the *madrasa* and was getting a rather rude introduction to life outside the seminary. Ruad, the mullah, looked as though he would prefer to be drinking and laughing with the soldiers—beside myself and Ibn Fahad there were four or five more of these—while Abdallah the prim-faced clerk looked as though *he* should be the one who never lifted his head out of the Koran. Well, in a way that was true, since for a man like Abdallah the balance book *is* the Holy Book, may Allah forgive such blasphemy.

There was one other, notable for the extreme richness of his robes, the extreme whiteness of his beard, and the vast weight of his personal jewelry—Walid al-Salameh, the under-vizier to His Eminence the Caliph Harun al-Rashid. Walid was the most important man of the whole party. He was also, surprisingly, not a bad fellow at all.

So there we found ourselves, the wrack of the caliph's embassy, with no hope but to try and find our way back home through a strange, hostile land.

The upper reaches of the Caucassians are a cold and godless place. The fog is thick and wet; it crawls in of the morning, leaves briefly at the time the sun is high, then comes creeping back long before sunset. We had been sodden as well-diggers from the moment we had stepped into the foothills. A treacherous place, those mountains: home of bear and wolf, covered in forest so thick that in places the sun was lost completely. Since we had no guide—indeed, it was several days before we saw any sign of inhabitants whatsoever—we wandered unsteered, losing half as much ground as we gained for walking in circles.

At last we were forced to admit our need for a trained local eye. In the middle slopes the trees grew so thick that fixing our direction was impossible for hours at a time. We were divining the location of Mecca by general discussion, and—blasphemy again—we probably spent as much time praying toward Aleppo as to Mecca. It seemed a choice between possible discovery and certain doom.

We came down by night and took a young man out of an isolated shepherd's hovel, as quietly as ex-brigands like ourselves (or at least like many of us, Ibn Fahad. My apologies!) could. The family did not wake, the dog did not bark; we were two leagues away before sunrise, I'm sure.

I felt sorry in a way for the young peasant-lout we'd kidnapped. He was a nice fellow, although fearfully stupid—I wonder if we are now an old, dull story with which he bores his children? In any case, once this young rustic—whose name as far as I could tell was unpronounceable by civilized tongues—realized that we were not ghosts or Jinni, and were *not* going to kill him on the spot, he calmed down and was quite useful. We began to make real progress, reaching the peak of the nearest ridge in two days.

There was a slight feeling of celebration in the air that night, our first in days under the open skies. The soldiers cursed the lack of strong drink, but spirits were good nonetheless—even Ibn Fahad pried loose a smile.

As the under-vizier Walid told a humorous story, I looked about the camp. There were but two grim faces: the clerk Abdallah—which was to be expected, since he seemed a patently sour old devil—and the stolen peasant-boy. I walked over to him.

"Ho, young one," I said, "why do you look so downcast? Have you not realized that we are good-hearted, Godfearing men, and will not harm you?" He did not even raise his chin, which rested on his knees, shepherd-style, but he turned his eyes up to mine.

"It is not those things," he said in his awkward Arabic. "It is not you soldiers but . . . this place."

"Gloomy mountains they are indeed," I agreed, "but you have lived here all your young life. Why should it bother you?"

"Not this place. We never come here—it is unholy. The vampyr walks these peaks."

"Vampyr?" said I. "And what peasant-devil is that?"

He would say no more; I left him to his brooding and walked back to the fire.

The men all had a good laugh over the vampyr, making jesting guesses as to what type of beast it might be, but Ruad, the young mullah, waved his hands urgently.

"I have heard of such afreets," he said. "They are not to be laughed at by such a godless lot as yourselves."

He said this as a sort of scolding joke, but he wore a strange look on his round face; we listened with interest as he continued.

"The vampyr is a restless spirit. It is neither alive nor dead, and Shaitan possesses its soul utterly. It sleeps in a sepulcher by day, and when the moon rises it goes out to feed upon travelers, to drink their blood."

Some of the men again laughed loudly, but this time it rang false as a brass-merchant's smile.

"I have heard of these from one of our foreign visitors," said the under-vizier Walid quietly. "He told me of a plague of these vampyr in a village near Smyrna. All the inhabitants fled, and the village is still uninhabited today."

This reminded someone else (myself, perhaps) of a tale about an afreet with teeth growing on both sides of his head. Others followed with their own demon stories. The talk went on late into the night, and no one left the campfire until it had completely burned out.

By noon the next day we had left the heights and were passing back down into the dark, tree-blanketed ravines. When we stopped that night we were once more hidden from the stars, out of sight of Allah and the sky.

I remember waking up in the foredawn hours. My beard was wet with dew, and I was damnably tangled up in my cloak. A great, dark shape stood over me. I must confess to making a bit of a squawking noise.

"It's me," the shape hissed—it was Rifakh, one of the other soldiers. "You gave me a turn."

Rifakh chuckled. "Thought I was that vamper, eh? Sorry. Just stepping out for a piss." He stepped over me, and I heard him trampling the underbrush. I slipped back into sleep.

The sun was just barely over the horizon when I was again awakened, this time by Ibn Fahad tugging at my arm. I grumbled at him to leave me alone, but he had a grip on me like an alms-beggar.

"Rifakh's gone," he said. "Wake up. Have you seen him?"

"He walked on me in the middle of the night, on his way to go moisten a tree," I said. "He probably fell in the darkness and hit his head on something—have you looked?"

"Several times," Ibn Fahad responded. "All around the camp. No sign of him. Did he say anything to you?"

"Nothing interesting. Perhaps he has met the sister of our shepherd-boy, and is making the two-backed beast."

Ibn Fahad made a sour face at my crudity. "Perhaps not. Perhaps he has met some *other* beast."

"Don't worry," I said. "If he hasn't fallen down somewhere close by, he'll be back."

But he did not come back. When the rest of the men arose we had another long search, with no result. At noon we decided, reluctantly, to go on our way, hoping that if he had strayed somewhere he could catch up with us.

We hiked down into the valley, going farther and farther into the trees. There was no sign of Rifakh, although from time to time we stopped and shouted in case he was searching for us. We felt there was small risk of discovery, for that dark valley was as empty as a pauper's purse, but nevertheless, after a while the sound of our voices echoing back through the damp glades became unpleasant. We continued on in silence.

Twilight comes early in the bosom of the mountains; by midafternoon it was already becoming dark. Young Fawn—the name had stuck, against the youth's protests—who of all of us was the most disturbed by the disappearance of Rifakh, stopped the company suddenly, shouting: "Look there!"

We straightaway turned to see where he was pointing, but the thick trees and shadows revealed nothing.

"I saw a shape!" the young one said. "It was just a short way back, following us. Perhaps it is the missing soldier."

Naturally the men ran back to look, but though we scoured the bushes we could find no trace of anyone. We decided that the failing light had played Fawn a trick—that he had seen a hind or somesuch.

Two other times he called out that he saw a shape. The last time one of the other soldiers glimpsed it too: a dark, man-like form, moving rapidly beneath the trees a bow-shot away. Close inspection still yielded no evidence, and as the group trod wearily back to the path again Walid the under-vizier turned to Fawn with a hard, flat look.

"Perhaps it would be better, young master, if you talked no more of shadow-shapes."

"But I saw it!" the boy cried. "That soldier Mohammad saw it too!"

"I have no doubt of that," answered Walid al-Salameh, "but think on this: we have gone several times to see what it might be, and have found no sign of any living man. Perhaps our Rifakh is dead; perhaps he fell into a stream and drowned, or hit his head upon a rock. His spirit may be following us because it does not wish to stay in this unfamiliar place. That does not mean we want to go and find it."

"But . . . ," the other began.

"Enough!" spat the chief clerk Abdallah. "You heard the under-vizier, young prankster. We shall have no more talk of your godless spirits. You will straightaway leave off telling such things!"

"Your concern is appreciated, Abdallah," Walid said coldly, "but I do not require your help in this matter." The vizier strode away.

I was almost glad the clerk had added his voice, because such ideas would not keep the journey in good order . . . but like the under-vizier I, too, had been rubbed and grated by the clerk's highhandedness. I am sure others felt the same, for no more was said on the subject all evening.

Allah, though, always has the last word—and who are *we* to try to understand His ways? We bedded down a very quiet camp that night, the idea of poor Rifakh's lost soul hanging unspoken in the air.

From a thin, unpleasant sleep I woke to find the camp in chaos. "It's Mohammad, the soldier!" Fawn was crying. "He's been killed! He's dead!"

It was true. The mullah Ruad, first up in the morning, had found the man's blanket empty, then found his body a few short yards out of the clearing.

"His throat has been slashed out," said Ibn Fahad.

It looked like a wild beast had been at him. The ground beneath was dark with blood, and his eyes were wide open.

Above the cursing of the soldiers and the murmured holy words of the mullah, who looked quite green of face, I heard another sound. The young shepherd-lad, grimly silent all the day before, was rocking back and forth on the ground by the remains of the cook-fire, moaning.

"Vampyr . . . ," he wept, ". . . vampyr, the vampyr . . ."

All the companions were, of course, completely unmanned by these events. While we buried Mohammad in a hastily dug grave those assembled darted glances over their shoulders into the forest vegetation. Even Ruad, as he spoke the words of the holy Koran, had trouble keeping his eyes down. Ibn Fahad and I agreed between ourselves to maintain that Mohammad had fallen prey to a wolf or some other beast, but our fellow travelers found it hard even to pretend agreement. Only the under-vizier and the clerk Abdallah seemed to have their wits fully about them, and Abdallah made no secret of his contempt for the others. We set out again at once.

Our company was somber that day—and no wonder. No one wished to speak of the obvious, nor did they have much stomach for talk of lighter things—it was a silent file of men that moved through the mountain fastnesses.

As the shadows of evening began to roll down, the dark shape was with us again, flitting along just in sight, disappearing for a while only to return, bobbing along behind us like a jackdaw. My skin was crawling—as you may well believe—though I tried to hide it.

We set camp, building a large fire and moving near to it, and had a sullen, close-cramped supper. Ibn Fahad, Abdallah, the vizier, and I were still speaking of the follower only as some beast. Abdallah may even have believed it—not from ordinary foolishness, but because he was the type of man who was unwilling to believe there might be anything he himself could not compass.

As we took turns standing guard the young mullah led the far-from-sleepy men in prayer. The voices rose up with the smoke, neither seeming to be of much substance against the wind of those old, cold mountains.

I sidled over to the shepherd-lad. He'd become, if anything, more close-mouthed since the discovery of the morning.

"This 'vampyr' you spoke of . . . ," I said quietly. "What do your people do to protect themselves from it?"

He looked up at me with a sad smile.

"Lock the doors."

I stared across at the other men—young Fawn with clenched mouth and furrowed brow; the mullah Ruad, eyes closed, plump cheeks awash with sweat as he prayed; Ibn Fahad gazing coolly outward, ever outward—and then I returned the boy's sad smile.

"No doors to lock, no windows to bar," I said. "What else?"

"There is an herb we hang about our houses . . . ," he said, and fumbled for the word in our unfamiliar language. After a moment he gave up. "It does not matter. We have none. None grows here."

I leaned forward, putting my face next to his face. "For the love of God, boy, what else?"—*I knew it was not a beast of the Earth. I knew.* I had seen that fluttering shadow.

"Well . . . ," he mumbled, turning his face away, ". . . they say, some men do, that you can tell stories. . . ."

"What!" I thought he had gone mad.

"This is what my grandfather says. The vampyr will stop to hear the story you tell—if it is a good one—and if you continue it until daylight he must return to the . . . place of the dead."

There was a sudden shriek. I leaped to my feet, fumbling for my knife . . . but it was only Ruad, who had put his foot against a hot coal. I sank down again, heart hammering.

"Stories?" I asked.

"I have only heard so," he said, struggling for the right phrases. "We try to keep them farther away than that—they must come close to hear a man talking."

Later, after the fire had gone down, we placed sentries and went to our blankets. I lay a long while thinking of what the Armenite boy had said before I slept.

A hideous screeching sound woke me. It was not yet dawn, and this time no one had burned himself on a glowing ember.

One of the two soldiers who had been standing picket lay on the forest floor, blood gouting from a great wound on the side of his head. In the torchlight it looked as though his skull had been smashed with a heavy cudgel. The other sentry was gone, but there was a terrible thrashing in the underbrush beyond the camp, and screams that would have sounded like an animal in a cruel trap but for the half-formed words that bubbled up from time to time.

We crouched, huddled, staring like startled rabbits. The screaming began to die away. Suddenly Ruad started up, heavy and clumsy getting to his feet. I saw tears in his eyes. "We . . . we must not leave our fellow to s-s-suffer so!" he cried, and looked around at all of us. I don't think anyone could hold his eye except the clerk Abdallah. I could not.

"Be silent, fool!" the clerk said, heedless of blasphemy. "It is a wild beast. It is for these cowardly soldiers to attend to, not a man of God!"

The young mullah stared at him for a moment, and a change came over his face. The tears were still wet on his cheeks, but I saw his jaw firm and his shoulders square."

"No," he said. "We cannot leave him to Shaitan's servant. If you will not go to him, I will." He rolled up the scroll he had been nervously fingering and kissed it. A shaft of moonlight played across the gold letters.

I tried to grab his arm as he went past me, but he shook me off with surprising strength, then moved toward the brush, where the screeching had died down to a low, broken moaning.

"Come back, you idiot!" Abdallah shrieked at him. "This is foolishness! Come back!"

The young holy man looked back over his shoulder, darting a look at Abdallah I could not easily describe, then turned around and continued forward, holding the parchment scroll before him as if it were a candle against the dark night.

"There is no God but Allah!" I heard him cry, *"and Mohammad is His prophet!"* Then he was gone.

After a long moment of silence there came the sound of the holy words of the Koran, chanted in an unsteady voice. We could hear the mullah making his ungraceful way out through the thicket. I was not the only one who held his breath.

Next there was crashing, and branches snapping, as though some huge beast was leaping through the brush; the mullah's chanting became a howl. Men cursed helplessly. Before the cry had faded, though, another scream came—numbingly loud, the rage of a powerful animal, full of shock and surprise. It had words in it, although not in any tongue I had ever heard before . . . or since.

Another great thrashing, and then nothing but silence. We lit another fire and sat sleepless until dawn.

In the morning, despite my urgings, the company went to look for trace of the sentry and the young priest. They found them both.

It made a grim picture, let me tell you, my friends. They hung upside down from the branches of a great tree. Their necks were torn, and they were white as chalk: all the blood had been drawn from them. We dragged the two stone-cold husks back to the camp-circle, and shortly thereafter buried them commonly with the other sentry, who had not survived his head wound.

One curious thing there was: on the ground beneath the hanging head of the young priest lay the remains of his holy scroll. It was scorched to black ash, and crumbled at my touch.

"So it *was* a cry of pain we heard," said Ibn Fahad over my shoulder. "The devil-beast can be hurt, it appears."

"Hurt, but not made to give over," I observed. "And no other holy writings remain, nor any hands so holy to wield them, or mouth to speak them." I looked pointedly over at Abdallah, who was giving unwanted instructions to the two remaining soldiers on how to spade the funeral dirt. I half-hoped one of them would take it on himself to brain the old meddler.

"True," grunted Ibn Fahad. "Well, I have my doubts on how cold steel will fare, also."

"As do I. But it could be there is yet a way we may save ourselves. The shepherd-boy told me of it. I will explain when we stop at mid-day."

"I will be waiting eagerly," said Ibn Fahad, favoring me with his half-smile. "I am glad to see someone else is thinking and planning beside myself. But perhaps you should tell us your plan on the march. Our daylight hours are becoming precious as blood, now. As a matter of fact, I think from now on we shall have to do without burial services."

Well, there we were in a very nasty fix. As we walked I explained my plan to the group; they listened silently, downcast, like men condemned to death—not an unreasonable attitude, in all truth.

"Now, here's the thing," I told them. "If this young lout's idea of tale-telling will work, we shall have to spend our nights yarning away. We may have to begin taking stops for sleeping in the daylight. Every moment walking, then, is precious—we must keep the pace up or we will die in these damned, haunted mountains. Also, while you walk, think of stories. From what the lad says we may have another ten days or a fortnight to go until we escape this country. We shall soon run out of things to tell about unless you dig deep into your memories."

There was grumbling, but it was too dispirited a group to offer much protest.

"Be silent, unless you have a better idea," said Ibn Fahad. "Masrur is quite correct—although, if what I suspect is true, it may be the first time in his life he finds himself in that position." He threw me a wicked grin, and one of the soldiers snickered. It was a good sound to hear.

We had a short mid-day rest—most of us got at least an hour's sleep on the rocky ground—and then we walked on until the beginning of twilight. We were in the bottom of a long, thickly forested ravine, where we promptly built a large fire to keep away some of the darkness of the valley floor. Ah, but fire is a good friend!

Gathered around the blaze, the men cooked strips of venison on the ends of green sticks. We passed the water skin and wished it was more—not for the first time.

"Now then," I said, "I'll go first, for at home I was the one called upon most often to tell tales, and I have a good fund of them. Some of you may sleep, but not all—there should always be two or three awake in case the teller falters or forgets. We cannot know if this will keep the creature at bay, but we should take no chances."

So I began, telling first the story of The Four Clever Brothers. It was early, and no one was ready to sleep; all listened attentively as I spun it out, adding details here, stretching a description there.

When it ended I was applauded, and straight away began telling the story of the carpet merchant Salim and his unfaithful wife. That was perhaps not a good choice—it is a story about a vengeful djinn, and about death; but I went on nonetheless, finished it, then told two more.

As I was finishing the fourth story, about a brave orphan who finds a cave of jewels, I glimpsed a strange thing.

The fire was beginning to die down, and as I looked out over the flames I saw movement in the forest. The under-vizier Walid was directly across from me, and beyond his once-splendid robes a dark shape lurked. It came no closer than the edge of the trees, staying just out of the fire's flickering light. I lost my voice for a moment then and stuttered, but quickly caught up the thread and finished. No one had noticed, I was sure.

I asked for the waterskin and motioned for Walid al-Salameh to continue. He took up with a tale of the rivalry beyond two wealthy houses in his native Isfahan. One or two of the others wrapped themselves tightly in their cloaks and lay down, staring up as they listened, watching the sparks rise into the darkness.

I pulled my hood down low on my brow to shield my gaze, and squinted out past Walid's shoulder. The dark shape had moved a little nearer now to the lapping glow of the campfire.

It was man-shaped, that I could see fairly well, though it clung close to the trunk of a tree at clearing's edge. Its face was in darkness; two ember-red eyes unblinkingly reflected the firelight. It seemed clothed in rags, but that could have been a trick of the shadows.

Huddled in the darkness a stone-throw away, it was listening.

I turned my head slowly across the circle. Most eyes were on the vizier; Fawn had curtained his in sleep. But Ibn Fahad, too, was staring out into the darkness. I suppose he felt my gaze, for he turned to me and nodded slightly: he had seen it too.

We went on until dawn, the men taking turns sleeping as one of the others told stories—mostly tales they had heard as children, occasionally of an adventure that had befallen them. Ibn Fahad and I said nothing of the dark shape that watched. Somewhere in the hour before dawn it disappeared.

It was a sleepy group that took to the trail that day, but we had all lived through the night. This alone put the men in better spirits, and we covered much ground.

That night we again sat around the fire. I told the story of The Gazelle King, and The Enchanted Peacock, and The Little Man with No Name, each of them longer and more complicated than the one before. Everyone except the clerk Abdallah contributed something—Abdallah and the shepherd-boy, that is. The chief-clerk said repeatedly that he had never wasted his time on foolishness such as learning stories. We were understandably reluctant to press our self-preservation into such unwilling hands.

The Armenite boy, our guide, sat quietly all the evening and listened to the men yarning away in a tongue that was not his own. When the moon had risen through the treetops, the shadow returned and stood silently outside the clearing. I saw the peasant lad look up. He saw it, I know, but like Ibn Fahad and I, he held his silence.

The next day brought us two catastrophes. As we were striking camp in the morning, happily no fewer than when we had set down the night before, the local lad took the waterskins down to the river that threaded the bottom of the ravine. When a long hour had passed and he had not returned, we went fearfully down to look for him.

He was gone. All but one of the waterskins lay on the streambank. He had filled them first.

The men were panicky. "The vampyr has taken him!" they cried.

"What does that foul creature need with a waterskin?" pointed out al-Salameh.

"He's right," I said. "No, I'm afraid our young friend has merely jumped ship, so to speak. I suppose he thinks his chances of getting back are better if he is alone."

I wondered . . . I *still* wonder . . . if he made it back. He was not a bad fellow: witness the fact that he took only one water-bag, and left us the rest.

Thus, we found ourselves once more without a guide. Fortunately, I had discussed with him the general direction, and he had told Ibn Fahad and myself of the larger landmarks . . . but it was nevertheless with sunken hearts that we proceeded.

Later that day, in the early afternoon, the second blow fell.

We were coming up out of the valley, climbing diagonally along the steep side of the ravine. The damned Caucassian fogs had slimed the rocks and turned the ground soggy; the footing was treacherous.

Achmed, the older of the remaining pike-men, had been walking poorly all day. He had bad joints, anyway, he said; and the cold nights had been making them worse.

We had stopped to rest on an outcropping of rock that jutted from the

valley wall; and Achmed, the last in line, was just catching up to us
when he slipped. He fell heavily onto his side and slid several feet down
the muddy slope.

Ibn Fahad jumped up to look for a rope, but before he could get one
from the bottom of his pack the other soldier—named Bekir, if memory
serves—clambered down the grade to help his comrade.

He got a grip on Achmed's tunic, and was just turning around to catch
Ibn Fahad's rope when the leg of the older man buckled beneath him and
he fell backward. Bekir, caught off his balance, pitched back as well, his
hand caught in the neck of Achmed's tunic, and the two of them rolled
end over end down the slope. Before anyone could so much as cry out
they had both disappeared over the edge, like a wine jug rolling off a
table-top. Just that sudden.

To fall such a distance certainly killed them.

We could not find the bodies, of course . . . could not even climb back
down the ravine to look. Ibn Fahad's remark about burials had taken on
a terrible, ironic truth. We could but press on, now a party of five—myself, Ibn Fahad, the under-vizier Walid, Abdallah the clerk, and young
Fawn. I doubt that there was a single one of our number who did not
wonder which of us would next meet death in that lonesome place.

Ah, by Allah most high, I have never been so sick of the sound of my
own voice as I was by the time nine more nights had passed. Ibn Fahad,
I know, would say that I have never understood how sick *everyone* becomes of the sound of my voice—am I correct, old friend? But I *was*
tired of it, tired of talking all night, tired of racking my brain for stories,
tired of listening to the cracked voices of Walid and Ibn Fahad, tired to
sickness of the damp, gray, oppressive mountains.

All were now aware of the haunting shade that stood outside our fire
at night, waiting and listening. Young Fawn, in particular, could hardly
hold up his turn at tale-telling, so much did his voice tremble.

Abdallah grew steadily colder and colder, congealing like rendered
fat. The thing which followed was no respecter of his cynicism or his
mathematics, and would not be banished for all the scorn he could
muster. The skinny chief-clerk did not turn out to us, though, to support
the story-circle, but sat silently and walked apart. Despite our terrible
mutual danger he avoided our company as much as possible.

The tenth night after the loss of Achmed and Bekir we were running out of tales. We had been ground down by our circumstances, and were ourselves become nearly as shadowy as that which we feared.

Walid al-Salameh was droning on about some ancient bit of minor intrigue in the court of the Emperor Darius of Persia. Ibn Fahad leaned toward me, lowering his voice so that neither Abdallah or Fawn—whose expression was one of complete and hopeless despair—could hear.

"Did you notice," he whispered, "that our guest has made no appearance tonight?"

"It has not escaped me," I said. "I hardly think it a good sign, however. If our talk no longer interests the creature, how long can it be until its thoughts return to our other uses?"

"I fear you're right," he responded, and gave a scratchy, painful chuckle. "There's a good three or four more days walking, and hard walking at that, until we reach the bottom of these mountains and come once more onto the plain, at which point we might hope the devil-beast would leave us."

"Ibn Fahad," I said, shaking my head as I looked across at Fawn's drawn, pale face, "I fear we shall not manage . . ."

As if to point up the truth of my fears, Walid here stopped his speech, coughing violently. I gave him to drink of the water-skin, but when he had finished he did not begin anew; he only sat looking darkly, as one lost, out to the forest.

"Good vizier," I asked, "can you continue?"

He said nothing, and I quickly spoke in his place, trying to pick up the threads of a tale I had not been attending to. Walid leaned back, exhausted and breathing raggedly. Abdallah clucked his tongue in disgust. If I had not been fearfully occupied, I would have struck the clerk.

Just as I was beginning to find my way, inventing a continuation of the vizier's Darian political meanderings, there came a shock that passed through all of us like a cold wind, and a new shadow appeared at the edge of the clearing. The vampyr had joined us.

Walid moaned and sat up, huddling by the fire. I faltered for a moment but went on. The candle-flame eyes regarded us unblinkingly, and the shadow shook for a moment as if folding great wings.

Suddenly Fawn leaped to his feet, swaying unsteadily. I lost the strands of the story completely and stared up at him in amazement.

"Creature!" he screamed. "Hell-spawn! Why do you torment us in this way? Why, why, why?"

Ibn Fahad reached up to pull him down, but the young man danced away like a shying horse. His mouth hung open and his eyes were starting from their dark-rimmed sockets.

"You great beast!" he continued to shriek. "Why do you toy with us? Why do you not just kill me—kill us *all,* set us free from this terrible, terrible . . ."

And with that he walked *forward*—away from the fire, toward the thing that crouched at forest's edge.

"End this now!" Fawn shouted, and fell to his knees only a few strides from the smoldering red eyes, sobbing like a child.

"Stupid boy, get back!" I cried. Before I could get up to pull him back—and I would have, I swear by Allah's name—there was a great rushing noise, and the black shape was gone, the lamps of its stare extinguished. Then, as we pulled the shuddering youth back to the campfire, something rustled in the trees. On the opposite side of the campfire one of the near branches suddenly bobbed beneath the weight of a strange new fruit—a black fruit with red-lit eyes. It made an awful croaking noise.

In our shock it was a few moments before we realized that the deep, rasping sound was speech—and the words were Arabic!

". . . It . . . was . . . you . . .," it said, ". . . who chose . . . to play the game this way . . ."

Almost strangest of all, I would swear that this thing had never spoken our language before, never even heard it until we had wandered lost into the mountains. Something of its halting inflections, its strange hesitations, made me guess it had learned our speech from listening all these nights to our campfire stories.

"Demon!" shrilled Abdallah. "What manner of creature are you?!"

"You know . . . very well what kind of . . . thing I am, man. You may none of you know *how,* or *why* . . . but by now, you know *what* I am."

"Why . . . why do you torment us so?!" shouted Fawn, writhing in Ibn Fahad's strong grasp.

"Why does the . . . serpent kill . . . a rabbit? The serpent does not . . . hate. It kills to live, as do I . . . as do you."

Abdallah lurched forward a step. "We do not slaughter our fellow men like this, devil-spawn!"

"C-c-clerk!" the black shape hissed, and dropped down from the tree. "C-close your foolish mouth! You push me too far!" It bobbed, as if agitated. "The curse of human ways! Even now you provoke me more than you should, you huffing . . . insect! *Enough!*"

The vampyr seemed to leap upward, and with a great rattling of leaves he scuttled away along the limb of a tall tree. I was fumbling for my sword, but before I could find it the creature spoke again from his high perch.

"The young one asked me why I 'toy' with you. I do not. If I do not kill, I will suffer. More than I suffer already.

"Despite what this clerk says, though, I am not a creature without . . . without feelings as men have them. Less and less do I wish to destroy you.

"For the first time in a great age I have listened to the sound of human voices that were not screams of fear. I have approached a circle of men without the barking of dogs, and have listened to them talk.

"It has almost been like being a man again."

"And this is how you show your pleasure?" the under-vizier Walid asked, teeth chattering. "By k-k-killing us?"

"I am what I am," said the beast. ". . . But for all that, you have inspired a certain desire for companionship. It puts me in mind of things that I can barely remember.

"I propose that we make a . . . bargain," said the vampyr. "A . . . wager?"

I had found my sword, and Ibn Fahad had drawn his as well, but we both knew we could not kill a thing like this—a red-eyed demon that could leap five cubits in the air and had learned to speak our language in a fortnight.

"No bargains with Shaitan!" spat the clerk Abdallah.

"What do you mean?" I demanded, inwardly marveling that such an unlikely dialogue should ever take place on the earth. "Pay no attention to the . . ." I curled my lip, ". . . holy man." Abdallah shot me a venomous glance.

"Hear me, then," the creature said, and in the deep recesses of the tree seemed once more to unfold and stretch great wings. "Hear me. I must kill to live, and my nature is such that I cannot choose to die. That is the way of things.

"I offer you now, however, the chance to win safe passage out of my domain, these hills. We shall have a contest, a wager if you like; if you best me you shall go freely, and I shall turn once more to the musty, slow-blooded peasants of the local valleys."

Ibn Fahad laughed bitterly. "What, are we to fight you then? So be it!"

"I would snap your spine like a dry branch," croaked the black shape. "No, you have held me these many nights telling stories; it is story-telling that will win you safe passage. We will have a contest, one that will suit my whims: we shall relate the saddest of all stories. That is my demand. You may tell three, I will tell only one. If you can best me with any or all, you shall go unhindered by me."

"And if we lose?!" I cried. "And who shall judge?"

"You may judge," it said, and the deep, thick voice took on a tone of grim amusement. "If you can look into my eyes and tell me that you have bested *my* sad tale . . . why, then I shall believe you.

"If you lose," it said, "then one of your number shall come to me, and pay the price of your defeat. Those are my terms, otherwise I shall hunt you down one at a time—for in truth, your present tale-telling has begun to lose my interest."

Ibn Fahad darted a worried look in my direction. Fawn and the others stared at the demon-shape in mute terror and astonishment.

"We shall . . . we shall give you our decision at sunset tomorrow," I said. "We must be allowed to think and talk."

"As you wish," said the vampyr. "But if you accept my challenge, the game must begin then. After all, we have only a few more days to spend together." And at this the terrible creature laughed, a sound like the bark being pulled from the trunk of a rotted tree. Then the shadow was gone.

In the end we had to accede to the creature's wager, of course. We knew he was not wrong in his assessment of us—we were just wagging our beards over the nightly campfire, no longer even listening to our own tales. Whatever magic had held the vampyr at bay had drained out like meal from a torn sack.

I racked my poor brains all afternoon for stories of sadness, but could think of nothing that seemed to fit, that seemed significant enough for the vital purpose at hand. I had been doing most of the talking for several nights running, and had exhausted virtually every story I had ever heard—and I was never much good at making them up, as Ibn Fahad will attest. Yes, go ahead and smile, old comrade.

Actually, it was Ibn Fahad who volunteered the first tale. I asked him what it was, but he would not tell me. "Let me save what potency it may have," he said. The under-vizier Walid also had something he deemed suitable, I was racking my brain fruitlessly for a third time when young Fawn piped up that he would tell a tale himself. I looked him over, rosy cheeks and long-lashed eyes, and asked him what he could possibly know of sadness. Even as I spoke I realized my cruelty, standing as we all did in the shadow of death or worse; but it was too late to take it back.

Fawn did not flinch. He was folding his cloak as he sat cross-ankled on the ground, folding and unfolding it. He looked up and said: "I shall tell a sad story about love. All the saddest stories are about love."

These young shavetails, I thought—although I was not ten years his senior—*a sad story about love.* But I could not think of better, and was forced to give in.

We walked as fast and far as we could that day, as if hoping that somehow, against all reason, we should find ourselves out of the gloomy, mist-sodden hills. But when twilight came the vast bulk of the mountains still hung above us. We made camp on the porch of a great standing rock, as though protection at our backs would avail us of something if the night went badly.

The fire had only just taken hold, and the sun had dipped below the rim of the hills a moment before, when a cold wind made the branches of the trees whip back and forth. We knew without speaking, without looking at one another, that the creature had come.

"Have you made your decision?" The harsh voice from the trees sounded strange, as if its owner was trying to speak lightly, carelessly—but I only heard death in those cold syllables.

"We have," said Ibn Fahad, drawing himself up out of his involuntary half-crouch to stand erect. "We will accept your wager. Do you wish to begin?"

"Oh, no . . ." the thing said, and made a flapping noise. "That would take all of the . . . suspense from the contest, would it not? No, I insist that you begin."

"I am first, then," Ibn Fahad said, looking around our circle for confirmation. The dark shape moved abruptly toward us. Before we could scatter the vampyr stopped, a few short steps away.

"Do not fear," it grated. Close to one's ear the voice was even odder and more strained. "I have come nearer to hear the story and see the teller—for surely that is part of any tale—but I shall move no farther. Begin."

Everybody but myself stared into the fire, hugging their knees, keeping their eyes averted from the bundle of darkness that sat at our shoulders. I had the fire between myself and the creature, and felt safer than if I had sat like Walid and Abdallah, with nothing between the beast and my back but cold ground.

The vampyr sat hunched, as if imitating our posture, its eyes hooded so that only a flicker of scarlet light, like a half-buried brand, showed through the slit. It was black, this manlike thing—not black as a Negro, mind you, but black as burnt steel, black as the mouth of a cave. It bore the aspect of someone dead of the plague. Rags wrapped it, mouldering, filthy bits of cloth, rotten as old bread . . . but the curve of its back spoke of terrible life—a great black cricket poised to jump.

Ibn Fahad's Story

Many years ago [he began], I traveled for a good time in Egypt. I was indigent, then, and journeyed wherever the prospect of payment for a sword arm beckoned.

I found myself at last in the household guard of a rich merchant in Alexandria. I was happy enough there; and I enjoyed walking in the busy streets, so unlike the village in which I was born.

One summer evening I found myself walking down an unfamiliar street. It emptied out into a little square that sat below the front of an old mosque. The square was full of people, merchants and fishwives, a juggler or two, but most of the crowd was drawn up to the façade of the mosque, pressed in close together.

At first, as I strolled across the square, I thought prayers were about to begin, but it was still some time until sunset. I wondered if perhaps some notable *imam* was speaking from the mosque steps, but as I approached I could see that all the assembly were staring upward, craning their necks back as if the sun itself, on its way to its western mooring, had become snagged on one of the minarets.

But instead of the sun, what stood on the onion-shaped dome was the silhouette of a man, who seemed to be staring out toward the horizon.

"Who is that?" I asked a man near me.

"It is Ha'arud al-Emwiya, the Sufi," the man told me, never lowering his eyes from the tower above.

"Is he caught up there?" I demanded. "Will he not fall?"

"Watch," was all the man said. I did.

A moment later, much to my horror, the small dark figure of Ha'arud the Sufi seemed to go rigid, then toppled from the minaret's rim like a stone. I gasped in shock, and so did a few others around me, but the rest of the crowd only stood in hushed attention.

Then an incredible thing happened. The tumbling holy man spread his arms out from his shoulders, like a bird's wings, and his downward fall became a swooping glide. He bottomed out high above the crowd, then sped upward, riding the wind like a leaf, spinning, somersaulting, stopping at last to drift to the ground as gently as a bit of eiderdown. Meanwhile, all the assembly was chanting "God is great! God is great!" When the sufi had touched the earth with his bare feet the people surrounded him, touching his rough woolen garments and crying out his name. He said nothing, only stood and smiled, and before too long the people began to wander away, talking amongst themselves.

"But this is truly marvelous!" I said to the man who stood by me.

"Before every holy day he flies," the man said, and shrugged. "I am surprised this is the first time you have heard of Ha'arud al-Emwiya."

I was determined to speak to this amazing man, and as the crowd dispersed I approached and asked if I might buy him a glass of tea. Close up he had a look of seamed roguishness that seemed surprising placed against the great favor in which Allah must have held him. He smilingly agreed, and accompanied me to a tea shop close by in the Street of Weavers.

"How is it, if you will pardon my forwardness, that you of all holy men are so gifted?"

He looked up from the tea cupped in his palms and grinned. He had only two teeth. "Balance," he said.

I was surprised. "A cat has balance," I responded, "but they neverthe-less must wait for the pigeons to land."

"I refer to a different sort of balance," he said. "The balance between Allah and Shaitan, which, as you know, Allah the All-Knowing has cre-ated as an equilibrium of exquisite delicacy."

"Explain please, master." I called for wine, but Ha'arud refused any himself.

"In all things care must be exercised," he explained. "Thus it is too with my flying. Many men holier than I are as earthbound as stones. Many other men have lived so poorly as to shame the Devil himself, yet they cannot take to the air, either. Only I, if I may be excused what sounds self-satisfied, have discovered perfect balance. Thus, each year before the holy days I tot up my score carefully, committing small pecadilloes or acts of faith as needed until the balance is exactly, exactly balanced. Thus, when I jump from the mosque, neither Allah nor the Arch-Enemy has claim on my soul, and they bear me up until a later date, at which time the issue shall be clearer." He smiled again and drained his tea.

"You are . . . a sort of chessboard on which God and the Devil con-tend?" I asked, perplexed.

"A flying chessboard, yes."

We talked for a long while, as the shadows grew long across the Street of the Weavers, but the Sufi Ha'arud adhered stubbornly to his explana-tion. I must have seemed disbelieving, for he finally proposed that we ascend to the top of the mosque so he could demonstrate.

I was more than a little drunk, and he, imbibing only tea, was filled nonetheless with a strange gleefulness. We made our way up the many winding stairs and climbed out onto the narrow ledge that circled the minaret like a crown. The cool night air, and the thousands of winking lights of Alexandria far below, sobered me rapidly. "I suddenly find all your precepts very sound," I said. "Let us go down."

But Ha'arud would have none of it, and proceeded to step lightly off the edge of the dome. He hovered, like a bumblebee, a hundred feet above the dusty street. "Balance," he said with great satisfaction.

"But," I asked, "is the good deed of giving me this demonstration enough to offset the pride with which you exhibit your skill?" I was cold and wanted to get down, and hoped to shorten the exhibition.

Instead, hearing my question, Ha'arud screwed up his face as though it was something he had not given thought to. A moment later, with a shriek of surprise, he plummeted down out of my sight to smash on the mosque's stone steps, as dead as dead.

Ibn Fahad, having lost himself in remembering the story, poked at the campfire. "Thus, the problem with matters of delicate balance," he said, and shook his head.

The whispering rustle of our dark visitor brought us sharply back. "Interesting," the creature rasped. "Sad, yes. Sad enough? We shall see. Who is the next of your number?"

A cold chill, like fever, swept over me at those calm words.

"I . . . I am next . . . ," said Fawn, voice taut as a bowstring. "Shall I begin?"

The vampyr said nothing, only bobbed the black lump of his head. The youth cleared his throat and began.

Fawn's Story

There was once . . . [Fawn began, and hesitated, then started again.] There was once a young prince named Zufik, the second son of a great sultan. Seeing no prospects for himself in his father's kingdom, he went out into the wild world to search for his fortune. He traveled through many lands, and saw many strange things, and heard tell of others stranger still.

In one place he was told of a nearby sultanate, the ruler of which had a beautiful daughter, his only child and the very apple of his eye.

Now this country had been plagued for several years by a terrible beast, a great white leopard of a kind never seen before. So fearsome it was that it had killed hunters set to trap it, yet was it also so cunning that it had stolen babies from their very cradles as the mothers lay sleeping. The people of the sultanate were all in fear; and the sultan, whose best warriors had tried and failed to kill the beast, was driven to despair. Finally, at the end of his wits, he had it proclaimed in the market place that the man who could destroy the white leopard would be gifted with the sultan's daughter Rassoril, and with her the throne of the sultanate after the old man was gone.

Young Zufik heard how the best young men of the country, and others from countries beyond, one after the other had met their deaths beneath the claws of the leopard, or . . . or . . . in its jaws. . . .

[Here I saw the boy falter, as if the vision of flashing teeth he was conjuring had suddenly reminded him of our predicament. Walid the undervizier reached out and patted the lad's shoulder with great gentleness, until he was calm enough to resume.]

So . . . [He swallowed.] So young Prince Zufik took himself into that country, and soon was announced at the sultan's court.

The ruler was a tired old man, the fires in his sunken eyes long quenched. Much of the power seemed to have been handed over to a pale, narrow-faced youth named Sifaz, who was the princess's cousin. As Zufik announced his purpose, as so many had done before him, Sifaz's eyes flashed.

"You will no doubt meet the end all the others have, but you are welcome to the attempt—and the prize, should you win."

Then for the first time Zufik saw the princess Rassoril, and in an instant his heart was overthrown.

She had hair as black and shiny as polished jet, and a face upon which Allah himself must have looked in satisfaction, thinking: "Here is the summit of My art." Her delicate hands were like tiny doves as they nested in her lap, and a man could fall into her brown eyes and drown without hope of rescue—which is what Zufik did, and he was not wrong when he thought he saw Rassoril return his ardent gaze.

Sifaz saw, too, and his thin mouth turned in something like a smile, and he narrowed his yellow eyes. "Take this princeling to his room, that he may sleep now and wake with the moon. The leopard's cry was heard around the palace's walls last night."

Indeed, when Zufik woke in the evening darkness, it was to hear the choking cry of the leopard beneath his very window. As he looked out, buckling on his scabbard, it was to see a white shape slipping in and out of the shadows in the garden below. He took also his dagger in his hand and leaped over the threshold.

He had barely touched ground when, with a terrible snarl, the leopard bounded out of the obscurity of the hedged garden wall and came to a stop before him. It was huge—bigger than any leopard Zufik had seen or heard of—and its pelt gleamed like ivory. It leaped, claws flashing, and he could barely throw himself down in time as the beast passed over him like a cloud, touching him only with its hot breath. It turned and leaped again as the palace dogs set up a terrible barking, and this time its talons raked his chest, knocking him tumbling. Blood started from his shirt, spouting so fiercely that he could scarcely draw himself to his feet. He was caught with his back against the garden wall; the leopard slowly moved toward him, yellow eyes like tallow lamps burning in the niches of Hell.

Suddenly there was a crashing at the far end of the garden: the dogs had broken down their stall and were even now speeding through the trees. The leopard hesitated—Zufik could almost see it thinking—and then, with a last snarl, it leaped onto the wall and disappeared into the night.

Zufik was taken, his wounds bound, and he was put into his bed. The princess Rassoril, who had truly lost her heart to him, wept bitterly at his side, begging him to go back to his father's land and to give up the fatal challenge. But Zufik, weak as he was, would no more think of yielding than he would of theft or treason, and refused, saying he would hunt the beast again the following night. Sifaz grinned and led the princess away. Zufik thought he heard the pale cousin whistling as he went.

In the dark before dawn Zufik, who could not sleep owing to the pain of his injury, heard his door quietly open. He was astonished to see the princess come in, gesturing him to silence. When the door was closed she threw herself down at his side and covered his hand and cheek with kisses, proclaiming her love for him and begging him again to go. He admitted his love for her, but reminded her that his honor would not permit him to stop short of his goal, even should he die in the trying.

Rassoril, seeing that there was no changing the young prince's mind, then took from her robe a black arrow tipped in silver, fletched with the tail feathers of a falcon. "Then take this," she said. "This leopard is a magic beast, and you will never kill it otherwise. Only silver will pierce its heart. Take the arrow and you may fulfill your oath." So saying, she slipped out of his room.

The next night Zufik again heard the leopard's voice in the garden below, but this time he took also his bow and arrow when he went to

meet it. At first he was loath to use it, since it seemed somehow un-
manly; but when the beast had again given him injury and he had struck
three sword blows in turn without effect, he at last nocked the silver-
pointed shaft on his bowstring and, as the beast charged him once more,
let fly. The black arrow struck to the leopard's heart; the creature gave a
hideous cry and again leaped the fence, this time leaving a trail of its
mortal blood behind it.

When morning came Zufik went to the sultan for men, so that they
could follow the track of blood to the beast's lair and prove its death.
The sultan was displeased when his vizier, the princess's pale cousin, did
not answer his summons. As they were all going down into the garden,
though, there came a great cry from the sleeping rooms upstairs, a cry
like a soul in mortal agony. With fear in their hearts Zufik, the sultan,
and all the men rushed upstairs. There they found the missing Sifaz.

The pale man lifted a shaking, red-smeared finger to point at Zufik, as
all the company stared in horror. *"He* has done it—the foreigner!" Sifaz
shouted.

In Sifaz's arms lay the body of the Princess Rassoril, a black arrow
standing from her breast.

After Fawn finished there was a long silence. The boy, his own
courage perhaps stirred by his story, seemed to sit straighter.

"Ah . . . ," the vampyr said at last, "love and its prices—that is the
message? Or is it perhaps the effect of silver on the supernatural? Fear
not, I am bound by no such conventions, and fear neither silver, steel,
nor any other metal." The creature made a huffing, scraping sound that
might have been a laugh. I marveled anew, even as I felt the skein of my
life fraying, that it had so quickly gained such command of our unfamiliar tongue.

"Well . . . ," it said slowly. "Sad. But . . . sad enough? Again, *that* is
the important question. Who is your last . . . contestant?"

Now my heart truly went cold within me, and I sat as though I had
swallowed a stone. Walid al-Salameh spoke up.

"I am," he said, and took a deep breath. "I am."

The Vizier's Story

This is a true story—or so I was told. It happened in my grandfather's time, and he had it from someone who knew those involved. He told it to me as a cautionary tale.

There once was an old caliph, a man of rare gifts and good fortune. He ruled a small country, but a wealthy one—a country upon which all the gifts of Allah had been showered in grand measure. He had the finest heir a man could have, dutiful and yet courageous, beloved by the people almost as extravagantly as the caliph himself. He had many other fine sons, and two hundred beautiful wives, and an army of fighting men the envy of his neighbors. His treasury was stacked roofbeam-high with gold and gemstones and blocks of fragrant sandalwood, crisscrossed with ivories and bolts of the finest cloth. His palace was built around a spring of fragrant, clear water; and everyone said that they must be the very Waters of Life, so fortunate and well-loved this caliph was. His only sadness was that age had robbed his sight from him, leaving him blind, but hard as this was, it was a small price to pay for Allah's beneficence.

One day the caliph was walking in his garden, smelling the exquisite fragrance of the blossoming orange trees. His son the prince, unaware of his father's presence, was also in the garden, speaking with his mother, the caliph's first and chiefest wife.

"He is terribly old," the wife said. "I cannot stand even to touch him anymore. It is a horror to me."

"You are right, mother," the son replied, as the caliph hid behind the trees and listened, shocked. "I am sickened by watching him sitting all day, drooling into his bowl, or staggering sightless through the palace. But what are we to do?"

"I have thought on it long and hard," the caliph's wife replied. "We owe it to ourselves and those close to us to kill him."

"Kill him?" the son replied. "Well, it is hard for me, but I suppose you are right. I still feel some love for him, though—may we at least do it quickly, so that he shall not feel pain at the end?"

"Very well. But do it soon—tonight, even. If I must feel his foul breath upon me one more night I will die myself."

"Tonight, then," the son agreed, and the two walked away, leaving the blind caliph shaking with rage and terror behind the orange trees. He could not see what sat on the garden path behind them, the object of their discussion: the wife's old lap-dog, a scrofulous creature of extreme age.

Thus the caliph went to his vizier, the only one he was sure he could trust in a world of suddenly traitorous sons and wives, and bade him to have the pair arrested and quickly beheaded. The vizier was shocked, and asked the reason why, but the caliph only said he had unassailable proof that they intended to murder him and take his throne. He bade the vizier go and do the deed.

The vizier did as he was directed, seizing the son and his mother quickly and quietly, then giving them over to the headsman after tormenting them for confessions and the names of confederates, neither of which were forthcoming.

Sadly, the vizier went to the caliph and told him it was done, and the old man was satisfied. But soon, inevitably, word of what had happened spread, and the brothers of the heir began to murmur among themselves about their father's deed. Many thought him mad, since the dead pair's devotion to the caliph was common knowledge.

Word of this dissension reached the caliph himself, and he began to fear for his life, terrified that his other sons meant to emulate their treasonous brother. He called the vizier to him and demanded the arrest of these sons, and their beheading. The vizier argued in vain, risking his own life, but the caliph would not be swayed; at last the vizier went away, returning a week later a battered, shaken man.

"It is done, O Prince," he said. "All your sons are dead."

The caliph had only a short while in which to feel safe before the extreme wrath of the wives over the slaughter of their children reached his ears. "Destroy them, too!" the blind caliph insisted.

Again the vizier went away, soon to return.

"It is done, O Prince," he reported. "Your wives have been beheaded."

Soon the courtiers were crying murder, and the caliph sent his vizier to see them dealt with as well.

"It is done, O Prince," he assured the caliph. But the ruler now feared the angry townspeople, so he commanded his vizier to take the army and slaughter them. The vizier argued feebly, then went away.

"It is done, O Prince," the caliph was told a month later. But now the caliph realized that with his heirs and wives gone, and the important men of the court dead, it was the soldiers themselves who were a threat to his power. He commanded his vizier to sow lies amongst them, causing them to fall out and slay each other, then locked himself in his room to safely outlast the conflict. After a month and a half the vizier knocked upon his door.

"It is done, O Prince."

For a moment the caliph was satisfied. All his enemies were dead, and he himself was locked in: no one could murder him, or steal his treasure, or usurp his throne. The only person yet alive who even knew where the caliph hid was . . . his vizier.

Blind, he groped about for the key with which he had locked himself in. Better first to remove the risk that someone might trick him into coming out. He pushed the key out beneath the door and told the vizier to throw it away somewhere it might never be found. When the vizier returned he called him close to the locked portal that bounded his small world of darkness and safety.

"Vizier," the caliph said through the keyhole, "I command you to go and kill yourself, for you are the last one living who is a threat to me."

"*Kill* myself, my prince?" the vizier asked, dumbfounded. "Kill *myself?*"

"Correct," the caliph said. "Now go and do it. That is my command."

There was a long silence. At last the vizier said: "Very well." After that there was silence.

For a long time the caliph sat in his blindness and exulted, for everyone he distrusted was gone. His faithful vizier had carried out all his orders, and now had killed himself. . . .

A sudden, horrible thought came to him then: what if the vizier had *not* done what he had told him to do? What if instead he had made compact with the caliph's enemies, and was only reporting false details when he told of their deaths? *How was the caliph to know?* He almost swooned with fright and anxiousness at the realization.

At last he worked up the courage to feel his way across the locked room to the door. He put his ear to the keyhole and listened. He heard nothing but silence. He took a breath and then put his mouth to the hole.

"Vizier?" he called in a shaky voice. "Have you done what I commanded? Have you killed yourself?"

"It is done, O Prince," came the reply.

Finishing his story, which was fully as dreadful as it was sad, the under-vizier Walid lowered his head as if ashamed or exhausted. We waited tensely for our guest to speak; at the same time I am sure we all vainly hoped there would be no more speaking, that the creature would simply vanish, like a frightening dream that flees the sun.

"Rather than discuss the merits of your sad tales," the black, tattered shadow said at last—confirming that there would be no waking from *this* dream, "rather than argue the game with only one set of moves completed, perhaps it is now time for me to speak. The night is still youthful, and my tale is not long, but I wish to give you a fair time to render judgment."

As he spoke the creature's eyes bloomed scarlet like unfolding roses. The mist curled up from the ground beyond the fire-circle, wrapping the vampire in a cloak of writhing fogs, a rotted black egg in a bag of silken mesh.

" . . . May I begin?" it asked . . . but no one could say a word. "Very well. . . ."

The Vampyr's Story

The tale *I* will tell is of a child, a child born of an ancient city on the banks of a river. So long ago this was that not only has the city itself long gone to dust; but the later cities built atop its ruins, tiny towns and great walled fortresses of stone, all these too have gone beneath the mill-wheels of time—rendered, like their predecessor, into the finest of particles to blow in the wind, silting the timeless river's banks.

This child lived in a mud hut thatched with straw, and played with his fellows in the shallows of the sluggish brown river while his mother washed the family's clothes and gossiped with her neighbors.

Even *this* ancient city was built upon the bones of earlier cities, and it was into the collapsed remnants of one—a great, tumbled mass of shattered sandstone—that the child and his friends sometimes went. And it was to these ruins that the child, when he was a little older . . . almost the age of your young, romantic companion . . . took a pretty, doe-eyed girl.

It was to be his first time beyond the veil—his initiation into the mysteries of women. His heart beat rapidly; the girl walked ahead of him, her slender brown body tiger-striped with light and shade as she walked among the broken pillars. Then she saw something, and screamed. The child came running.

The girl was nearly mad, weeping and pointing. He stopped in amazement, staring at the black, shrivelled thing that lay on the ground—a twisted something that might have been a man once, wizened and black as a piece of leather dropped into the cookfire. Then the thing opened its eyes.

The girl ran, choking—but he did not, seeing that the black thing could not move. The twitching of its mouth seemed that of someone trying to speak; he thought he heard a faint voice asking for help, begging for him to do something. He leaned down to the near-silent hiss, and the thing squirmed and bit him, fastening its sharp teeth like barbed fishhooks in the muscle of his leg. The man-child screamed, helpless, and felt his blood running out into the horrible sucking mouth of the thing. Fetid saliva crept into the wounds and coursed hotly through his body, even as he struggled against his writhing attacker. The poison climbed through him, and it seemed he could feel his own heart flutter and die within his chest, delicate and hopeless as a broken bird. With final, desperate strength the child pulled free. The black thing, mouth gaping, curled on itself and shuddered, like a beetle on a hot stone. A moment later it had crumbled into ashes and oily flakes.

But it had caught me long enough to destroy me—for of course *I* was that child—to force its foul fluids into me, leeching my humanity and replacing it with the hideous, unwanted wine of immortality. My child's heart became an icy fist.

Thus was I made what I am, at the hands of a dying vampyr—which had been a creature like I am now. Worn down at last by the passing of millennia, it had chosen a host to receive its hideous malady, then died—as *I* shall do someday, no doubt, in the grip of some terrible, blind, insect-like urge . . . but not soon. Not today.

So that child, which had been in all ways like other children—loved by its family, loving in turn noise and games and sweetmeats—became a dark thing sickened by the burning light of the sun.

Driven into the damp shadows beneath stones and the dusty gloom of abandoned places, then driven out again beneath the moon by an unshakeable, unresistable hunger, I fed first on my family—my uncomprehending mother wept to see her child returned, standing by her moonlit pallet—then on the others of my city. Not last, or least painful of my feedings was on the dark-haired girl who had run when I stayed behind. I slashed other throats, too, and lapped up warm, sea-salty blood while the trapped child inside me cried without a sound. It was as though I stood behind a screen, unable to leave or interfere as terrible crimes were committed before me. . . .

And thus the years have passed: sand grains, deposited along the river bank, uncountable in their succession. Every one has contained a seeming infinitude of killings, each one terrible despite their numbing similarity. Only the blood of mankind will properly feed me, and a hundred generations have known terror of me.

Strong as I am, virtually immortal, unkillable as far as I know or can tell—blades pass through me like smoke; fire, water, poison, none affect me—still the light of the sun causes a pain to me so excruciating that you with only mortal lives, whose pain at least eventually ends in death, cannot possibly comprehend it. Thus, kingdoms of men have risen and fallen to ashes since I last saw daylight. Think only on that for a moment, if you seek sad stories! I must be in darkness when the sun rises, so as I range in search of prey my accommodations are shared with toads and slugs, bats, and blindworms.

People can be nothing to me anymore but food. I know of none other like myself, save the dying creature who spawned me. The smell of my own corruption is in my nostrils always.

So there is all of *my* tale. I cannot die until my time is come, and who can know when that is? Until then I will be alone, alone as no mere man can ever be, alone with my wretchedness and evil and self-disgust until the world collapses and is born anew . . .

The vampyr rose now, towering up like a black sail billowing in the wind, spreading its vast arms or wings on either side, as if to sweep us before it. "How do your stories compare to this?" it cried; the harshness of its speech seemed somehow muted, even as it grew louder and louder. "Whose is the saddest story, then?" There was pain in that hideous voice that tore at even my fast-pounding heart. "Whose is saddest? Tell me! It is time to *judge* . . ."

And in that moment, of all the moments when lying could save my life . . . I could not lie. I turned my face away from the quivering black shadow, that thing of rags and red eyes. None of the others around the campfire spoke—even Abdallah the clerk only sat hugging his knees, teeth chattering, eyes bulging with fear.

". . . I thought so," the thing said at last. "I thought so." Night wind tossed the treelimbs above our heads, and it seemed as though beyond them stood only ultimate darkness—no sky, no stars, nothing but unending emptiness.

"Very well," the vampyr said at last. "Your silence speaks all. I have won." There was not the slightest note of triumph in its voice. "Give me my prize, and then I may let the rest of you flee my mountains." The dark shape withdrew a little way.

We all of us turned to look at one another, and it was just as well that the night veiled our faces. I started to speak, but Ibn Fahad interrupted me, his voice a tortured rasp.

"Let there be no talk of volunteering. We will draw lots; that is the only way." Quickly he cut a thin branch into five pieces, one of them shorter than the rest, and cupped them in a closed hand.

"Pick," he said. "I will keep the last."

As a part of me wondered what madness it was that had left us wagering on story-telling and drawing lots for our lives, we each took a length from Ibn Fahad's fist. I kept my hand closed while the others selected, not wanting to hurry Allah toward his revelation of my fate. When all had selected we extended our hands and opened them, palms up.

Fawn had selected the short stick.

Strangely, there was no sign of his awful fortune on his face: he showed no signs of grief—indeed, he did not even respond to our helpless words and prayers, only stood up and slowly walked toward the huddled black shape at the far edge of the clearing. The vampyr rose to meet him.

"No!" came a sudden cry, and to our complete surprise the clerk Abdallah leaped to his feet and went pelting across the open space, throwing himself between the youth and the looming shadow. "He is too young!" Abdallah shouted, sounding truly anguished. "Do not do this horrible thing! Take me instead!"

Ibn Fahad, the vizier, and I could only sit, struck dumb by this unexpected behavior, but the creature moved swiftly as a viper, smacking Abdallah to the ground with one flicking gesture.

"You are indeed mad, you short-lived men!" the vampyr hissed. "This one would do nothing to save himself—not once did I hear his voice raised in tale-telling—yet now he would throw himself into the jaws of death for this other! Mad!" The monster left Abdallah choking on the ground and turned to silent Fawn. "Come, you. I have won the contest, and you are the prize. I am . . . sorry . . . it must be this way. . . ." A great swath of darkness enveloped the youth, drawing him in. "Come," the vampyr said, "think of the better world you go to—that is what you believe, is it not? Well, soon you shall—"

The creature broke off.

"Why do you look so strangely, man-child?" the thing said at last, its voice troubled. "You cry, but I see no fear. Why? Are you not afraid of dying?"

Fawn answered; his tones were oddly distracted. "Have you really lived so long? And alone, always alone?"

"I told you. I have no reason to lie. Do you think to put me off with your strange questions?"

"Ah, how could the good God be so unmerciful!?" The words were made of sighs. The dark shape that embraced him stiffened.

"Do you cry for *me? For me?!*"

"How can I help?" the boy said. "Even Allah must weep for you . . . for such a pitiful thing, lost in the lonely darkness . . ."

For a moment the night air seemed to pulse. Then, with a wrenching gasp, the creature flung the youth backward so that he stumbled and fell before us, landing atop the groaning Abdallah.

"Go!" the vampyr shrieked, and its voice cracked and boomed like thunder. "Get you gone from my mountains! *Go!*"

Amazed, we pulled Fawn and the chief clerk to their feet and went stumbling down the hillside, branches lashing at our faces and hands, expecting any moment to hear the rush of wings and feel cold breath on our necks.

"Build your houses well, little men!" a voice howled like the wild wind behind us. "My life is long . . . and someday I may regret letting you go!"

We ran and ran, until it seemed the life would flee our bodies, until our lungs burned and our feet blistered . . . and until the topmost sliver of the sun peered over the eastern summits. . . .

*   *   *

Masrur al-Adan allowed the tale's ending to hang in silence for a span of thirty heartbeats, then pushed his chair away from the table.

"We escaped the mountains the next day," he said. "Within a season we were back in Baghdad, the only survivors of the caravan to the Armenites."

"Aaaahh . . . !" breathed young Hassan, a long drawn-out sound full of wonder and apprehension. "What a marvelous, terrifying adventure! I would *never* have survived it, myself. How frightening! And did the . . . the creature . . . did he *really* say he might come back someday?"

Masrur solemnly nodded his large head. "Upon my soul. Am I not right, Ibn Fahad, my old comrade?"

Ibn Fahad yielded a thin smile, seemingly of affirmation.

"Yes," Masrur continued, "those words chill me to this very day. Many is the night I have sat in this room, looking at that door—" He pointed. "—wondering if someday it may open to show me that terrible, misshapen black thing, come back from Hell to make good on our wager."

"Merciful Allah!" Hassan gasped.

Abu Jamir leaned across the table as the other guests whispered excitedly. He wore a look of annoyance. "Good Hassan," he snapped, "kindly calm yourself. We are all grateful to our host Masrur for entertaining us, but it is an insult to sensible, Godly men to suggest that at any moment some blood-drinking Afreet may knock down the door and carry us—"

The door leaped open with a crash, revealing a hideous, twisted shape looming in the entrance, red-splattered and trembling. The shrieking of Masrur's guests filled the room.

"Master . . . ?" the dark silhouette quavered. Baba held a wine jar balanced on one shoulder. The other had broken at his feet, splashing Abu Jamir's prize stock everywhere. "Master," he began again, "I am afraid I have dropped one."

Masrur looked down at Abu Jamir, who lay pitched full-length on the floor, insensible.

"Ah, well, that's all right, Baba." Masrur smiled, twirling his black mustache. "We won't have to make the wine go so far as I thought—it seems my story-telling has put some of our guests to sleep."

Shave and a haircut Two Bites

by Dan Simmons

O utside, the blood spirals down.

I pause at the entrance to the barbershop. There is nothing unique about it. Almost certainly there is one similar to it in your community; its function is proclaimed by the pole outside, the red spiralling down, and by the name painted on the broad window, the letters grown scabrous as the gold paint ages and flakes away. While the most expensive hair salons now bear the names of their owners, and the shopping mall franchises offer sickening cutenesses—Hairport, Hair Today: Gone Tomorrow, Hair We Are, Headlines, Shear Masters, The Head Hunter, In-Hair-itance, and so forth, ad infinitum, ad nauseum—the name of this shop is eminently forgettable. It is meant to be so. This shop offers neither styling nor unisex cuts. If your hair is dirty when you enter, it will be cut dirty; there are no shampoos given here. While the franchises demand $15 to $30 for a basic haircut, the cost here has not changed for a decade or more. It occurs to the potential new customer immediately upon entering that no one could live on an income based upon such low rates. No one does. The potential customer usually beats a hasty retreat, put off by the too-low prices, by the darkness of the place, by the air of dusty decrepitude exuded from both the establishment itself and from its few waiting customers, invariably silent and staring, and by a strange sense of tension bordering upon threat which hangs in the stale air.

Before entering, I pause a final moment to stare in the window of the barbershop. For a second I can see only a reflection of the street and the silhouette of a man more shadow than substance—me. To see inside, one has to step closer to the glass and perhaps cup hands to one's temples to reduce the glare. The blinds are drawn but I find a crack in the slats. Even then there is not much to see. A dusty window ledge holds three desiccated cacti and an assortment of dead flies. Two barber chairs are just visible through the gloom; they are of a sort no longer made: black leather, white enamel, a high headrest. Along one wall, half a dozen uncomfortable-looking chairs sit empty and two low tables show a litter of magazines with covers torn or missing entirely. There are mirrors on two of the three interior walls, but rather than add light to the long, narrow room, the infinitely receding reflections seem to make the space appear as if the barbershop itself were a dark reflection in an age-dimmed glass.

A man is standing there in the gloom, his form hardly more substantial than my silhouette on the window. He stands next to the first barber chair as if he were waiting for me.

He *is* waiting for me.

I leave the sunlight of the street and enter the shop.

"Vampires," said Kevin. "They're both vampires."

"Who're vampires?" I asked between bites on my apple. Kevin and I were twenty feet up in a tree in his back yard. We'd built a rough platform there which passed as a treehouse. Kevin was ten, I was nine.

"Mr. Innis and Mr. Denofrio," said Kevin. "They're both vampires."

I lowered the Superman comic I'd been reading. "They're not vampires," I said. "They're *barbers.*"

"Yeah," said Kevin, "but they're vampires too. I just figured it out."

I sighed and sat back against the bole of the tree. It was late autumn and the branches were almost empty of leaves. Another week or two and we wouldn't be using the treehouse again until next spring. Usually when Kevin announced that he'd just figured something out, it meant trouble. Kevin O'toole was almost my age, but sometimes it seemed that he was five years older and five years younger than me at the same time. He read a lot. And he had a weird imagination. "Tell me," I said.

"You know what the red means, Tommy?"

"What red?"

"On the barber pole. The red stripes that curl down."

I shrugged. "It means it's a barbershop."

It was Kevin's turn to sigh. "Yeah, sure, Tommy, but why *red?* And why have it curling down like that for a barber?"

I didn't say anything. When Kevin was in one of his moods, it was better to wait him out.

"Because it's blood," he said dramatically, almost whispering. "Blood spiralling down. Blood dripping and spilling. That's been the sign for barbers for almost six hundred years."

He'd caught my interest. I set the Superman comic aside on the platform. "OK," I said, "I believe you. Why is it their sign?"

"Because it was their *guild sign,*" said Kevin. "Back in the Middle Ages, all the guys who did important work belonged to guilds, sort of like the union our dads belong to down at the brewery, and . . ."

"Yeah, yeah," I said. "But why *blood?*" Guys as smart as Kevin had a hard time sticking to the point.

"I was getting to that," said Kevin. "According to this stuff I read, way back in the Middle Ages barbers used to be surgeons. About all they could do to help sick people was to bleed them, and . . ."

"Bleed them?"

"Yeah. They didn't have any real medicines or anything, so if somebody got sick with a disease or broke a leg or something, all the surgeon . . . the barber . . . could do was bleed them. Sometimes they'd use the same razor they shaved people with. Sometimes they'd bring bottles of leeches and let them suck some blood out of the sick person."

"Gross."

"Yeah, but it sort of worked. Sometimes. I guess when you lose blood, your blood pressure goes down and that can lower a fever and stuff. But most of the time, the people they bled just died sooner. They probably needed a transfusion more than a bunch of leeches stuck on them."

I sat and thought about this for a moment. Kevin knew some really weird stuff. I used to think he was lying about a lot of it, but after I saw him correct the teachers in fourth and fifth grade a few times . . . and get away with it . . . I realized he wasn't making things up. Kevin was weird, but he wasn't a liar.

A breeze rustled the few remaining leaves. It was a sad and brittle sound to a kid who loved summer. "All right," I said. "But what's all of this got to do with vampires? You think 'cause barbers used to stick leeches on people a couple of hundred years ago that Mr. Innis and Mr. Denofrio are *vampires?* Jeez, Kev, that's nuts."

"The Middle Ages were more than five hundred years ago, Niles," said Kevin, calling me by my last name in the voice that always made me want to punch him. "But the guild sign was just what got me thinking about it all. I mean, what other business has kept its guild sign?"

I shrugged and tied a broken shoelace. "Blood on their sign doesn't make them vampires."

When Kevin was excited, his green eyes seemed to get even greener than usual. They were really green now. He leaned forward. "Just think about it, Tommy," he said. "When did vampires start to disappear?"

"Disappear? You mean you think they were *real?* Cripes, Kev, my mom says you're the only gifted kid she's ever met, but sometimes I think you're just plain looney tunes."

Kevin ignored me. He had a long, thin face—made even thinner looking by the crewcut he wore—and his skin was so pale that the freckles stood out like spots of gold. He had the same full lips that people said made his two sisters look pretty, but now those lips were quivering. "I read a lot about vampires," he said. "A *lot.* Most of the serious stuff agrees that the vampire legends were fading in Europe by the Seventeenth Century. People still *believed* in them, but they weren't so afraid of them anymore. A few hundred years earlier, suspected vampires were being tracked down and killed all the time. It's like they'd gone underground or something."

"Or people got smarter," I said.

"No, think," said Kevin and grabbed my arm. "Maybe the vampires were being wiped out. People knew they were there and how to fight them."

"Like a stake through the heart?"

"Maybe. Anyway, they've got to hide, pretend they're gone, and still get blood. What'd be the easiest way to do it?"

I thought of a wise-acre comment, but one look at Kevin made me realize that he was dead serious about all this. And we were best friends. I shook my head.

"Join the barber's guild!" Kevin's voice was triumphant. "Instead of having to break into people's houses at night and then risk others finding the body all drained of blood, they *invite* you in. They don't even struggle while you open their veins with a knife or put the leeches on. Then they ... or the family of the dead guy ... *pay* you. No wonder they're the only group to keep their guild sign. They're vampires, Tommy!"

I licked my lips, tasted blood, and realized that I'd been chewing on my lower lip while Kevin talked. "All of them?" I said. "Every barber?"

Kevin frowned and released my arm. "I'm not sure. Maybe not all."

"But you think Innis and Denofrio are?"

Kevin's eyes got greener again and he grinned. "There's one way to find out."

I closed my eyes a second before asking the fatal question. "How, Kev?"

"By watching them," said Kevin. "Following them. Checking them out. *Seeing* if they're vampires."

"And if they are?"

Kevin shrugged. He was still grinning. "We'll think of something."

I enter the familiar shop, my eyes adjusting quickly to the dim light. The air smells of talcum and rose oil and tonic. The floor is clean and instruments are laid out on white linen atop the counter. Light glints dully from the surface of scissors and shears and the pearl handles of more than one straight razor.

I approach the man who stands silently by his chair. He wears a white shirt and tie under a white smock. "Good morning," I say.

"Good morning, Mr. Niles." He pulls a striped cloth from its shelf, snaps it open with a practiced hand, and stands waiting like a toreador.

I take my place in the chair. He sweeps the cloth around me and snaps it shut behind my neck in a single, fluid motion. "A trim this morning, perhaps?"

"I think not. Just a shave, please."

He nods and turns away to heat the towels and prepare the razor. Waiting, I look into the mirrored depths and see multitudes.

*   *   *

Kevin and I had made our pact while sitting in our tree on Sunday. By Thursday we'd done quite a bit of snooping. Kev had followed Innis and I'd watched Denofrio.

We met in Kevin's room after school. You could hardly see his bed for all the heaps of books and comics and half-built Heath Kits and vacuum tubes and plastic models and scattered clothes. Kevin's mother was still alive then, but she had been ill for years and rarely paid attention to little things like her son's bedroom. Or her son.

Kevin shoved aside some junk and we sat on his bed, comparing notes. Mine were scrawled on scraps of paper and the back of my paper route collection form.

"OK," said Kevin, "what'd you find out?"

"They're not vampires," I said. "At least my guy isn't."

Kevin frowned. "It's too early to tell, Tommy."

"Nuts. You gave me this list of ways to tell a vampire, and Denofrio flunks *all* of them."

"Explain."

"OK. Look at Number One on your stupid list. 'Vampires are rarely seen in daylight.' Heck, Denofrio and Innis are both in the shop all day. We both checked, right?"

Kevin sat on his knees and rubbed his chin. "Yeah, but the barbershop is *dark,* Tommy. I told you that it's only in the movies that the vampires burst into flame or something if the daylight hits them. According to the old books, they just don't *like* it. They can get around in the daylight if they have to."

"Sure," I said, "but these guys work all day just like our dads. They close up at five and walk home before it gets dark."

Kevin pawed through his own notes and interrupted. "They both live alone, Tommy. That suggests something."

"Yeah. It suggests that neither one of them makes enough money to get married or have a family. My dad says that their barbershop hasn't raised its prices in years."

"Exactly!" cried Kevin. "Then how come almost no one goes there?"

"They give lousy haircuts," I said. I looked back at my list, trying to decipher the smeared lines of pencilled scrawl. "OK, Number Five on your list. 'Vampires will not cross running water.' Denofrio lives across the *river,* Kev. I watched him cross it all three days I was following him."

Kevin was sitting up on his knees. Now he slumped slightly. "I told you that I wasn't sure of that one. Stoker put it in *Dracula,* but I didn't find it too many other places."

I went on quickly. "Number Three—'Vampires hate garlic.' I watched Mr. Denofrio eat dinner at Luigi's Tuesday night, Kev. I could smell the garlic from twenty feet away when he came out."

"Three wasn't an essential one."

"All right," I said, moving in for the kill, "tell me *this* one wasn't essential. Number Eight—'All vampires hate and fear crosses and will avoid them at all cost.'" I paused dramatically. Kevin knew what was coming and slumped lower. "Kev, Mr. Denofrio goes to St. Mary's. *Your church, Kev.* Every morning before he goes down to open up the shop."

"Yeah. Innis goes to First Prez on Sundays. My dad told me about Denofrio being in the parish. I never see him because he only goes to early Mass."

I tossed the notes on the bed. "How could a vampire go to your church? He not only doesn't run away from a cross, he sits there and stares at about a hundred of them each day of the week for about an hour a day."

"Dad says he's never seen him take Communion," said Kevin, a hopeful note in his voice.

I made a face. "Great. Next you'll be telling me that anyone who's not a priest has to be a vampire. Brilliant, Kev."

He sat up and crumpled his own notes into a ball. I'd already seen them at school. I knew that Innis didn't follow Kevin's Vampire Rules either. Kevin said, "The cross thing doesn't prove . . . or disprove . . . anything, Tommy. I've been thinking about it. These things joined the barber's guild to get some protective coloration. It makes sense that they'd try to blend into the religious community too. Maybe they can train themselves to build up a tolerance to crosses, the way we take shots to build up a tolerance to things like smallpox and polio."

I didn't sneer, but I was tempted. "Do they build up a tolerance to mirrors, too?"

"What do you mean?"

"I mean I know something about vampires too, Kev, and even though it wasn't in your stupid list of rules, it's a fact that vampires don't like mirrors. They don't throw a reflection."

"That's not right," said Kevin in that rushy, teacherish voice he used. "In the movies they don't throw a reflection. The old books say that they avoided mirrors because they saw their *true* reflection there . . . what they looked like being old or undead or whatever."

"Yeah, whatever," I said. "But *whatever* spooks them, there isn't any place worse for mirrors than a barbershop. Unless they hang out in one of those carnival funhouse mirror places. Do they have guild signs, too, Kev?"

Kevin threw himself backward on the bed as if I'd shot him. A second later he was pawing through his notes and back up on his knees. "There was one weird thing," he said.

"Yeah, what?"

"They were closed on Monday."

"Real weird. Of course, every darn barbershop in the entire *universe* is closed on Mondays, but I guess you're right. They're closed on Mondays. They've got to be vampires. QED, as Mrs. Double Butt likes to say in geometry class. Gosh, I wish I was smart like you, Kevin."

"Mrs. Doubet," he said, still looking at his notes. He was the only kid in our class who liked her. "It's not that they're closed on Monday that's weird, Tommy. It's what they do. Or at least Innis."

"How do you know? You were home sick on Monday."

Kevin smiled. "No, I wasn't. I typed the excuse and signed Mom's name. They never check. I followed Innis around. Lucky he has that old car and drives slow, I was able to keep up with him on my bike. Or at least catch up."

I rolled to the floor and looked at some kit Kevin'd given up on before finishing. It looked like some sort of radio crossed with an adding machine. I managed to fake disinterest in what he was saying even though he'd hooked me again, just as he always did. "So where did he go?" I said.

"The Mear place. Old Man Everett's estate. Miss Plankmen's house out on 28. That mansion on the main road, the one the rich guy from New York bought last year."

"So?" I said. "They're all rich. Innis probably cuts their hair at home." I was proud that I had seen a connection that Kevin had missed.

"Uh-huh," said Kevin, "the richest people in the country and the one thing they have in common is that they get their haircuts from the lousiest barber in the state. Lousiest barbers, I should say. I saw Denofrio drive off, too. They met at the shop before they went on their rounds. I'm pretty sure Denofrio was at the Wilkes estate along the river that day. I asked Rudy, the caretaker, and he said either Denofrio or Innis comes there most Mondays."

I shrugged. "So rich people stay rich by paying the least they can for haircuts."

"Sure," said Kevin. "But that's not the weird part. The weird part was that both of the old guys loaded their car trunks with small bottles. When Innis came out of Mear and Everett's and Plankmen's places, he was carrying *big* bottles, two-gallon jars at least, and they were heavy, Tommy. Filled with liquid. I'm pretty sure the smaller jars that they'd loaded at the shop were full too."

"Full of what?" I said. "Blood?"

"Why not?" said Kevin.

"Vampires are supposed to take blood *away,*" I said, laughing. "Not *deliver* it."

"Maybe it was blood in the big bottles," said Kevin. "And they brought something to trade from the barbershop."

"Sure," I said, still laughing, "hair tonic!"

"It's not funny, Tom."

"The heck it isn't!" I made myself laugh even harder. "The best part is that your barber vampires are biting just the rich folks. They only drink premium!" I rolled on the floor, scattering comic books and trying not to crush any vacuum tubes.

Kevin walked to the window and looked out at the fading light. We both hated it when the days got shorter. "Well, I'm not convinced," he said. "But it'll be decided tonight."

"Tonight?" I said, lying on my side and no longer laughing. "What happens tonight?"

Kevin looked over his shoulder at me. "The back entrance to the barbershop has one of those old-style locks that I can get past in about two seconds with my Houdini Kit. After dinner, I'm going down to check the place out."

I said, "It's dark after dinner."

Kevin shrugged and looked outside.

"Are you going alone?"

Kevin paused and then stared at me over his shoulder. "That's up to you."

I stared back.

There is no sound quite the same as a straight razor being sharpened on a leather strop. I relax under the wrap of hot towels on my face, hearing but not seeing the barber prepare his blade. Receiving a professional shave is a pleasure which modern man has all but abandoned, but one in which I indulge every day.

The barber pulls away the towels, dries my upper cheeks and temples with a dab of a dry cloth, and turns back to the strop for a few final strokes of the razor. I feel my cheeks and throat tingling from the hot towels, the blood pulsing in my neck. "When I was a boy," I say, "a friend of mine convinced me that barbers were vampires."

The barber smiles but says nothing. He has heard my story before.

"He was wrong," I say, too relaxed to keep talking.

The barber's smile fades slightly as he leans forward, his face a study in concentration. Using a brush and lather whipped in a cup, he quickly applies the shaving soap. Then he sets aside the cup, lifts the straight razor, and with a delicate touch of only his thumb and little finger, tilts my head so that my throat is arched and exposed to the blade.

I close my eyes as the cold steel rasps across the warmed flesh.

"You said two seconds!" I whispered urgently. "You've been messing with that darned lock for *five minutes!*" Kevin and I were crouched in the alley behind Fourth Street, huddled in the back doorway of the barbershop. The night air was cold and smelled of garbage. Street sounds seemed to come to us from a million miles away. *"Come on!"* I whispered.

The lock clunked, clicked, and the door swung open into blackness. *"Voilà,"* said Kevin. He stuck his wires, picks, and other tools back into his imitation-leather Houdini Kit bag. Grinning, he reached over and rapped 'Shave and a Haircut' on the door.

"Shut up," I hissed, but Kevin was gone, feeling his way into the darkness. I shook my head and followed him in.

Once inside with the door closed, Kevin clicked on a penlight and held it between his teeth the way we'd seen a spy do in a movie. I grabbed onto the tail of his windbreaker and followed him down a short hallway into the single, long room of the barbershop.

It didn't take long to look around. The blinds were closed on both the large window and the smaller one on the front door, so Kevin figured it was safe to use the penlight. It was weird moving across that dark space with Kevin, the penlight throwing images of itself into the mirrors and illuminating one thing at a time—a counter here, the two chairs in the center of the room, a few chairs and magazines for customers, two sinks, a tiny little lavatory, no bigger than a closet, its door right inside the short hallway. All the clippers and things had been put away in drawers. Kevin opened the drawers, peered into the shelves. There were bottles of hair tonic, towels, all the barber tools set neatly into top drawers, both sets arranged the same. Kevin took out a razor and opened it, holding the blade up so it reflected the light into the mirrors.

"Cut it out," I whispered. "Let's get out of here."

Kevin set the thing away, making sure it was lined up exactly the way it had been, and we turned to go. His penlight beam moved across the back wall, illuminating a raincoat we'd already seen, and something else.

"There a door here," whispered Kevin, moving the coat to show a doorknob. He tried it. "Drat. It's locked."

"Let's *go!*" I whispered. I hadn't heard a car pass in what felt like hours. It was like the whole town was holding its breath.

Kevin began opening drawers again. "There has to be a key," he said too loudly. "It must lead to a basement, there's no second floor on this place."

I grabbed him by his jacket. "Come on," I hissed. "Let's get out of here. We're going to get *arrested.*"

"Just another minute . . ." began Kevin and froze. I felt my heart stop at the same instant.

A key rasped in the lock of the front door. There was a tall shadow thrown against the blind.

I turned to run, to escape, anything to get out of there, but Kevin clicked off the penlight, grabbed my sweatshirt, and pulled me with him as he crawled under one of the high sinks. There was just enough room for both of us there. A dark curtain hung down over the space and Kevin pulled it shut just as the door creaked open and footsteps entered the room.

For a second I could hear nothing but the pounding of blood in my ears, but then I realized that there were *two* people walking in the room, men by the sounds of the heavy tread. My mouth hung open and I panted, but I was unable to get a breath of air. I was sure that any sound at all would give us away.

One set of footsteps stopped at the first chair while the other went to the rear wall. A second door rasped shut, water ran, and there came the sound of the toilet flushing. Kevin nudged me, and I could have belted him then, but we were so crowded together in fetal positions that any movement by me would have made a noise. I held my breath and waited while the second set of footsteps returned from the lavatory and moved toward the front door. *They hadn't even turned on the lights.* There'd been no gleam of a flashlight beam through our curtain, so I didn't think it was the cops checking things out. Kevin nudged me again and I knew he was telling me that it had to be Innis and Denofrio.

Both pairs of footsteps moved toward the front, there was the sound of the door opening and slamming, and I tried to breathe again before I passed out.

A rush of noise. A hand reached down and parted the curtain. Other hands grabbed me and pulled me up and out, into the dark. Kevin shouted as another figure dragged him to his feet.

I was on my tiptoes, being held up by my shirtfront. The man holding me seemed eight feet tall in the blackness, his fist the size of my head. I could smell garlic on his breath and assumed it was Denofrio.

"Let us go!" shouted Kevin. There was the sound of a slap, flat and clear as a rifle shot, and Kevin was silent.

I was shoved into a barber chair. I heard Kevin being pushed into the other one. My eyes were so well adjusted to the darkness now that I could make out the features of the two men. Innis and Denofrio. Dark suits blended into black, but I could see the pale, angular faces that I'd been sure had made Kevin think they were vampires. Eyes too deep and dark, cheekbones too sharp, mouths too cruel, and something about them that said *old* despite their middle-aged looks.

"What are you doing here?" Innis asked Kevin. The man spoke softly, without evident emotion, but his voice made me shiver in the dark.

"Scavenger hunt!" cried Kevin. "We have to steal a barber's clippers to get in the big kids' club. We're sorry. Honest!"

There came the rifle shot of a slap again. "You're lying," said Innis. "You followed me on Monday. Your friend here followed Mr. Denofrio in the evening. Both of you have been watching the shop. Tell me the truth. *Now!*"

"We think you're vampires," said Kevin. "Tommy and I came to find out."

My mouth dropped open in shock at what Kevin had said. The two men took a half step back and looked at each other. I couldn't tell if they were smiling in the dark.

"Mr. Denofrio?" said Innis.

"Mr. Innis?" said Denofrio.

"Can we go now?" said Kevin.

Innis stepped forward and did something to the barber chair Kevin was in. The leather armrests flipped up and out, making sort of white gutters. The leather strops on either side went up and over, attaching to something out of sight to make restraining straps around Kevin's arms. The headrest split apart, came down and around, and encircled Kevin's neck. It looked like one of those trays the dentist puts near you to spit into.

Kevin made no noise. I expected Denofrio to do the same thing to my chair, but he only laid a large hand on my shoulder.

"We're not vampires, boy," said Mr. Innis. He went to the counter, opened a drawer, and returned with the straight razor Kevin had been fooling around with earlier. He opened it carefully. "Mr. Denofrio?"

The shadow by my chair grabbed me, lifted me out of the chair, and dragged me to the basement door. He held me easily with one hand while he unlocked it. As he pulled me into the darkness, I looked back and caught a glimpse of my friend staring in silent horror as Innis drew the edge of the straight razor slowly across Kevin's inner arm. Blood welled, flowed, and gurgled into the white enamel gutter of the armrest.

Denofrio dragged me downstairs.

*   *   *

The barber finishes the shave, trims my sideburns, and turns the chair so that I can look into the closer mirror.

I run my hand across my cheeks and chin. The shave is perfect, very close but with not a single nick. Because of the sharpness of the blade and the skill of the barber, my skin tingles but feels no irritation whatsoever.

I nod. The barber smiles ever so slightly and removes the striped protective apron.

I stand and remove my suitcoat. The barber hangs it on a hook while I take my seat again and roll up my left sleeve. While he is near the rear of the shop, the barber turns on a small radio. The music of Mozart fills the room.

The basement was lighted with candles set in small jars. The dancing red light reminded me of the time Kevin took me to his church. He said the small, red flames were votive candles. You paid money, lit one, and said a prayer. He wasn't sure if the money was necessary for the prayer to be heard.

The basement was narrow and unfinished and almost filled by the twelve-foot slab of stone in its center. The thing on the stone was almost as long as the slab. The thing must have weighed a thousand pounds, easy. I could see folds of slick, gray flesh rising and falling as it breathed.

If there were arms, I couldn't see them. The legs were suggested by folds in slick fat. The tubes and pipes and rusting funnel led my gaze to the head.

Imagine a thousand-pound leech, nine or ten feet long and five or six feet thick through the middle as it lies on its back, no surface really, just layers of gray-green slime and wattles of what might be skin. Things, organs maybe, could be seen moving and sloshing through flesh as transparent as dirty plastic. The room was filled with the sound of its breathing and the stench of its breath. Imagine a huge sea creature, a small whale, maybe, dead and rotting on the beach for a week, and you've got an idea of what the thing itself smelled like.

The mass of flesh made a noise and the small eyes turned in my direction. Its eyes were covered with layers of yellow film or mucus and I was sure it was blind. The thing's head was no more defined than the end of a leech, but in the folds of slick fat were lines which showed a face which might once have been human. Its mouth was very large. Imagine a lamprey smiling.

"No, it was never human," said Mr. Denofrio. His hand was still firm on my shoulder. "By the time they came to our guild, they had already passed beyond hope of hiding amongst us. But they brought an offer which we could not refuse. Nor can our customers. Have you ever heard of symbiosis, boy? Hush!"

Upstairs, Kevin screamed. There was a gurgle, as of old pipes being tried.

The creature on the slab turned its blind gaze back to the ceiling. Its mouth pulsed hungrily. Pipes rattled and the funnel overflowed.

Blood spiralled down.

The barber returns and taps at my arm as I make a fist. There is a broad welt across the inner crook of my arm, as of an old scar poorly healed. It *is* an old scar.

The barber unlocks the lowest drawer and withdraws a razor. The handle is made of gold and is set about with small gems. He raises the object in both hands, holds it above his head, and the blade catches the dim light.

He takes three steps closer and draws the blade across my arm, opening the scar tissues like a puparium hatching. There is no pain. I watch as the barber rinses the blade and returns it to its special place. He goes down the basement stairs and I can hear the gurgling in the small drain tubes of the armrest as his footsteps recede. I close my eyes.

I remember Kevin's screams from upstairs and the red flicker of candlelight on the stone walls. I remember the red flow through the funnel and the gurgle of the thing feeding, lamprey mouth extended wide and reaching high, trying to encompass the funnel the way an infant seeks its mother's nipple.

I remember Mr. Denofrio taking a large hammer from its place at the base of the slab, then a thing part spike and part spigot. I remember standing alone and watching as he pounded it in, realizing even as I watched that the flesh beneath the gray-green slime was a mass of old scars.

I remember watching as the red liquid flowed from the spigot into the

crystal glass, the chalice. There is no red in the universe as deeply red,
as purely red as what I saw that night.

I remember drinking. I remember carrying the chalice—carefully, so
carefully—upstairs to Kevin. I remember sitting in the chair myself.

The barber returns with the chalice. I check that the scar has closed,
fold down my sleeve, and drink deeply.

By the time I have donned my own white smock and returned, the barber is sitting in the chair.

"A trim this morning, perhaps?" I ask.

"I think not," he says. "Just a shave, please."

I shave him carefully. When I am finished, he runs his hands across
his cheeks and chin and nods his approval. I perform the ritual and go
below.

In the candlelit hush of the Master's vault, I wait for the Purification
and think about immortality. Not about the true eon-spanning immortality of the Master . . . of all the Masters . . . but of the portion He deigns
to share with us. It is enough.

After my colleague drinks and I have returned the chalice to its place,
I come up to find the blinds raised, the shop open for business.

Kevin has taken his place beside his chair. I take my place beside
mine. The music has ended and silence fills the room.

Outside, the blood spirals down.

Robert Bloch (1917–1994) is known worldwide as the writer of the book *Psycho,* the basis for Alfred Hitchcock's famous film of the same name. He got his start writing stories for pulp magazines such as *Weird Tales, Fantastic Adventures,* and *Unknown.* Later in his career he wrote the novels *American Gothic, Firebug,* and *Fear and Trembling,* among many others. He also edited several anthologies, including *Psycho-paths* and *Monsters in Our Midst.*

Philip K. Dick (1928–1982) wrote novels and stories which examined "reality" in all of its myriad forms, letting his protagonists, along with his readers, try to sort out what was real and what wasn't. His novel *The Man in the High Castle* won the Hugo award in 1962, and he also received the John W. Campbell Memorial award. His work has also inspired films, most notable the Ridley Scott-directed *Blade Runner.*

Best known for writing a hard-edged military science fiction, including the Hammer's Slammers series, **David Drake**'s horror output has lessened in recent years. But what he did write is as powerful as any of his other fiction. The best of his dark fiction can be found in the collections *Old Nathan* and *From the Heart of Darkness.* He has edited a number of anthologies, including *Men Hunting Things, Things Hunting Men,* and *A Century of Horror: 1970–1979.*

Tanith Lee has made her reputation by successfully mixing science fiction, heroic fantasy, and fairy tales into a unique mix all her own. Often turning fantasy conventions upside down, her examination of the ambiguities of moral behavior can be found in her novels *Death's Master, Dark Dance,* and *Darkness, I.* Her work can also be found in *Warrior Enchantresses* and *Rivals of Dracula.* A World Fantasy Award winner, she lives in London, England.

Eric Lustbader is well-known for his novels which combine the martial arts and the Far Eastern underworld with eroticism and intrigue for a powerful combination matched by few other authors. Before turning to writing full time, he worked at Elektra Records and edited *Cash Box* magazine. Recent novels include *The Kaisho, Floating City,* and *Second Skin.*

Richard Matheson is one of the most respected writers of the past forty years. His novel *I Am Legend* is considered one of the seminal vampire novels, a classic tale of the last man on an earth populated entirely by the undead. His books *The Shrinking Man* and *Hell House* also broke new ground in the horror field. His work has been adapted for television as well, most notably as several episodes of original *Twilight Zone.*

Robert McCammon is the author of 11 novels, including the New York Times Bestsellers *Goin' South, Boys' Life, Mine* and *The Wolf's Hour.* A superior stylist who evokes a sense of dread out of the most commonplace events, his short fiction packs just as powerful a punch. A native of Birmingham, Alabama, he lives there with his wife and daughter.

Daniel Ransom's latest novel, *Zone Soldiers,* explores a future United States weakened by the collapse of society and sectioned off into different areas where humans are sent to live. He has also written another science fiction novel, *The Fugitive Stars.* Other stories by him appear in *Monster Brigade 3000, Future Net,* and *Dracula: Prince of Darkness.* He is also a successful horror writer, as evidenced by his novels *The Serpent's Kiss* and *The Long Midnight.*

Dan Simmons's fiction is known for its minute attention to detail and lush settings, whether they be tropical forests in *Fires of Eden* or the world of vampires in *The Hunger and Ecstasy of Vampires,* expanded from his novella of the same name. Wherever and whomever he chooses to write about, the results are guaranteed to be classified among the most effective horror fiction of today. He lives in Colorado.

S.P. Somtow is the author of the Vampire Junction series featuring Tommy Valentine, a vampire trapped in the body of a child whose story is told in *Vampire Junction* and *Vanitas: Escape from Vampire Junction.* He has written many other novels, including *Jasmine Nights* and *Moon Dance.* A native of Thailand, he currently makes his home in California, with regular visits to his homeland.

Brian Stableford is a British author who combines science fiction with horror for a disturbing mix unlike anything else. He has written over 45 novels and non-fiction books, including editing the Dedalus series of dark fantasy and horror anthologies. He has also written a study of the James Blish as well as essays on science fiction's master writers. He makes his home in England.

Karl Edward Wagner (1945–1994) wrote the first of what was later to be termed "dark fantasy" fiction with his series character Kane, who is based in the biblical Cain, a wandering immortal who takes up arms in the eternal battle of good versus evil. He has also collaborated with other authors, notably David Drake in the space alien meets Roman Empire adventure novel *Killer*. He continued the exploits of one of the pulp era's mightiest heroes, Conan the Barbarian. A prolific editor, his annual *Best Horror Stories* anthology showcased the most powerful tales of terror of the preceeding year, the series continued until his untimely death. A four-time recipient of the British Fantasy Award, he also won the World Fantasy Award twice.

Tad Williams has held some unusual jobs before turning to fiction, among them a singer in a rock and roll band as well as working for Apple Computers. He made his mark in fantasy fiction with the substantial Memory, Sorrow and Thorn trilogy, consisting of *The Dragonbone Chair, Stone of Farewell,* and *To Green Angel Tower.* He has also written the evocative *Caliban's Tale,* a retelling of William Shakespeare's *The Tempest* from the viewpoint of Caliban. His latest novel is *Otherworld.*

World Fantasy Award winner **Jane Yolen** has written well over 150 books for children and adults, and well over 200 short stories, most of them fantasy. She is a past president of the Science Fiction and Fantasy Writers of America as well as a 25-year veteran of the Board of Directors of the Society of Children's Book Writers & Illustrators. She lives with her husband in Hatfield, Mass. and St. Andrews, Scotland.

Roger Zelazny (1937–1995) burst onto the science-fiction writing scene as part of the "New Wave" group of writers in the mid to late 1960s. His novels *This Immortal* and *Lord of Light* met universal praise, the latter winning a Hugo award for best novel. His work is notable for his lyrical style and innovative use of language both in description and dialogue. His most recognized series is the Amber novels, about a parallel universe which is the true world with all others, Earth included, being mere shadows of Amber. Besides the Hugo for *Lord of Light,* he was also awarded three Nebulas, three more Hugos and two Locus awards.